Praise for *The Last of What I Am*

"What really haunts us—our own mistakes, or the weight of history. Based closely on the true story of her own uncanny encounters in an inherited antebellum Virginia farmhouse and old letters she found there, Abbie Cutter has crafted a novel that plumbs the painful history of a common soldier in the Civil War and the burdens he cannot set down. A riveting read, rich in historic detail and moral complexity."

—Geraldine Brooks, *New York Times* bestselling author
and Pulitzer Prize winner of *Horse* and *March*

"Abigail Cutter has rendered the Civil War and its consequences with a rare power and eloquence, combining literary imagination with fidelity to history. She has allowed people who lived and breathed in the past to live and breathe again, telling us of loss and suffering we need to remember."

—Edward Ayers, author and winner of the Bancroft Prize for
In the Presence of Mine Enemies: Civil War in the Heart of America

"*The Last of What I Am* is a richly imagined tragedy of a Rebel soldier whose regret for ill-chosen allegiance haunts him from the moment of enlistment through the horrors of a Union prison. It follows him into the afterlife, where he lingers in his ancestral home, unable to shed his shame for fighting for the cause of slavery. Masterful historical research and detail of the nineteenth century invest this story with a reader's pleasure in a felt life. All of this with an ear for the poetry that lives in disaster."

—John Rolfe Gardiner, author of *Newport Rising*
and O. Henry Prize winner

"Abigail Cutter's *The Last of What I Am* digs down to the dark and bloody roots of the Civil War that cling to us today. Graceful, unflinching, and wise, the book unearths one family's tragedy and the ghosts that haunt it through four generations. This is a very well-told tale, set in the Shenandoah Valley, which Cutter knows in her bones."

—John Pancake, former Arts editor at the *Washington Post*

"A searing, brilliant, moving, and utterly original Civil War novel, told by the guilt-ravaged Virginia infantryman Tom Smiley, whose own war never ended—at least not until a young couple move into his now-historic childhood home and start renovating, literally taking the past apart brick by brick, pots and pans, faded velvet curtains, cedar chests and china dishes and rusted hairpins, and even the tattered blue handkerchief box that contains his medals from the Battle of Gettysburg twenty-fifth and fiftieth reunions . . . bringing it all back. A stirring meditation on guilt and redemption."

—Lee Smith, *New York Times* bestselling author of *The Last Girls*

"Is a fascinating and readable look at love and heartbreak in Civil War America. Highly recommended."

—Patrick Anderson, author and book reviewer for the *Washington Post*

THE
LAST
OF
WHAT
I AM

THE LAST OF WHAT I AM

ABIGAIL CUTTER

UNION
SQUARE
& CO.

NEW YORK

**UNION
SQUARE
& CO.**

NEW YORK

UNION SQUARE & CO. and the distinctive Union Square & Co. logo are
trademarks of Sterling Publishing Co., Inc.

Union Square & Co., LLC, is a subsidiary of Sterling Publishing Co., Inc.

First published in 2022 as *Long Shadows* by She Writes Press,
a division of SparkPoint Studio, LLC.
This 2023 paperback edition published by Union Square & Co., LLC.

ISBN 978-1-4549-5178-0
ISBN 978-1-4549-5179-7 (e-book)

Library of Congress Control Number: 2023012944
Library of Congress Cataloging-in-Publication Data is available upon request.

For information about custom editions, special sales, and premium purchases,
please contact specialsales@unionsquareandco.com.

Printed in Canada

2 4 6 8 10 9 7 5 3 1

unionsquareandco.com

Cover design by Jo Obarowski
Cover art © Yolande de Kort/Trevillion Images; Library of Congress (porch and shadow)
Interior design by Richard Hazelton

"Whoever pretends not to believe in ghosts of any sort, lies to his own heart."

—Lafcadio Hearn, "The Eternal Haunter," 1898

PART 1

1

SOME MIGHT THINK THERE'S NO LIFE IN THE HOUSE, BUT I KNOW otherwise. I've made friends with the mighty black snakes who take up winter residence. One has grown from a thin, stringy, mean-looking fellow to a thick band almost six feet long and round as my wrist. He enters the house when the days shorten by climbing the gnarled, vine-covered tree hovering over the back porch. Dropping from a low-leaning branch, he traverses the roof and stretches upward along the wood siding to enter the attic window, triangular snout tap-tapping, seeking entry. Hail has splintered the windowpanes, and he slides over the edge into the attic to hibernate. Sometimes he noses his way through the lime and horse-hair mortar on the central fireplace chimney and drops into the rooms below in search of mice.

His compulsion is uncomfortably familiar, though in my case the brown river rat was my prey. Prisoners' fare. So much time has passed, yet those months in a miserable Union prison camp are as real to me today as then. Famished, I slit my quarry from ear to naked tail, tossed aside the oozing hide, and punctured the pink, shiny body with a stick. Twisting it past bone and gristle, I roasted the flesh over fire until it curled crisp. Oblivious to spikey hair and whiskers, I welcomed it to my tongue, as warm, juicy fat dribbled on my chin. The image thins to a film of nausea and is then gone.

Here in my childhood home, the mice are a constant. Their daily occupations exhaust me with their ill-conceived, Herculean efforts. They struggle for days, dragging acorns half their own size through cracks in the stone foundation, hoisting them through the interior walls, gnawing ragged holes in the baseboards, shoving them across the halls, hopping with them up the stairs, and then thrusting them through openings chiseled in the backs of dresser drawers—all just to find the perfect storage place. It's a treacherous trip through the house when the coiled monster with flicking tongue is lying in wait to bulge his belly before the winter's sleep. The whole thing casts me low in spirit; their activity reminds me of the futility of so many human endeavors.

And I remember. Folks say you take nothing with you when you go to meet your maker, but I'm here to tell you that memory tracks your every step like a rabid dog. Things learned and retained in the mind are a pestilence that not even God can dispel—causing me to wonder if the strange power of remembering isn't the Devil's device. Even now, when my worn-out body has fallen away and the past is more vivid than the present, I am plagued by mistakes grand and small. There's no remedy for remorse—memory's dark shadow—and no fleeing from the mind. As days turn into months and months into years, I remember, I remember until more than a century has passed.

Soothing visions of boyhood innocence and my marriage have been my only salvation, wrapped round like a soft blanket to ward off the rest. Here in this house lies a way. Here's where I'm beyond the reach of the harrowing war years. In the corners of my mind, I can find the soothing touch of my beloved wife Ellen, my sister Mary's playful smile, and my little daughter Cara's pigtails flapping as she skipped toward me. It's there that I dwell.

Now, after decades when nothing interrupted my solitary recollections—not even time's passing—everything has changed. A month ago, in the early afternoon, I heard two sets of footsteps, one heavy, the other lighter, clump on the porch stairs and then rustle through the fall leaves banked against the old screen door. My knees trembled and I couldn't find my voice. No one has approached my front door in over twenty years. Alarmed, but a little curious too, I floated in the hall near the ceiling as a key twisted in the rusty lock. Two strangers, a young man and a young woman, barged in, followed by their inquisitive black dog.

I couldn't believe my eyes. What right did these people believe they had to enter my house? Where did they get a key? And both were dressed like hoodlums. He was clad in a collarless shirt with writing on it as though he was a poster board, and she was in long denim pants like a boy. To my mind, the only womanly touch was the silver ear hoops that peeked through her hair when she moved.

This couple wasn't put off by the black snake that slithered from the sofa cushion and escaped up the fireplace chimney or discouraged by the ribbons of faded wallpaper that rippled across heaps of crumbled plaster cluttering the floors. Nothing seemed to deter them! They explored each room, handled the books, used a letter opener to pry up the lid of the cedar chest safeguarding my sisters' high-necked blouses and bustled skirts. They even pawed through the tattered blue handkerchief box that contains my medals from the Battle of Gettysburg twenty-fifth and fifti-eth reunions. The dog flopped on the parlor rug, of all places, after mak-ing a ruckus about the snake and then sniffing every corner. I couldn't think what to do; my mind was a blank. Stunned helpless by this invasion, I reeled back, as though punched in the gut.

The woman spread out on the dresser top the crumpled reunion ribbons of crimson and indigo, ornate with rectangular silver bars and gold medallions. She held up to the light the yellowed newspaper article describing how Confederate and Union veterans clapped one another warmly on the shoulder as if we'd shared some mutual rite of passage, nothing more. "Here, take a look at this," she said. The man's hand passed right through me as he reached for the paper, but he paid no mind. Finally, I found my voice and yelled at the top of my lungs, "What the hell are you doing here? Get out! Get out right now!" The woman only shivered and knitted her dark brows together. She looked momentarily annoyed, as though a horsefly had buzzed her ear, and then continued to rifle through drawers. There was no reaction from the man. I wondered if these interlopers were stone deaf, although no one ever seemed to hear or see me. It used to break my heart in the years after I passed, when my wife Ellen was still alive. I yelled again, "Don't you dare touch my things! Or else!" But with no effect. I began to sense that threats would be useless. Panic clawed at my throat.

Now these harbingers of doom invade every weekend, armed with mops, odd liquid soaps, and a noisy machine that sucks up dirt. They show up out of nowhere, she with long brown hair twisted on top of her head, ready for messy work, and he in another shirt with a meaningless message. They unsettle everything—piling sheets, hairbrushes, combs, dented pots and pans, my sister Mary's sewing remnants, my daughter Cara's aprons, faded velvet curtains, and whatever else they deem disposable in a heap of glossy black bags in the backyard. I look anywhere but at their industry, feeling queasy in my stomach and weighted in my heart. They are senseless to the distress they are causing.

What has happened to my years of silence broken only by birdsong, the hum of rain, and the wind's murmur? That calm has been destroyed by buzzing machines that slice wood, the whack-whack of pounding hammers, and the dog's piercing bark. The riot of noise drives me to the opposite end of the house, but even there I find no peace.

They have no respect for the fact that even though my shell and those of my family were borne away to the cemetery behind the church, everything else, including dried-out face cream and rusted hairpins, has stayed where the last hand placed it.

My daughter, Cara, was the last to live in the house. Childless and widowed in her late twenties, she had moved back home into the embrace of her family. Eventually, my parents, two sisters, wife, and I were gone too. Then she had relied on the things we'd left behind to keep her company, same as I do now.

These new people act as if the wide wings of the armchair don't still hold an impression from Pa's daily ritual of reading the latest issue of the *Staunton Spectator*, or the silver-handled hairbrush isn't imbedded with the touch of Mary's hand. Or that my dark serge coat, the special one I wore to Sunday services every week and that still hangs in the upstairs cupboard, doesn't remember the slope of my shoulders.

These intruders seem ignorant of the fact that I'm still here, that this is my home, that every object, as I touch or catch sight of it, floods me with warm memories that reaffirm my sense of who I am. I won't stop being Tom Smiley as long as evidence of my life surrounds me. And as long as I'm Tom, I'm safe from whatever happens to unworthy souls.

But now they are stripping away that evidence, piece by piece, memory by memory. I'll lose my grip if they continue. First, the outer layers will slide away, like an onion in the hands of a cook. Those layers are the man reflected within my home's four walls and its furnishings—the guileless boy, loyal husband, and law-abiding citizen. The knife's edge next will slice into the core, leaving disconnected bits of soldier Tom scattered about. Finally, with the last cuts, the secret I've kept from everyone will lie exposed, radiant in the dark. I'll erode to nothing more than a formless shade that yields to Hell's gravity. The Heavenly judges who decide a soul's fate will then have no choice but to speed my fall. This man and woman will destroy me.

How their presence makes me ache for my own family and their affection, when my home stirred with a multitude of their voices and activities. Ma, Pa, my sisters Mary and Tish, and then my wife Ellen and our four—Grier, Argyle, Will, and Cara—still sound in my ears. Our only grandchild, sweet little Helen, would shriek with summer joy when Grier drove up with her in his smoke-belching Ford, all the way from Kentucky.

Of my own offspring, Cara was the last to perish. I watched her grow old alone at the farm, into her eighties. Cara's thick, ebony hair that her mother used to plait and tie with silk ribbons faded to a wispy white halo with pink flesh showing through. Age contorted her hands into painful claws. She ventured out less and less and kept a lonesome journal that mostly tracked the weather. Most nights, she indulged in a dram of alcohol and groped her way up the stairs to her bedroom at the back of the house. As a father, it wracked my soul to see my daughter fall into such a state.

When she was gone, there was no one left to care about. Over time, the house has soaked into my being, and I've expanded out into it until there is no difference between it and me. The dry rustle of a roach scooting across the floor, the construction efforts of a nesting chimney swift, the drilling of a borer bee in a porch beam—all merge with who I am.

I've overheard these peculiar people speak of "modernizing" the farmhouse for a weekend place as if it's theirs, as though my presence matters not one whit. By damn, I won't permit it.

In addition, on warm days this woman strides about unconcerned that her slip of a dress immodestly displays her long, bare legs. What in God's name is she thinking? Perhaps this is all for the man's sake. He calls her Phoebe and watches her with a happy gleam in his eye. I suppose some might consider her pretty, but my wife never revealed her legs or wore her hair loose in that way, long brown strands swaying with every step, except in private moments. This woman also has a sprinkling of freckles across her nose, frowned upon in my day when flawless pale skin was prized, and she's almost as tall as her male companion. I don't see the appeal.

My dear Ellen was diminutive and plainer than this woman, but her upbringing in a Lutheran minister's family instilled qualities of forgiveness and forbearance that were attractive to me. I met her a decade after the war. I remember spying her for the first time across the oak pews at New Jerusalem Presbyterian Church. What a graceful neck, what slender wrists! Not one loose strand escaped from the raven-black hair twisted tightly on the back of her neck. The tenderness with which she calmed fidgeting siblings and tended to her elderly aunt beguiled me. When she felt the heat of my stare, I struggled to glue my eyes to the hymnal. Such thoughts rampaged through my mind! A woman like her might save me from myself. I imagined how the touch of her hand would replace my despairing moods with shivers of pleasure. She'd love me despite my shortcomings, just as she seemed to love and have patience with her family. Her serenity appeared contagious. I fell for her that very first morning and determined to win her. My ten-years' seniority didn't put her off and, after six months of unrelenting courtship, she broke down and became my wife.

Poor Ellen had no idea what she'd gotten herself into. The private pleasures of new marriage kept my sickness of heart at bay for several months, but one day she found me in despair, head bowed. "What's wrong?" Tears flooded her soft eyes. "You spoke so impatiently to me this morning when I asked your plans for the day. It was as if you despised my very presence. Is it something I've done or said?"

"No, Sweet. Please forgive me." I paused, the heaviness in my chest choking the words. I couldn't bear to look at her. "I'm not worthy of you, or anyone, for that matter. It was a mistake for me to coax you into my life." She averted her face so that I wouldn't see her pain and clenched the flowered fabric of her full skirt until her knuckles were white. I arose from the sofa, abandoning her in the middle of the library. The porch door banged shut behind me, and I headed for the overgrown cow paths along the fence line on the hill above the house. There I paced until I wore myself out.

Over the years, Ellen found a way to cope with my moods and irritable temperament. When our children were born, she ran off to her mother's in Greenville, North Carolina, for as long as six months for each child. She claimed she was going for reasons of health, but she didn't fool me. For the last baby, Argyle, she enrolled Cara in school for a semester and didn't come home for Christmas. The best I could do was send letters enclosing the bedtime stories that I usually recited to my three little ones, or small gifts, such as a puzzle or a wool scarf pattern for Cara, who was eight and learning to knit.

During my bad times, Ellen tried to talk me into a better state of mind. She said, "Why can't you accept that you are a good man? And find peace in that. Why must you be so hard on yourself?"

"I can't help it. I would do anything to change, if I could. I hate causing you pain, but it's due to something you would never understand."

"You've never tested my understanding." She smiled and added, "Although you do test my patience sometimes." She touched my arm tenderly. "If only you'd give me a chance to learn what ails you so." But I could never risk that. Not ever. "I feel I never see anything of you but your shadow," she said, her voice trailing off.

Then Ellen seemed to gain resolve and shook her head in frustration. "The children and I love you because you've never taken a switch to them, regardless of how disobedient, and you listen patiently to my needs and troubles with a generous and understanding heart. That should count for something." She nodded her head emphatically as if she'd settled the matter.

But it wasn't enough. Every morning, the old brown rooster on the chicken house roof awakened me to an inescapable dark state of mind. I'd lie motionless and track the black mood as it radiated from behind my eyes, slid down to my heart and then plumbed my limbs until it claimed even my toes and fingers. Against this burden, I strove daily to prove the value of my existence. Ellen had no idea how hard it was to lift my head from the pillow, much less to soldier on for one more day.

Yes, I was even a good citizen in some people's minds. Folks reelected me for six terms to the county Board of Supervisors, and it's true I championed ways to make their lives easier, such as paving the county roads. Now they can haul their vegetables and meats to market during the spring muddy season. Later, in 1901, when the state wanted to restrict voting rights of Blacks by forcing them to prove they could read, all the while exempting whites, I railed against this injustice. I spoke in community halls and on the steps of the courthouse and thumped on flag-draped lecterns in protest. Folks only turned sour faces toward me and heaved rotten eggs at our front door. They elected someone else as their delegate to the state convention, but I had fought hard for the right thing. And, as Ellen often said, "After all those years as Sunday school superintendent, look at you. You're a church Elder, one of the most respected positions in our community."

But these efforts never made up for my failings. Ellen was heroic for trying, but not even an angel could disentangle me from the web of shame I'd woven. I was guilty of a rash and naive act that resulted in the killing of someone I cared for. For whom I was responsible. I might as well have killed him with my own hands, wrapping my fingers around his neck and squeezing until there was no breath left. Never a day passed in my life that I wasn't reminded that this was yet another day he wouldn't see.

Ellen didn't suspect I hadn't started out as a devout churchgoer. Faith had nothing to do with it. It was because religion was the only prescription for a diseased mind in those days. And after the war, I had a diseased mind. Folks were convinced that lack of faith in God and His Son was the reason melancholia took root. I never considered either trustworthy, but I continued to hope that churchgoing would provide a cure, even to the very end.

I do believe in one thing. Hell is real. I know it lurks just beyond these four walls. New Jerusalem preachers' fiery exhortations, year in and year out, persuaded me of its truth. Beyond a doubt, the demon realm exists.

To be honest, my good works were entirely a form of atonement. A hedge against an eternity of hellfire and damnation. They were a wager that my four decades of church work and my community service were payment enough for my sins. But the debt was never fully paid. My utmost dread was for my family and friends to discover what I'd done, the shameful secret I'd buried for so many years. I couldn't bear for them to know what a sorely unfit man I was, and then, finally, for me to be driven from the gates of Heaven, if such a place exists.

While I've been distracted by these thoughts, that strange woman has been digging through the library like a terrier after a rat. She has scattered across the floor piles of dog-eared and dusty books from shelves stretching from floor to ceiling.

What a mess she's made of the room. After all, it is my room. Strolling around edges of the sunlit library, I lightly tap my sons' engineering texts and college annuals and glide my fingers across the soft leather spines of books about Biblical times and the many ladies' novels that consumed Ellen's and my sisters' afternoons. The Brontë sisters' works were their favorites.

Here also are my parents' tiresome texts on Presbyterian Church history, as well as favorite classics of English literature. I can still hear Pa's sonorous voice reading from Dickens's spirited *Oliver Twist*, as we three children listened wide-eyed. Inspired by Longfellow's great romantic saga *The Song of Hiawatha*, I memorized long passages during my twelfth summer, perched on the sturdiest limb of my favorite oak beyond the pasture, the words rustling in my skull. The poem's melancholy Milky Way—a broad, white pathway guiding ghosts of plumed warriors heavenward across a frozen sky—too often comes to me in an evening.

Now the woman's fingertips have brushed something behind the newly exposed bookshelf—something misplaced a century before she was born. She strains to disengage a moldy packet wrapped with a twist of shattered twine. I feel a jolt. They are the letters my younger sister Mary wrote to me during the war! I haven't seen them for more years than I can remember. "Get away, Emma. Shoo," the woman says to the dog snuffling at the thin sheets. She lifts away one or two papers, and after scanning through the stack for a few minutes, places the packet on the oval sofa table. She suddenly looks up, stares in my direction, and hesitates as if she senses something. Shaking her head, she hastens away from the room with the black dog, its neck hairs bristling, pressing into her calf as if its life depends upon it. Mary's letters remain on the table.

2

ARE YOU SURE YOU WANT TO DONATE THIS THING TO THE SALVATION Army?" The man rubs his fingers across the dining room table's surface. "Don't you think we should sell it instead?"

The woman has been clattering old pots and pans in the kitchen, but now she joins him. With a bright yellow wrist encased in a work glove, she brushes strands of hair away from her eyes. "It would be great if we could. Extra money would help a lot. But this table will never sell."

"Why not?'

"Well, for the same two reasons I don't want it." She tells him that nowadays dealers can't sell heavy, brown furniture from the middle of the nineteenth century. People won't buy it unless it's at junk store prices, and maybe not then. "That's what most everything in this house is. I guess it was all bought at the same time, like a big redecorating project. I don't care for it much either. Besides, this table is in terrible shape." She points a yellow finger at the many irregular pale patterns splotching the surface. "See these? They're mouse pee stains."

"They're what? How do you know?"

"They're wherever I find mouse nests and droppings. They're all over the dresser tops upstairs." She pauses, pointing at something else. "And look at these wide cracks in the wood. I think they're too bad to be fixed, and it would cost more than the table is worth, even if they could be. Frankly, I can't imagine who'd want this thing, but maybe someone will, if it's almost free." She looked at him sympathetically. "Think about our house at home. Everything's 1950s mid-century modern. Most people prefer chrome, glass, and leather these days."

The man nods. "Okay, I'll take it into town in the pickup later today, after I help you with the kitchen." They pass close to me on the way out of the room, unaware of my choking rage.

Their careless disregard for my possessions sets my head on fire. I literally see waves of red. That table was the center of our family life. Kept polished to a fine sheen, the walnut surface bore the food that sustained us and was the scene of many events, joyful and solemn. Pa's open wood coffin lay on its gleaming surface while neighbors kept candlelight vigil for three nights, guarding against mice and bearing witness that his spirit was gone. It served the same function for my coffin. But I remember most clearly when I was eighteen, and my family, seated around its oval surface, heard an announcement that I've regretted ever since.

An ordinary journey to town was the start of it all. New blades of grass pushed through the early March snow as Sam Lucas's father set out to Staunton to acquire sacks of coffee, sugar, and rice at the general grocers. Sam and I were boyhood comrades in those days, and his father had asked us to come along. Our young backs would come in handy if the wagon wheels skidded off the ice-slicked road.

The three of us hunched forward in silence as the wagon jostled us along the frozen ruts of the road from Bethel to Staunton. Blink, and you might miss my hometown of Bethel—not much there but a black-smith shop, the general store, a handful of houses, and the few farms edged by the road. Staunton, the county seat and the closest town of any size, was a world away: a good fifteen miles and a six-hour round-trip journey by horse. Bethel was long behind us when a dark silhouette came into view.

"It's old Mr. Tatternook with his dogs. The damn fool has blocked our way," Mr. Lucas muttered as he drew back on the horses' reins. A coarsely woven, irregularly fitting overcoat swaddled the man in black, and a pack of scraggly curs, wolf breeds, wild-eyed bear dogs, and yapping rat terriers encircled his feet. Under his breath Mr. Lucas let go a stream of oaths before he said, "What are you up to, Tatternook?"

There was no response from under the low, broad brim of the flapjack hat that almost obscured a patch across one eye. I expected the man and his dogs to approach Mr. Lucas, but as snow crunched under his boots, Tatternook shuffled to where I perched on the wagon's boards. He stared me dead in the eyes. Heat surged in my cheeks, and I recalled where I'd seen him. It had been one steamy, boring day last summer.

During the past year, I had settled into a routine of helping Pa with his mill and farm work. All summer and fall I'd lugged burlap sacks of wheat and then corn from farm wagons to a heap by the grinding stones, marked their number in the mill book, and watched the circular stones crush the grain as the huge water wheel forced them around. Then Pa and I scooped up the flour or cornmeal and bagged it for the farmer. While we worked, he'd mutter about how too much rain or too little rain was affecting wheat crops, and then he'd worry over his account book. Four bags of wheat ground for Mr. Lucas. Ten bags of corn ground for Mr. Hogshead. Who owes, who doesn't? The tedium of it, day in and day out, drove me mad.

The only thing I looked forward to was spending time with my friend Sam. While everyone sought his invitation for adventures, he most often chose me. I counted myself extremely lucky. No one ever paid any attention to the fact he was slightly bowlegged. Sam could still outrun almost any creature on two or four legs, once even a mad hound dog. He might have been considered short, but the muscles bulging his sleeves and straining his shirt across his chest made anyone think twice about mocking him. The son of a Bethel tavern keeper, he was springy as a cat and full of fire. He never got his fill of anything. He'd respond to even the crabbiest remarks with a wide, toothy grin and an open expression. That's when you noticed his dimples and strong chin, both pleasing to girls. He's the one who taught me to fire a hunting rifle, not Pa. And taught me before we were ten years old to swear as good as any sailor by mimicking what he'd heard in his father's tavern.

"Goddamnit, get your horse's arse over here," he'd yell.

"Not on your life, you yellow-bellied bastard," I'd holler back, and we'd laugh so hard at those forbidden words that we'd tumble onto the ground.

If I could have had my wish in those years, it would have been to be just like Sam, rather than the serious boy I was. No one ever accused him of being a bookworm.

Sam often sought out danger to leaven endless summer days, and he easily persuaded me to join in. I was eager to prove I was as much fun as his other friends, boys a year or two older. It was hard to compete with their tales of taking down ferocious bears and timber rattlesnakes, supposedly encountered during afternoons roaming the forest with rifles.

One August afternoon, Sam and I climbed into Mr. McKimmie's pasture to taunt his bull. The game was to flap a crimson kerchief before his broad snoot while whooping and hollering and then to run like the devil with the beast snorting at our heels until we catapulted over the fence. We kept at it until the bull had no more breath or energy. At one point, I spied a fellow clad in crow-black off in the distance but paid him no mind. Now, on the wintery road to Staunton, he stood before me. He hesitated a moment, then inquired, "Boy, do you remember me?"

My voice cracked as I responded, "I believe I've seen you around these parts once or twice, sir."

"You're correct there, Tom Smiley," he spoke softly. He hesitated for effect and then said, "Heed my warning, young man. Your rash nature and false pride will lead to nothing but remorse all your life. Unless you learn to curb them." His one piercing eye glittered as it locked onto my gaze. A chill flowed down my spine like a winter stream over rocks. Then, without further conversation, Tatternook abruptly moved away from the wagon with his dog pack and continued in the direction of Bethel. Sam and I looked at one another.

"What the devil? Just what did you do to provoke that old fellow?" Sam said. I shrugged my shoulders and rolled my eyes, hiding my unease.

Mr. Lucas thwacked the leather reins on the horses' flanks. "Pay no heed to that man. No one knows where he came from or who his folks are, and God knows what blinded him. Probably provoked someone into poking him in the eye. He's as odd as a three-dollar bill. All of Bethel is fortunate he keeps to himself." And we lurched forward.

Sam's father went his own way in town, and we were drawn toward the courthouse, curious about loud shouts echoing from that direction. When we rounded the corner, we found the source. A crowd had set up a rhythm of stamping feet and waving fists, cheering at the top of their lungs, "Seventy-six, seventy-six." The day's chill was forgotten as we pushed our way through to the center where fire in an iron barrel warmed the hands and hind parts of dozens of boys. The crowd looked to be our age but included a few older men on the sidelines. A uniformed man had taken the center of the courthouse broad stone porch as we drew closer. He drew himself up with an important air, and the crowd grew silent.

"Who's that?" Sam asked a boy standing close.

"Everyone knows he's Captain John Imboden, leader of the West Augusta Guard, the county's volunteer militia. Where've you been?"

"I don't know. What's this about?"

"You didn't hear about Lincoln's inaugural speech? It came in by telegram hours ago. He said that no state may withdraw from the Union. That's got people pretty riled up. Enough to think there might be a war. Imboden's looking for recruits for the Guard, I hear."

We listened to a tirade aimed at a group of boys barely old enough to shave. Imboden bellowed, "If there's no other way to defend our right to withdraw from oppressive rule, we'll band together to bear arms!" A lean, hawk-nosed man, he paced back and forth, shouting and spitting, while he fiercely pounded his clenched fist on his open palm. "Our patriotic ancestors cast off the yoke of tyrannical rule in 1776. We can do it too! Has this president forgotten the example set by the Founders and the colonies? We must defend our God-given rights! We must protect the inherent freedoms that Lincoln and his bogus new party will surely trample!"

A wave of "Seventy-six, seventy-six" swelled again from the crowd. The blaze that ignited the speaker's eyes and the hint of danger that rippled through his spare form were what riveted my attention. When Imboden paused to swig from a hip flask, I spotted someone waving at me. He grinned widely, revealing the familiar gap between his top teeth. It was Tayloe Hupp, a Staunton boy I'd known when we were children. He beckoned us to join him.

"Tom, you're here too? You look pretty much the same, but taller."

"You too." I didn't tell him that his teeth were the only way I recognized him. "My friend Sam and I rode into town with his father. We heard the ruckus and came only to satisfy our curiosity. I didn't imagine it would be anything like this."

"It's really something, isn't it? I think I'm going to sign up. It's one way to keep my old man from forcing me into his law practice. What about you fellows? Why don't you join me?"

Sam's brown eyes were dancing. His elbow nudged my ribs. "This is a heck of a lot better than spending our days charging McKimmie's bull, I'd say. Let's do it; let's enlist."

"I don't know. I'll have to think about it." I studied my boots rather than meet his challenging eyes. Joining the volunteer militia was something I'd never considered, not even for a minute.

"Come on. I won't do it without you." He playfully punched me on the shoulder. A broad grin covered Tayloe's face. Sam said, "You might have a better chance with Lizzie Fackler if you're in a uniform." He winked and waited for my response. I wished he had left Lizzie out of it. Her blue eyes fringed with dark lashes and the cupid's bow of her plump, inviting lips flashed to mind, along with the warm scent of the rose water she dabbed on her pale wrists. A month earlier she had held hands with me at the Saturday church social on two occasions, hiding our clasped fingers within the folds of her skirt and pressing them against her thigh. Then she'd allowed me to walk her home and steal an inviting, lingering kiss. I could still feel the damp softness of her mouth on mine. Without explanation, from the next day forward, she refused to even glance at me and wouldn't speak, either. I'd made the mistake of asking Sam about the peculiar ways of women. But to volunteer for the militia, I needed a bit more convincing than Tayloe's encouragement and Sam's goad about Lizzie.

Now Imboden was cunning, playing to the young crowd's rejection of authority. "Let's not forget George Washington was damn proud to be called a rebel, and we should be too!" A roar surged forth.

The voices faded into a dull buzz, and I was adrift in a daydream. Mountains and villages miles beyond my father's farm loomed in my mind's eye, as I imagined my heroic deeds. Staunton was the most I had ever journeyed, and I feared that would hold true all my life. Pa had never been farther than Staunton or Lexington, both no more than fifteen miles distant. He had no interest in visiting the state capital when Mr. Lucas invited him to accompany him a few years earlier. For the most part, he had no desire to see anything of the world beyond what he already knew, unless it was by absolute necessity. I, on the other hand, was desperate to exist awhile right on the edge of life and death—to feel truly alive in a manner that working in my father's fields and mill could never provide. It didn't occur to me then that the route to that high state required a deep numbness the remainder of the time.

Imboden's passionate rhetoric paid off. A long queue of boys formed before the table on the courthouse steps to sign up. Tayloe waited among them to scrawl his name on the muster roll, and Sam joined him. He raised an eyebrow at me and strode forward, dipping the pen in ink and firmly signing his name with a grand gesture. He then turned expectantly. With only a flicker of hesitation, I joined the line and signed when it was my turn. The three of us were now militiamen, partners in a pact with the unknown, and we strolled away from the courthouse—proud as pigs in mud.

And yet, during the three-hour wagon ride home, the thrill began to drain away. I dreaded telling my folks. Sam and I traded secretive, sly glances, but then sank into thought as Mr. Lucas's plodding team of farm horses parted the twilight landscape. Neither of us much considered that we had set ourselves on a traitor's path, joining a militia hell bent on over-throwing the United States government, if the call came. Nor had we given any thought to the reasons behind the conflict.

As the paneled front door thudded behind me, Ma cried out from the kitchen, "Is that you, Tom Smiley? We're sitting down to eat any minute now, so wash up quickly." I recall my mother so well from before the war. In those days, she was a person of habit and orderliness. She insisted that her kitchen be scrubbed spotless, not a splash of grease on a kettle or pot, and that we appear at the dining table for every meal on time, hair combed, hands washed. Her delicate face could become fierce in a flash if we dawdled long enough for food to chill but then could brighten quickly afterward. She also cared that no locks stray from the soft brown braids wrapped round her head and that her lace-collared dark dresses were stiffly pressed. But most specifically, she was generous with her maternal devotion and scrutiny, and, as her only son, I was the recipient of their greatest share.

Now I responded to her call. My image flared out of the hall mirror as I headed toward the kitchen, and I doubled back to check if I might look any different. I twisted my head this way and that. No, the same gangly fellow stared back, taller than most and capped by an unruly tousle of brown hair that refused to slick down. My long-nosed face tried on a sober expression, but I was still an awkward youth who had sprung up too fast for his clothes and features to keep pace. There was no new aura of manliness or derring-do. Nevertheless, the blue eyes above the sharp cheekbones were not those of the boy from the morning. These eyes burned with the promise of adventure.

Word flies across the county miles. The minute Mr. Lucas discovered Sam's deed, my parents would be quick to find out. I'd be in a far worse pickle if they got the news from a Bethel neighbor. The best time would be after everyone had gathered around the table for supper that night. Thinking of Pa's reaction, my palms grew sweaty, but the presence of my sisters and mother might soften his disapproval. They would be in opposition at first—not to the notion of a seceded Virginia, but to my thrusting myself into harm's way if war was to come.

Early nightfall had already tinted the shallow snow a deep indigo beyond the tall dining room windows when Ma and the girls finally settled china tureens and platters on the table's homespun linen cloth. The warm aromas of freshly baked corn bread, smoked ham from our own hogs, and green beans stewed with pork hocks held no lure for me. Through cracks in the thick, winter curtains, the gas lamps banded the powder-cloaked shrubs with golden light. I cast my gaze there rather than at the cheery faces around the table and allowed my mind to drift back to Tayloe at the courthouse.

I met him six years earlier when we were both twelve. Pa had need of a lawyer, and I had insisted on riding the three hours with him to Staunton. I was loafing next to the office door with my nose in one of my favorite books, *Ivanhoe,* when a fellow about my age trotted around the corner.

"What are you reading?" he asked, without any preliminaries, his bright eyes friendly and curious. "By the way, I'm Tayloe."

"I'm Tom. Tom Smiley," I said. Then I showed him the book's cover and asked, "Have you read this? It's powerfully good."

He nodded. "It's one of my favorites. I'll read any book about knights and kings."

"Me too." I tried to think of something more to say. "Is this where you live?" He glanced at the spacious brick house with the wide porch behind us and nodded again. "Well then, my father is paying a business call on your father," I said.

"I guess so." He paused a moment. "Do you play dominoes? We could sit on the porch while you watch for him."

"I'd like that," I said, trying not to stare at the conspicuous gap in his front teeth.

He strode off on the brick walk leading to the columned porch and I followed along. Just as we reached the steps, the formal front door swung open and a middle-aged Black woman dressed in blue calico and a white apron beckoned to Tayloe. She had a red kerchief around her head, and wisps of gray curls escaped around the edges. She placed her hands on her thin hips.

"Your mother says get on into this house. It's time for piano lessons, and you needn't be talking to boys you don't know." My eyes widened in wonder that a house slave was giving Tayloe orders, even if they started with his mother. I'd never known anyone with a house slave, and I quickly looked away, unsure of how to act.

Tayloe made a grimace and turned toward me. "Next time your father comes to town, get him to bring you by the house. We'll play dominoes then." I accepted his invitation only a couple of times. His mother treated me as though I wasn't a worthy guest by aiming a hard expression my way whenever she saw me at the door. Obviously, she didn't want her boy to befriend a farmer's son.

One thing I know, we were proud to have been tradespeople for several generations, and Scotch-Irish Presbyterians to boot. And there was not one slave on our place, or on our neighbors' lands. Folks in the Valley raised wheat and rye, not cotton, tobacco, and rice that required backbreaking labor. Those plants don't do well in the Valley's limey soil. Besides, we Virginians at the southwestern end of the Shenandoah Valley believed our own hard work built character. We couldn't abide the lazy Tidewater Virginia aristocrats with their English ways and indolent habits. They forced enslaved people to provide for all their needs. Tayloe's people had recently come from that part of the world and were no different.

With Tish and Mary's help, Ma did her own cooking, gardening, butchering, house cleaning, sewing, churning, milking, weaving, and putting up vegetables in crocks after the growing season. Pa's income from the mill just a quarter mile down the road, as well as livestock grazed on the farm, permitted us to live in a newly expanded four-bedroom woodsided house, drive a fashionable buggy, and to eat as fine and as often as we wished.

The toe of Mary's buttoned boot thwacked my ankle and brought me back to the present. Heads were bowed, ready to say grace. After Pa offered thanks to the Lord for providing the ample meal before us, his angled face grew stern, and his brows slanted toward his prominent nose. His eyes were stern behind his glasses. "Tom, do you know anything about an incident over at Mr. Ware's place? He says somebody has been using the back of his barn as target practice with eggs pilfered from his chicken coop. When I met him today on the road, he swore he spied you and the Lucas boy scurrying off behind his shed. You wouldn't be involved in some nonsense like that, would you?" He waited, elbow on the table and one hand cupped around his gray-bearded chin.

Caught off guard, I paused a second and then said, "No, sir. I can't imagine what fools would do such a half-witted thing—wasting a man's egg supply and spoiling his barn. Sam and I had nothing to do with it, you can be sure of that." But I couldn't meet his eyes directly. We'd thought the Wares weren't home—that they were off at a church supper with my parents. It was the sharp, quick thwack of the hard shell against the wood and the slow, messy aftermath that we found so pleasurable. Years later, the sound would trigger night terrors.

"Well, I hope not to hear of anything like this in the future." To my relief, he seemed satisfied and returned to his meal.

Sixteen-year-old Mary looked over at me with eyes that brimmed with mischief and a smile working the edges of her mouth. "Tom, just where have you been all day in such wretched weather?"

Ma and Pa both glanced up quickly from their plates as my face and ears flushed. Mary knew me well enough to suspect that I'd been up to something, and she was going to catch me out in front of our parents. Eyes glued to my fork, I muttered, "Sam and I went with Mr. Lucas to town today. What more do you need to know?"

Ma said sternly, "That's no way to talk to your sister. Answer the question that was put to you."

Now I'd have to tell them: I had committed myself to bear arms for the South, if it came to that. "Sam and I signed up with the West Augusta Guard today when we were in town," I stuttered. Forks clattered back to their plates, and everyone stared. "You should have heard all the speechifying. If you'd seen that fellow Imboden strutting and inciting the crowd like we did, you'd have been hard-pressed not to sign up yourselves."

My parents exchanged knowing looks. In their view, I was headstrong, and there was some truth to it. The schoolteacher took switches to my calves more often than the other fellows. Pa's tone was gruff. "Why now? There's been no call for volunteers, at least not that I know of, and those fellows in Richmond at the state convention don't seem anywhere ready to vote for secession. They've been at it for months, toing and froing on the subject. What's gotten into you, boy?" I had no good answer, sputtering and fumbling for words until abandoning the fruitless effort. My parents' faces darkened with a shared alarm.

Ma chimed in, "Do you have any knowledge of these militia hotheads you've joined yourself up with?"

"Do you?" I asked.

"I do indeed. They're a bunch of hooligans and reckless fools. It won't do you one whit of good to associate with the likes of them." Her eyes burned into mine. "Or to be impudent to your mother."

"Aw, Ma, they seem not such a bad lot. The leader is John Imboden, a high-falootin' Staunton lawyer who hobnobs with all the bigwigs in the State Capital. I ran into Tayloe Hupp at the rally. Remember him? He's the son of Pa's lawyer, and he thinks Imboden makes the sun rise and set."

"That's where you're both mistaken," Pa said. "Most people know he's a man of poor judgment and abrupt reactions—not a fellow to whom I would entrust my son." He placed both hands on the table and leaned forward. "For Lord's sake, withdraw before it's too late. This secession convention in Richmond may lead to a catastrophe." He glanced at Ma for confirmation. "I'll acknowledge that there's many a wager that there'll not be enough votes to secede—but if troubles are coming, you'll have committed yourself to the storm's center. If you hadn't done this outrageous thing, you might never be called to fight."

Ma nodded her head and then muttered something under her breath about bad influences. I was certain I heard Sam's name.

But they knew nothing of this business I'd signed up for. They were born too late for the American Revolution and were barely born in time for the War of 1812. There were no old veterans in the Bethel area, and my father hadn't ever been an army man. He had never believed that fighting just for fighting's sake was noble.

I usually could count on Mary, younger by two years, to support me, even if she had sparked this uncomfortable discussion. She and I were most alike. When I was ten and she was eight and wore braids, she entered my room one summer day and found me bent over a piece of paper on my desk in a bar of sunlight. I held a large magnifying glass a few inches above the white surface and peered through it so intently that I didn't hear the door creak open.

"What's that?" she said loudly, causing me to drop the glass to the carpet. When I jerked around in my chair, her expression revealed the same wonder at the insect's appearance that I had felt. I hadn't the heart to scold her for startling me.

"It's a snaketail dragonfly. In Latin, it's called an *O-phi-o-gomphus*," I told her, slowly sounding out the syllables of the unfamiliar word I'd found in Dr. Asa Finch's *Science of Entomology*.

"Oh, fie on gomphus," she yelled and burst into giggles. "Gomphus is a terrible sickness. Fie on it! You'd better not let Ma hear you talk about that!"

"It's not a disease, Silly. Come here and look more closely. I caught it down by the stream." I put the magnifying glass in her hand and shoved the paper across my desk toward her. A four-winged insect with a thin, armored tail lay pinned to the surface. Its bulbous blue eyes reflected a tiny image of the window's light.

"It's beautiful and scary," she said.

"Now let me have my glass back."

"Not yet." She bent lower over the paper. "Did you see how the belly is patterned like a snake?"

"Abdomen, not belly. You have to learn the terms." I gave her brown braid a sharp tug. She kicked me in the shin and fled, hollering for Ma.

From that afternoon on, she shared my love of collecting and studying insects. I made her a long-handled net to match mine with discarded strips of our mother's hat veiling sewn to a bent piece of willow. When we finished with summer chores, Mary would run with me along the stream or in the field grass. We'd lie quietly on our bellies in the baking sun and wait for an unsuspecting grasshopper or an eastern Hercules beetle to scurry by. Then we'd scoop it up, drop it in an old apothecary bottle, and plug the glass mouth with a cork until we carried it back to the house to identify it in the insect book. I showed Mary how to draw the carapace, six spiny legs, stalk-like antennae, and to write the Latin name in her best script beneath. With practice, she became an even better draftsman than I was.

And, like me, she was restless to see more of the world, but was pretty enough to attract a fine husband who would settle her down. At least, that's what we thought then. Our mother's sapphire eyes shone from Mary's fine-boned face, but Mary's were always alight with a wry humor. Even though I teased her mercilessly, she was the one with whom I shared my doubts and worries.

Now she said softly to our parents, "Allow him a chance to speak before you judge him harshly." She turned toward me with wide eyes. "You must have a good reason, don't you, Tom?" But I honestly couldn't think of one worthwhile explanation for my actions at the courthouse. It seemed the better course to stay silent.

At twenty, Letitia was the oldest of us three and I always thought she was a bit jealous of my status as the only son. She said, "Why must you always be so rash? Pa needs you at the mill and around here in the fields. He depends upon you. How will he possibly manage?" Her tone became sour. "I agree with Pa. You could at least have waited until matters are more decided."

At first, I didn't want to acknowledge what she said. But later that evening, her words about abandoning my father to do all the work and Mary's concern for my safety had a sting. I began to regret my decision. In truth, Pa often complained of sore arms and an aching back, and he'd recently become more dependent upon my younger muscles for help with heavy work. But it was too late to withdraw. My earlier euphoria was reduced to a leaden feeling in my stomach. I wondered how Sam was faring with his family.

3

WHAT UNMITIGATED NERVE THAT INVADING WOMAN HAD TODAY! She hired two burly fellows to haul away the parlor's grand piano. They cussed and sweated, inching its awkward bulk through the doors, chipping off bits of the black varnish. Ma would have been beside herself to see the long scratches and to hear the splitting wood as the piece was upended and shoved down the porch steps. Maybe the instrument did take up half the room, as the woman complained, and maybe never could be properly tuned again. But its music had given life to the house.

My beloved Ellen would pound the keys as she worked the brass floor pedals. Mary would stand with her hands on Ellen's shoulders, as they warbled their hearts out. "Rock of Ages" soared through every room, as well as "Onward Christian Soldiers." I can also see little Cara biting her lip in concentration, practicing for Miss Marley's recitals and then making us proud. The house will not be the same again.

That stout-legged instrument was Ma's last sizeable purchase—in March 1861—before the war and the pinched aftermath. Pa proudly hauled it home in time for the Saturday social to which Ma had invited most of the Bethel neighbors and the New Jerusalem minister.

After sufficient gossip was shared over tea and Ma's lemon pound cake, the guests congregated in the parlor to view the new acquisition. "Play something, Christiana. Let's hear what this marvel sounds like," said Mrs. Calliston, with barely concealed envy. Tight rolls of curls bobbed beside her cheeks while she spoke. She wiped her plump face with a lace handkerchief and gave the group a coy smile, revealing yellowed wooden teeth. Another neighbor begged Mary to sing "The First Rose of Summer" accompanied by her mother, and soon everyone joined in. Their sweet voices led by Ma's and Mary's harmonizing soared through the parlor.

When the men's impatience to discuss the current political crisis became unbearable, they moved to the library. There would be a heated discussion, but only after they filled their pipes and clipped their cigars. I followed and settled inconspicuously against the wall. No one had commented on my itchy new beard. "Is there news this week from the State Capital on the secession debate?" asked Mr. Lucas, after a long draw on his pipe. "It's been going on too damned long."

Mr. Beard watched with hands jammed in his pockets, but now he spoke with frustration in his voice. "Our delegate will never change his mind. He's dead set against secession, like so many in this county." His bald head reflected a square of light from the window, and he rubbed his hand back and forth, polishing its surface.

"Our delegate is damned right," said portly Mr. Hogshead, his jowls wobbling. All eyes turned to him; the group respected his opinion because he was the wealthiest farmer among them. "For God's sake, Beard, what are you thinking? This is treason!" His face was tomato red. "Do you believe the federal government is going to stand by while the states secede, one after another?" Scarlet splotches now bloomed above his collar. "You secessionists aren't being rational about the consequences. We'll have a war on our hands, I guarantee it."

Reverend McIntyre had studied the floor during this exchange, but his hands had clenched into tight fists by his side. He'd been minister at New Jerusalem Presbyterian Church for at least a decade and was well regarded by the men in the room. Now he couldn't hold back any longer. "Gentlemen, you're missing the point." He paused and his eyes traveled the room, looking to engage each man. "Be certain you are clear about something. This is not a theoretical debate about the federal government interfering with states' rights. It's about whether one man can keep another in bondage, keep him uneducated and without property, and sell his wife and children away in real life. And why do the slaveholders in our state legislature want to secede? So they can protect their wealth built on this heinous practice." He pounded his fist on the table and roared, "They're all slave holders! The Southern position is about monumental greed, nothing more. A greed that flourishes because of a vast evil." The room was silent, with only the uncomfortable shuffling of a few feet to be heard. In a lower tone, he acknowledged that none of the men in the room owned slaves, but those who did would be damned in the eyes of God. "You can bluster all you want about states' rights, but the debate is really whether Virginia's wealthy, and their kind farther south, can persist with this abomination. We are at a profound moral crossroads." Several men turned their heads away, unable to meet McIntyre's challenging eyes, and the room was quiet.

Mr. Beard finally spoke. "There won't be a war, even if Virginia secedes. Seven states have already seized Federal forts and left the Union months ago. What did President Buchanan do? Nothing! Sure, slavery is outlawed in new territories, but when they're states and they send representatives to Congress, who's to say they'll pitch in with Northerners to overwhelm Southern interests? That's what scares these slave owners. But nobody can guarantee that's going to happen. These people are letting nonsense sicken their minds, splitting off from the Union."

"Well, a threat to slavery seems inevitable to me and a lot of other people. Important people," muttered one man.

Mr. Beard's voice drowned him out. "And Lincoln has promised he won't mess with slave-owning states. I'm betting he won't do anything more than the last fellow." Several listeners nodded in agreement.

Reverend McIntyre's face paled. "Don't be so cock sure of yourself there. No question about it, secession is treason, and Virginia may be the tipping point. We already know Lincoln's view on the matter. And then what? War." He pointed his finger at the closest man. "And make no mistake what it's about. Not this states' rights nonsense. Do you really want to risk your boys' lives to perpetuate slavery?"

Mr. Beard cleared his throat. "I don't think anyone in this room wants to go to war," he said. Most of the men murmured agreement. Mr. Beard was wrong about one of us. I wanted to go to war. I'm profoundly ashamed to say I hadn't given the plight of slaves much thought. The only encounter with a slave that had made any impression upon me was at Tayloe's house years earlier, and I was merely curious for the short time she appeared at his family's door. To tell the truth, at this moment, I only hungered for a change.

McIntyre then quickly moved toward the door, grabbing his hat from the hook. Some later said they heard him say, "If it takes a war to end slavery, then I'd be for it."

When his footsteps sounded on the porch steps, Pa said, "Look here. We lose nothing if slavery is outlawed. No investment, no lazy manner of living we'd have to give up." Pa then gave me a hard look. "And the idea of fighting to protect the wealth of a bunch of slave owners far away in eastern Virginia is preposterous. These rich men in Richmond want to drag all of us toward disaster with them."

A chorus of "Hear, hear!" and "Amen" followed, as the neighbors, relieved, agreed on that one thing. They hadn't been convinced by Reverend McIntyre of slavery's evil, a practice which they simply accepted, but none of older men in the room wanted to take up arms or have their sons do so. It seemed as if Bethel and the entire nation were holding their breath those early spring months.

Several times a week in March and early April, Sam and I joined the other militia volunteers who marched left and right in ragged rows behind the house. Looking back, I wonder at our innocence, at how little the militia leader, Imboden, knew. A few hours of shooting family rifles at targets nailed to trees was no preparation for real war. Most of the boys were restless youths like us, but we were joined by a few older men—pro-slavery fanatics, every one of them. After drill practice and when they were out of sight, Sam would mimic a fellow named Harris who hated Lincoln. Using two fingers to squeeze his nose, he'd capture the man's thin, venom-filled speech, while I'd double over laughing at his perfect impersonation.

Finally, before breakfast on April 17, John Hite, a fellow of my age who lived two miles north, charged up the farm roadway on his horse. Barely knotting the reins to the fence, he bounded onto the front porch, skipping plank steps two at a time. Ma heard his boots thudding and was at the door before he could knock. His voice reached me in the upstairs hall, "Tell Tom that Imboden dispatched a telegram from Richmond to all West Augusta Guard officers late last night. He ordered them to gather their men. They're to meet at the train station before noon today."

Her brow wrinkled. "What's the meaning of this? Surely you can come in for a moment and tell us more."

He thanked her but refused. "I can't tarry. Anyway, that's all I know. The message didn't say where they were headed. Just tell Tom to get to town double-quick."

As he flung himself off the porch, he hollered back over his shoulder. "And tell him to bring whatever weapons he has!" By the time I yanked on my boots and tore down the stairs with laces flapping, his horse was receding in the dust.

Pale as the moon, Ma met me in the hall, wringing her hands. "I feared this was going to happen. Imboden is up to no good, and you're being dragged into it. Now the man orders you to run off to some unknown destination, with weapons, no less. It makes no sense. That boy didn't say one word about a vote in the state convention to secede." She hurried toward the kitchen without giving me a chance to respond.

I found her at the scarred pine table with a butcher knife in hand, ready to slice smoked ham for my travels. But first she prayed, with no concern that I had entered the room. "Oh, Lord, praised be Thy Name. Watch over my son and let this trouble pass quickly, whatever it may be. He may not be one of your flock, but he's a good boy, the only one I have, and he deserves your protection."

"Ma, stop that rubbish! For once, leave God out of it." She startled and dropped the knife on the table. Her lips quivered, and her slumping shoulders tugged at my heart. Hoping to soften the harshness of my words, I wrapped my arm around her and stooped to give her a quick kiss on the check. Under my fingers, her shoulder blades pressed through the thin fabric of her linen blouse.

"You're forgiven." She managed a wan smile, but her eyes were wet. She then gently pushed me out of her way.

The previous week, when I returned from drill in the afternoon, Ma had met me at the door with a wooden cooking spoon in hand. She'd been so kidnapped by her thoughts that she hadn't remembered to put the spoon down. She waved it at me as she spoke. "I'm worried sick about this soldier business, even if you aren't. You should be more concerned, Tom Smiley, about the state of your soul before you go endangering your life."

"For cripes sake. I'll be fine." I knew that she believed my lack of faith guaranteed she would never see me in Heaven. When Gabriel blew his trumpet, my soul would be chained to the cemetery headstone.

She was absolutely right about my not being one of God's flock. If my parent's oversight was unbearable, the idea of an omnipotent spy in the heavens was even worse. Ma's moral lectures got under my skin, and now that I was old enough to have a say in the matter, I kept my distance from Sunday services. I left her bustling in the kitchen and went upstairs to gather my belongings.

For weeks, I'd been considering what I would carry if the militia were called up suddenly. A sketchbook, pencils and stationery, my mother's kitchen table oilcloth for rain-garb and protection for the rolled blanket, a volume of Longfellow poetry, two pairs of thick wool socks, and three changes of clothing bulged the sides of my sack. I tucked in a moth-eaten rabbit's foot and Mary's pressed four-leaf clover for luck. After removing the book and extra clothing, the sack was light enough for marching— considering I'd also have to haul a rifle, ammunition, and supplies.

Proudly eyeing that lumpy haversack propped at the ready by my bedroom door, I had allowed myself to daydream. Waves of men herded captives off the battlefield, as my courageous actions led to yet another victory. An officer's commission and a horse would soon follow. But that was nonsense. The first months of the war quickly taught me that only wealthy highborn men could become officers, not tradesmen's sons like Sam and me.

Now Pa's voice drifted up from the kitchen below. "Don't fret so," he told my mother. He reminded her of how Imboden and his useless militia ran off to western Virginia to protect citizens during John Brown's hanging when they had some lunatic notion of a slave revolt. It all came to nothing, and the militia came home in two weeks.

"That was different, William. The nation wasn't in such turmoil. My worries won't be shooed away, although I know you mean well," Ma said. The tremor in her voice told me she was probably dabbing at her eyes with her apron corners as she returned to her tasks.

While I checked my knapsack's contents one last time, Mary and Tish joined my mother in the kitchen. Silent in their worry, the women prepared a basket of provisions, neatly tucking in Ma's sliced smoked ham, dried beef, apples, biscuits, corn bread, and slices of minced meat pie that might last for several days, all wound up in flour-sacking. That evening on the train, I found a religious tract that Ma had poked in, and Mary had scribbled a message reminding me to take care. Tish had contributed nothing.

All three gathered in the front hall to say goodbye before I trotted up to join Pa at the barn. My oldest sister leaned against the wall with her arms folded and muttered, "Take care of yourself," but Mary was bursting with demands.

"Be sure to write, Tom, the very minute you know where you'll be going. And don't leave anything out. Promise."

"I will write, don't worry."

"You didn't promise. Swear that you'll let us know everything. Write every day. And tell us what Sam is doing, too."

"I said I'll write. I promise."

"That's better." And then she pushed into my hand a small, rolled rectangle of paper tied with a ribbon. "A going away present," she whispered and gave my earlobe a gentle tug.

I tucked the paper carefully under the flap of my haversack without unrolling it. Later, on the train, I untied the knot and saw the meaning of her gift. It was her most treasured and skillful drawing, a page of eastern June bugs marching in rows, their brilliant green and brown bodies colored in glowing ink. The sweet smell of the farm's field grass and the excitement of our discoveries would come back to me every time I unfurled it.

Ma had been waiting solemnly until Mary finished, but then she stepped toward me and pulled me wordlessly into a tight hug, just as she did when I was a small boy. She stepped back, touched my face with the back of her hand as though she could feel the excited fever coursing through me, and hastily retreated to the kitchen. Mary rolled her eyes and then shoved me toward the door.

"Pa's waiting, so get going. Come home soon as you can."

When I arrived at the barn door, I saw that Pa had fetched Wilbur, one of his two plow horses, for the long ride to the Staunton train station. I'd be astride behind him with my haversack over my shoulder. Pa was a man in his fifties—he and Ma didn't begin a family until they were in their third decade. He groaned with the effort as he threw the leather saddle over Wilbur's back and bent to fasten the straps under the horse's broad belly. Withholding judgment after John Hite's arrival that morning, he now straightened up, scowled through his wire-frame glasses, and said, "You know I'm a more cautious man than you. I wouldn't have rushed to enlist, even when I was your age." He shook his head, "I wish there was something I could do to change your mind."

"It's too late for that, Pa. But don't worry. I'll be fine." I put my hand on his shoulder.

"How can I not worry, if we have a war on our hands? You know Ma and your sisters will be powerfully upset if that's the case. Especially Ma."

There was a long, uncomfortable silence between us. Slowly, he pulled a wad of money from the small leather bag at his belt and said, "Here, Son, you might as well take these bills for your train fare. You can't pay for such a trip yourself." Then he awkwardly clasped me to him. "There's some in the pouch for the way back, too." His words were partially muffled by my coat collar. We broke apart and pretended nothing had happened. I couldn't bear to look at him. I worried my resolve might crack, and, worse, that Pa might detect my impatience to leave and would be hurt by it.

In a defeated voice he said, "I suppose there's some consolation if those boys, Sam and Tayloe, are headed off with you." He turned toward Wilbur to tighten the stirrups one more time. As we trotted down the barn lane, I saw that my mother and Mary had come into the yard. Mary put her arm around Ma's waist, and they leaned into one another. Both raised their hands and waved. Veering onto the road to Staunton, I heard Ma's farewell fade away.

Bewildered by Imboden's telegram, Pa counted on passengers from the overnight Richmond train to provide clarification. He urged poor Wilbur to a feverish gait, forcing the big beast to sweat and strain forward with his double burden. There was no news. There was no war. Ma proved to be dead right about that scoundrel Imboden. We were traitors and then became the state's first cannon fodder.

4

IN THE KITCHEN THIS MORNING I SAW THE WOMAN REGISTER THE train's whistle coming from miles away, tilting her head as she swirled suds on the breakfast dishes. Ellen's finest, the ones with delicate sprigs of corn flowers around the scalloped edges. My wife would be so grieved to see that her porcelain plates are now chipped from careless use. Christmas goose and sweet potatoes, Cara's currant and rum wedding cake, and countless birthday feasts were served up on that china. As the settings glistened on the linen cloth, Pa's face glowed with pride that his wife and girls had once again created such a bounty from his labor. Now look at those plates. But dwelling on them will only deepen my increasing misery.

The long wail of the train reminds me of the frenzy of excitement when construction on the new railroad line was finished a few years before the war, and Staunton was finally connected to the rest of the world. Until the day I boarded the train with Imboden's militia boys, I'd never ridden one of the new steam horses. It was an auspicious start for an adventure.

Some older fellows, summoned so quickly there was no time to change, sported dress suits. Sam had arrived at the Staunton rail station with a formal top hat perched at an angle on his head, capping off his bandy-legged swagger. His slingshot, carved from a knotty hickory branch, protruded from one pants pocket, and the sack of stones he'd collected from Tinkling Creek along the Bethel road, bulged the other. Many fellows bristled with pistols strapped to their thighs or stuck in their pants' waistbands. Sheathed hunting knives dangled from belts. I toted one of Pa's hunting rifles.

The train chugged north through the Valley. The boys boarding at Orange were convinced we were headed to the nation's capital, but no one could imagine what we'd do there. At the Culpeper stop, a fellow who sat behind me swore we were off to Alexandria. He'd heard rumors about tearing up the docks and disrupting shipping. Sam, Tayloe, and I unlatched and pushed up the windows. Leaning out, we hollered at every living thing—men, women, children, cows, horses, pigs, chickens—as the train plowed through the countryside. For most of us, the ride was the greatest novelty ever. To celebrate, boys around us broke out flasks of liquor, fueling boisterous boasts and cussing as the sun went down. Ma's voice was still too recent in my ears for me to be tempted to share in the boozing, but Sam gleefully guzzled the proffered spirits.

We rumbled along by rail all night, finally reaching Strasburg in the early gray light. A subdued crowd, we stumbled out of the cars, rubbing our eyes and hoisting haversacks for a twenty-mile walk toward a Winchester train. We hadn't gone far when I heard a commotion in the crooked line ahead.

"Something's going on," Sam said, and sprinted ahead to get wind of it. He hooted like a banshee and tossed his hat in the air.

"It's happened! We've seceded! The vote was 85 to 56 in favor!" he shouted. A hot buzz of voices swirled around us. Chest heaving, Sam again fell into step next to me. Then his face suddenly became grave. The ham bone I'd been gnawing fell to the ground. The lines straightened up, and each boy was, for the first time, a real soldier.

"Sam," I said in a low voice, "Did you ever believe this day would come? Now that it's real, there's no turning back." He didn't answer. He just strode forward with a pensive air.

An older man overheard. "Don't be so glum, boys. Have y'all forgotten? We're a bunch of farmers and hunters. We know how to use a gun." He paused to shift a chunk of tobacco to the other cheek. "Those citified Northerners who ain't never shot nothin' will scurry back home with their tails between their legs. Just like coon dogs who failed to git the coon." He spat to the roadside and bit off another plug. "We'll be back in the fields before summer harvest."

"I'm not so sure about that," Sam said. But the fellow already had wandered off.

By the time we reached Winchester, heel blisters had risen and popped, and my shoulders throbbed from the weight of the haversack. Exhaustion had dampened our enthusiasm. It was then that we heard we were bound for Harpers Ferry, famous as home of the country's largest gun-manufacturing plant and arsenal, the very place John Brown had failed to seize two years earlier. Our goal was the same—to seize the arsenal and the weapons. But for the possible Confederacy this time, not a slave revolt. An anxious undercurrent coursed through the car. "Look what happened to John Brown," Sam said. "The Feds strung him up for treason and ripped his gang's guts out. I heard they cut off one fellow's ears, shot and hanged some others, and sliced off their arms and legs afterward. Some weren't even given a decent burial." I felt the blood rush from my face and saw others turn pale.

"That scum Imboden tricked us," Sam growled. This was a side of Sam I'd never seen, a Sam who was less sure he would come out ahead in any situation. I was shaken and turned away lest he sense it.

Tayloe looked like he'd seen a ghost. "What if we fail too? Why would they treat us any different than they treated Brown and his gang?" The air seemed to thicken in our car and boys' shoulders slumped.

This was the first time I'd faced the possible consequences of what we were doing. To buoy myself, I reminded them that Brown had only seventeen men; we had many more.

Night fell. Fellows propped their backs against the freight car walls or curled up on the floor with their heads on knapsacks, unconscious until morning light pierced the cracks. Sam dozed within hollering distance while, too stirred up to close my eyes, I leaned against the wooden wall all night and saw the industrial town as it came into view at dawn. Carved out of limestone cliffs, there was scarce room between rock and river for any buildings. An ominous curtain of greasy black smoke stretched along the riverbank and hovered over rooftops. Boys began to stir. "What's that stink?"

"I dunno," one fellow said. "Smells like a blacksmith forge to me." He squinted his eyes and sniffed the air.

The train brakes screeched to a stop on the trestles leading across the narrowest section of the Shenandoah River. The engineer waited for the signal to move forward. In the early morning light, I caught sight below of a man squatting at the bridge's stone base. His movements were jerky; he seemed uneasy. Twenty small wooden kegs lay about as he tinkered with something. Then he charged up the hill like his tail was on fire. Without a word, Sam thrust aside his haversack, cast off his hat, and dove through the open doors. He almost flew down the hillside.

"Well, there goes our first deserter. Don't take much to scare that fellow," the boy who stood next to me said.

We crowded the open rail car door, boys craning their necks to get a view. On the riverbank, Sam stomped on flames inching along a rope that trailed toward the kegs.

"Dynamite! That son-of-a-bitch tried to blow up the train and kill us!"

The other fellows had finally realized why Sam had leapt from the car. Ashen-faced and fists pounding, he raced uphill, leaping over rocks and clumps of wire grass to reach the train just as it began to roll. He ran alongside, picking up speed with the freight cars. Gasping for air, he hollered my name, then Tayloe's. "Come on," I yelled. "We'll pull you in." He propelled himself halfway into the car opening, legs flailing over the tracks. Tayloe and I gripped his arms and the back of his jacket and tugged him the rest of the way.

I whacked his shoulder, "You're a war hero already."

"Boy, I sure couldn't have acted so fast," a fellow standing nearby said. I flushed with pride that Sam was my friend.

He bent half over, hands on knees, gasping for breath. His hair tumbled over his sweaty face. "How did someone know that soldiers were headed to the Ferry?" he finally sputtered.

"Oh no. If the Feds got word, they might have a full army there by now," the fellow swaying next to Sam said. His eyes were huge.

"I knew it. I knew this was a bad idea," said Tayloe. He grabbed for the pistol he had stuck in his belt and clutched it in a shaking hand.

Safely across the bridge and into the station, we straggled off. I paused for a moment, feeling newly alive now that death had passed us by. But sounds of four hundred confused and milling boys, plus a nostril-searing odor of hot iron, quickly dispelled my sense of awe.

I was scared. Tayloe kept running his tongue across his lips, a sign he was scared too. I think the smell threw everyone off, including the militia commanders. This wasn't what we'd expected, even though I'd caught a glimpse of smoke from the train.

"Prepare to march," hollered the militia leaders, and the three of us fell into a scraggly line behind some Staunton boys. We nervously opened and closed our powder canisters and jiggled minié balls as we waited, praying our weeks of practice at home would be enough. Boys from Culpeper were an exception. They had no weapons. Instead, they scouted the train yard for sticks and then stuffed stones from between the rails in their pockets. Nobody, not even the so-called officers, appeared to know what was called for next. On command, our entire band of four hundred hesitantly moved out into Potomac Street and saw something that made my jaw drop. Weapons clattered to the ground as boys gaped in stunned shock.

The armory was a smoldering mess of bricks and mortar, a few tottering pieces of wall, molten lumps of metal, and twisted girders. Small flames still licked at the building shell. There were no Feds.

All order collapsed, and despite the militia leaders' protests, Tayloe, Sam, and I, along with most of the other boys, wandered off to discover the cause. And if truth be known, to explore the town.

Beyond the armory debris on Potomac Street, we saw another astonishing sight. Townspeople strained at wheelbarrows piled with tools, clothes, hams, fowl, and children. It was a noisy procession with parents urging older children to hurry and neighbors shouting to one another. Cruel jeers of "Good riddance, Lincolnites" and "Take this, you Unionists" followed them as pro-secession youngsters hurled eggs and chunks of clay at their backs. Infants bawled and struggled in their parents' hold, and toddlers swung onto their mothers' skirts as the throng surged forward, ignoring the insults and blows in their haste to depart.

Sam and Tayloe were impatient to explore, so I let them go ahead of me. I wanted answers for why the armory had burned. I caught the eye of a sallow-faced man leaning against a doorjamb watching the scene as he rolled a cigar. He poured a little more tobacco from a leather pouch onto the brown paper and then licked the edge. After placing the unlit cigar in his mouth, he seemed willing to talk.

"Why isn't a federal army here? Did another rebel group beat us to the Ferry?" I asked. My boots crunched glass underfoot. Not a window remained intact for several blocks near the factory ruins, and building facades were marked with swaths of soot.

The man sucked on his stogie, hitched up his canvas pants, and replied, "Another rebel group? So that's who you are. I knew I hadn't seen your face before." He looked as though he was debating how much to tell me. Finally, he said, "Hell, no. The durn fool Federals done this to themselves. A fellow returned to the Ferry yesterday evening from the Virginia Convention and snitched to the armory guards that the state had seceded. That you boys were on your way for weapons."

"A snitch? I can't believe it. Of all the danged luck!"

"Yep," he said. "Anyway, as of last winter, the arsenal commander had only a dozen guards on hand. The poor fellow begged higher ups for more, but none were sent. Now he and his men have fled before y'all could get here."

"Can you tell me how it happened?"

"It was in the midst of a big uproar. You never saw folks so heated up when the news of secession spread. Why, even my neighbor and I threw punches at one another during a brawl in our local tavern. I never suspected he'd be a Union sympathizer. You can't tell about folks sometimes," he said. "The fellow was getting the better of me, had my shoulders pinned to the floor, until we both heard an explosion so strong that glasses behind the bar crashed to the ground. That brought us and the other brawlers to our senses, and we ran outside to see what had happened. Word spread fast that the federal arsenal commander had blown the armory to kingdom come to keep the weapons out of your hands. And the dangest thing was that he used explosives left over from when John Brown brought them to the Ferry to blow up the arsenal. How about that!"

We were both silent for a moment, taking in the strangeness of it all. Then I remembered all those pitiful folks at the end of Potomac Street.

"Why are all of these people leaving town? Who are they?" I asked.

"Foreigners," he said and then spat into the street. "Damned European immigrants come down from the North to work in the munitions plant. Nothing but pariahs now that we've seceded."

Just at that moment, I saw Tayloe and Sam stepping gingerly through the debris at the end of the street. I thanked the man and hurried off in their direction to find lodgings.

5

I'VE HEARD IT SAID THAT DOGS AND CATS SEE HAUNTS, AND THIS BLACK canine has given truth to that legend. She prowls the library doorway with a ruff the envy of any lion, snarling while peering straight at me. She makes me laugh, but I'm gratified to say, she distresses her mistress. "C'mon, c'mon now, Emma. Stop that foolishness." The dog looks at me out of the corner of her eyes and growls one last time. The woman drags her away by her pink collar, glancing furtively over her shoulder into the room, hoping to see nothing. Sometimes this dog, when contented, puts me in mind of Old Susie. An admirable creature, she showed up during the early days in Harpers Ferry.

Sam, Tayloe, and I benefited mightily from others' misfortune—finding an abandoned cottage up on Ridge Street along the row of arsenal workers' housing. The floor was littered with odds and ends from a hasty departure: a baby quilt, yards of linen, woolen pants and coats, a book or two, as well as chests and empty bedsteads too cumbersome to be hauled away. I fingered a delicate lace glove dropped by the door and tried to conjure its owner. Maybe she was a fair, soft-skinned young woman. One with a waist so small I could span it with my two hands. But Sam's call from within the house destroyed my reverie.

There were soon twelve of us competing for a spot to sleep. Our place was as overrun as the rest along that street—each crammed with boys persuaded that for daring an early raid they deserved this luxurious shelter. Thousands of latecomers squatted in flimsy tents ringing the town.

About a week after we'd settled in, several of us reclined on the porch steps during sundown. Some swigged brew peddled by enterprising mountain folks who had found an eager market in boys new to inebriants in such quantity and regularity. Sounds and smells of retching wafted through the evening air. Imboden hadn't foreseen the need for food, and the shelves of every merchant had been swept clean days earlier. We prayed for the arrival of fathers, uncles, and brothers driving wagons loaded with eatables.

"This entire town is nothing but a stinking hole, and this hovel's no better," Tayloe griped.

"You don't smell much like a rose yourself," I said. "I bet those clothes you're wearing haven't seen soap and water in weeks."

"Look who's talking," he said.

At that moment, we spotted one of the Mississippi boys sauntering along the street, dragging behind him a sorry yellow dog with a noose around its neck. Its head bobbed low, and its tail sagged along its flanks.

"Say, hold up! Where you going with that miserable creature?" Sam had risen to his feet, top hat at an angle. The scrawny lad stopped in his tracks. He was struggling to sprout a beard, and a cowlick sprouted from spikes of greasy hair. He scratched his belly under his shirt before answering.

"This is a goddamned Union dog, left behind by those filthy Lincolnites. The boys and I are about to teach it something about the new Confederacy." We barely understood his drunken drawl, but it was clear that whatever activity he had planned would be the animal's last. She yelped as he kicked at her skinny ribs.

Sam's eye fell on a piece of rope draped over a chair back. "Wait a minute now. I have something you may want more than that useless cur. An item that is rare and valuable, of some historical merit. Come over and take a look." As the drunken fellow peered through the dusk at Sam's hand, he continued. "This here was torn down from the gallows in Charles Town in '59. It was part of the rope that swung that devil John Brown.

I hate to part with it, but I've always wanted to get myself a dog—and a yellow one at that."

The boy paused. The idea of having such a thing clearly tickled his fancy. "Where'd you get that? I heard some chap is hawking genuine John Brown souvenirs, but I don't have the money to get none. I seen chunks of a stump that Governor Wise dismounted on and strips of pine planking from the gallows. But the rope that hung John Brown would impress the bejesus out of folks at home."

"Hell, this piece could have been the one to choke Brown dead. Right across his Adam's apple." Sam angled his hand across his neck to make the point. He then held out his rope in exchange for the one that throttled the dog. The Mississippian agreed, smug with confidence he had gotten the better deal. The dog used every last bit of her energy to put her paws on Sam's knees and swipe a lick of gratitude across his cheek.

That's how we came by Susie Louise Dedrick, Old Susie for short, named by Sam after a girl back home who'd stolen his heart. It would be hard to find a better or more appreciative animal. After giving up a profound sigh of contentment, she'd sleep at night with her head on one of our chests, liquid eyes occasionally half-open to lather her saviors in adoration.

Just as we thought we might starve due to Imboden's complete poverty of planning, my father and Mr. Lucas drove three days to the Ferry with a wagon loaded with hams, dried beef, apples, potatoes, and bread. When Pa jumped from the wagon to greet us, I almost knocked him down with a hug. Laughing heartily, he slapped me on the back. That food never tasted better, even at home. Old Susie got the leftover fat and tough bits and licked crumbs from my chin and fingers. Afterward, she sighed with the same deep happiness that I felt as she curled at my feet. Every day, Susie padded along to the arsenal as we dismantled any useable equipment for shipment to Richmond. She skulked about the thousands of heat-bent weapons while she tried to rustle up a meal of river rats. I grew dependent upon her company, the feel of her warm head under my hand, her silken ears between my fingers, and her exuberant greeting whenever she spied us. She eased my growing homesickness.

One day in late April before Tom Jackson arrived to take charge, a group of Georgia boys hailed us to join them in some merriment. A United States mail train had been detained, and a quantity of incoming Harpers Ferry letters lay undelivered in the rail cars. Springing up through the yawning doors, boys ripped into the bags, spilling envelopes and packages everywhere. Some lads perched on unopened sacks. Others reclined on the car floor and read as Sam and I rifled in vain for love missives we could pretend were intended for us. Susie had leaped into the car and entertained herself pouncing through the stacks, envelopes cascading over her nose.

Tayloe ripped through the envelopes like a man gone mad and then yelped, "Got one! Listen to this!" In a falsetto voice, batting his eyelashes like a girl, he read a letter from a young wife in Virginia to her husband in Ohio. Sam and I howled like coyotes when he got to the part where she described yearning to be enfolded in his arms again. Susie added a yowl or two to our chorus.

The Georgians were looking for a different kind of declaration—one that linked the recipient to the Union. They were speedily rewarded with a letter addressed to William McCoy from a relative in Pennsylvania. McCoy was a neighbor close by up on Bolivar Street. As he strolled past our cottage, I remarked in my homesickness that he was of my father's age and bearing.

"Let's pay a call on this William McCoy and show him who's in charge now," one boy hollered.

"Huzzah, huzzah," shouted others, pumping their fists. "Let's do it!" They jumped from the mail car and huffed up the hill, snatching up stones as they ran. The three of us tagged along, curious to see what they might do. When we arrived, sorely out of breath, stones were already bouncing off the Bolivar Street house. Glass had splintered into the hedges, and the picket fence had collapsed under battering boots. Somebody had kicked in the wooden door. McCoy emerged with arms raised, shielding his face. Nevertheless, rocks found their mark on his chest and belly, and blood trickled from a cut above his bristling white eyebrows. His denials counted for nothing against the accusatory shouts of his attackers. Truth be known, I'm sorry to admit that we heaved some stones too. Sam, Tayloe, and I trailed after as the mob prodded and pushed the broken man to the town's center. To his relief, I'm certain, he was locked up in the local jail. His confiscated property immediately became officers' lodgings, and we heard from our Culpeper captain that McCoy would be shipped penniless out to Ohio.

Later that month, not long after Commander Thomas Jackson came to town to take control, I passed near the same boys again strolling down Bolivar Street. I followed far enough behind not to attract attention but listened to their chatter. They were mocking Jackson behind his back. "The man don't know nothing about soldiering. He ain't even got a uniform," one said.

"He dresses no better than my daddy," another said.

This was before Commander Jackson banned all liquor, demoted the Ferry's officers, formed up daily muster and parade details, and forbade those troublemakers from coming into town. I'm sure they had plenty worse to say about him then.

The smartest thing Jackson did was to band all of us fellows from the same localities into distinct companies. He knew we'd fight more fiercely to protect boys we had known at home. Tayloe, Sam, and I joined the rest from Augusta and neighboring Rockbridge County in Company D, although it would be another month before there would be a real Confederate army.

And Jackson worked us like dogs, unlike the officers who came with us to the Ferry. He forced us to parade in parallel rows six hours a day under baking sun and pelting rain. Every day, a number of us boys fell out from fatigue. My feet swelled in my boots until I had to fight to pull them on, which was torture with so many seeping blisters. Old Susie lazed under trees on the sidelines, scratched her floppy ears, panted, and occasionally chased after a squirrel. She then padded at our heels as we trudged back to the house on the ridge. At the end of the day, the adoring swipe of her tongue on my cheek and the love radiating from her brown eyes almost made up for all the discomfort.

By late May, I doubted I was cut out to be a soldier. This was nothing like my imagining. We had been ordered to wreck the rail lines passing through Harpers Ferry that carried coal from western Virginia east to the coast. This meant hefting a sledgehammer above your head and smashing it down against iron rails. Grunting and cussing, we'd then shove them beyond the rail lines, and do it again. To make the time pass, I counted the strokes. As many as a thousand times a day, I'd swing that leaden sledgehammer. As the sun dove behind the mountains, Tayloe, Sam, and I dragged wooden ties to bonfires alongside the former track, where they were incinerated. At night, my throbbing muscles seemed to have come unstuck from the bones.

"Have you heard anything about Union troops gathering for an assault on the Ferry?" Sam asked one evening while we were resting on the porch. He leaned back on his elbows, allowing his legs to slope down the porch steps.

I was studying the nimbus of clouds forming around the moon, a sure predictor of rain. "Let them come," I replied. "It'll give us something to brag about when we're back home."

Jackson's orders to destroy everything the Yanks might find useful at the Ferry led us to believe they were coming for us soon. Explosions under the Baltimore and Ohio rail bridges were so loud that they rocked the house up on Bolivar Street. We could see the smoking metal carcasses from the upper windows as their twisted struts were lapped by the river tides. Every day we attacked the water towers with sledgehammers until their supports finally began to crumble. With an earsplitting crack, the wooden tanks slid sideways, and we leaped out of the way before they toppled with a mighty crash. If townspeople thought our arrival had brought chaos and destruction, our departure would be worse.

The wait for the Yanks' arrival dragged on and on. And then they never came. Our captain finally ordered us to cook five days' provisions and said we'd be setting out in the morning for a two-day march to Manassas.

"Hogsbreath. Manassas? All this time we've been waiting to do what we came for in the spring—to defeat the Yanks at the Ferry," said Tayloe. The others shared his disappointment, and truth be known, fear.

"We know the Ferry's ins and outs," I said. "I'd rather fight the enemy on familiar ground. We don't know anything about Manassas!"

The sad day was drawing near when we would have to bid farewell to Old Susie. Tagging beside a regiment of soldiers with uncertain fates was no prospect for a dog. Whenever there was thunder, she'd tremble by my side and then burrow under my bedroll. I knew she'd suffer greatly from the blasts of artillery fire that would roll across battlefields—if she had not first been blown to smithereens. Rebel sympathizers on our street had shared their meager food with us before we were regarded as a scourge, and I persuaded them to take Susie.

She must have sensed our intent because in the preceding hours she circled and whined, her tail hanging low as one betrayed. She'd lean into our legs as she made her circuit, as if her touch could persuade us to change our minds. It broke my heart to give her up. The family would be taking her and moving on not long after the troops departed. The Ferry would become a wasteland, populated only by looters who wheeled barrows to the larger houses and carted off what we hadn't destroyed.

Nevertheless, I kept a lookout for Susie in the coming years as we circled around the Ferry area. I searched for her in the starving packs of dogs that occasionally begged around our campgrounds, just in case. But I never saw her again. Toward the bitter last, the population of all creatures smaller than man sharply declined. I preferred to think that Susie lived out her days contentedly, away from the dangerous world that would soon be ours. I didn't realize it at the time, but giving her up would be the first of many heartbreaks.

6

THE PACKET OF STRING-BOUND LETTERS IS STILL ON THE LIBRARY table. Some of Mary's correspondence, sadly, didn't survive the fighting or was devoured by silverfish within a few years. But in the letters that remain, I can find her again. She's right there in the scrolling words that drove her pen across the paper. The pale sheets of vellum still hold the echo of her touch. There is precious little this couple does to deserve gratitude, but finding the letters is the great exception. Long ago, crouched on a stump or log in camp, I read and reread these missives from my sister. I carefully preserved them in my haversack and then hauled them home on furlough. In each letter, Mary's soft, clear voice was as real to me as the voices of the boys in the camp. I saw her eyes crinkle with laughter and sensed her lively spirit—just as I do now after so many years. Because her stories of home gave me the courage to carry on, I saved every one.

As I read her words, I envision my little sister at sixteen, seated with her back ramrod straight at the tall desk, sunlight haloing the fine wisps of dark hair caught back by a ribbon. Her high-collared pink linen blouse has tugged loose from the waistband of her floor-skimming, brown striped skirt. Her brow is furrowed as she carefully scribes each word across the page, praying the scroll pen won't splat ink across the lines. She cusses under her breath when it does and then absently twists a flyaway lock with her free hand. Fine penmanship was a source of pride, and as a girl she imagined herself a writer, inventing stories and then concealing them in a thick folder in her bureau chest. I'd sneak a look and quote lines to torment her. I miss her almost as much as I do Ellen.

May 1861. From Mary.

Dear Tom,

It feels like longer than a month since you and the others left. I wish you could have seen us—Ma, Tish, and at least twenty girls and women from the neighborhood—being so industrious on your behalf. Now that the state has officially seceded and has called for three-month volunteers, there is a powerful load of work to be done.

Last Tuesday morning, Pa, Mr. Lucas, and Mr. Beard ferried our sewing machine and others loaned by Bethel folks to Hupp's General Store. You wouldn't have recognized the place. Barrels of flour and cornmeal were shoved out of the way against the walls, bundles of brooms and towers of wash-tubs were moved outside, and tins of tea crowded the high shelves. The men lined up sewing machines in rows across the room. Several of the women hadn't ever seen the new invention, and Ma and Tish had to demonstrate pumping the foot pedals and threading the wheels. Then the men went off to borrow chairs to set before the machines. By late morning, the wagons returned loaded with teetering stacks of rush-seated kitchen and carved-back parlor chairs. Ma even told Pa to bring Grandma's old slat-backed one. By this time Pa was plumb worn out, and he complained about his back.

While they were gone for the chairs, we busily sorted through bolts of homespun fabric and beige canvas. Everyone had rifled through their chests and trunks for material suit-able for uniforms and had brought it to Hupp's. The long oak counters overflowed with it.

As the machines whirred, there was a festive mood while fellows lined up to be measured. Mr. Lucas volunteered for

*that task, saving us women from an improper job. The boys
loitered in front of the store and flirted with all the girls, and
we girls happily flirted back until Ma and the older women
realized work had lagged and then shooed them away. You
can always count on Ma to spoil a good time! You should have
seen those boys strut about. I expect they were considerably
puffed up by the idea of outfits that would set them apart as
daring. We cobbled together as best we could all manner of
pants, shirts, and jackets, and I stitched buttonholes until the
pads of my fingers bled. But we were all content to be doing
something helpful. Some girls were especially eager to sew for
the boys they were sweet on, but I hoped that my labor would
benefit you in some way.*

*I expect you'll be pleased to know that Pa and other
neighborhood men are headed your way up the Valley road
with wagons stocked with the new uniforms, fresh blankets,
and more important, baskets packed with last winter's yellow
and red apples, smoked hams and sausages, loaves of bread,
crocks of preserved vegetables, and spring greens. They should
be there at the Ferry by the time this letter arrives. Tish and I
were mighty proud of our part and know that without everyone's efforts, you boys would go wanting for however long this
war lasts.*

Your loyal sister, Mary

This closure makes me laugh now, as it did every time she signed this
way during the war.

June 1861. From Mary.
*Tom, you wouldn't believe how folks around here get
exercised about the arrival of anything from Harpers Ferry*

sent by you boys. I swear that by the time the stagecoach driver has planted a foot on the front porch, word has traveled and everyone for miles around swarms like hornets. The barnyard looks like a farm auction with horses, the Hogshead's Rockaway buggy, and so many farm carts pushed up against the fence. Last Sunday the weather was stormy, so the parlor was bursting with folks pressed against the walls after every seat was claimed. Pa read your latest message to a hushed group breathless for any mention of their sons' whereabouts. On fairer days, families stand about on the lawn and listen to a letter's contents as Pa reads to the assembled congregation from the porch. You'd think he's the local minister. He drones through each letter, glasses perched on his pointy nose. Folks beg him to repeat it all so that the precious words can feel like more. No letter is ever lengthy enough to satisfy.

Ma says to write anything personal on a small, separate piece of paper and tuck it inside the longer letter to keep the rest of the neighborhood from hearing. If word comes that the Lucas family has mail, people make just as mad a dash there, but Sam's not the scribe that you are. Letters arrive only two days after they are written, so don't think you can use mail delays as an excuse to shirk your brotherly duty.

We hear that as many as 800 Augusta boys have responded in the past few weeks to Governor Letcher's call for three-month volunteers. You'd be hard-pressed to find any healthy boys around here anymore

Ma and Pa never seem to have anything written in time when the mail stage drives by, but this evening Ma will add a note to this envelope. Be forewarned. I suspect it will be the usual.

June 1861. From Ma.

It's with a trembling hand and sad heart that I take this pencil in hand to drop you a line, as I fear that there may never be another opportunity. I exhort you once more to put your trust in the Almighty God of Jacob. Take Jesus Christ as your Savior. Then if you fall on the battlefield you'll be saved, and we'll be gloriously reunited in Heaven at the Last Judgment. There have been fervent prayers for you and the other boys. Oh, won't you pray for yourself!

Nothing more from your affectionate mother, C. Smiley.

July 1861. From Mary.

Tom, you know how Ma keeps no secret from Aunt Ellen, including her worries about your lack of faith? After church this past Sunday, Aunt Ellen lay in wait for me on the portico. Before I could slip past, she grabbed my arm and pulled me aside. She implored me to persuade you to enlist under Jesus's banner and to observe the Sabbath. As though I could influence you on such matters! She also stuffed into my pocket a scrap of paper that has a diarrhea remedy, saying she found it in a book penned by a man who has served in foreign countries. Here it is: take a tablespoonful of wheat flour and mix with two or more of water and drink. In most cases, one dose stops the flux instantly. I pass this on but try it at your own risk.

What my sister and Aunt Ellen couldn't imagine was that flour would quickly be in short supply, while diarrhea would be as constant as a soldier's shadow.

I have thought hard about you or Sam standing solitary guard duty around the steep bluffs that folks say encircle the

Ferry. What if you lost your footing on the treacherous stone and tumbled to the bottom one starless night, and no one knew you were below with a broken arm or leg? Pledge to me that you'll have Sam or some other fellow stand with you. Don't either of you stand guard alone. Tish and Ma also want to remind you not to sleep in wet clothes if you've been drenched by rain, as you know you might become ill. You are probably muttering under your breath "Enough of that motherly advice!" so I'll cease for now.

How does housekeeping go? At home you always thought our work was so easy, but I reckon you know a little about it now. I guess YOU will be the chief cook and dish washer. Do you sleep in tents or out in the open air with the sky as your cover?

Nothing significant is happening here, but that fidgety Mrs. Jim Calliston has lost her mind with all the war talk and was carried to the Staunton Lunatic Asylum. Speculations of war fill the air, and I guess it just drove her mad. No one seems concerned with anything else but rumors that the Northerners are nothing but warmongers, raving mad for battle. Everyone is scared to death. I do wish folks would be more interested in going to Harpers Ferry to check on you and the other boys from home, rather than being so distracted by all these dark imaginings.

You might be interested to know that because you fine, strapping boys have deserted us, the older men formed a thirty-man Home Guard three weeks after you left. Some of the remaining boys who haven't mustered the courage to join you, have joined them. Folks worry that "bad elements" will misuse the unprotected women and elderly now that everyone responsible for law enforcement has gone. A few are also convinced that slaves will seek revenge on all white people.

Do you remember Johnny Hutchens, my friend Eliza's brother who is several years your senior? I can't fathom why he was elected Captain of the Home Guard because everyone knows the Hutchens family has been staunchly pro-Union all along. Convincing Eliza Hutchens and her nine siblings to give up their Union sympathies, although now they aren't so bold about expressing them, would be like trying to convince the sun to shine in Bethel at night.

The Home Guard's purpose is to go where there's danger— but a vote of members determines every move. In my opinion, they can be depended upon to always vote to stay home. They march weekly in the small field to the south of our house, as the other fields in Bethel are in pasture, but most don't know "face right" from "face left." Almost all should have volunteered to be in the real army, especially those who brag they can whip five Yankees by themselves.

Johnny Hutchens didn't last long as Captain. Last Thursday was drilling day for the Guard and was also when the oath of allegiance to the Confederacy was administered—sworn to by all but the two Lacy brothers and their Captain Johnny. Johnny says he's too religious to fight, and anyway he won't fight against his relations, who are nearly all Northerners. If he went to battle, he swears that he couldn't fire one bullet at the Yankees and doesn't know whether he'd order his company north or south. He was speedily turned out of office, and Captain Hite was elected instead. Do you agree Johnny ought to have the words 'traitor' branded on his forehead—as "heretic" was in ancient Greece? Have you boys heard that President Davis has proclaimed that everyone who won't pledge loyalty to the sovereignty of the Confederacy must leave the state within forty days? After that time, they'll be arrested and thrown in the brig.

I have nothing more to write. Your most loyal sister, Mary

Those Lacy boys, just two years apart in age and strong, dark-haired fellows, avoided the Confederate army in the end. They were found dangling by ropes lapped round a broad beam in their father's weathered barn a month or so after the draft was announced in early '62. It beats me why they didn't just hightail it north instead, but the times were so exceedingly strange that no man's actions can be judged by usual measure.

7

AFTER THE BATTLE OF MANASSAS IN LATE JULY, I RECEIVED A LETTER
from my first cousin, Maggie Martin. Two years younger than I, she
was a companion of Mary's. Her family lived just a mile south of Bethel
and down the road toward Lexington. Maggie was convinced she was
mighty attractive and thus was quite a coquette, with a porcelain complexion and her hair twisted in brown ringlets. Her letter demonstrated
how those at home had no idea of what we'd lived through during that
terrible July day in Manassas. She wrote some silliness, asking if we were
putting on plays in camp or having dance socials with local girls, and if
there were very many tall boys like me. She said she loved to see tall boys
having to stoop lower to put their arms around girls, and she complained
there now was nothing but "little bits" of boys left at home. What could I
possibly say in response?

I could have told her about arriving at Bull Run on July 21 in the midst
of cannons bellowing, artillery rounds blasting, and smoke on the field
that blinded my vision. And that we were the victors of a one-day battle
that we believed had won the Southern states the right to secede. I could
have told her that.

But there wasn't much else I could say that she could bear to hear. I
couldn't tell her that the night before dawn on July 21 was the worst I had
ever spent. For eighteen hours we marched north from Winchester to the
quiet village of Piedmont Station, located at a railroad junction. We waited
there until the next morning when freight trains arrived to carry our horde
to Manassas. Our officers hoped to turn back Northern troops on their

way to attack the new Confederate capital in Richmond. Sam, Tayloe, and I lay jittery on the ground, side by side, newly minted army weapons pressed against our thighs. The late afternoon hours had been time enough to boast and prophesy, but as the shadows lengthened, there was also plenty of time to doubt and then quake right down to the soles of my boots. The sound of murmured prayer periodically lifted on the summer night air.

As the sun was sinking behind Cobbler Mountain, a fellow who said his name was William Valentine spotted room next to us for an extra blanket and asked, "Do you boys mind if I join y'all here?"

"Not a bit. Feel free," Sam said and then threw his arm over his eyes to signal his wish to be left alone.

Valentine laid his blanket on the rocky ground next to mine and squatted on it. Next to him, he placed his rifle and a small oval object he withdrew from his knapsack. In the dim light, I couldn't make out what it was. But then he spoke to it in a low voice.

"What the hell do you have there?" I asked him.

"It's my good luck box turtle. Name's Roscoe. He's been with me ever since I left home. He stays inside his shell during drills, and then I let him forage in the grass for bugs and worms when I'm resting." I stared at Valentine incredulously for a minute. Barely eighteen, and maybe not that, he was a little fellow, scrawny and pale with white-blond hair and sad eyes. He appeared not to have had any good luck—and certainly not to have had anybody who fed him well.

"Well, I guess you could catch up with a turtle easy enough if he tried to get away. Why aren't you bedding down with your own company?" I asked.

"They're just over the rise. But when I spotted you fellows as I walked by, I decided this was a decent place to stop. I can see my own company well enough from here to join them in the morning. Besides, I don't know none of 'em any better than you."

"Where are you from?"

"Just outside of Pulaski, down in western Virginia," he said.

Tayloe had propped himself up on his haversack and was listening. "Really? Aside from turtles, aren't there Indians and buffaloes still lurking around those hills?" he joked.

"Buffaloes have been gone so long, I don't know when the last one was chased off," Valentine replied. "I 'spect there's some Indians still around though. You might think living ain't so good there, but my pa had his own still, and people came from all around to buy his licker. Folks said it was the best they'd tasted anywhere. We had a milk cow, a roof over our heads, and a patch of land to grow vegetables. There wasn't much we wanted for."

"Sounds like a good enough life," I said.

He studied his ragged fingernails. "Yes, but things turned bad. The revenuers caught on to my pa," he said. "One night eight years ago, Pa dismantled the still, packed up the copper pipes, and run off. We never heared from him again. Ma tried the best she could, but we had less and less. She finally died two months ago; I suspect she was plain tuckered out."

"I'm sorry about that." I paused before asking, "How have you been getting by?"

"A cloth peddler gave my twelve-year old sister and me a ride on his cart up to Roanoke and helped us find odd jobs. She works as a scullery maid's helper in The Roanoke Hotel, and they let her sleep in the kitchen. I volunteered for the Confederate army. That's shelter, food, and a trifling wage for me. At least for three months." His story made me consider how lucky I'd been so far, even if I might die the next day. We both fell quiet, and then he stretched out on his blanket, staring blankly at the sky.

I remained upright, taking in a sight the likes of which I'd never seen. Thousands and thousands of boys stretched across the field on their backs, narrow lumps silhouetted by a full moon. They were spread as far as the horizon, waiting for dawn and the train to Bull Run. A chill swept down my spine, making me wonder about premonitions. Finally, I lay down, but sleep escaped me.

After a while, I heard muffled sobs and saw that Valentine was crying into his bent elbow to hide the sound. I reached across and touched his arm.

"Aw, man, buck up," I whispered, hoping he wouldn't detect the uncertainty in my voice. "This'll be over before you know it. We'll all be bragging about it by tomorrow evening."

He snuffled. Finally, he made no more sounds. I dozed off for a bit until I felt his hand shaking my shoulder.

"Are you awake, Tom? I need to ask a favor."

I rose up on my elbows to face him. "Sure. What is it?"

"If I get kilt tomorrow, I want you to promise that I get buried. You hardly know me, but I don't have anyone else to ask," he whispered in the darkness.

"I promise. But we might get through this unhurt or only wounded."

"I don't want to be wounded. No sir. I'd be useless then, and I don't want that. If I'm shot, I want to be shot straight through the heart," Valentine said.

"It won't happen. Just get some sleep," I told him and closed my eyes.

But there was still no sleep for me. Lying there, I was ambushed by odd thoughts. Would any of the girls in Bethel mourn my death? Would Lizzie Fackler be tormented by guilt for having spurned me? She might even regret she'd missed her chance, if she ever considered changing her mind. Then I worried about how my parents would find my dead body. And how they would haul it home for burial at New Jerusalem Church, or even better, on the hill above the house. What would my tombstone say? I hoped they would leave off my middle name, Martin; I'd never liked it much. These morbid thoughts fanned my fear to the point that sleep was impossible.

The morning dawned with a clear sky and with orders from our captain to join the noisy throng of soldiers teeming around the little station. This was the first time that troops had ridden trains to battle. An ear-splitting cheer arose as each train whistled and chugged forward, packed with boys departing for Manassas Station. Sam, Tayloe, and I rested wordlessly against the car's wooden wall with our backs bumping to the rhythm of the wheels, their rumble drowning out any conversation. When the train halted at Manassas, a steady roar of guns and cannons peppered the air in the distance. A racing heart propelled me during the short march from the station, across the wooden bridge over Bull Run, over trampled wheat grass and up Henry Hill to a fringe of dark oaks. Above the crowns of the trees, dense smudges of artillery smoke splotched the sky. Unleashed by heat and terror, salty sweat dripped from my brow into my eyes. Another pause while our commanders awaited a signal, and then the order went down our line: "Forward march! Double quick!" With Sam on one side of me, Tayloe on the other, and William Valentine trailing behind, we trotted through the trees toward the inferno. Branches whipped our faces and thorny blackberry bushes snatched at my pants. My breath came in desperate gasps, and a sour taste coated my mouth.

Cries of "Let's get some bluecoats!" and "Damn the Yankee bastards!" merged into one unbridled animal bellow that soared above the crash of trampled underbrush and thundering boots. It drove our feet forward like pistons, while the metallic stench of gunpowder stung my nostrils and smoke leached tears from my eyes. Frank Richards, a Bethel boy, broke ranks and scurried away. He cowered behind leafy foliage with his quivering arms over his head, shutting out the day. No one paid him, or several others with waning courage, any mind. When Sam,

Tayloe, and I cleared the tree trunks at the crest of Henry Hill, we saw the most terrible vista. I looked around to check on William, but I'd lost sight of him in the great surge forward. The valley below was heaped, in some places four-deep, with dead bodies and the wounded. The battle had been raging for hours, begun half a day before our group arrived as reinforcements.

On command, we let loose a terrific volley of musketry and continued to do so for another two hours. And then an astonishing thing happened. The whole lot of Yankees turned and ran like a wave drawn by a powerful tide toward the horizon. They let loose their belts, cast away their arms, knapsacks, haversacks, clothes, provisions, medicines, and anything else that might slow them down. I later wondered if some of those boys showed up in Washington naked that night. Artillery wagons crashed into supply wagons and rose into twisted knots of iron and splintered wood, while horses were flattened beneath. We watched with jaws agape, and then a terrific cheer tore down the lines. Not only had our company of a hundred men survived without a single casualty, but we believed our victory concluded a brief war, and the disagreement was over.

It rained all night after the battle ended, a night punctuated by piteous cries of "Water, please someone . . . bring me water," merging with moans and screams that nearly drove me mad with helplessness. When dawn came, I slogged through the hellish landscape to bury our dead and those of the enemy. The Yankees had fled so rapidly that they'd left theirs behind. Thousands of bodies still lay out in the weather, slick with water and mud.

As Tayloe and I crossed the field, I thought I recognized a body slumped face down on the ground. With a terrible foreboding, I grabbed the boy's shoulder and rolled him over. It was William Valentine. His sopping, white-blond hair was plastered to his bony forehead. His face was frozen in a look of terrific surprise. It seemed as though he had died instantly in the act of loading his gun. One hand was tight around his weapon, the other clasped a cartridge. He had been shot dead straight through the heart. I sat down on the ground next to him and cried right there, not caring who saw. Cried loud, wrenching sobs. I couldn't help it. He'd been alive just like me only the day before, talking about his home and his sister. It wasn't fair for him to have had such a short, hard life with no chance to make it better.

I then wondered: how many Union boys had my bullets struck? And how were those boys any different in their fears and hopes from William? We were all made of the same stuff, the bowels, brains, stomachs, and masses of red pulp now spread across the field. Dreadful sights that should remain hidden from any human eye.

Tayloe kindly turned away, leaving me alone to spend my tears. Remembering after a moment that it didn't look well for a soldier to cry, I stood and wiped my face with the back of my hand. I decided never again to allow myself this weakness.

William's knapsack had fallen to his side, and as I spotted it, the image of his brown and gold turtle sprang to mind. Bending over, I stuck my fingers inside the bag and felt the rippled shell tightly sealed. I placed the armored creature under a laurel bush and bade him farewell. He set off on his stubby legs for tall grass. Tayloe and I grabbed Valentine under the armpits and dragged him to the edge of the soggy field, where a burial crew hastily shoveled red clay. I penciled "William Valentine" on a scrap of paper from my haversack and tucked it between the thin hands we placed across his messy chest, even as I knew that no one would read it.

We waited to make certain that he was blanketed by the earth and then returned to our regiment, arrayed by company to march through a massacred landscape and the ashes of what had been Manassas Junction.

An unnatural season had caused not only the green leaves to shrivel and fall but had shredded and blackened every tree limb and gnarled trunk in the process. The trains we'd proudly arrived on were nothing more than charred and twisted wreckage. Aching legs and blistered feet would now have to bear us away, deeper into the Valley.

8

August 1861. From Mary.

Dear Tom,

    I take my pen in hand this morning to write to you a few lines, as the mail stage will come soon.

    We are well at present but hear that you are laid up in the Staunton hospital with measles. We finally learned about it from letters Sam wrote home. Not one letter came from you for about three weeks, and we were sick with worry. I forced myself to search the newspaper casualty list after Manassas, while my hands trembled so I could barely read the type.

    What a relief not to find you there! But then your name was never mentioned in any letter that came to the neighborhood, and it was not until day before yesterday we got the news. Ma was especially uneasy. You know she always expects the unspeakable. I suppose you thought it best not to let us know, but please promise never to do that again. Truth is always better than uncertainty. But enough of the measles—I hope that you're soon finished with them for good. I reckon when Tish had them, and Ma and Pa expected us to come down with them next, you never dreamed that you'd catch them as a soldier. Ma says if your eyes are sore from the measles and it impedes writing, send a message home by someone else.

Shortly after, she shared the most grievous news.

Tom, the very worst things are happening to folks around here. It seems like every day someone in the neighborhood takes sick and dies. The Roysters' little Tilly, Robert, Edward, and Sam were all four taken by the pox last week. Ma called on Mrs. Royster to offer solace for the death of her four little ones, then came home and wept for hours. The substitute minister at New Jerusalem says he has never preached as many final services for children and old folks, at least two a week. He says he thinks as many perish at home as on the battlefield. There are so many new tombstones in the grave-yard, Mr. Bailey, the stonecutter, says he can hardly keep up with demand.

And do you remember Mrs. Whidbey? Both her baby boy and husband died shortly after she returned from Frystown, where she nursed her youngest sister Polly Crawford who was down with the fever. Her nephew Peter was home from sol-diering for a visit with his mother but was not up to the task.

And I heard the most sorrowful news about William Rosen, from over toward Leonardtown. His wife, mother, father, three children, and his brother have all died within the month. It was a blessing that he was home on furlough when they passed away. Ma says the Angel of Death is overworked in these times and believes these terrible losses at home are part of the Lord's mysterious doings.

I don't rightly know what to think, but we are doing our utmost—keeping out of dampness, drafts, and the like. Folks stay to themselves, venturing out only when necessary, and will barter anything for a little eucalyptus oil to sprinkle on cloths held to their noses when they do go forth. It takes a funeral these days to get them to church.

Ever your loyal sister, Mary

Even before our first battle in Manassas, sick soldiers streamed by the multitudes down the Valley to the Staunton hospital. It was no wonder so many fell ill. We all tented for weeks near creeks where we washed our filthy bodies and clothes and then drank the scummy water. Tens of thousands of men urinated and defecated nearby daily. Our First Lieutenant Baylor, whose Lexington family Ma and Pa knew, died of sickness in the early days—without seeing one serious fight.

August 1861. From Mary.
Dear Tom,

Beards is coming your way soon. He has enlisted, and he stopped by the house on Monday before he left for the train. He wanted to tell Ma and Pa that he'd keep eye on you. And that he'd be sure that you got home safe soon. Pa was grinding at the mill and Tish was visiting Aunt Ellen, so Ma and I invited him into the parlor. I think he is the handsomest man in the county, but in his uniform, I expect he may be the best looking in the state of Virginia. Except for you, of course! Don't get a swollen head over that compliment.

Ma went to the kitchen because Mrs. Lucas came by to purchase some eggs, and Beards and I were left alone, awkwardly avoiding each other's glance. "We . . . I will miss you, Jeremy," I finally said. I confess, tears came to my eyes at the idea of him going away. It has been so lonely around here without you, and then to have Beards gone as well was too much. When he spied my wet cheeks, he reached out for my hand so tenderly. It was the first time. "Will you promise to write regularly, Mary?" he asked. He looked down, embarrassed to meet my eyes. "I've grown so accustomed to seeing you when I'm visiting Tom. I'll miss you terribly." He said leaving Bethel and me behind would be the hardest thing he'd ever done. That those many times he came to see you, he was also hoping to see me. To say such, he must have thought he was going off to die!

I told him, "I had no idea. But for some time now, I've dreamed you would like me as much as I like you. Of course, I'll write." His cheeks flushed bright red, and then he asked if we might be sweethearts when the war is over. My mouth dropped open with surprise. I must have appeared a moron, and then a rush of happiness triggered more tears. But he didn't care. He reached for my shoulders and then hugged me close. Of course, I said yes. He was staring so deeply into my eyes that I was forced to reveal my feelings. We'd just stepped apart when Ma came back into the room. She looked quizzically at our flushed faces, but I don't think she suspected anything. Now you need to take special care of Beards for me. He's the sweetest, most thoughtful boy I'll ever know. I tell you, Tom, I've never felt like this before—not knowing whether to be sad or happy.

While I've discovered a sweetheart, Ma and Pa have lost good friends. Mr. and Mrs. Hogshead, outright opponents to secession, won't speak to the Lucas' or the Beards, and Mr. Hogshead won't even tip his hat for Ma and me. The Callistons are just as bad. Reverend McIntyre, who has shocked much of our congregation by preaching abolition from the pulpit for the past month, has packed up his wife and children and headed north to stay with relatives in Pennsylvania. The priory sits forlorn and empty these days without the McIntyres. There's a call out for a new preacher, but I don't expect anyone will answer it soon.

Please remind Beards to let me know how things are going with him. I promised to write him regularly, but he needs to hold up his end of the bargain too.

Your loyal sister, Mary

9

I N NOVEMBER, JACKSON LED FIVE THOUSAND OF US NORTH FROM Winchester to Martinsburg. As usual, we foot soldiers had no more idea where we were going, or why, than the folks at home. After Manassas, we'd done nothing much but tramp lockstep for five months in square formations, first one way, then another, with our rifles on our shoulders. Every now and then around the eastern town of Alexandria, our soldiers on watch at night would exchange fire with Union pickets who came to spy. By the time of this winter march, we were ready to do anything that would get us away from camp.

Our mess was a tight group of five Augusta boys and two from Rockbridge, the adjoining county: Sam Lucas, Tayloe Hupp, Jeremy Beard, Jim Blue, Zeke Skinner, Otis McCorkle, and me. Those six fellows were as fine as any in the whole army, all with strong hearts and most of them from around home. We shared tents, cooked meals, and foraged together. It had been a happy day when Jeremy Beard showed up in the late summer, responding to the volunteer call-up shortly after Manassas. He was as good a friend as Sam from when we were small boys in Bethel. We were also neighbors, one farm over the ridge. Early on, Pa fondly gave him the nickname of Beards, and it stuck.

Sam and Beards were polar opposites, both in appearance and temperament. Slender and taller than Sam by several inches, Beards was quiet and watchful. His large gray eyes speckled with brown took in every nuance of expression and movement, and he was an intent listener, always curious about human nature. He could tell you why you'd done something long before you figured it out. He spoke slowly, as though he was considering the impact of every word before letting it roll out of his mouth. Where Sam was like the flame at the end of a fuse, Beards was like the quiet just before dawn. He was the one who drew his penknife in the earliest days and suggested each of us vow with a blood oath to defend the others. No one hesitated.

Now that we were soldiers, I quit teasing Beards about being sweet on Mary. I suspected it long before he'd admit it to himself. He was a solid man and was handsome enough. The sideways slant from a broken nose only added to his appeal, my sister informed me. Even the most perfect appearance benefits mightily from a slight flaw, she insisted.

Beards, in his accustomed way, this day wandered from mess to mess seeking familiar faces and gathering information. The second evening as we camped near Martinsburg, he came charging back after a stroll. "Boys! I've got news! Jackson plans to destroy dams on the Potomac River." He watched us with a crooked grin, waiting for a reaction.

Nobody said anything. Jim Blue looked at Beards in amazement and then regarded our puzzled faces with impatience. "Don't you fellows understand what this means? This could put a stop to the whole darned war. If the dams are broken, no river water will flow into the canal that runs alongside, and it dries up. That canal carries the Feds and material all the way from Washington to Ohio and back."

"How can you be sure that's right? I never heard anything about canals," Zeke said. Flyaway eyebrows slanting upward toward his nose gave him a permanently quizzical look, compounded by his perpetually ruffled brown hair. He prodded the campfire coals with a stick and laid another potato in the hottest area to roast. Then he stood to give Blue's explanation his full attention. Once again, I noted his erect posture and envied that he felt no need to stoop, as I habitually did. He carried his broad shoulders with pride.

"I learned about the Potomac canal and the Erie canal, too, in Jackson's engineering class at VMI. Can't you see for yourself? The river around here is impassable with huge boulders. The canal with its barges makes up for it. If we destroy the dams that feed the canal, we'll stop the Yanks dead in their tracks." Jackson had been Blue's professor at the Virginia Military Institute, and Blue had proudly worn his dress uniform to war. We had teased him for looking like a toy soldier until the uniform became soiled beyond recognition.

"I'm in favor of that!" Zeke was now smiling broadly.

"Maybe if folks in Washington are freezing this winter because they don't have coal from the west, they may change their minds about how badly they want war."

"I'm in favor of that too," said Zeke.

This news set my heart racing. Ever since Manassas, I was tired of only playing at soldiering. Destroying a dam was a hell of a sight better than sitting around camp.

On the sixteenth of December, the rumors proved true, and we set out marching the next morning with plans to try our luck on Dam Number 5. Once again, Beards came running, out of breath. "Listen to this. I met up with some fellows just back from stealing skiffs along the riverbank all night. They tied the boats up in the brush below the dam. There'll be some action tonight—I swear it." We all strained to peer in the river's direction, hoping to catch sight of the stolen crafts, but trees and underbrush disguised the curving shoreline. The dam was within clear view. Double wooden walls with foundations buried in the riverbed ran parallel, four feet apart. The space between was filled with chunks of quarried rock. Their length stretched from shore to shore.

Our company and one other were ordered to the stolen skiffs that evening a little before midnight. We yelled to Jim Blue to hurry up. He was in the bushes, suffering from his finicky innards, which heaved up whenever there was danger. Beards, Tayloe, and I packed one of the little boats with pickaxes, crowbars, picks, shovels, and a blanket for drying off, if need be, and a shame-faced Jim Blue joined us, wiping his mouth with his shirttail. That particular night was an odd choice for a secret maneuver because the full moon was luminous enough to read a book by. Every whisker of Tayloe's unshaven beard seemed to have a life of its own, as did the buttons on Sam's jacket, even at ten feet. Any movement of our band of thirty men would be detectable from across the river on the Northern side. My gut cramped.

Tayloe disguised his fear with indignation. "What the hell is the captain thinking? It's insane to send a band of soldiers out in boats under a full moon." He continued to gripe as we tugged the heavy-laden vessel from the shore on the downside dam wall, using its mass as cover from the Union troops supposed to be camped somewhere upriver. Stealthily, we joined the other men bobbing along on the silver surface. A wiseacre rasped from Sam's boat floating next to us, "You girls be sure to keep your heads down, now." Tayloe made a rude gesture in his direction.

A freezing veil of water splashed over the wall, soaking our faces, hands, and chests. The air was warm for December, but the river was fed by soul-chilling mountain streams. "Goddarnit, we gentlemen aren't properly dressed for this outing," Jim Blue stage whispered. Beards and I snorted with nervous laughter. I took a poke at Blue.

When the skiffs bumped the face of the dam, Blue and I lifted a rope-bound stone to the gunwale on the count of three and eased it soundlessly under the rush of the river. The little vessel lodged next to the dam. We then lowered ourselves into the waist-high water. I stifled a cry of shock when the cold struck my thighs and stomach. Blue sank up to his chest when he lost balance on the rocky riverbed and his foot slipped into a crevice. He cursed under his breath and was damn lucky not to have twisted an ankle. At least it was a warning to the rest of us to step cautiously.

The only remedy to the cold was to work like a fiend. After a while, the axe's thunk and the splitting of wood was distracting, but it didn't fully cure my anxiety or the chattering of my teeth. I feared my eyes might rattle out of my skull. I kept up a steady internal dialogue, telling myself the mission would be a great success. I might even win a special citation. All the while, my freezing legs and hands seemed no longer attached to my body. When there was a sizeable hole in the wooden wall, Tayloe and Beards reached into the opening and rolled rocks into the water, where they sank onto the river floor. When all the rocks were removed, water would gush through the hole, depriving the canal of enough water to float a barge. Every now and then one of us would crawl back into the boat to huddle for warmth under the blanket, causing the skiff to jump and quake along with the body inside. Inactivity in wet clothes caused as much discomfort as hard labor in the icy water.

So far, there was no evidence that any Northern troops were watching. But you could never be sure when that would change. Blue began to softly hum the popular song "Do They Miss Me at Home" as he worked. I couldn't have heard it except for being right next to him. How was he relaxed enough to hum? To cover my nervousness, I started to sing aloud with each blow. Immediately, Tayloe hissed, "For tarnation's sake, stop that before you get us killed!"

"You fellows sound like girls. There's no Yankees around here. I'll prove it." I don't know what got into me. I suppose I was afraid my singing hadn't convinced the others—most especially my idol, Sam, in the adjacent boat—that my trembling was in response to the cold, not fear.

Fingers gripping the lip of the wooden frame, I hauled myself up on the dam to peer around before balancing on its top in the reflecting moonlight. I tested a jig step or two on the water-slicked rocks piled between the two walls. The three boys barely had time to stare up in disbelief at my flickering white form when bullets whistled above my head from the Maryland side of the river. I tumbled down into the skiff, violently rocking it and sloshing icy water on the fellows' shoulders and faces. Tayloe snarled, "You goldarned fool! You almost got us shot! What a danged idiot you are!" Turns out there were Yanks camped close by on the Maryland shore.

"Why the hell did you have to go and give away our position?" Blue demanded. "You may have ruined everything! All this freezing goddamn work for nothing!"

Tayloe and Blue showered oaths on me that would sear bristle off a boar's hide. Beards just glared, which was worse. I couldn't see or hear Sam's reaction in the other boat.

We continued working only because Yankee smooth bore rifles lacked accuracy and range. They couldn't reach us on the far side of the shore, closer to Virginia. But their barrage of bullets peppered the water just short of the skiff for most of the night. The small craft provided cover as we hacked at the dam's structure, but every now and then a bullet would slap the water only yards away. In their urgency, the boys forgot their anger, but my face smarted whenever my thoughts returned to my stunt.

Near dawn, the Yanks got their hands on long-range Enfield rifles, but didn't use them until the rising sun improved their aim. They must have sent a scout upriver to another encampment to procure the rifles. Hiding behind trees, they opened fire. Their bullets now could reach the skiff as well as our artillerymen waiting on the Virginia shore. If the water hadn't been so cold, and our limbs hadn't been so stiff, we might have finished before they'd gotten the better guns. But now we were unable to work the few more necessary hours in the daylight.

Ducking volleys from both sides, we paddled hell-bent to reach the riverbank. Bullets kicked up white ruffles of water just to the side of our skiff, right and left. My trembling arms worked the oars awkwardly in the oarlocks, but Tayloe begged the mercy of his Lord and paddled in a fury. The minute the boat ground ashore, we leapt from it as if it were afire. Tent stakes were yanked as bullets spat dirt in our faces, and we high-tailed it back to Winchester. It wasn't long before the Yanks repaired our bit of damage, and troops and supplies once again flowed between Washington and Ohio. The war didn't end there, any more than it had at Manassas.

If I hadn't performed that cursed foolishness in the moonlight, there's a chance we might have irreparably broken that dam. Maybe there would have been too little time for the Yankees to make major repairs before really cold weather set in. Jim Blue, Beards, and Tayloe didn't tell the officers just what drew the Union fire that night, but for long after, they teased me mercilessly.

10

O N THE FIRST DAY OF 1862, SOON TO BECOME THE MOST BATTLE-TORN year of the war in Virginia, the morning unfolded beneath pewter clouds and a temperature mild for winter. It wasn't a bad day for nine thousand men to set off from Winchester, headed west across eight mountain ranges toward Romney, Virginia.

With Ma's oilcloth cast about my shoulders to ward against drizzle, the softness of the weather set me to daydreaming. My body was light as a turkey feather. A wagon bore my knapsack and blanket, leaving only my gun and ammunition for my back, and my feet automatically followed those of the man in front of me. Jim Blue and Sam walked to my left and, from time to time, sang a scrap of hymn or a verse from "The Girl I Left Behind Me." They demonstrated that they knew all the words to "Lorena," unconcerned that neither could carry a tune. Several of the men drowned them out by boisterously singing to the tune of "Dixie":

> *"Old Missus marry Will de Weaver*
> *Williams was a gay deceiver—*
> *Look away, look away, look away,*
> *Dixieland!*
> *But when he puts his arm around 'er*
> *He smiles as fierce as a forty-pounder,*
> *Look away, look away, look away,*
> *Dixieland!"*

Friendly shoves and jabs were shared between the two choirs, each trying to silence the other. Such nonsense leavened the drudgery of one foot endlessly planted in front of the other.

By late afternoon, needles of sleet pelted our faces. We had reached a higher altitude where the roaring wind tore at my collar and scarf. Shortly, my pants were soaked clear through and froze into planks of wool that rubbed my shins raw. My feet skated in the frozen ponds of my shoes. Every step forward was exhausting, lifting one foot above the drifting snow to repeat that movement with the other. By dusk it must have been close to zero degrees, and even shoving my ice-encrusted gloves into my coat armpits didn't warm them. Ice hung in daggers from visored caps, slicked men's cloaks in ragged sheets, and frosted brows and beards. Jim Blue and Sam's beet-red faces reflected silvery dust in the lantern light. With my free hand, I clung to my blanket under the oilcloth and shoved the edges around my eyes to meet the now-greasy skullcap knitted by Aunt Ellen. I could barely see but had little choice but to keep going forward. Sleet still dove beneath my upturned overcoat collar, and it crusted there. My blanket would have wet patches that night.

Finally, the howling died away. We lumbered along, trailed by hundreds of food and artillery wagons, until the horses' hooves began to skid out of control. Whinnies of fright pierced the snowy silence that had muffled our voices and footsteps. Falling men broke ribs, some broke legs, some broke arms. When the wagons finally halted that night, Sam, Jim Blue, and the rest of our mess tore up fence posts and railings with our numb hands and laid them as a barrier between the frozen ground and our thin blankets. Everything rested on thorny brush. Tents would keep snow from mounding on our heads, although by morning their sides would be slabs of ice. Dispirited, we fell into a troubled slumber on the side of Mount Stevens.

Fights broke out the next morning, even between comrades, for a spot alongside the wagons. No one wanted to suffer the fates of those who had slipped the day before. Elbowing others aside, Zeke grabbed the side rail of a wagon and clung to it for hours as the horse-drawn vehicle led his lanky body forward. With rags bound around his boots for traction, he thought he was prepared for the steep, icy road. He was absently humming a tune when he felt the wheels start to spin. In an instant, he threw himself clear of the wagon and scrambled up a wide ledge above the road. The wagons ahead began to slide backward and sideways. Screams and curses rent the air. Heavily loaded with gun caskets, the vehicles swayed and then fell like dominoes, plunging over fallen horses and soldiers, crushing whatever lay in their path. They finally exploded against the cliff walls, casting their contents onto blood-streaked snow. Zeke had saved himself by quick reflexes and a sharp intuition. I had stayed out of the morning's melee and had kept pace ahead of the wagons, steadied by my own efforts to remain standing. Now I was on a higher part of the road and, sickened, observed the disaster from above.

Everything halted while animals were shot and dragged aside, wounded and dead men were gathered up, and splintered wagons were cleared away. From my vantage, the impasse of tumbled conveyances and boxes trailed down the slope as far as eyes could see. There was no way to gin up any body warmth through movement, and stamping my feet only sent needles of agony through my stiffened toes.

We huddled together the second night with only a blanket and oil-cloth. Tents and supplies were trapped miles behind. Forms spooned together, sharing two blankets for extra thickness as the falling snow gathered on our heads and shoulders and filled the hollows in between. I'd never imagined that Jim Blue's warm breath on the back of my neck would be so welcome.

Lying out there on those icy rocks, I recalled how Blue and I once shared something else when we were lads—our mutual disdain for New Jerusalem Sunday School. We plotted our mutual expulsion, to be achieved by mimicking the teacher's pompous orations behind his back but where all the class could see. The teacher's face washed purple with rage as students giggled and pointed. But no one wanted to be guilty of expelling the grandson of a former minister, Reverend Winthrop Blue. He founded our neighborhood Presbyterian church near the start of the century and was just as renowned for marrying the last person in our area to be kidnapped by Indians and then rescued. Jim Blue would wrinkle his slightly turned-up nose and then launch into tales of family ties to Indians, generally irking everyone within earshot.

In the dark that night, a voice softly asked, "Do you ever wonder why anyone believed this was worth doing? Were we crazy? Why did we leave home for this?" It was Otis McCorkle, who had joined us only a month before this march to western Virginia. His deep sigh enfolded us. We'd noted by the first day's end that McCorkle was cursed with a melancholic streak. To make matters worse, he was sorely missing his wife and baby. He was dark inside and out: thick black hair framed his plump face, one rarely brightened by a smile. Bushy brows were often drawn together in morbid contemplation. We steered clear of him when we could because he too often reminded us of things we didn't want to consider. McCorkle and Zeke had been the last members to join our mess. They had walked into camp together from Rockbridge County in late November and were immediately assigned to our group. That's about all they had in common. Zeke thought about things at least as seriously as Beards, but he never let anything get him down. He always had a twinkle in his eyes and a ready laugh. McCorkle floundered in his unhappiness so often that he couldn't notice what lay outside of it.

A few feet away I heard Beards reciting, "A man has to live by his decisions and then drive himself forward, one step at a time. One step at a time." He uttered it as a sacrament, as if to convert a resistant part of himself. The rest of us, who might have agreed with McCorkle's view and Beards' resolution, made no comment. We couldn't afford to acknowledge either of them. I fell asleep with the rabbit's foot in my grip, its raggedy fur a reminder of home.

On the morning of the third day, severe hunger pangs radiated from my stomach to my legs and hobbled every step. I stumbled along, oblivious to the vague rumbling and low cacophony of voices coming closer. When it could no longer be ignored, I saw over my shoulder that the increasing commotion heralded the arrival of the food wagons. You never heard such jubilant cheering as when the first one wobbled over the hill. The brittle, tasteless hardtack was as welcome as Ma's fresh-baked lemon cake.

About fourteen miles along, the acrid odor of wood smoke stung our noses, and swirls of gray floated above low hills. Zeke was ahead of us and reached the break in the trees first.

"My God, what happened there?" He pointed his thin arm in the direction of the valley below. "Get up here and take a look!"

We sped up the path and stopped next to him. Our dark line of soldiers threaded from the hilltop toward a small town in ruins below. We gawked, then set off in its direction. Brick chimneys slumped over charred foundations, and the residents had clearly fled the flames and perhaps something else they feared just as much. Slaughtered cattle and pigs dotted the fields.

A sober hush fell upon the lines ahead of Company D as we crossed the town's perimeter. Steps faltered, and a pall fell over the group even as the officers loudly berated fellows to keep moving.

I asked Sam, "What's slowed things down in front?" He was several men ahead of me.

"Damned if I can tell." He craned his neck. "I can't spy anything yet." A dozen strides along, I saw some of the fellows in front of us avert their faces and heard others gag. An unnatural odor of burning fat assaulted my nose. Then we saw it.

A man's corpse, intentionally laid out face up and hands crossed, was smoldering in still glowing embers within his incinerated home. White teeth sparkled in his coal-black skull. The remnants of house, body, and the murky circle of watery soil around the foundation were the only melted parts of the frozen yard. His slain cattle and pigs were heaped by the side of the road, their throats circled by icy collars of gore. I assumed that the man had been suspected of spying for the Confederates.

"Jeeezus! This stinks just like pork left too long on the spit." Sam stared for a second with his scarf pulled across his nostrils and then turned abruptly from the scene.

Meat. That's all this man was now—flesh flaking from bone and fat sizzling in the flames. No history, no dignity, no name—only a sign, a warning.

Later that night, there was dispirited conversation. McCorkle said, "I don't know about the rest of you, but this past week has set me against this entire business." All of us but Zeke looked away.

His eyes darkened above his sharp cheekbones. "I'm there with you, McCorkle. We are in this hell of a fix because of a bunch of fat cats who are looking out for their investments. And now some of them command this army and control our lives. Which are nothing to these sons-of-a-bitches." He spat into the campfire.

"You're damned right," I admitted. I didn't add that Reverend McIntyre's comments in the parlor the previous spring about the evil of one human owning another had begun to gnaw at me. My questions ran deeper than Zeke's, but I blocked them whenever I could.

11

IN MID-FEBRUARY, SIX WEEKS AFTER WE'D LEFT ROMNEY, JIM BLUE'S
father waited for an opening in the weather and then, driving his weath-
erworn wagon, braved the frozen Valley road to haul bundles of food and
clothing from our families. He also toted letters from home and newspapers. Beards settled down on a log with the *Staunton Spectator* spread on
his knees and a salty ham biscuit in one hand. Contentment played across
his features until he read the headlines. "Look at this! It says the Confederate government plans to draft men for two more years, or until the end of
the war. That can't be."

"What's a draft? I never heard of a draft," McCorkle said. He spat
toward the campfire and scratched his ankle. All of us were peppered with
red lice bites.

"I think it means they're going after every man fit to fight and won't
let him go until they're finished with him. It's something new. It's got
nothing to do with volunteering or free choice, as I understand it," said
Jim Blue.

"Let me see that," Zeke said. Frowning, he held the grease-stained
paper before his nose for a few minutes. "Well, I'll be damned. If that's not
a poke in the eye. What about that noble speechifying on people's rights
we heard from the new government? They must have forgotten about all
that." He then read aloud that we could re-enlist now with our current
company—that being Company D—or we could go home, lay about for a
few weeks, and then for absolute certain, be called back to fight.

Pa also saw the news and sent me a letter outlining what he viewed to
be my options. First, he recommended that I re-enlist where I was. That way

I'd remain with long-time Augusta comrades on whom I could depend and the leaders whom I knew. Strangers wouldn't value my fate as highly, and new leaders would have unpredictable flaws. Jackson's Brigade was guaranteed to stay in Virginia. If drafted, I might be sent to Kentucky, Mississippi, Texas, or who knows where, too far to furlough home and out of reach of home provisions. He also speculated that anyone who deserted now would be in serious trouble. Pa was safe from the draft. Besides being too old, he was a miller, and like blacksmiths, worked at a profession vital for supplying the army.

Zeke was deluded to think we'd ever had much of a choice. Sure, we'd enlisted voluntarily, but quickly our three-month term had been extended to a year. Now the government had us by the scruff of the neck until the end of the war, and who could say when that would be. By the time of this latest news, most boys couldn't tolerate their officers and didn't much fancy being shot at or killing others. I was one of those, but in addition, the agonized screams of men and horses in battle now haunted me. Nightly I heard them as I trudged, shivering and teeth chattering, through icy dreamscapes with towering peaks of snow.

In a shrinking realm of choices, another was to just plain quit soldiering. During the first year, boys wandered off because they couldn't stand erect—much less fight—while sick with chronic dysentery, measles, mumps, and typhoid. Afterward, they just stayed home. They sauntered off to visit friends engaged in battles elsewhere, journeyed down the Valley to visit an ailing wife or child, or chose to linger awhile in areas unaffected by the war. Drifting back into camp, they paid for their sins with a night or two in the guardhouse or sloshing the officers' laundry in a nearby creek. But that all changed after the draft and the first full winter of the war.

I had a passing late acquaintance with a deserter—Dallas Bunn from Wake County, a plug-short, straw-headed fellow whose superior skills on the mouth harp drew our notice. Everyone called him Jug, as his protruding ears resembled handles. He was only eighteen when he was drafted with his cousin Wesley Bunn, ten years older. A year must have seemed aplenty, because the Bunn cousins then ran off with eight other North Carolina boys in May '62, just after our second battle of the year, First Winchester. In camp we were used to hearing the North Carolinians grouse even louder than Virginians about being forced to fight. They had less at stake; their homes weren't being invaded. As an older man when I studied books analyzing the war, I learned another reason they were less enthusiastic. Seventy-five percent of folks in the entire South owned not one slave and got no benefit from the practice. But with the draft, they were all forced to defend it.

When we got wind that Jug had been among the captured, Beards and I trudged over to the log brig to visit. The number of armed guards patrolling the perimeter was a bad sign. "Hey, Jug! Are you somewhere in there?" Beards hollered toward the window. A mournful-eyed Dallas Bunn appeared behind the bars, his pale face scratched red from his time in the brush.

"Yep. Can't go no place else." A sigh so deep it sounded like it was dug from the ground came out of his chest.

"You're in a fine kettle of fish, boy. What the hell happened?" Beards had met Jug during his campground tours in the evenings. Dallas drew closer to the opening. He looked both ways before speaking in a low voice.

"Someone must have snitched on us. That's the only way I figure we ended up here. I never fathomed this outcome yesterday when we lit off for the foothills. We're mountain folk and figured we'd be out of catching's way in that tough terrain before word got out," he said. "Someone snitched for sure." His knuckles whitened on the cell bars. "I'll make him pay if I ever find out."

"How'd you get caught?" I asked.

"All in all, it was rougher going than we reckoned. On foot we couldn't get much ahead of the mounted scouts if they knew where we was headed."

He sighed again and shifted his weight. "Goddamned snitch. Otherwise, I'd be gone by now."

"I know how hard going that country is," I said. I'd once gone bear hunting with Pa in the Blue Ridge Mountains. It was a custom for all thirteen-year-old males. I was amazed to see how, up and down the Valley, barn-sized boulders braced one another—tumbled eons ago from their perch at the top. They littered the forest. Rocky terrain and serpentine tree roots ensnared boots and made climbing difficult work. Dense growths of blueberry bushes, laurel, and rhododendron crowded the slopes and at times made them impassable. Under their branches laden with pink and white blossoms in late May, toxic poison ivy sprang up and twisted its hairy tendrils into nearby trees. Poison ivy is everywhere in Virginia, but it's even worse in the mountains. An unwary passerby was guaranteed days of itchy welts and seeping blisters after contact with its leaves—unless he knew about the antidote of a smear of jewelweed. We soldiers rejoiced whenever we saw poison ivy's watery pimples speckling the faces of Yankee corpses—boys who a day or so earlier had flopped down in the midst of the unfamiliar weed to take aim at us.

Jug told us how, when the ten of them finally reached the summit, they found a toothless crone, wrinkled as a cabbage, squatted in front of a poor shanty. She had a wounded rabbit laid across her lap that she was cutting loose from a crude leather and stick trap. It appeared to be near dead with fear.

"My word, where'd y'all come from?" she cried, dropping the creature. One look told her the boys were runaways. "Lightening should be about here, yet there was nary a sound. It's a mystery why he didn't warn me of you fellows." She looked to and fro, and then keened out his name.

Jug told us how her wolf-like dog scared them to death when he bounded into the clearing, but the dog wasn't interested in them. He hurled himself toward the rocky ledge, baying his heart out. The old woman said the dog's barking must mean that more folks were coming their way, and she suspected this time they were trackers. She hurried the boys to a dilap-idated pigsty behind her shack and instructed them to lie low. Grabbing the rigid rabbit by its hind legs, she ran into her shanty and slammed shut the rickety slab door. A heavy crossbar thunked into place inside.

Beards was aggravating a pebble back and forth with his shoe while Jug talked. "Unh-oh, that spells trouble," he said.

"It sure as hell was," Jug said. "A heap more trouble than we needed. Pretty soon two Confederate scouts rode over the ridge, that dog yammer-ing at their heels. The soldiers foraged around for sturdy tree branches and then rammed the door through and drove the old woman into the yard, butcher knife in hand. My mouth waters now just thinking what a fine stew that rabbit would have made." He said the old woman dropped her knife like a hot stone and cried out when the soldiers threatened her with drawn pistols. She was quivering and shaking so, he felt bad about bring-ing trouble upon her.

"Did you recognize either of the soldiers?" I asked.

"No, but the tall blonde one threatened to burn down her shanty if the old woman didn't confess where the runaways were hiding," he said. She jabbed a scrawny finger to where Jug and the others were bunched up peering through the pigsty's knotholes. The soldiers hollered, "We know you cowards are in there. Show your faces, and we might go easy on you." The boys were frozen in place, speechless. "You get one more invitation to join me and my friend out here, or we'll set you afire," they hollered.

"That last threat must have scared you aplenty," I said.

"You bet it did, but we were quiet as church mice except for my cousin Wes. His piss made a noise splashing the ground." He said the light-haired soldier lit a branch from a match struck on his boot heel and approached the back of the hovel. Eyes bulging, Wes set the tip of his rifle against a large knothole. Jug said he poked him and made motions not to shoot, but Wes fired anyway. They couldn't tell if he meant to, or if his trigger finger was trembling so hard that terror made it happen. His bullet struck the short one with the beard, an officer named Malleck. An oath flew out of his mouth as well as a shower of teeth, blood, and mess before he tumbled over.

"Son of a bitch!" Beards stopped fiddling with the pebble. My mouth had dropped open at that piece of news.

"My god, you're really in for it now," I said.

A sob choked Jug's voice. "None of us wanted that man to die. Wes just intended to stop him from setting us afire. We never meant to hurt nobody."

"What'd you do next? You had no place to run to," Beards said.

Jug said he and the boys had kicked open the door and fallen out in a frightened pile, tripping over themselves with their hands raised. They believed that surely the remaining soldier would see it was an accident and give them clemency for turning themselves in. "They'd promised it," he said.

He took a long pause. "But that's not what they have in mind now. Oh Lord, I'd like to see Ma and Sis one more time." His voice trailed off at the end, and sobs welled up. He sobbed until he couldn't get his breath.

Beards passed his hand through the bars and squeezed Jug's shoulder. "Oh, man, I'm sorry," he said.

I shook my head in sympathy. "Me too," I said bleakly. But there was nothing we could do to help. He gave a hopeless shrug and disappeared into the cell's darkness.

I saw them all die. Jackson detailed an equal number of shooters from each company, and they were divided into ten squads, one for each deserter. An additional ten reserve shooters were also chosen. In all, one hundred and ten men were selected. Imagine that—being ordered by your commanding general to mow down the very boys who'd covered you in battle and with whom you'd enlisted. These boys were not our enemies, but our brothers. I'd rather have been shot myself than to be a shooter.

At the bugle call after breakfast, Tayloe, Beards, McCorkle, and the rest of us gathered into winding double lines that snaked along three sides of a broad wheat field. Thousands of men gathered there in formation— Jackson's entire brigade. Not a sound was uttered as we waited. Across from us on the fourth side of the field were ten upright logs dug in the ground earlier that morning. Each was a little taller than a man's head. I couldn't look at that scene but wondered at the peacefulness of the moment. Breezes ruffled the wheat and hinted at the advancing warmth of summer. A red-tail hawk caught the uprising drafts and circled overhead, wings tipped toward the sun.

Finally, guards paraded the ten deserters around the division to wooden posts. I tried to catch Dallas Bunn's eye, but each condemned man bore his head high and eyes straight ahead like he was proud to be singled out. Beards repeatedly cleared his throat next to me, and nervous coughs disturbed the silence.

A guard bound the boys' hands behind the stakes, bandaged their eyes with white strips of cloth, and then gave a hand signal to the firing party. Ready, aim, shoot and a hundred muskets belched forth. All spat bullets at the same moment, but not all found their mark. The ten reserves were then called out to stand before their squads. They were ordered to fire again. Their reduced number and prominence on the field made it impossible to intentionally aim a bullet too low or too high. When all was done—when death finally quelled the last twitching and hushed the last moan—the division paraded past those boys, now sliced almost in half by the volley of bullets. Most of them, like Dallas, were only nineteen years of age.

Zeke, famous for his precision aim, had been chosen from our company to join the execution squads. I could see Zeke clearly from where I stood. He tried to conceal his weeping and the tremor in his hands, but I knew. Many of us feigned protecting our eyes from the sun's glare to hide the disgracing tears. It's one thing for a man to take aim at pillagers, but it is quite another to witness fellows shot dead for yielding to feelings familiar to the rest of us. As we trudged past the bodies, I heard a boy behind me pray, "May you all rest in peace with the angels of God around His throne on high." Camp was somber that night, with packed attendance at prayer meeting.

12

GENERAL LEE DECIDED AFTER JACKSON'S SIEGE OF ROMNEY THAT WAR shouldn't be waged in the winter. And not until after late spring, either. Spring rains melted dirt roads into ribbons of soupy mud that stuck supply wagons and cannon caissons to their surface like fly paper. The Civil War would become a seasonal thing. But by May 1862, we began a charge through Hell that didn't slow down until that December. We fought more major battles that year than any other year of the war, twelve of them including Antietam. Sometimes they were only a week apart without time for either horses or men to rest.

I dreaded sleep just as desperately as I needed it. Every night, headless ghosts in blue uniforms chased me through cornfields, a retreat was blocked by leaping flames, or I watched helplessly as a Union soldier drew a bead on Sam. Days were just as bad. When I raised my rifle to take aim, a voice repeated the Sixth Commandment, the one forbidding murder. It caused my rifle to waver. Another voice would rise against it, telling me that killing Yankees was my duty. Daily, my conscience was split in a deadly contest. War was winning, erasing the rules I had spent my brief lifetime learning.

Then there was theft—or confiscation, which was it? At Toms Brook in May, we captured Northern wagons loaded with grain for the horses, flour, rye, coffee, dried meat, medicinal opium, and quinine. We had no choice; we were at the mercy of the Confederate army's lack of experience providing for its soldiers. The horses had scarcely eaten in two weeks, and some boys had been living on lard candles gathered from nearby houses. Protruding ribs and hollowed cheeks marked man and beast.

Were we thieves after Port Republic under the early June sun, when we plucked guns, Federal-issue oilskin raincoats, knapsacks, ammunition, shoes, and pants from dead or fatally wounded Yanks so we could go back into battle? The most unnerving sight was men bent over the fallen, hands busy with shoelaces, buckles, coat buttons, in pockets, and in their haversacks. I, too, made that necessary, ghoulish search, competing with hordes of other men for something less raggedy, less caked with mud and body fluids than the poor excuse for clothing on my back. Was this disrespect for the dead? It seemed as great a sin to leave these useful items lying on the ground for years, fabric flapping loose around blood-filled shoes and desiccated flesh.

As I lay in my bedroll in his clothes, I couldn't shake the image of their redheaded former owner with his frozen expression and half-closed eyes. They had seemed to follow my hands as I rifled his pockets. In his haversack, I'd found a rabbit's foot just as worn as the one I rubbed for luck. Now that he was removed from battle, would this boy have understood my need and forgiven me?

The next morning, Sam noticed that I didn't join the others for breakfast but stayed inside my tent. He stuck his head through the tent flap. "What's ailing you?"

"Nothing. Leave me alone for a little while."

He sat down next to me. "Not on your life. Something's bothering you. What is it?"

Sam's open, accepting expression made it easier to tell him the reasons for my sleepless night. He became solemn. "I've been troubled too. But if you ever want to get home again, you've got to develop animal instincts. Don't think about anything but food and shelter, nothing else."

"I guess you're right."

"I know I'm right."

I grudgingly agreed, but to me, it was pure theft when our Lieutenant McDonald had a soldier lead to the back of the line his elegant, prancing Jack, sleek with a still healthy coat, because he worried he might lose his father's fine mount in the coming battle near Gaines Mill. He then covetously eyed a Confederate farmer's heavy-boned draft animal. Our company was marching alongside a pasture in late June when he spied the horse calmly feeding in the field. Our group of foot soldiers drew up behind McDonald when he abruptly halted by the fence and dismounted. He was in such a hurry to reach the sturdy animal that he swept right by me, knocking me off my feet. Grimacing, I stood up, wiggled each foot to check that it still worked, and brushed myself off.

"Here, boy. Come here, boy," the lieutenant teased, hand extended. The liquid-eyed stallion trotted toward him, innocent of its fate. McDonald stroked its velvet nose while whispering softly. The horse nudged him on the shoulder and gave a friendly whinny. The creature reminded me of Pa's Wilbur, who had carried us to Staunton so swiftly. Heartsick, I wondered if he'd been taken too, and how Pa would put in crops, haul wood, or get to town without him. If that were the case, my family would have to struggle against starvation and freezing weather for the length of the war.

Deftly slipping a bridle over its head, the Lieutenant coaxed the horse out of the farm gate and uprooted it from its safe pasture and the family for whom it was necessary. Worry about my own family cast a deep shadow across one more day.

I saw the stallion cut down five days later as a bullet pierced McDonald's saddle a finger's width from his thigh. It bored like a drill into the horse's muscled flesh. With a shriek, the animal hurtled to the ground and tossed the Lieutenant over his neck like an acrobat. Exhilarated by his escape from harm, McDonald guffawed as he brushed twigs from his uniform. He then leaped astride a comrade's mount, and the two men cantered off. I heard the rattle of the stolen draft horse's last breaths in the tall field grass.

Around this time, we stopped calling the war what it really was. A man would say as he dropped a blackened greasy rag after cleaning his rifle, "Well, now I'm ready to see the elephant." Or we'd say about a fellow who had fallen on the field that he'd "heard the hooty owl." We couldn't use words too close to the truth of the thing, so we kept it to animals or the weather. All these years I've done my best to avoid recollecting the cruelest particulars of the circus of war and the whisper of Death's wing.

13

July 1862. From Mary.

I feel quite pert after the cool rain we had yesterday. I hope it isn't as cold at night up the Valley. Tell Beards he didn't take all the rain away from here this time when he headed back to camp, and he also left the cold air behind. I suppose I shouldn't complain about the rain, it was welcome after such a dry May and June. Beards also left behind a bit of sadness, I confess. He came by to call, and because I told Ma about our vow to be sweethearts, she left us alone in the parlor for an afternoon. I believe I love him more with each passing week. You can tell him that he is sorely missed around here.

Law, Tom, your jaw would drop if you could see the poverty of the merchants in Staunton these days. Pa set off last week to get provisions, but there were none to be had. Mr. Sampson's market was shut tight, as were Mr. Wilson's bakery, the shoe stores, hardware and seed merchants, the American Hotel, and even all the taverns. Nary a crumb of sugar or coffee could be bought for all the gold in China! Prices for flour have risen from six dollars a barrel last year up to as much as forty dollars, and butter has risen from twenty cents a pound to as much as two dollars a pound. There simply is no salt, not even for rich people.

Pa finished his first harvest last Monday. He had no help, but for young Jackie Beard one day and old Mr. York, *who must be in his seventies, the next two. He could scarcely find time to be in the field because folks dragged one sack after another to the mill. Farmers around here are not storing their grains but are having them ground immediately after harvest. Pa says it's because they want to take advantage of current government prices.*

But I believe they are convinced that if their grain is in sacks rather than a silo, it can be better hid under floor-boards and in attics, safe from both armies' soldiers. I tell you, Tom, folks this year don't want to give up their all for the Confederacy. The summer's terrible drought and relentless army requisitioning is causing men around here to predict a sure famine. They say an agricultural catastrophe plagues the entire Valley.

In the flatlands around Richmond, I'd marched alongside dry fields filled with stunted brown corn stalks and topsoil spiraling upward in the slightest breeze. That's where we camped and fought that June and July. I'd witnessed the townspeople's faces marked with fear that they'd lose what was left of their crops when we marched through. But I had prayed that the Valley had been spared. This letter proved my worst fears were true.

In her next letter, Mary told me that cannon reports were heard every day, that they came more rapidly than she could write each word of her letter. That the booming kept rhythm with every beat of her heart. She wrote:

It seems powerfully strange for violent noises to fill the house, while I sit as usual on the library sofa, surrounded by famil-iar things like our childhood books and Ma's framed Currier and Ives prints. The morning sun shines just the same on the blue Chinese carpet. Outdoors, it looks like any summer day. Ma's fluffy pink and red roses are in full bloom, and clusters of snow-white daisies and fever-few are near the end of their season. Do you remember that the only machine sounds we used to hear were those of the horse-drawn thresher with the swish, swish of the blades in the fields, wagon wheels rumbling on the dirt road, and the hall clock ticking? Now, close by, there is the unrelenting noise of cannons and artillery.

At first, with no newspapers and only rumors to inform us, we had no idea how close those weapons were. We worried sick we'd be overrun by Yankees or be struck down by stray bullets whenever we went into the garden to fetch a potato. It's taken us a while to figure distance and to understand that cannon fire can be heard from battles as far away as sixty miles because the mountains pass along the sound. When we can bear it no longer, we lower the window sashes and swelter inside during the heat. To preserve sanity, the booming must be ignored, or we'll all join poor Mrs. Calliston in the lunatic asylum.

I'd worried for days over Mary's letters about the drought and hardships at home. Now, not far from Manassas again, the boys in my company and I were also suffering from heat, surrounded by tens of thousands of soldiers tramping ahead and behind us.

Grunting with effort behind a briar rosebush by the roadside, Sam tugged at his filthy canvas pants. Then off came the one-piece cotton drawers that covered him from shoulder to mid-thigh, and which were slung disdainfully aside. He quickly yanked the pants back on, but at least had shed the extra layer underneath. His shirt had been peeled off several miles back.

The August sun sizzled hot enough to boil a cup of Confederate rye coffee and pretty soon gave rise to blisters across Sam's muscular shoulders.

His clothing blended into the other drawers, shirts, handkerchiefs, and vests that littered the road and blanketed ditches with a continuous strip of white. Jim Blue walked next to me bare-chested, but his shirt draped his head like a biblical sheik of Arabia and partially shaded his back. A chorus of coughs and sneezes peppered the air, caused by grit stirred up by boots on the road. Our meager water was hoarded in tin canteens drawn from a nearby caramel-colored creek. Sweat blinded anyone without a bandana or torn strip of shirting knotted across his forehead.

"When I took these things off a second ago, it felt good enough to do it again and tramp naked down the road." Sam grinned mischievously and fiddled with his top pants button again. "These canvas pants are danged hot."

"You do that, and Winchester women will faint at your feet. I hope you'll spare a few for your old comrades." Tayloe wiggled shirtsleeves from his bare shoulders as he spoke. Along the route, women and children had come into their yards to cheer us on.

"Not a chance," Sam said.

Beards's complaints had grown fewer and weaker as the sun soared higher. "Tom, I cannot . . . do you," he mumbled. For several minutes he had rambled in his talk, but a headache pounded between my ears, and my vision swam. In my haze, I couldn't pay attention to anyone else.

"If you're going to say something, for tarnation's sake, make some sense," I grumbled.

Suddenly, he bent over double and spewed out the messy contents of his gut. This seemed different from Beards's vomiting habit whenever battle was nigh. He stumbled and grabbed my arm, panting. Then he crumpled at my feet. He lay there unmoving, his legs tucked under like useless wings.

"Water! Does anyone have water to spare? A man is down with sunstroke here," I hollered as I stooped to raise his head above the parched road. The flesh on the back of his neck felt on fire, and he was still as a corpse. Beards had been in my life as long as I could remember, right up through these worst of days. He couldn't abandon me now. And I wasn't the only one who would mourn his passing. What would I tell Mary? My breath caught in my throat. With the last of my canteen, I frantically sprinkled his head and slapped his reddened cheeks. His eyes fluttered, and he shoved my hand away. Pushing himself up with his elbows, he sat without support in the dust. Now that he was roused, Sam and I helped him stagger to a hospital wagon, where he could travel sheltered by its tarp. We settled him on the boards with his back propped against the side. Wiping his forehead with his hand, in a weak voice he said, "I owe you, my friend. I'll not forget." My heart near to burst with relief. Some boys had fallen, never to rise again. Thank God, Beards wasn't one of them. The wagon train gathered their prostrate bodies and hauled them to the next campground where their gaseous remains would be buried before they burst. Mary couldn't have lost Beards like that, nor could I.

For two weeks, we had marched twenty-five miles a day as blood pounded unceasingly through my ears. We marched even when the temperature must have soared above 100 degrees. A rifle, ammunition, a water canteen, and rations were all that was worth carrying. By the sides of the road, foam-speckled horses sprawled, done in by the sun. We hadn't passed a creek or pond for far too many hours. By nightfall, the army came upon a few houses with wells in their yards, but with thousands of men jostling for a position to get water, there was little hope of quenching one's thirst. Now we were a day from the brutal battle of Second Manassas where we'd find relief from the marching but not the infernal temperature. Those of us who survived Nature, through dumb luck or precaution, eventually became hardened like a gallstone to such discomfort.

14

OFTEN IN THE EARLY AFTERNOON WHEN I ABIDE IN THE FARM'S parlor, adrift in the slipperiness of time, I see the boys from Company D. They look just as alive as they did all those years ago. Yes, I think it's Sam who strides through the front hall to the back door. He doesn't notice me stretched out on the sofa just inside the parlor. He's a gray blur, really—and has passed before I can rise and call out his name. I think my mind is playing tricks; but the image carries me back to the last time I saw him alive.

We were near Chantilly, the last day of August 1862. I sniffed the air, sensing the undercurrent of coolness, and took note of the brittle yellow light that heralds the end of summer. Across the fields I witnessed a mob of solemn fellows, some cleaning their rifles, others chopping and hauling wood. A few quietly wrote letters while another group pulled huge cannons into place by the road for transport. Soldiers, wagons, encampments, horses, military bustle, and confusion spread out on the rocky fields. Some boys sat with minds drawn elsewhere.

I lowered myself down on a log and pulled one foot up across my knee to study it. My mud-crusted ankle emerged from nothing but a shoe top, tongue flapping for lack of laces. The sole was gone. In its place were wadded rags and straw, bound on with strips of cloth to protect my raw, oozing feet. I didn't know any man with proper boots after we had trudged over a thousand miles up and down the Valley of Virginia that year.

Hunched over a scrap of paper laid out on a Bible, Otis McCorkle was intently writing to his wife Lizzie and didn't see me approach. By craning my neck, I could see that he advised her to sell everything, all their geese, cows, and chickens. She could use the money to purchase food and necessities for herself and the baby before a new dispatch of our soldiers came to the southern counties to seize whatever cattle were left. In camp, McCorkle had heard that the men were on their way, seeking cattle hides for shoe leather. The beasts now were too scrawny for meat.

Zeke had sidled up behind me and mocked my awkward posture when he caught sight of McCorkle's letter. He grabbed McCorkle's arm, startling him so that he dropped pencil and paper. "How can you write such words? Look at my swollen feet; look at Tom's. Look at the wounds," he demanded. "You'd deprive us and others of shoe leather? We won't have a chance in hell against the Yanks if we can't chase them across a cornfield or walk down the road."

"You read my letter!" McCorkle shouted. "You had no business reading my private letter!" His eyes shot sparks, and his face looked like a ripe plum.

Zeke relaxed the arm he'd pulled back to punch McCorkle, and his voice softened. "You're right. I apologize. I had no right," he said. "But what are you thinking, saying such things?"

McCorkle's brow wrinkled in defense. "You don't know anything about it. I'm tormented every night, worrying about my Lizzie and the baby dying—just to benefit this effort." He wasn't at home to protect them from the depredations of either army, so this advice was all he had to offer. "Our horse is already taken, and Lizzie has no way to travel to market unless someone more fortunate offers her a ride in his wagon. How many of those folks are around these days?"

"None," we responded in a chorus.

He continued, "You're damned right. And our generous Confederate government gives a person less than half what their goods are worth. It's legal theft. She'll have nothing if she doesn't sell everything before they find her." After a bit, Zeke settled down, particularly when several of us concerned about our own folks at home admitted to sharing McCorkle's view. If officers had gotten hold of his letter, however, he would have been tossed in the guardhouse for a couple of days.

Wine-colored bruises and weeping blisters on my feet dashed any hope of walking home a hundred miles. How I ached to relax on the wide front porch with my ankles propped up on the railing. I'd listen to Mary's neighborhood tales and eat Ma's home cooking. I pined for a chance to lie on a down mattress with a pillow under my head, rain beating on a tin roof. If I were to see a table laden with Ma's vittles, I suspected I'd kill myself with gluttony. And to her horror, I'd pitch into everything with fingers and fists, not having used tableware for so long.

There was preaching in camp that morning. There would be preaching again that evening. Presbyterian, Methodist, and Lutheran ministers, it made no difference. They all came from Valley churches to take their weekly turns before us. They repeated propaganda from government-issued pamphlets designed to make it easy for us to draw a bead on a Yankee soldier. They told us the Yankee boys were evil, not sufficiently pious or God-fearing. "They deserve to die for their sins. You are doing God's work in doing battle with them," one had said, pounding his fists on a wood-crate lectern.

Their message reminded me of a letter written on my nineteenth birthday by my Aunt Ellen, Ma's favorite and youngest sister who lived on a farm near the Bethel road. She exhorted me to serve my country bravely as a soldier, but to serve as the Savior's warrior as well. Enlist under His banner, she'd said, and respond as cheerfully to His call as I had to my country's.

She meant well, but I saw no benefits to religion on the battlefield or in the camp hospital. Fellows who attended the preaching twice a day were just as likely to be sliced in half by a cannon's grapeshot as those who didn't. The minié balls didn't zing by overhead to cut down the non-religious while going out of their way to avoid the pious. I didn't know how the new minister preached, but from the looks of him, I thought I could do as well as him with two days' Bible study and a glass of whiskey.

I sometimes joined that crowd of fellows, their backs bulging out against the canvas walls. I'll admit there was some comfort in the repetition of the familiar words within the church tent where boys sought solace. Beards' face gleamed with more than lantern light when he recited the lines of the twenty-third psalm: "Yea, though I walk through the valley of the shadow of death, I will fear no evil; for Thou art with me." He swore those words brought him peace late at night as he lay on the ground. In moments of weakness, I too succumbed to hopes that if spoken enough times, the incantations might ward off death and injury.

The aroma of stew filled my nostrils. Kettles hung from horizontal branches propped up over small campfires. The men were preparing rations for three days, a sign we'd march and fight for at least that long. As usual, the direction of our march and the location of battle were a mystery.

These intervals between fighting ground down my spirit. On the other hand, combat fired up every cell of my being once I broke through the fear. My senses buzzed as bullets bore through the forests, unleashing a torrent of twigs and leaves. Foliage wafted in slow motion, each vein and stem magnified and trembling. Every moment intoxicated me with crystal detail.

Nothing in camp could touch it. At that moment, demons in my head groused about the captain's orders and made me long to be anywhere else. For distraction, I picked up my sketchbook, trying to find humor in our soldier's life by cartooning it. First, I surveyed the camp area.

I spied the boys of my mess—Sam Lucas, Tayloe, Beards, McCorkle, Blue, and Zeke. A small fire flickered where they prepared rations for the march. I had become indifferent to the camp's discarded paper and garbage that wreathed tents. An immense pigsty proliferated. The odor of horse manure was no stronger than our own human stink. Heaps of clothes, coffee-colored with diarrhea stains, lay about. I meandered up the field and stepped around an unidentifiable animal carcass that someone had hacked up. The fellows laughed over one of my cartoons, forgotten on a log where I'd been sketching. It depicted Sam watching as the day's pot of stew tumbled into the ashes from his poorly manufactured tripod. The others were rendered with mouths agape and arms raised in alarm as they saw their hopes for a meal disappear. Sam was often the butt of our jokes because he detested anything related to chores. His five older sisters back home had coddled him. He still had much to learn and plenty of complaining left in him.

Cartoon Sam's hair poked out in porcupine spikes, his face was darkened by sunburn, and a wiry beard sprouted below beady eyes. His head teetered above a stick body. The others didn't fare so well either. One thing about Sam—he could laugh at himself. And that's what he was doing when I hailed him.

As I drew close, I could see that his high spirits, contagious like a sneeze, had infected the men around the fire. They were all laughing as they stamped feet and shifted weight to loosen joints stiff from a night on damp ground. Suddenly, I heard a burst of rifle fire from over my shoulder, coming from the nearby woods. For a second, no one realized what had happened, even as Sam tumbled backward. Someone continued laughing. A Union sniper had anointed Sam, not another of us Augusta boys, to die that day. To accept the bullet that carved an exit through his skull. He was gone instantly.

How could it be that in the midst of guffawing right out loud— laughing from your deep gut with your head thrown back in abandon—as though all that matters is the itch working its way up from your innards to your brain—how could it be that you would be shot dead that very second through your open mouth? How could fate have allowed a bullet to penetrate such a pure expression of mirth, to turn merriment into a river of blood?

Not one of us moved. I stared at Sam's body on his back before us, wondering if I was next, but was too shocked to run. It felt as though I was watching the scene from the height of the thin clouds scrolling across the sky, too far away to attach a name to the body on the ground. Jim Blue was the first to shatter the horrified silence. "He should've kept his mouth shut! Don't you remember how Old Man Kiefer always ordered him to keep his goddamned mouth shut in Greek and Latin class? If he'd kept his mouth shut, this never would have happened." His words were choked with tears.

"For Chris'sake, Blue," Tayloe muttered.

The truth of the past few seconds finally broke through my stupor, and I snatched up my rifle on the run. "I'm going to kill the son-of-a-bitch who did this." The rest of the boys followed me. But as the tangle of wild grapevines and fallen branches clutched at our feet, the receding blue uniform disappeared into thin air. Finally, we straggled back to where Sam's body lay.

"That was a goddam Union sharpshooter with his telescopic rifle. They're the only ones who've got no respect for the rules of war," McCorkle raged. "Only a devil would look down a rifle barrel and draw a bead on an unarmed man relaxing with his mates."

"Sam didn't have a fighting chance," Beards muttered.

I remained silent. I was fighting to ignore the inky black sorrow that was crawling upward from my gut and seeping behind my eyes.

"Come on. We need to do something with his body," McCorkle said. "We can't just stand here all day." He moved toward what was left of Sam and the other four of us followed his example. I grabbed one warm, lifeless leg. Beards clasped the other. No one wanted to be anywhere near his bloody head, but finally Beards and Jim Blue each lifted an arm. I couldn't wrest my eyes away from Sam's teeth all lined up like small tombstones. I saw each clearly, as never before. The bullet had passed through Sam's mouth a hair's width away, without damage to any of them.

We laid the body down in a secluded spot at the edge of the woods.
Zeke then squatted to loosen Sam's boots. "He promised these to me in
case he died, and I now need them more than he does." He looked off
in the distance, avoiding everyone's gaze. I was repulsed yet fought my
desire to pull off his good pair of woolen pants recently sent from home.
I resented Zeke's acquisition, even if he was entitled to it, thinking how
those shoes would have allowed me to finally walk home on furlough.

Sam was buried as decently as circumstances would allow. We jabbed
our bayonet blades into the red clay and worked the weapons back and
forth, back and forth. Clawing at the wet, dense earth with our fingernails, we scrabbled out the bayonet-loosened clods and used a cooking
kettle for a scoop. Finally, we made a depression deep enough to keep out
the elements.

"Where is Sam's top hat?" Zeke shambled back to the camp to retrieve
it. "Can't bury him without his hat," he said sadly, placing the ragged
item next to the body. Not looking at anyone, I reached for it and clasped
the battered thing tight to my side. It was old to start with; probably had
belonged to Sam's grandfather. Its jaunty little tower had led us into battle
atop Sam's head more times than I could remember.

"I'm keeping this to remember him by. And maybe his folks might
want it," I said. The others nodded.

His body shrouded in his soiled blanket, dog-eared knapsack settled
on top, Sam was cocooned in his nest of red earth. Beards sacrificed a
scrap of paper hoarded in his knapsack and tucked it into the blanket's
folds with Sam's name and company scratched on it in pencil. Then we
piled dirt on what remained of Sam Lucas. We tamped it all down with
rifle butts and mounded branches on top to deter foraging dogs and wild
pigs. The whole time, I thought the walls of my chest would rupture with
the pressure of a silent howl. But not one of us dared show the strength of
our sorrow, in case we all broke down.

We couldn't just leave Sam without some kind of farewell ceremony. Nothing about it seemed right. Knit in a silent circle around the mound, each man probed his heart for words. I finally found my voice. "We'll sorely miss your high jinks and mischief, Sam. May your eternal soul rest in peace." No one else spoke but stood with shoulders sagging and heads bowed. We had lost the only one of our group guaranteed to make us laugh. He was also the bravest; he was the one who had saved a whole trainload of us that first morning at Harpers Ferry. I stroked the hat's frayed silk brim between my thumb and fingers, and later would find room for it in my backpack. From a hollowness more burnt-out than the big oak seared by lightening up in Pa's field three summers earlier, "What a Friend We Have in Jesus" emerged from my throat. It soared as the broken voices of the others joined in the second verse. After we finished singing, we all wandered off separately to deal with Sam's death.

Emptiness took root in my soul that day. Everyone was brought mighty low by Sam's loss, but I felt the most lonesome and apart from the others. I had lost a man as close as a brother. I couldn't get out of my head how empty Bethel would be without Sam. Every day would be like knowing the night sky would never again have stars.

I'd close my eyes but couldn't sleep. The Union sniper's bullet had struck Sam down, but I couldn't fully blame the sniper. After all, ours lured Union troops into battle and then quickly dropped behind the lines to kill our own boys—shirkers fleeing duty. I'd finally leave my blanket and spend hours at the tent flap staring into the dark while I cursed Jeff Davis, the entire Confederate government, the slave owners—including Bobby Lee and most of our officers—and everyone else who'd spouted states' rights and voted for secession. In truth, all those people cost me my closest friend. For days, I spoke only when necessary. If my grief was so vast and raw, how would Mr. Lucas and the rest of Sam's family deal with theirs? An upright, forked stick was all we had to mark the spot for his folks. It would be three years later when they came for him with a wagon and a tin box to unearth what was left and transport it home for burial.

Campground sounds and sights melt away, and I realize I've wandered near the farmhouse back door, confounded by shifting place and time. The sofa in the library is my destination, and I seek it through the blue shadows enfolding the rooms. The deep tranquility of the library is my touchstone, and I sink with relief into the soft sofa cushions. But not for long. A sense of great urgency seizes me. Where is Sam's top hat? I hadn't thought of it in many decades until this afternoon. Could it have been tossed out with everything else these strangers have pitched in the trash? That hat is all I have left of Sam. Like so many boys lost then, there was little to bring home and place under a tombstone.

15

IN MID-OCTOBER, WHILE MEN MORE RELIGIOUS THAN I WERE STILL trying to reconcile why God had dealt the South the powerful wound of Antietam four weeks earlier, I met a man with a different tale of theft. After an afternoon foraging for sassafras bark, pine needles for brewing tinctures, and chicken-of-the-woods mushrooms, I rested contentedly with my back against a broad loblolly pine. My overflowing haversack lay by my knee on the edge of a wood near Kearneysville. Too soon, I'd have to leave the fragrant forest and head back to camp. Every now and then, I thought I heard the cluck of a wild turkey hen, perhaps gathering her chicks. A hand to my brow, I searched the hedgerow edging the field in hopes of a bird for dinner. That was good enough reason to linger where I was.

Not long after, sounds of heavy breathing and twigs snapping startled me. A cavalry horse was tracking nearby through the underbrush, and a bulging sack twisted around the saddle's horn revealed the rider and I had been on the same quest. The man and his piebald mare lazily glided through tunnels of dappled light until they caught sight of me. The fellow drew back on the reins, rested his hand on his pistol, and demanded, "Hey, are you a Reb?"

I quickly recited my name and company to put him at ease.

"Julie Edwards, from Williamsburg," he said as he drew near.

He was no more than my age, but he sported the shiny sword of a cavalry posting. I stood to stroke the horse's mane, thinking how fine it must be to have four legs to carry you foraging rather than two exhausted and mostly shoeless feet. He leaned down to pat her neck.

"This is Lucky. You won't find a better soldier anywhere." After we shared disbelief about the Antietam rout, he asked about my company's losses and inquired about our commander. I assured him Captain Paxton was in good health.

Jeb Stuart was his commander, and Julie told me about a maneuver with that daredevil across the Potomac River to Maryland several weeks earlier. He had been ordered to join a thousand other cavalry soldiers for the five-day expedition.

"What good could come out of being on the northern side of the Potomac at this time?" I asked.

"Horses. The army was desperate for more after Antietam. There was no other choice but to go back into Maryland. There are certainly no horses left in Virginia!"

I stifled the memory of the thousands of dead animals scattered on the field in September and instead asked, "The locals weren't hostile?"

"No sir, people were so scared that they just stood by, jaws hanging. We could pilfer anything we pleased, as long as we got out of there quickly afterward."

He described how a mass of animals followed from town to town. The horses swelled out down the road in a choking cloud of dust that hid everything in their wake.

His eyes sparkled and his voice rose an octave. "You should have seen it. The lanes and roads were cluttered with empty four-horse wagons and carts after those animals were stolen, or confiscated, if you prefer. You can bet no horse was safe in its pasture, either." He said that farmers could only stare in shock at the receding rumps after he and the other troops had visited. I'd heard rumors about the raids, but Julie's account reminded me that Yanks could be doing the same around our farm. They always retaliated in kind, and both sides were running out of horses. A shadow fell across my mind, and I had trouble following his words for a few minutes.

But then Julie came to the heart of his story. His regiment had approached a small farm with a neat clapboard house and fresh manure in the barnyard. The captain waved his brimmed hat in the air as a signal to soldiers behind and galloped up to the weathered-board building. Julie and the other soldiers waited in the lane with their stamping and snorting charges. The captain made a show of jumping down from his horse and then he thrust back the broad barn door. "We could see him prowling through the vacant stalls. Just as he waved his hat to signal there was nothing there, he whirled around. A horse had snorted once, then twice, somewhere inside," Julie said. The captain pushed the barn door all the way open and motioned for Julie and the others to join him. Another snort sounded from behind hay bales stacked to the stall's ceiling. "We hurled hay on the ground until a chestnut flank came into view. Someone had hidden the mare behind a false wall of bales." The barn dust set everyone to sneezing, but Julie saw through a crack in the siding a young woman tearing toward the barn. He moved closer to the boards for a clearer view.

"She was hollering and shrieking, wavy brown hair and skirts flying behind her. I couldn't help but notice how pretty she was. She yelled at us to wait. She charged right across the ankle-high filth between the fence and the stable door, she was so panicked." She gasped out a plea to leave the horse, saying the captain must surely have enough mounts. She waved her hand toward the crowd of them in her barn lane. If he took her mare Lucy, she wouldn't be able to go for supplies or to fetch a doctor for her baby suffering from croup. What would she do if he became feverish? Holding her hands out in supplication, she begged all of us to have mercy on a woman alone, a woman forced to fend for herself.

"I was sorely tempted to plead on her behalf, but it wasn't my place to argue with a higher officer. I just kept my mouth shut." Julie said. He looked away. "The captain sneered at her, passed the reins of his steed to me and leaped astride her chestnut mare. The woman stumbled back as he shoved her aside with his well-polished boot and started slowly down the driveway mounted on her Lucy." Hooves splattered her dress with mud as she tagged after, begging us to spare her horse.

"Here's the part I can't forget." Julie still couldn't look at me but told how the captain pulled back on his reins and then turned slowly in the saddle. He smiled and beckoned to the woman. "I wondered at the sudden expression of hope that brightened her delicate pink face," he said. "Her eyes glowed with relief, but when she drew alongside, the captain whipped the horse forward and sped a little way down the road. That's when I understood he was playing a cruel game. She'd never see that horse again." He said she again ran after, her face dripping with tears and sweat. Wisps of hair were glued to her forehead when the captain slowed and stopped again. He waited for her to catch up. By this time, she struggled for each breath. He and the rest laughed heartily at her distress.

"Did you laugh? What were you doing all of that time?" I asked.

"I guess I protested, but pretty weakly. It didn't make any difference, though." Again and again, the captain taunted the woman. Julie could hear her racking sobs from where he sat on his horse. Finally, bored with the game, the captain trotted off, while the stolen mare strained to look back at its abject mistress.

His voice dropped to almost a whisper. "I last saw the woman limply braced against a fence post on the side of the road. She'd chased after us at least two miles and was completely spent. Her bodice was splotched with sweat, her head was bowed, and her hands hung limply by her side. I couldn't look her in the eyes as I rode past. It's been weeks, but I still spend nights wondering how that woman and her baby are getting by without that horse. And how long they will survive."

I scuffed at a patch of spongy moss with the toe of my shoe as Julie waited for my reaction. It was tough to find the right response. "Don't be so hard on yourself," I finally said. He gave me a rueful glance as he leaned forward in his stirrups and geed Lucky forward. I watched as he and the horse disappeared over the hill.

Even though my scavenging trip had been a success, Julie's words haunted me every step of the way back to camp. All of us were stained by the war. It wasn't clear to me we could ever be free of it. I'd like to have told Sam, to have heard his thoughts about Julie's story, and that made me miss him even more.

16

WHEN THEY ARE LEAST AWARE THAT ANYONE SEES—IN BED, THE TUB, the bathroom, strolling the yard, preparing and eating food—I admit to the guilty pleasure of spying on the man and woman in my house. At the same time, my conscience torments me. It's just that I'm so in need of the company of anyone other than myself that I can't resist. I was raised to be modest, and Ellen always dowsed the light before we made love regardless of my desire to see her supple body. But I can't help myself now.

These people are wanton in their intimate moments. They stride about the bedroom naked and sleep without any nightclothes. Although I'm content with the memory of being enclosed in Ellen's primordial warmth, I wish we'd allowed ourselves this couple's freedom. And these days, vicarious pleasure is the only kind I know.

Now in the empty house, mine once again without the weekend people, I recall my times with Ellen. All the touching, until only awareness pulsated—with no word for my wife, no name for myself. There were no labels, no analysis of what she'd said to me earlier in the day, no judgments about needs met, or not.

By my reckoning, it has been ninety-two years since anyone has spoken to me. Occasionally, the man or woman will step into my space close enough to brush my arm or face. Registering only a puzzling chill, they move away. In my solitude, I've considered how people briefly move against, or brush by, one another the way cattle in fields establish connections through touch—and how we are ignorant that this habit keeps us grounded. That is, until those with whom we are physically intimate are gone.

And where is Ellen now? At the age of eighty-five, she'd lived longer than me by eight years. I never minded the deepening crows' feet around her eyes, the thickening of her waist, and the graying of her hair. She was always beautiful in my eyes. After I was beyond her reach, my heart shattered as I saw her face distorted by joint pain, her mouth dragged down by losses, and her quick, graceful step become slow and tentative. I witnessed her confinement to bed, heard her cry out in her sleep—particularly during her last illness. I stroked her forehead and held her dear hand, but she had no idea of my presence or the comfort I wished to offer. I still seek her at night. Often, I dream that a young Tom and Ellen embrace in a sunny field, naked bodies oblivious to the rough terrain and the dampness of the earth. We never lay unclothed in a field. Ellen wouldn't have allowed it. But in the early days, we tasted this merging. After the dream, I vainly search to find myself reflected in her luminescent eyes again. Why do I never see her here in our home? Why does she appear to me only in this dream?

17

January 1863. From Mary.

Tom, do you remember Mr. Shumate's girl Sukie? A year before the war, we spied her along the road clutching a hand-written pass that permitted her to leave her master's property. She balanced a knobby bundle on her head under a sky that dumped buckets of rain. Pa offered her a ride on the back of the wagon. She seemed about my age and had a quiet nature. I recently saw her in the awfulest circumstances and have no one to confide in for fear of our parents' wrath.

Pa encouraged me on New Year's Day to accompany him on one of his usually futile visits to town with his sack of smoked possum and rabbit to trade for salt to preserve what meat we trapped. The government now distributes small quantities to the few shops, but salt is fetched up quick as a blink when set out for sale. Any diversion was welcome, and I had not been on such a long jaunt since that time several summers ago—you must remember it—when we rode into Staunton for that traveling minister's tent revival.

As Pa would be a while, I thought to stroll around by the train station. But as I neared the courthouse, I could hear a hubbub from as far away as two blocks. A crowd of finely dressed strangers milled around at the foot of the wide stone steps and stretched out down along Augusta Street. Law, I never heard such deep Southern drawls as they hailed one another. The street was a sea of black stovepipe hats that

bobbed alongside felt bowlers. They were atop gentlemen
dressed to the nines in sack coats, vests, and matched trousers. Some streamed from the American Hotel and must have
arrived the previous night by train, come all this way north
in such perilous times.

A crimson cloth banner bound to one column rippled in
the air as I climbed the porch steps to read the small bulle-
tins pinned at all angles to it. There was much jostling and
elbowing to get a good view, and I had only a minute to see
the headlines: "Negroes to Be Disposed of Today," and then
the lists. "Patience, fine seamstress with small boy child;
Moses, rented out for hotel waiter; Joseph, excellent carpen-
ter; James, fine cook; and Stephen, strong field laborer." And
there was Sukie's name next to the description "girl aged 19,
good laundress."

"What are you doing here, Miss? A refined young lady
doesn't belong at a slave auction. Go yonder back home with
your family where you belong," an uncivil fellow in a white
silk scarf growled as he shoved his way in front of me to better
read the notices.

You know we have never witnessed anything of this kind,
and I had an untoward inquisitiveness as well as being sorely
vexed about Sukie. The man was correct. I wish I had heeded
his rough counsel. Before I could think whether to leave or
stay, a fellow next to me gestured, "Look there, Josiah. Here
comes the coffle, straight from the jail behind the courthouse.
It's about time we get to see the merchandise. I hope there's a
strong buck there worth my traveling from South Carolina."

Well, Tom, that was just the beginning of the most miserable sights you could ever imagine. Down Augusta Street
out of Barrister's Alley came rows of Black men, two abreast,

shackled at the ankle by iron cuffs linked by heavy chain. The chains clanked on the cobblestones as the men stumbled along and the cuffs bloodied their ankles. Slowly behind them marched the women, arrayed in their finest calicoes with red bandanas wrapped on their heads, clasping children by the hand or against their breasts. Hemp rope tied one hand to that of another slave woman, and the ones with babes made the most pitiful cries. Certain of separation, they implored the heavens for mercy. Two stocky white men preceded and followed, each with a twitching cat-o'-nine whip. I was searching the lines for Sukie when a frantic scuffle ensued. When the lead slave was released from his fetters, he kicked and screamed, then shoved and punched the white men who rushed to detain him. Out came the whip, and down lashed the strips of knotted leather against his back until his shirt oozed red. He uttered not a sound during it all, but if looks could kill, that man with the whip would have died on the spot. I expect his owner thought the Black man's value as a marketable commodity was reduced then and there, and he was borne off with loud blaspheming to be sold another day to an unsuspecting set of customers.

I know I shouldn't have been tempted, but I was repulsed and yet craved to learn more. I sidled along the wall behind the stirred-up crowd to a crude warehouse door where some female slaves were being confined until their time for sale. Just as I pried the heavy door open a crack, I saw Sukie. Four potential buyers were ogling her when one drew her by the arm into light from a square, barred window across the empty brick space. Another pried her mouth open and jammed his finger inside to inspect her teeth. The third drew down her bodice and pinched and poked her breasts. And the one named Josiah pulled at her blue-checked skirt. He commented on the width of her hips and their potential for carrying a child. Her glance locked with mine over their heads as their uncouth hands pawed her. Scalding anger flashed my way. Confounded and dismayed, I realized that I too was a target of her rage in this heinous circumstance. Only later did I understand.

Outside, the auctioneer warmed to his task. Clad in stained, brown-striped pants, a grimy white shirt, and a moth-eaten green topcoat, he was the very picture of unwholesomeness as he paced around a strong, young black man. The slave was mounted upon a wooden block for all to appraise easily. "Who will offer the first bid for a strong Negro of good color? I am told he's industrious, so let me hear $200 in Federal greenbacks. Now do I hear $250 for this prime worker?" He did not write anything down, but just held up two fingers to signify sold when the raucous bidding finally reached $1,600. Even if I had some money, I would never have enough to buy Sukie and free her. I know for a fact that this sum is three times Pa's yearly income at the mill during the best of times. It would take years for a hardworking man to earn enough money to buy one slave, and that without spending a cent on his family, foodstuffs, and shelter.

But the worst was yet to come. Sukie and other women were displayed on the block with their chests exposed, blouses scrunched around their waists, afforded no more consideration than beeves at market. I was horrified for them, shocked at such a circumstance, and then finally outright shamed to be in such a situation surrounded by those men. I sheltered my eyes with my hand and turned away while those poor women were on the block. Even more grievous, a number of buyers declared the children an irksome burden, and the little ones were auctioned separately from their mothers to other bidders. The children howled piteously with arms stretching toward to their wailing mothers as the distance between them grew. It cleaved the heart right out of my chest.

By this time, I thought to flee then and there. But having come this far, I struggled to pull myself together and to endure until the bitter end. Coffles were formed up under direction of the new owners, with slaves again shackled and paraded this time up Augusta Street to the train station. Others gathered for who knows how long a march to locations far from a rail line. The sun was dropping, and I knew Pa would be most anxious if I didn't hasten to Beverly Street where we had agreed to meet, so I did not linger around the courthouse as the crowd dispersed. A few freed Blacks were scattered in the group. They solemnly wandered off down the street after their own desires, in heart-wrenching contrast to the coffles marching away.

My somber silence and downcast eyes were hard to ignore as we started on the tedious ride home, now after sundown. Pa finally asked, "What ails you, Mary? I've seldom seen you so sore-hearted." I mumbled a non-response, and he turned back to manage the wagon, its bobbing lantern casting brief patches of yellow onto the emerging landscape. Do you ever wonder about all the articles in The Spectator that quote this slave and that about how good their lot is, and how few could hope for a better life and kinder masters? Do you think the newspaper is in the sway of businessmen who make their living from the slave trade? And the politicians who depend upon them? I have only met slaves in town who serve as waiters, shopkeepers, and blacksmiths' helpers. I had no idea of *the falsehoods and deceptions those newspapers promulgate, and I'm sore ashamed to say I had never given the slaves' situation much thought.*

Finally, through the dreary silence, I said, "Pa, why didn't you tell me about slave auctions in Staunton, and that one would be held in town today?"

"I plumb forgot it was today. I guess it is New Year's Eve, after all. It's a once-a-year tradition." He hesitated and then said, "And as a girl, it's not something you needed to know."

"You do me no favors by hiding such things from me. I'm old enough to know lots of things," I told him, drawing myself up tall on the wagon seat.

"You reckon so, now?" he said. "Well, Staunton is a major stop on the rail line, easy to get to and leave. Which is why plantation owners and their managers come here from all over down South—though not as many as come to the Richmond auctions. Yes, indeed, selling slaves is mighty lucrative business. I've heard said that their value in Augusta is more than eight million dollars, and the slave trade is as profitable an enterprise as any merchandise slaves might produce. That's what's driving this war, you know. People in power don't want their incomes threatened."

I asked him, "But what about Lincoln's emancipation address in Gettysburg that everyone is talking about? Didn't that have any effect?"

"No. None at all here in Virginia. The state hasn't been defeated. Won't have any effect until that happens. As I understand it, that proclamation is legal only where the Feds are in control," he answered, and then fell silent.

The day presented me with an abundance to contemplate. I have been guilty of a failure to imagine a slave's plight. Why had I never conjured myself in their place? I couldn't bear to think of Sukie's future somewhere far away in the deep South. Where is her family now? What about those little children? How could they endure such a terrible separation from their mothers and home? What kind of scars would they bear for the rest of their lives? And then another question occurred to me. Where in the practice of slavery is the Christian compassion taught in Sunday School? Have you ever pondered this? Now I hadn't the temper for more conversation during the bumpy ride home. Please don't let on to Beards about my day in Staunton. He might think badly of me for going to the auction.

I remember how my hands shook after reading this letter the day the postmaster handed it over. I had barely noticed Sukie when Pa gave her a ride that rainy day before the war, and neither Mary nor I had witnessed an auction at that time. Only a vague knowledge of slave auctions had hovered on the edges of our awareness. But Mary's account had filled me with shame and grieving for those people.

18

ONE SPRING DAY IN '63, POSTMASTER JEREMIAH P. STUBBS, A FLINTY little man with curling hair that wove itself into a tangled beard, stood in his usual place beside the flap of the canvas postal tent. His mail sack hung over his shoulder. He solemnly passed out envelopes from a thin stack to the boys crowding before him on the campground. We hadn't seen action since December, which had given the Union troops ample time to destroy the remaining rail lines. Lately the sack had flapped almost flat against Stubbs's thigh, and his normally bland face had become grim. Our mess had elected me to trudge to Stubbs's tent to collect whatever mail had arrived for us. No one had wanted to make the long tramp across the campground to return empty-handed and disheartened. Dread slowed every footstep as I returned to our campfire. I couldn't bear to see the boys as disappointed as I was.

Beards called to me before I reached our tents. "Anything for me?" I shook my head no. The light went out of his eyes, and his shoulders slumped.

"This is about Mary, isn't it?" I asked. I wandered over to where he sat on a tree stump.

He nodded his head. "I haven't had a letter in far too long. She's forgotten our bargain. I was a fool to think she'd care for me all this time." His ears reddened and his eyes narrowed. "She's too fine a girl for some other fellow not to steal her. I bet that's what has happened."

"Did she ever give you any sign that she'd stopped caring?" I sat down beside him on a log. "I know she hasn't. It's not Mary; it's the mail. I'm not hearing anything from her either." I told him that the postmaster had blamed it on the Confederacy. The government hadn't paid its bills to the rail company contracted to deliver mail. "The company has quit running its trains. That on top of the Yanks ripping up the tracks."

He looked at me with disbelief and shook his head. "The part about the rail company makes no sense. How could such a thing be true? No, it's Mary." I'd been listening to his growing doubts about my sister for days. Now he'd convinced himself she'd been tending some injured boy at home who'd won her heart. "Well, if she has given up writing to me, I'm sure as hell not going to lower myself by writing to her," he said and stomped away. Something had gone sour within Beards in recent weeks that had nothing to do with Mary.

I continued to write home, even though I knew there was little hope anyone would receive the letters. For the few minutes that a pencil stuttered across the page, the faces of Ma, Pa, Tish, and Mary were vivid before me, and I found comfort in that. My letter to Aunt Ellen in May got through eventually, and she passed it on to Ma for safekeeping. It's the last in the bundle that the woman unearthed behind the bookshelves.

Dear Aunt,

I seat myself this morning to write you a few lines to let you know that I am well, with the exception of being tired out from the terrible suffering we've just passed through.

You no doubt heard news of the battle of Chancellorsville before this, and you may feel uneasy about me. I wanted to let you know I'm safe, with no broken bones. We lay in the line of battle for three days and three nights after the hard fight of May 3. On Tuesday evening, May 5, it commenced raining and didn't stop until Friday. That whole time we were forced to lie out or march through mud. This last battle is the most terrible we've had lately. Saturday night was spent in occasional skirmishes, and it was then that General Jackson lost his arm, which we all feel to be a sore bereavement.

The large brick house at Chancellorsville used as a hospital took fire and burnt up. Flames killed hundreds of Yanks who were already so hurt that they couldn't get out in time. Their own soldiers wouldn't help them any. Later in the day, the woods took fire. Many more helpless men perished. Their burial was no better than their death, and it was harrowing to view their charred bodies. There were so many that our men couldn't dig enough graves, but instead threw a few shovelfuls of dirt over each and passed on. My comrade Zeke joked that if the Yankees had stayed at home as they should have, they would've gotten a decent burial. I saw some who had been buried in shallow trenches and subsequently had the covering clay washed off in the rain. They were black as charcoal.

I grabbed a button from the coat of a fallen Yank and will send it home as a souvenir when I can. As my paper is nearly out, I'll close by asking you to excuse all mistakes, bad writing, etc. Give my love to friends and relations, especially Uncle James, and keep a due share yourself from your affectionate nephew, Thomas M. Smiley.

19

SHRIEKS CURDLE WITHIN MY SKULL UNTIL I DOUBLE OVER WITH HANDS to my ears. But that doesn't help; the sound doesn't ease any. At first, it's far away, but then it sneaks up, keening and howling. Stumbling about, I search for a place where I might escape from its ear-splitting sound. Then I have a startling realization: this ungodly noise is coming from me. It swirls around and around, while I slip into a bottomless hole. The opening at the top is reduced to a pinprick of light. And there's a foul vapor, like that from a rotting deer abandoned by vultures. Breathe. Draw the calming stream of air into my lungs. Forget today, when the man with a crowbar tore at the plaster in the kitchen and left ragged wooden lathes and beams exposed naked in the room, the cupboards in a broken heap on the floor. Breathe and remember something soothing. Sit in the porch rocker and listen to the music of leaves rustling and yellow flickers gathering to head south. After all, Nature's sounds bring a man closer to the contents of his heart. This is what I tell myself.

I do recall another a time when Nature was a balm. It began one June morning in Virginia near Culpeper as Beards and I lounged on the packed earth near our tents while we gnawed on our breakfast hardtack biscuits. He regarded the tooth-snapping material in his hand with disgust, and asked if I'd seen how many blackberry bushes we had passed yesterday on the march to the new camp.

"Let's go get some of those berries. Do you recall when we used to play for hours around the bushes along the farm fence? We stuffed our mouths until our chins and fingers ran purple." I then fell silent, allowing the pleasant memory of the summer berry hunt to replace, for at least a few minutes, the nightmarish images of recent days.

"Maybe Tayloe Hupp wants to go, and the three of us can share with the other fellows." Beards wiped hardtack crumbs from his mouth, stood up, and headed over to roust Tayloe from his tent. It didn't take much persuasion, and the three of us were off.

Anticipation of the berries' plump sweetness after the meager dry rations of the past weeks boosted our spirits, and we joked as we hiked away from the tents. No matter how far I wandered along the hillside above, waves of noise washed over me from the twenty thousand men bivouacked in camp. Strains of song, shouts of laughter, jesting, games of toss, arguing, horses' whinnying and stamping of hooves, clanking of moving carts and cannons, clacking of rifle butts, and general conversation filled my ears with a singular clamor. The steep hills, the forests at their crowns, and the cloudless sky were alive with it.

From this high vantage, my eye was drawn to a band of enslaved men at the edge of the encampment. Some sawed trees and others split logs for firewood. But the deep release I'd felt as my feet strode away from camp made me think about them down there. They might be doing the same work we foot soldiers did, but they labored with armed guards standing over them. Joy at my temporary freedom curdled. These men could never set off on a berry hunt. They could never dream of furloughs or a safe and a comfortable home far from the battlefield, could never be visited by family bringing food, clothing, or news. I averted my eyes and stumbled downhill, shame and sadness slowing my steps.

The berry bushes closest to the encampment had been denuded. The three of us had to travel several more miles along side roads to find any that were fully laden with fruit. Tayloe lagged behind, slowed down by a mending ankle twisted while charging through a cornrow. We discovered shrubs sprawled along former fence lines, their prickly branches arched over the grass, heavy with blackberries at the perfect moment of sweetness. Beards, Tayloe, and I spread out and wordlessly plucked from bush to bush, filling our knapsacks and eating an occasional stray. Initially, I picked in view of the others, but as I moved down the row and then along the edge of the dirt road, they were gone. I gathered fruit until I had an ample quantity and gingerly hoisted my rucksack to my shoulders so the berries wouldn't crush under their own weight.

I lost track of how far I'd journeyed from camp. Rye grass and wheat-covered hills rolled like waves down the valley. Fence posts had not yet been yanked up for firewood, and maple and oak trees clamped their roots into the earth as if they would be there forever. The camp sounds were only a faint drone in the background. The fellows yelled my name once or twice in the distance, but I kept walking. I longed to find a point when the babble and rankness of men no longer filled my senses. Striding ever more quickly, taking one hill and then another, I sought respite in the rapid movement of my feet from the bitter taste of summer battle. I cursed myself for not bringing a canteen. I could've dowsed my head and wet my throat. But then a peculiar thing happened. As the rumble of humanity diminished, another sound filled the space. It swelled to a high hum just where the other began to shrink. My ears weren't sharp enough to catch the precise second when the loss of old occurred and there was the gain of the new.

Creature noise inescapably enfolds you in the hills of summertime Virginia. Crickets in the grass with their high-pitched leg-rubbing, synchronized like group breathing—into my hearing, out of my hearing. Cicadas' scritch, scritch, scritching in the oak, cedar, locust, and walnut trees. All together in one place—it drifted out, then lifted altogether in another. At first it came in clumps, but I listened more carefully and detected the millions of dancing sounds separately. The cawing of sleek, ebony crows was a staccato in the orchestral buzz. Above it all was the melancholy cooing of the Carolina mourning dove—whoooo–who-who-who. I reckoned I might dissolve into a world of notes ever dividing. From time to time a cow lowed or a horse whinnied. But the insects were a constant—a mass that broadcast the same cry out into the universe. Or did it just seem that way from my limited human viewpoint?

The shade of a wide oak was irresistible, and after carefully situating my juicy sack against the trunk, I collapsed upon the soft moss and ferns at its roots. With legs outstretched, I crooked my arms beneath my head and looked up. A mammoth luna moth spanned his wings on a branch just above my head. Perhaps he'd just burst from his cocoon and waited for his lime green mantle to harden in the sunshine so that he could float off to find his love. Or he could have been wistfully peering at me, envying my longevity seconds before his life ended. After hours of memorizing the pages of Dr. Finch's insect book with Mary, I knew the luna moth lives most of its seven weeks as a caterpillar or in a cocoon. It is most glorious for only its last seven days on earth. The large, green wrinkled wings unfurl across a triangular body soft with the white fur of a Persian cat. As the insect pumps fluids into them, they are forced out to their full four-inch span. The moth then flies off to mate with a fury before death comes. Because it has no mouth, it must live on past experience, consuming itself. A luna moth can't eat.

I pondered the moth's fate. For him, a clock ticks down, and an alarm has already sounded. But for now, there's maybe the joy of sailing on the currents and the intoxication of living to mate. The eyes are huge and soulful. The head is flamboyantly adorned with two brilliant yellow stalks like ostrich ferns. Does it know it's doomed, and does this awareness deepen its desire to leave a legacy? The wings encompass four miraculous windows, false eyes to fool predators, but they are perfect transparent circles through which the world beyond is visible.

I wondered if, like the magnificent luna moth, all the tiny carapaced members of the insect orchestra filled the steamy afternoon with searching, yearning desire. Could any of these sounds be answered inquiries, invitations to assignations, offerings of tantalizing insect delights to come?

I lazed in the grass and watched the sun dip lower. With all of this thought of insect sex, I recalled infrequent glimpses of pearly bosoms just visible above dress bodices. Oh, how I missed the fairer gender. But I yanked my thoughts back to the immediate ocean of humming. Were the lives of men like those of the insects? If a man could hover far enough above the earth, would war, peace, and other human endeavors appear only as an indistinguishable mass of activity? Was this God's vantage point if He was, indeed, in a Heaven above us? Was it, in the end, just about reproduction of the species—an act of immense vanity if we are indeed made in His image? Had my mother known my mind at that moment, she would rightly fear for my soul. I sank back into the insect songs and remained there without thought until the sun fell to the tops of the trees.

Satisfied that I had enough berries to share with the boys, I carefully laid my haversack across my shoulders and covered the miles back to camp.

20

M ARY'S LETTER ABOUT SUKIE AND HER QUESTION ABOUT HOW THOSE who owned slaves could consider themselves Christians tormented me with self-doubt. What about those of us who were killing men to preserve slavery? I wasn't the kind of Christian that my parents were, and maybe wasn't one at all. But I did believe in the same principles. Six months after her letter, the issue rose to such a boil that I could no longer escape it. It was just a few days before Gettysburg.

At the end of June 1863, General Lee had led so many of us across the Maryland line into Pennsylvania that it took three days for troops to pass through a single small town. Those of us in the infantry were the last to file through, and by that time, fearful locals were wearied of the sight and no longer stood in their yards to gawk.

After setting up camp, our company and several others were ordered to capture every edible farm critter from miles around. Hundreds of us chased about in fields, pursuing panicked turkeys, ducks, and chickens in all directions. The promise of regular food put everyone in high spirits. Squawks, gobbles, quacks, and hisses filled the air. As I was grabbing for an elusive hen trembling under a wild rose hedge, I saw Zeke approach with a duck under each arm. Their orange feet frantically paddled the air. With a tight grip, he was trying to steer clear of their snapping bills, but one pinched his forearm. He dropped the duck like a hot coal, and it ran off until another fellow caught it. Feathers clung to our hair, made us sneeze, and carpeted the field like snow. The creatures' final destination was an acre so packed with fowl that you couldn't see an inch of ground. There they were quickly slaughtered, plucked, and cooked on spits laid over fires. Another field was crowded with wagons piled high with loaves of bread, cheeses, chunks of corned beef, sides of bacon, crocks of apple butter, barrels of dairy butter, and other edibles seized from surrounding houses. My stomach was in a state of continuous rumble, anticipating a real meal for a change.

A few days earlier, General Lee had issued a command that was read down through the ranks until it reached us. During this foray into Pennsylvania, we were forbidden to destroy property as Union troops had in the South and were to wage war only against armed men. The last night of encampment before we reached Chambersburg, thanks to Beards' wandering ways, we learned that very few soldiers intended to obey. Men were aching to retaliate for Union barbarity in the South. Beards had seen a copy of the *Richmond Times* handed around that called for troops to light a sea of flame in every Pennsylvania town. The newspaper claimed even that punishment wasn't enough for the theft of over 500,000 slaves, or fifty million dollars' worth of investment, since the beginning of the war.

"It's not just the officers," Beards said. "I heard a lot of angry talk around the campfires." He'd rejoined us as we loafed around our fire, enjoying the last bit of goose grease on our fingers and sucking marrow from leftover bones. "It's not easy to forgive burning Virginia farms and to forget the danger to our families."

Signs of disobedience became obvious the next day. While the fellows and I were on a hill chopping fence rails for firewood, I caught sight of a distant cloud of brown dust that seemed to swirl closer. Propping my axe against a tree, I walked toward the road to see who approached.

"Where are you going?" Beards yelled.

"I'll be back in a minute." I waved my hat at him and kept walking. The crack of splitting wood told me he'd returned to work.

As I waited by the road, the outlines of cavalry soldiers became clearer, and behind them streamed a line of Blacks on foot. Most of them were women and children, hands bound loosely with rope. Soldiers with rifles trotted alongside, enforcing order in the lines by screaming curses and pointing their rifles menacingly. The distant tide of sound now became a buzz of voices. Cries of "Mama" and despairing wails assaulted my ears. Women with exhausted children clinging to their backs stirred up the dry road. Soldiers clasped toddlers on the front of their saddles, while sobbing mothers who couldn't keep pace with the army horses trailed behind.

One Black woman passed close where I stood. She carried herself straight-backed as Ma and looked to be about the same age. She was dressed in a crisp calico dress, a white kerchief neatly knotted around her head. "Please, officer, I'm free," she cried out to a cavalry officer who rode nearby. His face was like carved stone, and he kept his eyes straight forward as though he was deaf. "I was born and raised right here in the North, in Franklin County!" she cried more loudly. "Oh, Lord, this ain't right! We're all freed or weren't never slaves to start with! Why are you taking us?" Again, her captive ignored her. She lifted her eyes to the sky and called out, "Lord Jesus, how have I failed you, to be punished this way?" Her head fell to her chest, and she moaned inconsolably as she trudged forward.

A soldier mounted on a black horse noticed me standing by the road and waved. "Look what we've got here" he called. "As fine a bunch of contraband as you'll see anywhere."

"Where are you headed?" I hollered back.

"Taking 'em to auction across the Mason-Dixon line. We'll sell every one of 'em to make up for what was stole from us. Too bad there ain't so many men amongst them so we'd get a better price. Guess they run off to join the Yankees." He raised his hat in farewell as he rode by. I forced myself to nod in response.

When he was out of sight, I sank down on the red earth by the side of the road. A powerful despair blackened my vision on the edges and made me weak. How could this be happening? How many others would suffer in this way? Now that we were no longer fighting to defend home ground, the evil underbelly of the war's purpose was inescapable. Saliva surged in my throat, and then I was on my hands and knees disgorging the contents of my gut. I puked until nothing but bile filled my mouth. Through my misery, I could hear the sounds of agony lingering in the air for what seemed an eternity as the dust cloud disappeared over the next hill. Emptied out, I sat with my head in my hands until I heard footsteps crunch in the dirt behind me. I looked up and found Beards by my side.

"What's the matter? You've been gone for a long time."

"Did you see that?" I asked him.

"Just the end of the line. It's pretty awful, isn't it?"

I nodded. There were no words for what was going through my head. I guess because I looked so out of sorts, Beards decided to wait with me. He squatted on the ground and joined my silence. Eventually, he picked up a twig and drew lines in the dirt. But I knew that something momentous had changed for me that afternoon. Like the other boys, I'd disliked the business of soldiering, slogging through rain and bone-numbing cold, the fear that loosened your gut, and bloody chores on the battlefield when fighting was over. Now a biting sense of revulsion toward the entire Confederacy and my own role took hold, stronger even than when Sam died. I choked back another surge of bile. I would disown anything to do with the Confederacy.

But what were my choices? As a deserter, I couldn't go home, and I'd be executed if I were caught. I was trapped. I had to stay where I was, but from this day forward, my goals would be pared down to only one thing, protecting my friends and saving myself. Nothing more. I had to return to my family at war's end. Given the Valley's wreckage, they would need me more than ever.

"We ought to be heading back now," Beards said. He threw his stick aside and stood up.

I silently got to my feet, brushed the clay from my pants, and slowly followed him to the fence post where I'd abandoned my axe, never imagining how, in just a few days, my resolve to return home alive would be sorely tested in the farm fields to the southeast near Gettysburg.

21

As the frost dissolved under a pale November sun in 1863, our regiment headed south one morning toward the rolling Virginia landscape of Orange Courthouse. We trudged behind the cavalry, and the artillery followed with cannons rumbling on the corrugated road. Miles of wagons spilled over with gear and bumped along behind. I entertained myself by watching beads of light sparkle on the icy fields and thinking we would soon retreat to camp for the winter. No more marching out on cold mornings, not until after the spring thaw. How welcome those days would be. This would be our third winter with an unknown number stretching ahead. My mind drifted to the crude log and mud shelter we boys had cobbled together in last winter's camp. With a makeshift chimney and fire pit, we'd kept passably warm. I continued to dream about a break from fighting, having no idea that just over a hill and through a dense stand of forest, lines of Union troops snaked for miles down the road, unaware of our parallel route.

Their commander then made a wrong turn at a crossroads near Mine Run, we learned later from captives, which is why a line of blue-jacketed soldiers appeared out of nowhere. They emerged from the forest on the hill above us, and we stared, dumbstruck by the sight. Their shock and ours quickly changed to panic. They couldn't retreat, blocked by their own soldiers, horses, wagons, artillery, and cannons. We were completely exposed in a valley boxed by rocky hills and by forests on their ridges, our artillery wagons stretched out on the low road. There had been no time to dig trenches, heap barricades, or position cannons to face the enemy. Our only hope was to gain the stand of trees above. With a dry mouth and a throbbing heart, I barreled after our Sergeant, Erin McGinniss, who bawled like a madman, "Pick up your feet, sonsabitches, and get to cover, goddamn it, get to cover!" His red-blotched cheeks were fiery in his fair Irish face. He raced upwards toward the trees.

Runners pitched forward on the slope's slick wet grass, tripping like dominoes those who charged behind them. Knots of our soldiers struggled to rise, only to be targets for Yankee shooters who had come to their senses. Bullets were pinging everywhere. My breath came in ragged bursts, but the trees now weren't so far away. Boys were visible between the trunks, readying their rifles. Beards, Blue, and Zeke ran nearby, following our sergeant's lead. But Tayloe was behind us, lower on the hill. I heard him cry out, and when I looked around, he had fallen face down, one leg bent beneath him, and his arms splayed out. My heart was in my mouth; getting to him would be almost impossible in the shower of metal. But I wheeled around, kept my head low, and ran down to where he lay. Tayloe's face was turned to the right away from me, his profiled aquiline nose and high cheekbones pressed to the earth. A shock of brown hair hid his eyes, and the ruddiness of his cheeks had vanished. Now blood ran from a rip in his scalp, oozing scarlet across his skull and over his collar. My breath stopped. First Sam and then Tayloe, the two who had been with me in this hell the longest. Placing my hand on the back of his grimy jacket, I prayed to feel his ribs expanding and contracting. Underneath the jacket's coarse texture, there was movement. And then Tayloe groaned, moved his left arm, and finally twisted his body over to peer at me with groggy eyes. The bullet had only grazed his head, knocked him unconscious, and torn several inches of skin aside above one ear. "Tom? You're a damned idiot. We'll both get killed," he mumbled. He tentatively touched his fingers to the wound and then stared at the blood smearing his hand. "How in the hell are we going to get out of here? My ankle hurts, too." The bullets passed overhead with renewed fury.

"Play dead. That's the only hope right now," I said, flattening myself next to him. "If we stand up, it's over."

When I'd seen him last, McGinniss had been on the hill's crest, flailing his arms and yelling at Company D to goddamn hurry up. He was a short, wiry fellow with hair that flew in tufts over his ears, a few years older than the rest of us and proud of being Irish tough. He was a devoted Catholic, although you'd never know it by the cussings we received. The entire company trusted him. He never forgot that we were his sacred duty to protect. Now he ran down the hill and threw himself on his knees next to Tayloe. He directed the Lord's wrath at us and simultaneously fired his rifle at the enemy. "Run! I'll cover you," he screamed. We rose, bent at the waist, and scuttled a few yards uphill, Tayloe ignoring the pain of his bad ankle. As McGinniss launched into a fresh set of epithets, I heard the thwack of a bullet hit him. "Holy mother, I've lost my leg," he bellowed. When I turned to grab him, he flailed at me with his rifle butt. "Get the hell out of here, you idiot." His leg was still attached, but crimson leaked from a round hole in his pants leg. He was pallid as snow.

"Do what he said, Tayloe. I'll deal with the sergeant," I hollered. Then I turned to McGinniss. "Straighten out that leg, and let's see if it's broken," I ordered, kneeling by his side and squeezing his bleeding thigh with both hands above the wound.

"You goddamn fool, it's not broken, it's shot off," he yelled. "Get your hands off me. Ow, Ow!"

"It's not shot off. Stick your goddamn leg out," I yelled back. "We can get you to cover easier and stop the bleeding if the bone's not broken." Clumps of grass and clay jackknifed into the air, popping me in the leg and arm as Yankee shooters missed their target. "I need to look at it!" I insisted. He finally agreed. The bullet had torn all the way through his thigh but seemed to have missed the bone.

Tayloe had crept back down the hillside and seized McGinniss's rifle to return fire. I grabbed McGinniss under his arms and pulled him along while he struggled on his good leg. He was faint with loss of blood, but managed to growl, "Leave me here. Save yourself."

Tayloe snapped, "No way in hell, Sergeant." After what seemed an eternity's climb to the hill's crest, Zeke raced out and helped drag McGinniss behind a stout fallen oak. Tayloe and I made it to cover behind the trees, and I scooted over to McGinniss. I tore the Sergeant's ripped pants from his injured leg. Tourniquet strips could be made with the fabric. "Help me with this," I said to Zeke. All the while, bullets bounced off the trunks and branches above our heads. I yanked the strip tight above the puncture while Zeke knelt and twisted a stick through our tourniquet to increase pressure. The gush of blood slowed to a modest flow. Tayloe was collapsed against a tree, wrapping his head with a piece of shirttail.

Zeke looked up for a second, away from the hand pressed on McGinniss's thigh, and tilted his head. "Listen for a second. What have the Yanks got hold of?" Above the ordinary rhythm of rifle fire there now was a steady stream of louder rat-a-tat-tats that ricocheted off the trees and never relented.

"Something that doesn't have to be reloaded," I said. Just then, we spotted figures moving beyond the thicket: regiment doctors readying tents for surgeries. Zeke and I lifted McGinniss' arms around our shoulders, crooked his useless leg over my arm so that it was elevated, and made our clumsy way across brambles and fallen limbs to the hospital area. Every few steps, McGinniss dug his fingernails into my arm. He bit his lip until it bled and moaned even though we stepped as carefully as we could. "Write my wife," he groaned. "Tell her that I loved her 'til the end . . . will see her in Heaven." His head fell forward.

"What? You're giving up? You're too brave for that," I told him. "You need to see Ireland one more time." I grunted as I adjusted his weight. "Nobody will let you into Heaven, anyway."

He attempted a faint smile, "Goddamn you, Smiley." We gently settled him on the ground with the other wounded as medical staff passed among them, and we raced back to our broad log. He wouldn't die, but we knew the camp doctor would amputate his leg to prevent gangrene.

Through the trees and over the hill's rise, we could see mangled bodies lying under the thick gun smoke. Bullets rained down without pause. Beards and the others were grim-faced as they reloaded their rifles after each shot. I leaned against a tree to gather my thoughts and surveyed the ridge across the valley. From time to time, the smoke parted and sunlight gleamed on bright metal in the direction of the mysterious blasts. Squinting to sharpen my focus, I spied a monster gun with six brass barrels pointing through the foliage. It was more delicate than a cannon and larger than a rifle. I'd never seen such a weapon.

Something rose up in me, ripened by Sam's death and the suffering I'd seen. It was righteous anger, but it mostly felt like an intention larger than myself. Grabbing my rifle, I called out, "Follow me." Zeke raised an eyebrow, then guessed my goal, and we were off, dodging through the brush, leaping over fallen limbs, and circling the curving ridge behind the rapid blasts. Every hundred feet, I searched upward through the bare branches, seeking the sun behind rather than in front of where we began. Our noisy progress was undetectable in the midst of the artillery blasts. When the infernal machine came within sight, we hid behind a giant sycamore. The rest of the Yankee force was far to the right of the blasts, distant from where we were. But through the gray trunks, two Yankee soldiers hefted buckets and dumped streams of bullets into a sleek mechanical hopper. Two other men rotated the barrels with a hand crank.

"Let's take it," I mouthed to Zeke. We both shouldered our rifles and on a count of three, fired together. The four Yanks ducked in surprise, so intent were they on reloading and aiming the machine that they never suspected our presence. A second volley from our rifles struck one man in the arm, and he ran off clutching the wound. The third volley quelled the action of the gun. Two artillerymen frantically fiddled with it, turning the barrels and snapping the trigger. The third grabbed up his rifle and was set to take fire toward us when the other two convinced him to flee. We waited until they were out of sight and then rushed to the weapon. It would do no more harm that day; the firing mechanism was shattered.

"Do you think we can get this back to our side? The boys will never believe us when we tell them what we discovered," Zeke said.

"We can try. The monster weighs as much as two men," I said as I leaned against the gun carriage. Zeke was tinkering with the hopper and the hand crank, trying to figure out how the thing worked. "Come on, you can look at it later."

But we had wasted too much time examining it. In the distance, splotches of blue were racing in our direction. And our hopes were greater than our strength, anyway. The two of us would never be able to drag the cumbersome carriage across the brambles and downed trees clogging the space we had crossed earlier. Not before they got to us. Zeke and I fled through the woods, back to the ridge held by our men. That was the only time I laid eyes on what I later learned was a Gatling gun, the first semi-automatic weapon.

After it was too dark to shoot, Zeke and I picked our way through downed branches toward the surgery tent. I held aloft a lighted stick wrapped with a flaming rag, and Beards and Blue followed behind. We wanted to see how McGinniss was faring. By torchlight, the mound of arms and legs discarded in buckets by the soiled hospital tent made a gruesome display. The salty smell of blood sullied the evening air. "He's gone home to Augusta, fellows," the nurse told us. "He was a brave man when we operated. He squeezed the devil out of my hand, and I'll never repeat a word he said, but he made it out alive. We put him on the wagon with the other wounded just an hour ago."

"It's good news for McGinniss that he's going home, but what in the hell will we do now?" I asked as we walked toward the flickering camp-fires. "No one else is tough enough to replace him."

"We don't have many to choose from; not like we used to. But we'll vote. It will work out," Beards said.

"I guess so, but you tell the company."

As we drew closer, one fellow cleaning his rifle called out to us, "What's going on with the Sergeant? Did he make it?"

Beards didn't answer but strode to the center of the group. He cleared his throat loudly to signal he had something important to say and solemnly waited for quiet. All eyes turned toward him.

"McGinniss lost the leg, and he won't be coming back. Do you fellows have any suggestions for a replacement?"

Tayloe called out, "I nominate Private Tom Smiley to be Sergeant of Company D, thanks to his heroic actions today."

My face reddened. Then another voice said, "We need someone who has a cooler head, who thinks before he acts. Is Tom that man? I'm not so sure."

Beards came to my defense. "He wasn't at first. But he's changed over the past two years. You've seen it yourself. Look around at what's left of our group. Is there anyone else here who would have done what he did today?" That silenced the boys for a minute.

"I suppose you're right," someone said. "His courage and quick thinking saved a bunch of lives."

"Well, what about it, Tom?" asked Beards.

I could feel my ears burn. "I'd be honored, but a lot of you deserve it more than I do."

Zeke stood. "That seals it. I second the nomination. I move that we vote now." He counted hands and squatted again beside Jim Blue, who was nodding his head in assent. That was how I became sergeant. Afterward, I spent all night worrying about filling McGinniss's big shoes. He'd never shown signs of the emptiness I felt.

22

I FEEL REDUCED, THINNED. WHEN I STROLL PAST THE HALL MIRROR, THE outlines of my body waver, fly off into the room. If I hold my hands before my face, they are transparent, just the same as looking through the lunar moth wing. I seize up with shudders of fear, my arms and legs paralyzed. For so long, I have depended upon my home and the things I own to keep Hell at bay. Now the man and woman have whittled these away until the most painful memories are all I have left. They are like dragonflies under the surface of a frozen pond, not dead but waiting until they can paddle upward toward the promise of a thaw, which is now upon me.

Here it is—the day we were captured in May 1864. It was the first week of combat after the battle at Mine Run following five long months in winter camp, and the morning couldn't have started off worse. The fields of Spotsylvania Courthouse were swaddled with cotton fog after rain so fierce that I could see no farther than Beards on one side and Zeke on the other. For five days, we'd done nothing but dig until a four-mile ditch unfolded, throwing up hillocks of clay in front of our line. Now spear-sharp tree trunks bristled outward from the mounds that formed a great shield. We huddled behind it, waiting for the enemy at first light.

Yankee noisemaking no longer frightened us. "That sounds too far away to be an attack cry," I told Jim Blue. He just grunted. No one was stirred up enough to rise to his feet.

"Why would they do something so danged stupid? Now they've wasted any element of surprise," Zeke said in a slurred voice. None of us had slept the previous night. We'd been on watch, and anyone who nodded off for even a few minutes risked being shot as punishment. "Never mind. We'll whip their asses in no time," he assured me, and perhaps himself.

"They must be as blinded by this fog as we are," I said. It seemed forever that we'd crouched there, although it was only a few minutes before a tide of the enemies' shots roared in our direction. It was then that we leaped to our feet, raised our rifles, and were ready when a line of blue-clad boys rose out of the mist and over the edge of the earthworks.

My rifle misfired with a forlorn little pop, and Beards hollered, "What in God's name!" as his did the same. A sea of Yanks charged toward us as we and the other boys nearby futilely loaded and reloaded rifles. We had shouldered our weapons and pulled the triggers, but nothing happened. Moisture had besotted our gunpowder.

One of our boys, a young fellow no more than seventeen, charged up the earthwork's steep incline. He shouted toward an oncoming Yankee, "I'll show you, you yellow-bellied bastard!" A bullet struck him in the eye. The force spun him around and then toppled him onto Beards. Before Beards could scream "What the hell?" Frye, the dead fellow's comrade, grabbed the dropped rifle, drew his arm back, and heaved his bayonet forward into the air. "Take that, you Yankee pig," he cried. The weapon whizzed past me and flew so forcefully into the Yank's chest that the blade burrowed into him at least six inches up the rifle barrel. You never heard such an unholy shriek as he fell backward, just beyond where I stood, the rifle poking straight out of his chest and saluting the sky.

Zeke and I followed Frye's example and frantically twisted bayonets onto our rifle muzzles. The short piece of sharpened steel was handy for digging, cutting meat, and sometimes as a candlestick, but our troops rarely used it to kill, not since first Manassas. Now it was all we had. The barricade we'd built as protection held us and the Yanks imprisoned, face to face. There was no room or time to reload rifles at that close range. We couldn't run, and neither could the Yanks once they were over the top. We were in a gutter of muddy water, our feet glued in the mire.

A dark-haired Yankee propelled himself toward me, steel flashing. I'll never forget the moment—how I felt his iron grip on my collar and saw his arm above with a bayonet pointed downward. Thrusting my shoulder into his chest, I writhed away and finally found enough space between us to stab upward with my blade. The jab of my bayonet brought the feel of shattering bone and the slippery slice of flesh right up through my arm muscles, and it crawled into my soul. For a second, images of this boy's life, likely similar to mine, flashed by. But after this first one dropped at my feet, the second wasn't as hard. You stared a man right in the eyes and attempted to kill him before he killed you, both of you screeching like maniacs and gnashing teeth.

In their ghoulish faces, only the desperate eyes of Beards and Blue appeared human. Enemy blood was splattered there and on their chests. I stayed close to Beards. We always fought side by side, but this time we needed the other's protection like never before.

When rifles and bayonets weren't enough, fellows around me dropped them, abandoned their clubs and knives, and grabbed for hatchets to hammer enemy heads into scarlet pulp. But the soldiers continued to surge over the barricade in a vast blue wave until there were thousands of them amongst us. At one point, Zeke climbed a little knoll and hollered across the din, "Fellas, look at me . . . look at me! If you doubted my powers of reasoning, think again! I've got brains all over me!" He threw his head back and roared with crazy glee in the midst of all that gore, teeth ablaze. "Only problem is, now I'll think like a Yankee!"

Around midday, rain again pounded the scarlet field, flooding sinkholes and the blood-soaked ground. One enormous depression was surrounded by at least a hundred wounded men, some groaning piteously. They had dragged themselves there on their bellies to slurp the water, crimson with blood. Other wounded fellows twisted onto their backs, mouths open toward the sky, attempting to moisten their parched tongues.

In the chaos, I lost sight of Beards and my company. Strangers screamed and thrust by my side, and rank made no difference. I searched in vain for a recognizable face but found none. In a landscape that teemed with bellowing lunatics, exploding bombs, roaring cannons, and tens of thousands of guns discharging in the distance, I was without a friend or acquaintance. Even worse, my men were without a sergeant.

As I bent over at the edge of a melee, hands on knees and gasping for breath, a Yank spotted me and plunged through the battling soldiers, headed in my direction. His feet flew nimbly over bodies littering the ground as he gained speed. I couldn't pull my wits together, and my hands seemed disconnected from my mind. Time slowed, and the Yank grew larger and more murderous looking by the second. *So this is how it is*, I thought as my heartbeat thrummed in my ears. *It's finally my time.*

Without warning, a young Confederate burst out of the nearby swarm. He rocketed toward me and lunged shoulder first into the approaching enemy. As the Yankee wobbled with the impact, my savior plugged him hard in the kidneys with his blade. After an abrupt grunt, the Yank toppled forward, a crimson fountain spouting from above his waistband. Had the Confederate seen my plight a second later, I would have been the one gasping my last breath. For a brief moment, this tall young man locked his brown eyes with mine and then disappeared into the thick of it. He was gone too quickly for words.

By late afternoon, bodies stacked five-deep hemmed me in, and I still didn't see anyone I knew. Dead had fallen on the living, and the survivors' desperate twitches and clawing animated the macabre piles before me. It was next to impossible to find a foothold, but that didn't stop me from swinging my rifle butt at yet another blue-jacketed attacker.

Suddenly I felt the hard mouth of a rifle barrel bite into my lower back and a gruff Northern voice rasp, "Drop your weapon and raise your goddamned hands in the air." A chill ran down my spine, and I jerked my head around to see my captors. Two enemy soldiers had surprised me from behind. This scene was repeated all around with cries of, "You boys better surrender! Throw down your weapons, or we'll stab bayonets in one side of you and out the other!"

A Rebel nearby clung to his musket, either too scared to release it or frozen with mad rage. One shot through the heart from the bluecoats, and he buckled over, his weapon tumbling from his fist. I wondered how Beards and the rest of my Company had fared, whether they were facing my fate or that of this poor soldier. In this mass of thousands ordered to the rear of the battlefield away from the shooting, I feared I might not know.

But then I heard someone call my name. It was Beards, with Jim Blue, Tayloe, and Zeke at his heels. A cry burst from my throat, startling me with its animal sound. We fell together, embracing and madly laughing, not with mirth but something I couldn't name.

Never has such a miserable looking group been assembled. Faces were begrimed with mud and gore and besmirched with sooty gunpowder. Tears cut white paths through the smut of some, though I couldn't know if they were tears of relief or grief at the loss of friends and brothers. We were clothed head to toe in the elemental materials of being human: feces, mucus, blood, guts, urine, and earth. Injured men leaned upon comrades, and those without wounds lent an arm or shoulder to those blinded or whose reason had given out. Later I met a fellow who had been deafened for life that day. Many boys could only hobble or limp, and the rough terrain of shattered tree trunks and sundered branches made the going even more treacherous.

The Yanks lost patience. Three guards moved behind our straggling line and cursed us. "Goddamned Rebels. You mince along like girls," one of them hollered. "We don't have all day. Double quick, walk, goddamn you." Several fellows in the line cried out as the guards prodded them in the back with the tips of their bayonets. At that, the five of us kept our eyes forward and tried to keep up the pace set by the Yanks. I prayed not to attract the guards' attention, but Beards was worn out and stumbled.

Before he could regain his step, a guard with a filthy shirt and blood-stained boots poked him close to his lower spine with his steel blade. Beards winced but stifled a cry. Then the same fellow turned his attention to Jim Blue. "What's the matter with you? Can't you keep up or are you a girl too?" He jabbed his blade against Blue's shirt, and a thin trickle of blood seeped through the small cloth tear. Blue gritted his teeth.

I'd had enough. I looked the fellow in the eyes and howled at the top of my lungs, "Stop that! Stop it now. We surrendered. You have no right!" I was in such a terrible rage that I could feel my ears burn and twitch. There was a long silence. Beards and the others froze on the spot, staring at me in disbelief. But nothing happened. The guard glared at me and then moved on. There was no more prodding. The others clapped me on the back, and we marched on. I was still their sergeant, and they were still my responsibility.

Strange as it may sound, capture was a huge relief. Only by accident had I survived. After three long years, I was withdrawn, without disgrace, from the center of Death's aim. A minié ball had been waiting for me; it just hadn't been fired yet. My knees trembled, and my hands quivered as I was overcome with gratitude that cannons, disease, and the surgeon's knife hadn't done me in. You might say it was a miracle. I was now finished with this business, and the prospect of prison was welcome. My fingers brushed Mary's rubbed-slick rabbit's foot in my pants pocket one more time.

PART 2

23

THE MAN SNORED, HIS LEFT ARM THROWN LOOSELY OVER HIS HEAD and one foot hung over the side of the bed. I could never squeeze my lanky frame onto the goose feather mattresses in this house, either. But the woman he calls Phoebe sat stiffly upright in the dark, her spine driven vertical by fear. Her eyes stared open wide, and her arms were tight bands around her thin ribs, holding her sides as though to keep a scream in.

She whispered, "Is someone there?" Then louder, in a halting voice, "Is anyone there?" She warily glanced at the windows once and then again, peering as if to catch a glimpse of something just beyond the black glass. But she was on the second floor. Who could press his face to the window at that height? Her neck strained toward the room's invisible corners, eyes searching past the bed's tall posts, and then she sighed. She turned to watch her husband sleep, considering whether to awaken him. Her hand moved toward his shoulder, but then withdrew at the last minute. The dog Emma stirred, opened her eyes, and sniffed the air. Her neck hair spiked above her silken ears, and she catapulted to the floor in my direction, leaving the warm nest of Ma's blue patchwork quilt at the end of the bed. Head forward and tail aloft, she emitted a guttural, threatening sound. This was when I made my move. I drifted to the room below.

One foot in front of another, I soaked into the library floor's pine planks, forcing them to vibrate, to send out sound waves that could be heard in the bedroom above. There was no mistaking the thud of my heavy boots. Sheets rustled as though pushed aside, and then the woman demanded, "Harry, wake up—did you hear that? There's somebody downstairs."

The man responded sleepily. "Umph, what? What are you talking about? Somebody in the house? I didn't hear anything."

"Can't you please, please, go down to see what it is? Grab the poker by the fireplace when you go." Her vocal cords seemed constricted by terror, so that she could barely force out the words.

"Feebes, you dreamed it. I'm not going downstairs—no burglar would stomp through the library. That's not what crooks do. There's nothing there." He patted her leg, and when he reached over to brush her cheek with his lips, the bedsprings squeaked. "Go back to sleep, Hon. We've got tons to do tomorrow." The man rolled over, and his snores soon competed with the hooting of the barn owls on branches beyond the window.

The woman lay stiff as a pine board next to him, eyes staring at the ceiling, unconvinced. I prayed that this time I had really frightened her.

Several weeks later, something happened that made me think I'd succeeded. A balding man in an oddly cut tweed jacket, brown-framed glasses, and neatly creased pants came knocking loudly at the front door. Phoebe certainly seemed glad to see this ordinary-looking fellow. He accepted her outstretched hand with a pleasant smile, and then looked curiously over her shoulder at me, where I watched from the shadows. My knees buckled; no one has so directly registered my presence since I'd shed my body. Afire to learn more about this man, I drew closer.

"Thanks for coming, Professor Liebowitz. I'm grateful to you for making the trip over the mountain from the university," she said. Once again, Phoebe wore long denim pants—hardly an outfit to greet a guest— and a loose, flowered blouse with lace on the cuffs that somewhat made up for it.

He followed her into the library. "No problem. I was glad to do it. Your phone call made me curious." He sat down on my old sofa. "I hope I can help you."

"I hope so, too. I've read about your research, but never thought I'd be calling you. I'm at my wit's end," she said, perched nervously on the edge of the ladder-back chair in front of the window. "I was so excited when we inherited this place from my husband's mother, but not anymore." She shook her head ruefully.

While she spoke, he surveyed the room, eyeing the old Currier and Ives prints on the walls and the antique tables and chairs. "You're clearly in the process of renovating, but this is really an interesting house. It seems frozen in the nineteenth-century. What's the story behind this place?"

She said that the farm had been in her husband's family for more than a century and a half, but no one had lived here since his great aunt had died thirty years earlier. By the mid-Sixties, the old plumbing had failed to meet county standards, and the toilets couldn't be flushed. An expensive new drain field was needed to fix the problem. Phoebe's in-laws, who had lived and worked in northern Virginia, couldn't afford to have one dynamited out of the native limestone or to maintain a second home. The house had been without inhabitants, slowing deteriorating.

The great aunt has to be my daughter Cara. This man Harry is my great-grandson? The same mischievous tyke who visited years ago before Cara passed away? That means he must be my only grandchild Helen's son. His baseball cap still hangs on the hook behind the front door. I guess the mystery of who these people are is solved, but it makes them no less threatening as they strip my world away.

She continued, "They left all the furniture, books—everything— exactly as it had been, I guess hoping some day they could afford to fix it up. Now that we own it, my husband Harry and I are renovating it for a weekend place. He's a lawyer in Washington, and we live not far from where he grew up," she said. She seemed mighty proud of all of their destructive work, I thought to myself.

"So all of this has been in the same family for one hundred and fifty years? That's remarkable. You don't hear of that much these days." His eyes sparkled.

Phoebe nodded.

"You're lucky. Few folks have even one object, much less an entire house filled with old things from their family." I thought I noted a hint of something else in his voice.

She grimaced. "I don't know about being lucky," she said. "At first I couldn't believe it. We never dreamed we'd have a second home in our early thirties. And certainly not a two-hundred-acre farm. But now I'm too scared to stay here at night. Honestly, I wish we could sell it. But that would break Harry's heart, and besides, no one would want to buy it with all that still needs to be done." Alarm flared in my chest. I listened even more intently.

"Well, selling may not be necessary. Let's start with what you've experienced," he said, now looking serious.

Phoebe sighed and stared at her folded hands in her lap. "You're the only person who might understand. Even my husband thinks I'm making it all up. But I swear I'm not." She brushed a lock of brown hair behind her ear, steadying herself. "I hardly know where to start. It's like someone is watching us, but not all the time." The color drained from her face as she shivered.

"What do you mean? Watching but not all the time?"

"It's only when we change things or throw stuff out. But someone knows about it every time." She hardly paused to catch a breath. "And then things get very strange. For instance, when we tore down the old kitchen cabinets, Harry's toolbox crammed with electric drills slid across the kitchen floor. It must weigh fifty pounds. I was alone while I watched it move at least three feet across the level surface." She told him that the night after they painted woodwork in the bedrooms, she heard the sound of interior doors repeatedly slam for maybe ten minutes, but the doors never moved. "When I had the old piano hauled away, someone stomped up and down the stairs most of that night."

The professor had leaned forward to catch her softly spoken words. She paused and then said, "I feel trapped. I could stay at home in northern

Virginia on the weekends and not help Harry work on the house, but there's too much for him to do by himself. And because he thinks I'm making this up, that would probably wreck our marriage." She explained that they couldn't afford to pay workmen to do it all. Since they'd owned the place, she'd taken courses in home restoration and bragged she was now handy with a table saw, could do heavy carpentry, apply wallpaper, and paint walls and woodwork. Harry was dependent on her help.

"I can't think of a solution. That's why I reached out to you." She twisted the strand of hair that had fallen forward again. "If you can tell me why the ghost is here, what it wants, maybe I can figure out how to get rid of it."

Professor Liebowitz said, "You hear and see these things, but your husband doesn't?"

She nodded.

"Have you had experiences like this in the past?"

She fidgeted with her gold wedding ring, turning it round and round before answering. "Not really," she said.

The professor appraised her for a minute. He then gently asked, "Why aren't you telling me the truth?"

Now she flushed deeply, the freckles across her cheeks disappearing. She looked at her shoes and spoke so quietly that Dr. Liebowitz had to lean forward again. "I've always had some kind of second sight since I was a little girl. Maybe this hearing thing is part of that."

He looked puzzled. "Isn't having second sight a good thing?"

"No! My parents convinced me that people would think I'm crazy if I let on about it, so I've learned to ignore it. I've never even told my husband." She said her father had grown up in a Bible-toting town in Alabama. Folks there believed such a talent came from the Devil. From the time she could barely talk, she'd accurately predict things. Her father would then punish her by locking her in the hall closet. She remembered his steely voice scolding her as he clasped her under his arm, her feet desperately kicking as they neared the door.

"Small, dark spaces terrify me. Even now, I can feel the long coats and dresses flapping against my face, piling on my head. The more I flailed and screamed, the more stuff fell from the hangers and landed on top of me. I struggled against the buttons and rough wool and was convinced my parents would never find me under that heap. That they'd open the door and, not seeing me, lock it again. To a little kid of only four or five, the possibility seemed very real." Her brows knitted together. "The trouble was, I never knew when stories about the future would pop into my head and then spill out of my mouth. I couldn't help it." She wouldn't lift her glance as she spoke.

"Was your mother more understanding?"

"Yes, but she was powerless against my father. She fussed at me to stop, but I think it was more to save me from punishment."

Phoebe told him she had felt unloved and ashamed. She eventually learned to stop the words before they escaped, and then finally learned to block that part of her mind.

"I'm trying to learn how to forgive them." Her glance flickered in the professor's direction.

My heart softened toward this woman. I knew how it felt to live with the burden of shame.

The professor regarded her solemnly. "That would have been so painful! But you mustn't believe what your parents made you think. You have a true gift, one you should celebrate. Best of all, it's something you can use to help others."

"I can?" Phoebe brightened for a moment.

"Yes, you can. And you could start right here." He smiled consolingly. "Now, let's see if we can find out what's going on."

He stretched his spine to his full sitting height, flattened his scuffed brown shoes on the polished floor, placed his hands on his knees, and closed his eyes. The wrinkles around them smoothed, and his mouth released any sign of tension. The rise and fall of his chest noticeably slowed. Both of them sat in silence as Phoebe studied her visitor intently.

Dr. Liebowitz's brow knotted and his mouth became cheerless, down-turned. "Ah, such sorrow here. Scenes of fierce battle, and then some kind of prison. Fear, too." He shook his head. "Powerful fear. Poor fellow."

Phoebe's eyes widened. "Who is it?"

Dr. Liebowitz opened his eyes and relaxed into his normal position on the sofa.

"I'm sorry." He shook his head. "I can't see anything more than I've told you. But I did see something in an upstairs room; it looked like old, yellowed papers." He paused. "They may hold some clues."

She wrinkled her nose. "I'll look. But how can someone who's dead do the things I've seen and heard? It makes no sense."

"I'll try to explain," he said. "Physics has taught us that our senses give us only a limited view of the world. For instance, they tell us that matter is solid. But a while ago, we learned that there's nothing solid about matter. Nothing at all. Matter is actually made up of subatomic particles in constant motion. But most of us aren't willing to think of our bodies in the same way—particles in constant motion."

Phoebe absently tapped on her wrist bone with her fingers, as if testing Professor Liebowitz's words.

"And now, physicists who study quantum mechanics have dramatically altered how we think about the past, present, and the future."

"Does that relate to what's going on here?"

"Certainly. But there's one more thing you need to know. Some of these physicists believe that our minds are part of a much larger consciousness. They are like sifters, straining the larger consciousness in their own individual ways. For a long time, scientists believed that without a brain, there is no mind. We don't think that anymore."

"So my brain is like a radio or a television picking up a signal?"

"Something like that."

"And what does this have to do with ghosts?"

"I can't speak in scientific terms about ghosts because that hasn't been my lab's primary focus. But I am sure of this: memory and personality last after death, at least for a while. You probably saw something about our research on our website."

"I did, but I don't get it—how you can be so sure about such a thing."

"I'm sure because my staff and I have thousands of case studies of American children, most of them so young they've only recently learned to speak and who claim to have been someone who died before they were born. They give names and minute details about people and places they couldn't possibly know now." He told her that department researchers had tracked down family members and information about these other people. "In every instance, the children's information was correct. Even if we discount the idea of reincarnation, these studies certainly suggest that memory survives without a physical brain." He said that most of the children lose these memories by the time they are five or six.

Phoebe regarded him with wide eyes. "But what do scientists know about memory and the brain? Can you talk a little bit about that?"

"It's the part of neuroscience that's still a big mystery. Memory isn't like something saved in a bank vault. It occurs in many places within the brain. There are some theories that part of memory is even located outside of our brain."

While Phoebe puzzled over what he'd told her, Professor Liebowitz looked around the room again. "This place, with everything pretty much as it's been for several lifetimes, is full of someone's memories." He watched her face intently and then said firmly, "You need to ask him why he's here."

Phoebe shook her head and her face clouded. "I don't want anything to do with a ghost. He, it, or whatever, is a complete stranger, an intruder who comes and goes in my house. And I have no way of knowing if he's harmless or what he'll do next. That's what frightens me."

The professor was silent again, then in a calming voice said, "This being won't harm you. He's in trouble. Think about it for a minute. How would you feel, stuck in your home after death, completely yourself in mind and heart but invisible? There'd be no one to laugh at your jokes, to praise you, to touch you with love, or sympathy. There'd be no one who understood your past." He asked again, "How would you feel?"

"I guess it would be unbearable," she said in a low tone. "I can't imagine such loneliness." Her expression softened.

"That's right. And if a house and its contents still remind you of who you'd been and the people you'd loved, you might cling desperately to them." He paused and looked intently at her. "Why not let go of your past to help someone else get free of his? If you succeed, you might have the house all to yourself. No ghosts."

Phoebe stared out of the window as if she hadn't heard him.

"This is not someone who means to hurt you," he said.

She sighed and said, "Okay. I'll try. How do I do it?"

"There aren't easy answers. You need to find a way on your own, but you will. For starters, strengthen your intuition. Let it out of the dark. And, as a bonus, you'll be more fully yourself."

Dr. Liebowitz rose from the sofa, signaling the session had ended.

Phoebe's face relaxed. "I'm so grateful. You don't know how much. Thank you." She walked with the professor to the door.

He turned toward her. "Stay in touch and let me know how you're doing. And keep notes. I'll be interested in reviewing what you discover."

When his footsteps on the porch stairs faded, Phoebe leans against the heavy wooden door and sighs. She lingers there a few minutes and then steps into the center of the front hall.

She takes the stairs two at a time. In the bedroom she and the man share, she searches for a rusty coat hanger. After twisting the hanger wire open, she heads to the back bedroom where she used the wire and some unladylike oaths to pry open the swollen closet door. Inside are crooked stacks of my daughter Cara's *Reader's Digest* magazines from the 1930s and '40s, boxes of mouse-gnawed handkerchiefs and dresser scarves, wads of rotted jet-beaded black lace, and a set of thigh-length, one-piece man's linen underwear with buttons to the neck. She pulls out and examines each item, then places it on the nearby dresser top. Now that the closet is almost empty, a wooden box is visible in the back of a lower shelf.

She tugs it out and lowers it to the floor. Mouse droppings skitter off the top onto the bedroom rug. This box was my first try at fine carpentry. I made it for my mother's February birthday from planed walnut boards from trees along the fence line. It was two years before the war, and I surprised her with it at breakfast. When she brought the steaming bowls of porridge from the kitchen, there it was on her dining chair. "Where in the world did this come from?" she asked. She clapped her hands in delight.

"Tom made it, Ma," Tish broke in.

"I'm so proud of you, Tom. This is the best gift I've ever received," she said. She planted a kiss on my cheek. "William, come see what our son has made for me!" she called to my father in the parlor. The splinters and my hammer-pounded fingers were nothing compared to this moment; my heart was near to bursting with pride.

Now the box is crammed with a jumble of notebooks, tattered yellow papers, envelopes, and broken bits of two porcelain cat and dog figurines. The woman squats and paws through it all—including 1930s tax forms and a rolled-up plan for rail lines to transport cavalry horses during World War I. These and several French postcards of naked women came home with my son William after his service in France.

At the bottom of the box are some crinkled vellum pages. She spreads them on the dresser and flattens the creases with the heel of her hand. The first is a letter from Aunt Ellen to Reverend Brown, the new substitute minister, who was traveling to Richmond to comfort our wounded soldiers in the hospital. He must have saved the letter for Ma and given it to her afterward.

> *March 30, 1865*
>
> *Sir, I have enclosed a little money which I place at your disposal to be used in any way you think will do the most good.*
>
> *There's one thing I must tell you. We have been hearing from Augusta County boys delivered to Richmond from Northern imprisonment that the Confederate government does nothing for them. They return south without a cent, and therefore can't procure any clothing, food, or a way home. This is a terrible shame after enduring so much for the Confederate cause. We are looking for two boys from our church: my nephew Tom Smiley and his friend Jeremy Beard, prisoners at Fort Delaware for the past year. If on your mission to the Confederate Capital you should see either destitute, please expend whatever is necessary for their comfort, and let me know. I will refund it.*
>
> *Your friend, Ellen Martin*

The second paper is my signed oath of allegiance to the United States of America, dated at the moment of my release from the Union prison, Fort Delaware, on June 15, 1865, and certified by the prison's Commander Schoepf. Phoebe studies it for a moment with a mournful face, as though the misery that single page suggests might be contagious. The last item at the bottom of the box is my likeness as a Confederate soldier. Mary begged me to sit for a photographer in the early days and then complained I looked too solemn. The woman turns it over and sees Cara's handwritten note: *My father Tom Smiley, 1845–1920.* "My god, this is Harry's great-grandfather. And he was a Union prisoner!" she says to herself.

Phoebe read and reread the letter from Aunt Ellen before putting it down on the dresser. Then, resting her back against the edge, she stares pensively through the wavy window glass. After several minutes, she squeezes her eyes shut and speaks to me. "Whoever you are, I know you're here. I want to help, but only if you stop scaring me."

It has been so long since someone addressed me, even if she didn't call my name. My heart thaws for a moment, and I believe her. She grabs the two pages along with my photograph, and rushes from the house to her car to drive home in the thinning light.

24

THE SECOND DAY AFTER CAPTURE, UNION SOLDIERS HERDED SMALL knots of us into a massive, depleted pack headed to the Potomac River. Four thousand prisoners were strung across desolate Stafford County's fenceless fields and splintered forests toward Belle Point Port for two steamboat trips to the Union prison. I plodded wearily beside one of the few other tall men in the crowd. At 6′3″ I was very conscious of others who shared my unusual height.

I'd heard his deep voice while we awaited our captors' order to move out. Every utterance sounded as though it was extracted by hook from his gut. He appeared younger than I by as many as four years, maybe he was as young as seventeen. There were cannon-fodder fourteen-year-olds who carried muskets in this war, but this fellow wasn't quite that young. His height caused me to take a closer look.

"My God, you're the soldier who saved my life yesterday!" I said. "I never had a chance to thank you. What's your name?"

"Private John Bibb, an artilleryman in Cutshaw's Charlottesville Artillery." He looked at me with sudden recognition. "I couldn't let you die. There's only a few of us beanstalks in this war."

"That's because most of them forgot to stoop when Union bullets were flying around," I said. "Well, this time I'm thankful to be tall. You were really heroic."

"It happened so fast, in a blur. Animal instinct, that's all. Nothing special about it," he said. "Sorry I didn't recall your face at first."

The ensuing silence gave me a chance to observe him more carefully. Crisp white laugh lines framed blue eyes in his open, filth-smeared face. Flaxen hair, bleached from sweat and several weeks without shelter, flopped across his forehead. He clearly was unaccustomed to his rapidly sprouting body. Gangly arms swung awkwardly at his sides as he leaned forward. His head preceded his long limbs and his pants legs ended inches above his ankles.

"I'm Sergeant Tom Smiley, Company D, Stonewall Brigade, or what's left of it," I offered. "My rank is due to a shortage of men, and I'm still pretty green at it. This last week's fighting was my first as sergeant. Where's home for you?" I asked.

He said he'd grown up in Charlottesville and had just reached legal age for enlistment two months earlier. On the morning of his seventeenth birthday, he had joined his brother's company. His distraught mother had been furious that the age for enlistment had been lowered and had heard the Confederacy wasn't training draftees any longer. He scoffed at her complaint that he was only one day past sixteen, was too tender to kill men, and was too inexperienced with weaponry for defense.

"If my mother hadn't been so dead set against it, I would've lied about my age and been on the battlefield a year earlier," he added. "Then I could have joined you fellows at Gettysburg and First and Second Manassas. But these past few weeks might make up for it."

His bravado showed how little he understood war's toll. Our souls were sheathed with its callouses—worn thick by acres of burned Yankee bodies at Chancellorsville and burnished by the Gettysburg landscape after three hot, sultry July days the year before. After the third afternoon, Jim Blue, Zeke, and I, along with the rest of our mess and thousands of the infantry had wandered the wheat fields and peach orchards under a white flag. We searched for any signs of life in the Confederate bodies sprawled across boulders and twisted in the grass. Zeke tugged the arms of a bloated corpse toward a shallow grave, and then suddenly vomited on its chest. He wasn't the only one whose gut heaved up. Beards, Blue, and I suffered the same in the midst of so many swollen horse and human carcasses. I later read that death lay heavy on the land for three months, and townspeople miles away couldn't venture forth without a scarf muffling their noses. John Bibb should thank his lucky stars he wasn't there.

Now as Union prisoners, he and I trod past a severely wounded boy propped against a sturdy log. The fellow reached into his pocket for a plug of tobacco, although he looked too young to chew. A wound gaped across his skull and oozed crimson and globules of gray. He poked the treasure into his mouth, then slowly toppled to the side with eyes rolled back in his head. Some bodies on the field in front of the earthworks had taken bullets from both sides for the entire battle. They were now only glistening sponge-like globs with what must have been thousands of bullet holes. The air reeked of smoke and the putrid scent of dead horses and humans. Mockingbirds earlier spooked by battle's roar warbled again from the split pine and oak branches overhead as though nothing had happened that day.

As I considered our situation, surrender was nothing to be ashamed of. The peculiarity was in surrendering my rifle. It was as though I'd severed my arm, and I felt naked and vulnerable.

John Bibb had it right; he had been to see the largest and fiercest of the elephants, and both of us had escaped the cry of the owl. Now he confessed his real reason for joining the Army. The Yankees had shot French, his oldest brother, at Chancellorsville. His truest motive was revenge.

"You might have seen my brother somewhere. He was an officer in a student volunteer unit from Virginia Military Institute that fought in the Valley Campaign."

"No, I never encountered him. I'm sorry to hear of your loss. What happened?"

John related how French had been shot by the Yankees in the upper right thigh, but the family didn't get word until he was already at an army hospital in Richmond. His father rode nonstop to the city and found that French's leg had been sawed off near the hip, and the wound was foul with gangrenous pus. Bibb told me how his father stayed by his delirious son for three weeks, soaking the fetid injury and softly beseeching French not to leave just yet.

"Your family must have taken it hard."

"I don't think they'll ever recover. He was the best of us five children. My father wanted French to follow him into the dry goods business, but he would have made a first-rate university professor or doctor. So that's why my mother was dead set against me going off to fight."

He paused and withdrew a scrap of paper from his pocket. "I saved a poem placed on his coffin during the funeral by a young lady he'd known." Shyly he handed it to me, and I read these lines:

> *His noble heart is now at rest;*
> *The young, the beautiful, the brave,*
> *We will not mourn his early grave.*
> *Then let him rest, till that glad sound Full on his*
> *raptur'd ear is pour'd,*
> *"Come forth, ye blessed of the Lord."*

It could have been for any fallen soldier, but the words gave him comfort. Sharing it with me was an invitation to friendship. His other brother, Albert Pendleton, had followed French into service, even though he'd been plagued all his life by asthma. He was quickly dispatched home on sick furlough, because he couldn't run without becoming breathless. It had fallen to John Bibb to avenge his brother's death.

I was moved by his friendliness and, sadly, his resemblance to my former, more innocent self. It made me want to protect him from what we'd come to know. And now that he'd saved my life, our fates were inextricably bound. I owed him something. I vowed then to make every effort to keep him safe. When we halted for the night, I invited him to join Beards, Jim Blue, and the others where we chose to lie down. They took to him as quickly as I had. "You're one of us, now, Bibb," Tayloe said. "You're a bona fide member of Company D."

"Welcome to the best damned company in the Confederate army," Zeke added. "What's left of it, anyhow. We need a new recruit."

"Thanks. My old company has disappeared. I'm grateful to be adopted," he said.

A cold drizzle fell through the moonless night. We kept to ourselves, wrapped only in our thoughts as we lay on the damp branches and brambles in the woods of Stafford County. Sounds of combat faded with distance, and we fell into deep unconsciousness, worn out after five nights of fighting, marching, digging, and more fighting.

When I woke, my gut was cramping. I'd seen a Confederate boy on the field pilfer hardtack from the pockets of a fallen comrade, discarding the bloody bits to eat the rest. Beards saw it too and reminded me, "I hope I'll never be that desperate. But I wouldn't mind having more of that greasy groundhog we shot two nights ago. We won't have such a good meal for a long time to come."

On the second day's march, we traded stories about home—anything that would draw Bibb into the group and distract my men from their misery. As a boy from the city, there was a lot Bibb didn't know about. For instance, his mother had always procured bacon from a market. We nurtured the hog from a piglet and slaughtered it fat in the fall. Now, because we had no food to eat, I thought talking about getting some might raise spirits. "Beards, tell Bibb what happens at hog slaughtering time. This city boy doesn't know a whit about where Virginia ham comes from. He's probably never seen a real live hog," I said. Bibb took a playful swipe at my cap, knocking it to the ground.

"You can do as good a job as I can, but I'll tell him how we all go to your Pa's place once the weather gets a little edge on it—just as the leaves begin to turn." Beards went into great detail, telling Bibb how families bring their fattest pig in a wagon—the pig all the time thinking he's on a fine ride to see the neighbors—and how they line the creatures up together and shoot them between the eyes at the same time, or they'll scream and holler when they see what's happened to the other hogs. "You've heard that expression 'screaming like a stuck pig'? You never heard such a pitiful and miserable racket when that happens," he said.

He described how the hogs' throats are slit, the bodies are hung upside down to drain, and how the dogs go crazy licking at the scarlet clots on the ground. Every single last part of the pig is dumped into a heavy black cauldron on fiery coals and filled with boiling water. After all the hair is singed off, the men whip out their sharpest knives and saws and slice the meat into hams, ribs, chops, bacon pieces. They save the head, feet, snout, ears, and brains for good eating, too.

Then he got to the best part, telling how the day ends in a feast with sausage made by shoving slabs of pork through a hand-cranked grinder and stuffing it into the cleaned intestines with spices and herbs. Fried, crunchy chitterlings and thick chops topped with apples fried with cinnamon are piled on plates. Ma's buttermilk biscuits are followed by plump fruit pies. When he finished, we all fell silent. This was the most we'd heard from Beards in weeks. His account had prompted such nostalgia for home and food that we felt worse, rather than better.

In an effort to distract us, and perhaps to put us in our place for our teasing, Bibb talked about his life. Charlottesville was Mr. Jefferson's city, Bibb said, and even though Jefferson had passed away thirty-nine years earlier, his presence was everywhere. John Bibb's great uncle had served as Jefferson's personal secretary up on the big hill at Monticello after the president returned from Washington.

Bibb related what might have been considered a ghost story. His uncle often rode with Jefferson through the countryside of Albemarle County, and one day they came upon a large, conical grassy mound that most regarded as a natural feature. Jefferson was convinced it was man-made, and measured it top to bottom and around with his father's old surveying instruments. He even made an astronomical investigation to see if the shape was aligned with the sun or the stars.

Later, when Bibb's uncle and Jefferson were feasting in the shade, they spotted two men making some sort of ritual walk around the hillock. The figures might be clothed as white men, but feathers entwined in raven braids and necklaces identified them as Indians. At the end, they laid their necklaces at the eastern and western sides. Then they retreated without being any wiser that they'd been seen. The mystery mound gnawed at Mr. Jefferson. On a moonless night, he ordered two slaves to dig into it and bring back whatever they found. He created a "curiosity cabinet" with leg bones, skulls, spear points, and some bits of decorated pottery in his formal entry hall at Monticello so that the hundreds of uninvited public, who arrived daily to peer at his home, might study the curious objects. Bibb said his uncle swore that ever after, slaves told of voices chanting in an unknown tongue late at night in that room. When they pushed back the doors, the space was deserted. But their stories were dismissed as only idle slave chatter.

"I'd wager Jefferson was haunted for stealing just to satisfy his curiosity," I said.

No one responded with more than a grunt. Spirits were too low. Trudging along afterward, I reflected on how Bibb's tale revealed his higher social status—with a brother enlisted as an officer, a great uncle who assisted Mr. Jefferson, and his idea of a good story being one about ideas and ethics. My parents treasured their books and valued learning but were country folk more directly engaged in survival. The hog-butchering story demonstrated what the other boys and I had in common.

Morning and evening along the route, Union officers halted their supply wagons and unloaded wooden crates of hard crackers. A melee of pushing, shoving, punching, and cursing would follow. Using my recently gained authority as sergeant—and with help from Beards and Jim Blue— we organized lines around the boxes so everyone had a fair chance. I also grabbed a handful for Bibb, who wasn't yet accustomed to the "every man for himself" culture we lived by. Then six hundred of us, many with branches as makeshift crutches, others with life-threatening wounds and laid out in wagons, willed ourselves forward under the barking commands of our captors.

We were two days from the battlefield. One more day lay between Aquia Harbor and Washington. From there we'd go by train to Baltimore and by steamboat again to the Union prison, Fort Delaware. The guards marching alongside had told us that much. I plodded along in the hobbling mob next to John Bibb. This time he spoke about plans for the future. The efforts of simply living day to day hadn't yet swamped his thoughts of home and events there.

"My father hoped to hang out a sign with the gilded letters Bibb and Sons Dry Goods over his store someday. But I'm not sure I want that tame life. With French gone, it's too quiet at home for me."

"What would you do instead?"

"Go west. Reports about gold in California make me long for adventure. I had thought I might even enlist in the army of the new Confederate nation after things settled down. Of course, there isn't much chance of that now."

He withdrew from his rucksack a picture of his sweetheart. Swirls of brown curls framed a delicate face, and a black ribbon with a cameo looped her graceful neck. Kind eyes focused dreamily beyond the photographer, perhaps visualizing the boy to whom this likeness would be given. He pushed the image toward me. "Another thing I might do is marry. This is Margaret Ellen. I've known her my entire life. We're neighbors on Ridge Street."

"She's a fine-looking girl; I can see why you'd be sweet on her."

"Her family has agreed, but I'll have to complete my education before we wed."

"But then you'll never taste the freedom of the West."

Bibb looked down and shook his head. "When I'm with Margaret Ellen, I think of nothing else but being with her. The whole situation binds me in knots. I can't decide what to do."

"I know about the power of women," I said. "There was this girl named Lizzie . . ." and then I stopped.

He looked off into the distance, not listening. "When this war is over, there'll be plenty of time to sort it all out, I guess."

Talk about home and adulthood unsettled me now that we were no longer soldiers. If prisoner exchanges occurred as in the past, we'd be regular civilians within two or three months. That thought triggered both longing and fear of how I might fit into my old life.

Looking back, I marvel that dread of prison had such a light grip, even though we had all heard stories of deadly disease, heartless officers, and no food. At that time, fewer men died in prison than on the field, and the stay was fairly brief. And if we were concerned about mistreatment from prison guards, we'd already seen enough from our own Confederate officers. Poor Zeke had plenty to say about that.

Several months earlier, he was on a two-day leave to visit Richmond, when our army unexpectedly dismantled its tents and set out from Louisa County to Orange County on the heels of some Yankees. The evening he was due, Beards walked up, powerfully disturbed. "Where's Zeke? Is he here yet?"

"Haven't seen him," I replied.

"Do you think he'll figure out where we've gone?"

"Maybe folks along the way have given him the word." I went back to idly gnawing on a wheat straw I'd picked up.

"Roll is being called right now, and anyone not here will have hell to pay later," Beards said. He strode off, hoping to find Zeke chatting with fellows down the row of tents.

By the time he caught up with the company, Zeke was too late for roll call. At dawn, we spied two soldiers yanking him along by rope twisted around his wrists as he peppered them with oaths. Our jaws dropped. Beards shouted, "Where are you taking this soldier? He's done nothing wrong!" They continued at a determined clip, Zeke's canvas-clothed buttocks bouncing along over rocks and branches.

"You bastards, let me go. I came back, for God's sake. This army is damned lucky to get me back, too."

"You tell 'em, Zeke!" I bellowed. We gave pursuit. Puffed up with my new status, I believed I could sway them with rank. I drew myself to full height and said in an authoritative tone, "I'm this man's sergeant. I'm the one to deal with him. Release him immediately."

One guard spun around, grappling for his rifle while maintaining his hold under Zeke's arm. "Our orders are from the commanding officer. That's not you, right? You got no say here. Get back to your camp. This is none of your business, but it will be if you come any closer." That quieted us pretty quickly. We had neared their destination, a grove of oak trees and scraggly cedars. It sheltered a quantity of fellows in strange postures on the forest floor. Their wrists were bound, and their arms were forced tight down over knees bent up to their chins. A stout branch was then threaded over one crooked arm, under their knees, and over the other arm, locking them in a painful position. The sharp edges of bayonets were lodged within their mouths by cord tied either end and then behind their heads.

Released at sundown with crimson slits at the corners of his stretched mouth, arms and legs like bruised boards, clothes stained with urine, and a voice gravelly from lack of water, Zeke was beside himself with fury.

"There'll be desertions tonight; bet good money on it. Fellows would rather risk execution than go through that humiliation again." He also swore the aggrieved men had "spotted" the commander for death on the battlefield the next chance they had. Luckily, the enemy targeted the wretch in the next day's battle.

Three long years we'd endured—what could a few more months mean? But an unforeseen standoff between Jeff Davis and Abe Lincoln changed all that shortly after our Fort Delaware arrival. Those of us who managed to survive would remain for more than a year—months after Lee surrendered.

25

I'M SCARCELY ABLE TO TELL THE DIFFERENCE BETWEEN NIGHT AND day, submerged as I am in a nightmare that regularly ambushes me now. Every sound reminds me of the past. Even the creek, my beloved creek below the house, is driving me mad. It assaults my hearing as it spills over its banks, flooded with rains from the fall hurricane off the distant Virginia coast. Clapping my hands over my ears makes the torment no less. The creek in its passage is chillingly similar to waves beating against Pea Patch Island, where I was imprisoned for thirteen months.

After a six-day hike from Spotsylvania, Union soldiers prodded us into cavernous freight cars waiting in Washington. The cries of wounded men drowned out the thrum of spinning metal wheels as we rolled first toward Baltimore, and then to the Union Fort McHenry. There, blue-uniformed officials stood behind wooden tables and piles of documents. With a sharp thwack of a red rubber stamp, they changed our identities from soldier to prisoner.

A packet steamboat that stank of recently transported livestock was moored at the end of a long dock jutting out from Fort McHenry. Our little group, along with hundreds of others, was forced into the lower hold. The space was foul with manure. Envy gnawed at me as our Confederate officers boarded in a separate line headed for upper decks where there was fresh air. We were packed together upright, not able to even crouch, for a twelve-hour journey in an airless enclosure with the rank scent of human illness everywhere. Beards and Jim Blue, already in ill health from lack of nourishment, were overwhelmed. Tears involuntarily drained from Beards' eyes.

"Boys, step aside or you'll be fouler than you already are," he muttered weakly and swayed. John Bibb, Jim Blue, and I strained away, but there wasn't an extra inch to spare. As those near Beards cringed, splatters of vomit added another indignity to our clay and bloodstained rags. By now, I was largely indifferent to unpleasant body fluids—from my own chronic diarrhea to liquids from others' bodies. Being transported in an animal packet steamer struck me as an appropriate continuation of the foot soldier's life. I prayed we weren't headed to slaughter, surely the previous passengers' fate.

When the boat began to sway more heavily from side to side, we knew we'd left the river and had entered the broad and turgid Chesapeake Bay. Exhaustion, injuries, and jolting waves would have toppled many by this time but for the pressure of bodies on all sides. Men around me fainted, and Bibb was one of them. I supported his weight, his arm limply across my shoulder and my hand on his belt. It was a small price for what I owed him. The ever-present moaning and stench of seasickness made this leg of the journey interminable, until we finally entered the mouth of the mile-wide Delaware River. There we were herded off a gangplank to our future home.

Wobbly-legged, I stepped onto an island of barely reclaimed swamp. Before us loomed a high-walled brick and granite fortress, crowned by one hundred cannons. Our company of common prisoners, however, would never see the inside of that pentagonal structure. Stretching before it was an immense twelve-foot-high wooden pen, capped by a walkway on which blue-uniformed men patrolled with weapons. This was where we were herded.

High on the wall, three officers stood, waiting for the hundreds of new prisoners to surge through the gate and fill the square below. The commanding general, a man named Schoepf, nervously toyed with the medals on his blue jacket, revealing the white handkerchief stuffed in his cuff. His pants were crisply pressed and without stains. He withdrew the handkerchief and held it to his nose as he waited for the crowd to settle. Then, with a thick European accent, he introduced himself and his two deputies. "You'll answer to different commanders now. I'm charged, along with my two deputies, Captain George W. Ahl and Sergeant Abraham Wolf, with the execution of President Lincoln's orders. You will unwaveringly follow them. Any violation of prison regulations, and you will pay the price." He paused and took stock of the scraggly crowd. "But if you heed my warnings well, you'll have no trouble here." His shiny boots thumped across the walkway to a ladder leading down to the separate officers' pen, as he left his underlings to oversee us. I felt an urge to better see what these men were made of. "Excuse me. Coming through," I muttered as I pushed through the crowd standing nearest the wall.

Maybe it was my height or bold movement, but I attracted Ahl's notice as I finally stood beneath him. I was close enough to see that his shirt strained across his bulging stomach and remnants of former meals marred his trousers. His army jacket was sloppily thrown across both bulky shoulders, and he gripped the crooked handle of a cane in his right hand. I could also see the glinting, soulless eyes that revealed the true man. When I looked up, those eyes locked on mine and fiercely glowered. I glared back, refusing to look away. A current of fear rippled through me from head to toe, and I shuddered.

Separated into groups of one hundred, we filed through a crude door in one of the two very long, flimsily constructed wooden barracks that stretched along the sides of the pen. Inside were tiered, six-foot wide shelves on which lay rows of thin wool blankets. The guards commanded us to empty our pockets and what rucksacks men still carried onto the rough wooden boards. They then confiscated everything we'd brought with us, including any extra clothes. Beards nudged my arm.

"We better pray we're home by winter. I bet a cold wind blows off the water through these plank walls." He gestured to the daylight streaming between the boards.

"It's mid-May. We'll be gone by then," I said. We'd all heard that the system of prisoner trades meant incarceration for only three months or so.

Jim Blue, Beards, and I staked places side by side on the second berth. Zeke Skinner and the rest of the Augusta fellows were close by, and John Bibb claimed a spot on the tier across the aisle.

These sleeping shelves were also our living accommodations. It was impossible for more than a few to stand in the narrow aisle between. On each side, fifty men slept with heads to the outside wall and feet to the center, shelved as common logs without bedding or even straw. The single federal-issue blanket was little protection from the splinters and would be none at all from the weather. I quickly learned to place half on the shelf and to wrap the other half around my body.

Directly below the barrack floors and bisecting the pen were watery canals. Twice a day as the tide rose there should have been sufficient flow to lift the waste that would then spill through sluice gates into the river. But nine thousand overcrowded inmates produced so much garbage and filth that the canals were clogged. The tides had no power to dislodge the accumulation. They thus became incubators for slime and animalculae. Any open wound festered after canal contact.

Luckily, in the morning's crowd of veteran prisoners I'd spotted Frank Armstrong, a member of the 5th Virginia Infantry. Company D had belonged to the 5th. Several years older than I, the stocky, curly-bearded fellow from Brownsburg had taught Sunday school classes at New Jerusalem Church. My parents had spoken admiringly of this young man who took the Bible so seriously, and Ma had suggested that I should emulate him. This, of course, meant I stayed far away from him, but now I approached with hand outstretched. "Frank, it's good to see you alive and with all your limbs. When did these Yankee devils catch up with you?"

At first his expression was blank, but then he recognized me. "I'll be darned. Tom Smiley, isn't it? Praise be to the Lord, although I can't say it's good to see you here." His mouth set in a grim line. "I've been in this place for a month, but it feels like years." He looked around to see if there was a guard nearby. "Let me tell you, you have to figure this place out on your own. Otherwise, you'll be gunned down. There's no second chance."

My stomach clenched. "How can I avoid that fate?" I asked.

"Well, you need to know that the guards take curfew very seriously. Don't dare mess with the barrack lantern after 8:00 p.m. lights out. If you do, they'll shoot you on the spot. Stay alert, take your time and watch, and do everything the guards tell you as quickly as you can."

He then added, "Here's another piece of advice. Choose a second-tier bunk, not an upper or lower one, whatever you do. The leaky roof soaks those on top, and the 'floor men' on the bottom get the canal vapors and any fluids from both tiers above." I felt some satisfaction that, with the exception of Tayloe, our group had chosen well. I would warn him to switch shelves.

"What about the commander and his sidekick Ahl? Ahl looks particularly dangerous."

Frank motioned me to move even farther from others and spoke softly. "Schoepf's not so bad. But he's very peculiar about health and cleanliness. Very peculiar. Fellows say he was driven mad by the death of his infant daughter shortly before the war, before he came over from Austro-Hungary. He blames 'foul vapors,' and there are surely plenty of those around here. It's why he's so pale. He rarely comes outside."

"That sounds like you don't see much of him."

"True. Ahl is the one who keeps an eye on us, and between you and me, he's the one really in control. He watches us like a hawk watches mice. No one can get to Schoepf unless they go through him, not even other officers or the guards. He and his flunkies censor all mail, incoming and outgoing." All mistreatment, Frank believed, originated from Ahl. "I hear he gained power over Schoepf by ratting him out to Washington as being too soft on us. Now he threatens to do it again if the commander shows any humanity. Believe me, stay far away from Ahl for your own good."

"What about Sergeant Wolf?"

"He's not any better, but he's not as much of a threat. He's responsible for the officers' pen. He's too fond of his whiskey, which makes him meaner, but also keeps him out of action."

"It sounds like Schoepf is the pawn of his two junior officers," I said. Frank nodded.

After the boys and I claimed our spots on the boards, we filed out into the vast pen. It teemed with thousands of idle men standing in knots talking or squatting against the walls. A gray-haired prisoner with a wheelbarrow struggled by, parting the crowd with his burden of corpses piled like so much corded lumber. He wearily called, "Make way, make way."

I searched for Frank and found him standing in the pen where I had left him. "What's this?" I asked, gesturing toward the grim scene.

"These poor souls are from the hospital. It's in the pen over yonder by the wall. The place overflows with men at all hours—plagued by loose bowels, measles, the pox, or whatever wound gnaws at them since the battlefield. Most of 'em will be dumped headfirst into trenches dug by inmates across the river." He explained that lime would break down their flesh, and then there will be room for more of us to join them in days to come.

Not long after, Tayloe, who hadn't followed my advice and was still berthed above me, couldn't muster out for morning drill. He murmured that he wasn't well enough to rise. Beards hollered out in Tayloe's place during roll call and did so for the week that Tayloe lay wasting of what looked like typhus pneumonia. He turned a deaf ear to our pleas to visit the surgeon's window in the pen wall where, once a day, men waited in long queues for a consultation.

"That damn doctor dispenses nothing but bread pills and some mysterious powder boys swear is flour," he said. "A stay in the hospital will surely kill me." He breathed in gasps but continued. "I'll take my chances right here with you fellows." I gently patted his arm and tried to smile for his sake.

As the days passed, we helplessly listened while he moaned feverishly on the boards above. Five of us sneaked bits of our cornbread and meat to share, but he pushed them away as his fever mounted. There was nothing to do but pray he wouldn't suffer for long. In the meantime, he lay in a puddle of excrement and vomit. Nights were the worst. He thrashed his arms about and called out words in a ragged voice that none of us could understand. "Tayloe, what is it?" I'd ask, hoping to ease his discomfort. But if he responded, it was only to moan in the dark. We took turns dipping a rag in tepid water and holding it to his forehead, but he remained clammy and feverish. Finally, on the sixth day in the late afternoon, Zeke, who had been resting below, noticed there was an unnatural silence from Tayloe's shelf.

"Tayloe, Tayloe, answer me," he called out. When there was no sound, he pulled himself up to Tayloe's level and held his hand beneath Tayloe's nostrils. No breath crossed his fingers. A palm to Tayloe's chest told Zeke what he dreaded. He ran into the yard where I was squatting in the shade of the wall.

"I think Tayloe is gone," he choked out. "Come see for yourself. I can't feel a heartbeat."

I leaped to my feet, crossed the barrack threshold, and stood next to the pale body curled on the shelf. Zeke was right. The whites of Tayloe's eyes were visible under half-closed lids and his mouth gaped open. When I put my head to Tayloe's chest, there was nothing. Pulling up the dry flesh of his lid, his eye stared unblinking at a place far beyond my reach. I paused for a moment, my hand on his shoulder, and looked long at what was left of my friend so that I might never forget. During those days as barely more than children in Staunton, neither of us could have predicted his death this way.

This was different from Sam's dying. The blood drained from my face, and my knees were weak. Throbbing pain behind my eyes made my head feel huge. But deep feelings of loss had been out of reach ever since we'd laid Sam in the ground. Zeke yelled to the other boys in our company to come in from the yard. We stood in a wordless row before Tayloe's body, each of us forming an inner farewell. Beards and I finally eased his emaciated corpse down from the boards, wrapped it in his blanket, and bade it farewell as the wheelbarrow man hauled it away. I spent the afternoon slumped against the pen wall with my head in my hands until the dinner signal was given.

Three weeks had passed since our arrival, and the prison was due for a visit from the Federal health inspectors. Schoepf was obsessed with demonstrating that he ran a clean operation. Two days before inspection, Ahl appeared on the wall above the pen. "All men muster out of the barracks!" he hollered.

We poured out of the doors and waited in the yard from the time the sun was highest and hottest until it was mercifully lower in the sky. Guards trooped in with mops and buckets sloshing with lye soap, and then with buckets of whitewash and brushes. Afterward, we were marched to the river where, under the close watch of rifle-toting guards, we scrubbed off months of grime and stink, as well as more than a few lice. It was a glorious time. I'll never forget the sensation of glistening hair and a scrubbed body.

On the tenth of June, after an early morning visit to the sinks, Beards returned to the barracks to rouse Jim Blue and me with a rumor he'd heard in the yard.

"Hey you fellows, wake up. There's going to be a big announcement before morning drill. Men are already out in the pen. Do you think Old Abe or Jeff Davis, either one, has come to his senses about our release? That prisoner trades are starting up?"

Bibb propped himself up on his elbows, suddenly alert. "Lord, could it be true?"

We sprang to our feet and lined up behind other stragglers for the usual eight o'clock drill. After roll call, Captain Ahl and Sergeant Wolf appeared above on the wall. We maintained our lines, each man savoring images of homecoming. With a smirk at our upturned faces, Ahl then recited loudly from an order clutched in his hand.

"I hereby inform all enlisted prisoners of Fort Delaware that as of today, anyone who risks public health by committing a 'nuisance' in or about the barracks will be given three verbal warnings to cease, and then will be shot or die by bayonet. This directive is straight from Commander Schoepf and will henceforth be known as Special Order Number 157." The sun gleamed white off the official paper as he read it. At the conclusion, his lips twisted as he relished the effect of his announcement.

Oh, how I suddenly hated this man. Rage and resentment made my chest feel it might explode. Straight from Commander Schoepf. Right? In my mind, Ahl no longer just represented evil stupidity. He became everything I despised about the past three years. Now it had boiled down to something smaller than the greed of Confederate legislators and their cronies but was no less threatening. This petty minded, cruel man had us completely under his thumb. The helplessness of it made me lightheaded. To my mind, this newest injustice reeked of Ahl, not Schoepf.

Astonishment surged through the crowd. Next to me, a fellow leaning on a wooden crutch muttered under his breath, "That goddamned Schoepf!" A wave of profanities swept through the pen.

"Do you all, every one of you, understand me?" Ahl continued. "Guards will be reminded of Special Order Number 157 every day before they stand duty. Every single day. It is your responsibility as prisoners never to forget it." Fellows spat more oaths under their breath, while others stared hopelessly at the ground. Zeke's ire pulsated across his pinched face as he stared upward at Ahl. The man felt the heat of Zeke's hatred and glared back, taking his measure and storing it away. Ahl's eyes then fell on me, standing next to Zeke, and lingered. Once again, I stared him down.

We had recently suspected that Schoepf was wary of men relieving themselves at the doorways of the barracks because the guards' warnings had grown increasing harsh. But now there would be serious consequences for men with raw wounds, amputated limbs, and serious illnesses who had trouble walking the narrow, board pathways across the muddy pen in the black night. The boards ran about seven hundred feet before reaching the bridges leading to privies or "sinks." These were nothing more than planks with side-by-side round holes sawn in them, set out over shallow water too low for the tide to wash away daily droppings. Meals of decayed meat, often covered with green flies, insured the spindly bridges and pathways were constantly lined with men shifting from foot to foot. Understandably, all of us preferred to stumble half asleep to tend to our needs just beyond a barrack exit.

That very day, a man from our barrack committed a "nuisance" on the bank of the Delaware River. Zeke and Beards had newly befriended him in the pen and joined in with others pitching a bar of soap back and forth in a slippery game of catch during the monthly bath. He was nineteen-year-old Wilbur Sparks from Madison, Virginia. I think he'd joined the army only recently, although he'd suffered some wounds in that time. A raw scar traveled across his nose and forehead. While the others waited for Beards to chase after the bobbing piece of soap, Wilbur stepped onto the sand, and turning his back, relieved himself. A guard screamed for him to halt, but the boy, unable to stop the flow midstream, hollered over his shoulder that the guard was "a Yankee son of a bitch." The bathing group burst apart, guessing the guard's angry response. The guard raised his rifle and took direct aim. The hapless fellow tumbled onto the sand, his pants flapping open below the bloody exit wound in his belly. He died quickly. This was a sobering demonstration of Schoepf's obsession, Ahl's application of it, and another incident to feed Zeke's and my wrath.

26

NOT ONE TREE OR SHRUB SHADED OUR PRISON PEN, AND THAT SUMMER the dirt baked into cracked clay and magnified the scalding sun's rays. Ahl called us out twice a day for drill, but after the morning activity, many boys cooled off by standing or lolling shirtless in the canals' toxic slime. Others flopped down on their backs, too sapped by the heat to move. Exposed skin burned and blistered, creating open wounds vulnerable to the canals' foul brew.

One blazing mid-August day, Zeke and I stood in the shade of the pen's wall watching Jim Blue and a fellow from the west barrack compete at chess with sacrificed shirt buttons. A board was scratched in the dirt, and a barrack against barrack contest was under way. From boyhood, Blue had been an ace chess player. We rooted loudly for him.

A commotion began to brew over by the gate. A new group of prisoners poured through. They'd been duly searched, all possessions confiscated, and then they were released into our midst. With calls of "Fish! Fresh Fish!" we abandoned the game to surround the new prisoners. We were starving for news, and its only source was those most recently outside. These newcomers had been captured near Petersburg and Richmond. A cacophony of voices yelled, "Did you hurt those Yankee bastards?" "What company y'all with?" "Where were you captured?" "Have they gotten any closer to Richmond?" "Is Granny Lee still alive?" "Did we win?" "Is this God-forsaken war going to be over soon?" "What happened after Spotsylvania?" "Where's Grant now?" "Have you seen—?" A thousand names followed the end of this question.

The din drowned out any answers. A heavy-jowled older man shouldered his way through his companions with his arms above his head and scaly palms forward. He had a face like a bulldog. "Hold on now! Settle down! Let me introduce myself. I'm Sergeant Martin Sorrell, and I'll address your questions. Any of you boys who came with me feel free to jump in and correct what I get wrong." He looked around for approval. A calm settled over our group as they realized this man was the only route to satisfied curiosity. A white roped scar traced a line from Sergeant Sorrell's right cheekbone behind his right ear, which was short a chip off the top. His right eye was swollen and bruised black. I couldn't tell whether stiffened blood or red Virginia clay colored his rusted outfit. Zeke and I joined the prisoners who sank to the crusty ground, squatting on their heels in attentive postures. Sorrell had the brash and aggressive manner of an elixir salesman, which I later found him to have been.

"First, you Southern boys can rejoice," he said. "We roundly routed the Yankee bastards in a glorious victory at Petersburg this last week." The cheering was rowdy enough to be heard in the civilized world across the wide Delaware. Minutes passed before he could quiet the exulting crowd. "Yes, that defeat merits great celebration, but as God is my witness, I declare this was a battle unlike any ever fought, which makes victory even sweeter." Scratching at the lousy varmints feasting behind his torn ear, he paused for that tidbit to sink in. "They employed two new weapons against us, both of them indecent and immoral, just like the Yanks themselves." His audiences made sounds of impatience to hear what those were.

Sorrell was visibly enjoying everyone's rapt attention. He told how, the morning of the attack, he and thousands of troops had been sleeping like babies, scattered at dawn across a Petersburg field after days of mounding up ten-foot walls of dirt around their position. Suddenly the ground heaved up with an infernal din and threw him what must have been three feet into the air. Miraculously, he fell to earth without a broken bone. "You won't believe what happened next. A giant fountain of red dirt rose high into the air, stretched out over the plain like a fierce thunderhead, and then let loose a barrage of broken timbers, planks, clods of clay, guns—all mingled with blackened arms, legs, heads, and every sort of body part." Waving his arms, Sorrell gave the appearance of a country minister describing Hell.

Zeke and I joined the collective gasp. The Federals had never deployed explosives of this force. Sorrell then told how the blast left a gigantic crater, larger than a wheat field. It was hollowed out ten to twenty feet deep, just where our boys blissfully dreamed. It was into this crater that the horrible debris rained. He said the Yanks had chiseled out a tunnel in the dark of night and planted hundreds of kegs of dynamite beneath our boys. They then trailed a fuse all the way back out of the tunnel to the Yankee side of the field.

"How did you find out?" someone yelled.

"We beat the hell out of a captive, that's how," Sorrell said.

Again, a torrent of questions arose, but Sorrell silenced them with an offhand wave. He paused for effect. "This is when the Yanks unleashed their second surprise: the United States Colored Troops." Again, the crowd erupted in shouts.

Sorrell spat a thick wad of chewing tobacco and said, "This is the first we'd seen of a blue-coated Black company hauling rifles. For our boys, it was like waving a red flag before a raging bull. You put guns in the hands of Coloreds, and after this war is over, they'll murder our women and children sleeping in their beds."

A torrent of epithets erupted and a chant of "Kill, kill, kill them now," floated above the crowd. One man yelled out, "White soldiers shouldn't have to fight Coloreds! It's a goddamned insult." Voices throughout the pen echoed the same sentiment.

Zeke muttered, "This is madness. These idiots assume slavery is the only thing standing between whites and a population of Black assassins."

The boldness of his words startled me, but then I hadn't recovered from seeing those free Blacks rounded up for sale near Gettysburg. However, I'd kept it to myself. Every nerve in my body was raw as Sorrell continued.

"Somebody swore that the advancing Coloreds yelled 'Show 'em no mercy!' That did it. Then we really had murder in our hearts."

He told how Union soldiers slid down the crater's walls for cover, but then were trapped like fish in a barrel. An Alabama company charged in after them, using clubs and muskets to horrible effect. By the time Sorrell and his troops reached the crest, about five hundred Yanks had hoisted flags of surrender down in the bottom, Coloreds and whites alike. Sorrell continued, "We stormed into the crater too, parting the Blacks from the white Yanks. You should have heard them Coloreds, begging us to spare their lives. But we executed every one of those turncoats. Shot 'em point-blank with our rifles."

He told how soldiers plunged bayonets in the Blacks' hearts, blew their brains out with their pistols, and knocked them in the head with their rifle butts. Afterward, some soldiers pranced around, whooping and hollering, and twirled over their heads steel blades coated with gore. He then related how he came upon a grievously wounded Black wretch who reached out to all who passed, as he begged them for just a drop of water. Sorrell said he hollered, "Drink your own blood. You'll have no need for water, anyway, not when I'm finished with you." And then he silenced the man forever with his bayonet. Sorrell paused for more cheering. Admiring prisoners enthusiastically applauded and stamped their feet again.

By this time, Zeke's head was lowered, the flush spreading on his neck a clue to his feelings. I was outraged. Everyone knew that a white flag of truce raised by surrendering troops means the opposition holds its fire as prisoners are taken, regardless of race. Glancing away from Sorrells to hide my revulsion, I busied myself with removing of a piece of lint that clung to my tattered pants. Again, Mary's image of Sukie and those free Blacks taken south seized my mind. What were we doing?

He finished his address by exhorting the men to butcher every Black cur that Lincoln sent against them when they were freed and went back into combat. "Don't capture a single one!" he hollered. "Not one, I tell you!"

"Huzzah! Huzzah!" poured forth when Sorrell stepped back, mopping his forehead after his oratorical exertions. Zeke's face was buried in his hands, and I felt hollow, empty as a deer strung up by its hooves to bleed out. Sorrell had described cold-blooded mass murder. This creature and his comrades should have been hanged for their crimes.

Head back and eyes closed, Zeke leaned against the wall after the snarling crowd broke up. I left him there and found another place to lean while I struggled with the anguish I'd been feeling for the past year. Yes, the Union held the moral high ground. I no longer had any doubt. They were also cruel invaders, but I couldn't get away from the fact that in defending our homes against them, we were also defending the abomination of slavery. When the conflict started, I hadn't the maturity or courage to give up my family, home, and friends on principle—to flee north like Reverend McIntyre. After Sorrell's account, screws of helplessness and guilt tightened in my heart and filled me with loathing.

27

THERE'S BEEN A DISASTER IN THE LIBRARY. BOOKS ARE STREWN ACROSS the blue rug, the spines gnawed off every one. Some were printed in the early 1800s, saved by Pa from his father's small collection and hauled all the way from Goshen when my family bought this farm. Now the books are ruined. On the heap is my favorite—Hiawatha's saga, nothing now but naked folds of paper sliding out of two pieces of printed cardboard.

For one hundred and seventy-two years, these books were safe in our house. But because my great-grandson and his wife neglected to turn off the heater in the library when they locked the front door for the winter, there is this tragedy. A squirrel, attracted to warm air floating up the chimney, clambered down and spent the winter feasting on the rabbit-hide glue that binds the books together. I heard the rustling in the library, the gnashing and ripping. The creature then defecated where it ate.

I screamed at the varmint, but it paid no more attention than the people. Stomping made no difference either. My moldering spirit is now so enfeebled that I'm powerless to frighten even a varmint.

Then I discovered something I'd never seen before. Splayed open across the top of the old traveling salesman set of encyclopedias was a volume with a faint pencil scrawl between the printed lines. I looked more closely. It was Mary's handwriting and easily recognized tone. She must have used the volume at a time when there was no paper. Ma and Pa never opened these books. They bought them solely for our education, and Mary knew her writing wouldn't be found. I strained to read her words.

The Worst Year Ever

Author Miss Mary Smiley

January 1, 1865. When Tom left for the war four years ago, Ma begged him to write every day what was happening to him. I guess she didn't imagine that we at home would have anything out of the ordinary to record. How wrong she was. I will set down in this book how grievous the old year has been and pray that the next will be no worse.

To begin with, I've lost both my mother and my brother. Not to death so far—mind you that might be easier because death brings certainty. Families mourn, and then, over time, there's healing

After the Wilderness and Spotsylvania battles, we heard that most of the Stonewall Brigade was killed or captured, but we had no way to know what had happened to Tom. Finally, we received his brief note from the Fort. At least we were certain he was alive!

And Ma has gone mad. When she heard Tom had been taken, she took to her bed most every day, and when she was up, she pored over her Bible from dawn until dusk and prayed for Tom's safety without any concern for the rest of us or her old life. Then the trickle of letters stopped.

Folks describe the prison as just this side of Hell. We've heard of boys taking ill and dying there—just like the first years of camp. Mrs. McClean's son Bill was in the Fort last spring and was so worn out and poorly fed that he died several weeks after getting home. And he was traded out after only a few months. This was before Lincoln called off all prisoner exchanges because the South considered Union Black soldiers to be property, not equal to a Southern soldier in trade. Mrs. McClean's heart is still profoundly broken. Such stories add considerably to Ma's burden.

Since 1862 there has been less and less of everything a body requires for living. And there has been more and more of what might frighten someone to death. All but crippled Augusta boys are gone, and there's no one left who's strong enough to put in crops by himself. I heard the substitute minister say that one hundred and eighteen boys from our church are on the battlefield. And all the horses are gone. There can't be any farming without horses. Our soldiers, wandering up and down the road in front of the house, come to the door and demand to be fed. They have such swollen bare feet and tatters for clothes that we can't refuse, but we risk starvation ourselves with each boy we feed. What they don't take is confiscated by the Army to appease starving troops. They say that when meat is found, one pound has to do for a whole day's ration for eight soldiers. Confederate currency is as useless as leaves fallen from trees. And it takes more bills to buy something miniscule than the leaves any one tree could shed. I hear a five-dollar cotton calico frock now costs as much as $500, if there are any frocks to be had in these parts.

Pa trapped a possum up in the woods for Christmas dinner this year, and we had some dried mushrooms left from foraging at the end of the summer. He skinned the pitiful thing, and Tish and I made a stew using the mushrooms and some sweet potatoes we'd buried in the cellar—although a possum hardly gives enough meat for more than one person. No one dares carry a hunting rifle for fear that Yanks who ride through here will think they are guerillas and shoot them dead on the spot, no questions asked. Ma had another of her terrible headaches and couldn't help with the dinner. It was a right gloomy gathering. So many people are missing family members now, and the holiday makes their absence strike deeper in the heart. We certainly missed Tom, and I secretly held Beards close in my thoughts.

I've learned to eat some things that would never have touched my lips before. It never occurred to me that I would try to suck the last sliver of meat from a stringy possum leg or seek ways to prepare acorns. I don't know what people in town do for food. We can wander up in our woods or in the fields to find eatables. Depending upon the seasons, we've had dandelion greens, wild onions, chanterelles, walnuts, blackberries, and what root vegetables we can grow and store. Tish and I everyday search on the ground and in the bushes for something digestible. There's no ammunition to shoot deer or wild turkey, but Pa's old rusty traps for rabbits and possums, sometimes squirrels, have saved our lives. We've not tasted sugar or coffee in the past three years. Nothing from across the seas gets past the Union boats barring the Southern ports.

I guess I'm taking my time getting to the hard parts to tell. I'll begin with June sixth, when the federal troops stormed Staunton. The familiar but dreaded roar of thousands of rifles fifteen miles away reverberated all day, starting at nine o'clock in the morning. I have heard that five or six thousand men fought around the town. Ma was still fretting over what had happened to Tom and kept to her room, huddled in bed with covers over her head and a pillow on top to block the sound. She bound a woolen scarf around her ears in a final attempt to muffle the noise. Tish paced, and Pa read his books, pretending that everything was just fine. I hummed to calm my nerves, but it did little good. Artillery had not been this near in all the years of the war, and we knew that if they took Staunton, the Yankees would continue southwest right past our house on the way to Lexington to destroy the military institute there. When the firing ceased, Pa went out on the Staunton road to see if anyone closer to town knew the outcome. He hurried back with a long face. Staunton's streets were overcome by Union troops. Ma had arisen from her bed and was fretting in a chair. "Do you know the date, children? It's June, the sixth month of the year, the sixth day of the month, and the year is in the decade starting with a six. 666 is Satan's mark. We've been sent a sign." Tish rolled her eyes at me and made a sour face.

None of us slept peacefully that night or the night after, each straining to hear any unnatural noise that might signal the advance of the enemy in the farm's direction. There's no light at night. Candles are impossible to obtain, so that we must go to bed when the sun sets unless we choose to sit with our hands in our laps in the blackness. That makes for an endless, sleepless night. I was terrified to drift off, lest soldiers come while I was unconscious. Some families have fared without too much hardship, but others have lost everything and been treated roughly. Tish and I began to bicker, substituting crankiness for the anxious gnawing at our innards. Ma came out of her room only for meals. She kept her Bible alongside as she chewed in silence. Every now and then she'd caress the cover with her thumb, rubbing it again and again over the gold embossed letters *Holy Bible*.

On Tuesday morning, I told Tish and Pa that I couldn't stay still another minute. I walked out the back to ascend the rise high above the house. Going past Pa's tiny kitchen garden hidden behind the barn in the midst of brambles, I was careful to keep my eyes on the ground, stepping cautiously between the rows of potatoes and squash vines. I wanted to avoid seeing what he'd nailed earlier in the day to a T-shaped stake in the middle of the few corn plants. The crows had been pecking the valuable ripening ears. A scarecrow of clothing and straw would attract army foragers' attention to our stalks, so Pa had hidden in the brambles with a sturdy slingshot and expertly downed one of the crows with a stone to the head. No form of meat can be wasted these days, so the dark bird was gutted, and its flesh was put aside for Ma to make a pie. The carcass's majestic, sparkling black wings were spread broad and affixed with nails to the stake's crossbar in the garden to warn other crows. Pa had stepped back to register its sinister appearance when another crow approached. It caught sight of its dead brother and, with agonized screams, rent the early morning sky. It instantly pivoted in the air and lifted on the current. The alarmed cawing could be heard echoing across the hills. The dead bird with its broken head and dulled eyes surely was a dark omen, but of what I wasn't certain. Compelling my feet to move as rapidly as possible, I moved past the garden and started the climb through the pasture.

There are no more cattle to graze the grass short in the upper field. They had been seized two years previous, and the movement of my skirts scything through the waist-high stems and leaves sent disturbed grasshoppers and tiny sweat bees spiraling upward in a cloud. Thorns snagged the fabric, and the trip took longer than usual because I had to repeatedly disentangle myself from their grasp. Reaching the crest, I found a soft patch of grass and stretched out on my back to watch the hawks soar between the top of the hill and the clouds.

But calm was forgotten when I arose to return to the house. Toward Staunton a plume of black smoke bulged into the air. It couldn't be a house or barn fire.

It was larger than anything I'd ever seen. A bewildered moment passed until I realized that I was witnessing the burning of the town. I tore down the big hill to alert the family, ripping my skirts as I raced through the briars. The town's destruction struck terror in my heart for what then might happen to unguarded farms. When I ran hollering onto the back porch, Pa leaped up from his seat in the library to see what so ailed me. My breathless account drew Ma out of her room at the top of the stairs, and she began to shriek, "I told you so, I told you. This is a continuation of the prophesied Tribulations."

Ma recently has spent more and more time studying the books of the Old and New Testament. She's taken the wild prophesy of the Book of Revelations as her guide these days. Ma is a good woman devoted to her family and God, but she's put her trust in the author of tracts who divines the world's end by 1865 in almost every verse of the Bible's two books. To Ma's thinking, Northerners are precipitating mankind's doom. They have abandoned the ways of the Lord and are attempting to destroy His institutions.

With neighbors struggling to get by and feeling low in spirit, social calls have fallen off in the past two years. Ma has had few distractions from time spent cross-referencing Bible pages with apocalyptic religious tracts. When Tish and I mourned so over the death of Sam Lucas, she tried to console us by advising us to study the Book of Revelations. She believes that God's love brings these terrible losses to make us stronger so that at the end we will be among the multitude summoned before Him on Judgment Day. She reminded us that unlike our brother, Sam came over to the Lord at church when he was home on furlough the last time. "He'll stand right alongside us on that glorious day. Oh Lord, if only I knew if Tom was saved," she insisted. We stopped listening to her Biblical rants and litany of concerns about our brother's soul.

After Tom was captured, Ma became much more agitated and bitter about the war. At the dinner table she lectured Pa that all of the South's suffering is for the sake of purifying her peoples' faith. That God has risen up these Babylonians in Washington, these evil forces, to bring judgment on the world for its sin. "Now, Christiana, it's not possible for man to know God's will, nor can we predict the future," my father said.

But she continued. "For certain, Abe Lincoln is the Antichrist. It's all prophesied in the Book of Revelations. Don't you believe the Bible?" Pa just looked at his hands and didn't respond. "The South has been chosen as the New Jerusalem, and this purified land will be where the Savior returns," Ma insisted. She scarcely looks like herself these days, with her lips set tight and her eyes so hard.

Pa shows sore-hearted patience toward her vehement preaching, but at least his mind can be occupied with other thoughts. He's concerned with our survival. Ma has got so she only sleeps, reads her book, and berates us when she's awake. She seems not to care about us anymore. If we chide her or speak our hurt, she responds with some quote to reinforce her position. With each death from illness, battlefield killing, and decrease in food she finds evidence of the work of the Horsemen who bring famine, plague, and civil war. She says they are in our midst already. The fourth, Pale Death, she's begun to see in recurring dreams that rouse her shrieking from her bed. Sometimes we think Ma rests in her chair, but she'll be staring at something in the distance and then will cry out some verse about the hour of judgment.

This was her unfettered state of mind while Pa, Tish, and I feared that at any moment several thousand enemy troops might come stalking down our road. Pa believes that a deserted house fares far worse from the soldiers' depredations than one where the family remains. He was steely in his resolve to stay where we were. Nothing Tish and I said, no matter how forcefully or pitifully we pleaded, could discourage this view.

If Pa had his way in this, Ma might be in true danger. We've heard that folks were sent away to federal prison for saying something only slightly insulting. Ma's hostile ravings might cause the enemy to shoot her. Pa decided that Tish should guide Ma into the cellar where they would hide. If Ma made any outburst, the thick stone walls would muffle its meaning. Pa and I would stay in the main part of the house.

While we were forming our plan, there were horses' hooves on the road toward Staunton. Pa darted out and located Mr. Lucas. Confederate soldiers who'd been defeated in the battle for that town had been spotted in the area; some companies had scattered toward Lexington. Mr. Lucas told Pa that a group had begged at his door for food and boots that morning. Hastening to the window, I saw quite a number of our men toting rifles and loping hunched over through side fields toward the Beard's place. Pa raced through the door and hollered at Tish, "Take your mother and get to the basement." Ma loudly protested but hiding suited both of them better. They were too distracted with hand wringing and whimpering to find a secure place anywhere else. There was nothing to be done but sit side-by-side with our father on the library sofa and wait. I could hardly breathe. He patted my arm, trying to maintain his own composure.

After what seemed days but was probably an hour, faint strains of the "Star-Spangled Banner" reached our ears. Folks said that invading Yankees like to sing their anthem as an insult to Southerners. My teeth were clacking in my head, and my body quaked. Pa continued to pat my hand, but I could see that he trembled too. The singing grew more distinct. The lilting tune seemed to be an anthem of death. There was a shot fired. The song abruptly stopped and was replaced by men yelling and more shots—all coming from the center of Bethel.

Blasts echoed from the hills as well as lower on the road. As the chaos of men's voices and gunfire grew nearer, Pa and I flew toward the back hall, the room farthest from the road and with only one window. We dove onto the floor and cowered behind the stairs. I couldn't tell you how long the dreadful cries and loud reports of rifles erupted from the battle below the house. The odor of gunpowder seeped into the hall, and puffs of smoke drifted past the window. Glass shattered in the front room and crashed to the floor like hail. With a sharp crack, a bullet slammed into the limestone foundation near the porch. I held my breath, every muscle frozen as I pressed into the floor. My head was turned away from Pa, but I could hear his ragged breath and knew that he was frightened too. Eventually most of the clamor moved on down the road toward Lexington, but the shouts of a few men were still audible near the front of the house. Pa and I remained rigid on the floor, not knowing when it would be advisable to get up. Now we could clearly hear Ma's incoherent howls of rage directed toward our invaders. Fortunately, at this point we were the only ones who would have been able to make out her words.

Then voices were at close range, and footsteps sounded on the porch. A man called out as he pounded his fist on the door, "Please, can you help us here? If anyone is there, we need help desperately. We have a seriously wounded soldier who needs care." Pa and I looked at one another. There was such urgency in the tone that the request seemed sincere.

Pa cracked the door apiece while I hovered behind. "What's going on here? Who do you have there?" he spoke through the opening. Two disheveled and filthy Confederates supported a bleeding man who was slumped over. He had a severe head wound. A third soldier coaxed a riderless horse into the yard.

"Our company's run off to thwart the enemy before they attack Lexington, but we can't desert our comrade wounded like this. Can you shelter him and care for his horse?" He looked over my father's shoulder and said, "Miss, you remain in the house. There are dead men on the road—sights you shouldn't see."

Pa directed them to put the man down on the parlor floor. He then told the soldiers to tie the bay mare up in the woods at the top of the hill where it would be invisible from the road. The poor animal looked famished. Its ribs poked out like barrel staves. Ma and Tish came up out of the cellar with Pa's "All's safe!" cry, and they hurried into the parlor to view the unconscious visitor on the floor. Although Ma's reason seems destroyed, she was able to move quickly to deal with the wounded boy. She ordered me to heat water and fetch the mustard plaster, and she commanded Tish to drag a mattress from the spare bedroom and assemble some blankets. Blood so obscured the boy's face that it was hard to tell how old he was, but when Ma sponged him with warm water, I saw that the fellow was about Tom's age. He had a vicious gash on the right side of his head with shattered bone visible through shredded flesh. The right side of his face was misshapen with bruises and swelling. I'd never witnessed such gore and had to stifle bile as it rose in my throat. I'd be no use to anyone if I'd given in to my revulsion.

The next few days were quiet. All the while, the wounded soldier lay senseless in the parlor with Ma tending to him. There was no laudanum, morphine, or even whiskey to be had anywhere and no other potions to ease his pain. The federal blockade on the coast made sure of that. The patient's cries of agony added another reason for sleeplessness. Before he arrived, we spent nights straining to hear enemy boots and horses. Afterward, I heard Ma's quiet footsteps on the stairs for many a night. She would sit vigil with him, humming the lullabies we heard as babies and alternating with hymns. Her sweet, crooning voice seemed to soothe away some of his distress.

"If only I had some honey. This wound needs honey or it will fester, and we'll lose him," Ma fretted to Pa.

He looked thoughtful for a moment and then said, "I think I may be able to get you some. I can't promise you, but I'll give it my best effort." We have no bees, and anyone who does, conceals the precious sweet from others, but Pa has traps and occasional meat. The next day, he walked into Bethel with a freshly trapped possum in his rucksack and returned with a most valuable container of honey to heal our wounded soldier.

Here's how it came to be that Ma's desperate plea was granted: Pa told us that on a trip back from Staunton in Mr. Lucas' wagon a month earlier, he had noticed a swarm of bees near old Mr. Tatternook's house at the gable end near the roof line. He and Mr. Lucas reined in the horse, curious to see what the bees were doing so far away from a hive or wild tree nest. They observed a horde flying into the octagonal attic window. Mr. Lucas immediately suspected that Old Tatternook had captured himself a queen and had her there under his roof.

No one in the community knows the old man well because he keeps to himself, and he's ignored by most. He's scary looking with a black eye patch and broad-brimmed black hat that almost conceals his other eye and beak nose. Ma says he looks like a Catholic priest with his shiny black suit and white shirt, and she deeply dislikes Catholics. I've seen him once or twice shuffling along, hunched over and seemingly indifferent to the passing landscape.

Pa asked Mr. Lucas what he made of the fact that this fellow never attends church. Reverend McIntyre had reported that when he went to call a few years ago, the old man said that he has no need for a wrathful God who waits to punish him for every misstep.

"That's blasphemy!" Mr. Lucas said.

Pa replied, "To make things worse, he told Reverend McIntyre some nonsense about how his God speaks to him daily through the fragrant breezes in the cedar trees, the melodies of the whippoorwill, and the pattering rain on the forest floor." When the minister warned Tatternook against being drawn into evil, Tatternook said there is no evil. He believes that it's man's ignorance of who he really is that causes him to harm other creatures, and that self-righteous people claiming to speak for God have done the greatest harm throughout history.

"So, what do you make of this kind of talk?" Pa asked.

Mr. Lucas then reminded Pa of the time when Tatternook warned Homer Reynolds to keep his boy Dennis away from the hind ends of horses while they waited in Reynolds' blacksmith barn to be shod. And not two days later, eight-year-old Dennis was kicked in the belly by the Beard's mare. He died within the week.

Pa replied that he thought the incident with Dennis was nothing more than coincidence.

Mr. Lucas disagreed. "Don't you recall that Jenny Beard took sick after the old man knocked at the door and presented Mrs. Beard with herbs to treat typhus? Jenny came down with a fever the next day, and her mother is convinced that the girl's life was saved only through the old man's foresight. She was so desperate when Jenny was close to dying that she made her mind up to ignore suspicious talk about Mr. Tatternook. I think he knows things the rest of us don't."

"Well, I'm reserving judgment until there's better proof," Pa said as Mr. Lucas lay the reins across the horse's back. The wagon rumbled the two men toward home.

So it was Old Tatternook that Pa approached to trade his possum for honey. But he said that when he offered the animal to the old man, he told Pa that he didn't kill or eat animals. What Pa had was of no use to him, and Pa would have to go elsewhere to barter. Mr. Tatternook shook his head as he sadly stroked the possum's dull fur.

"If you'll not have this meat, might I persuade you to share just a little of the honey I know is hidden in your attic hives? We have a critically injured soldier in our parlor, and honey is needed to knit his flesh together," pleaded Pa. "A man's life is at risk."

The old man looked surprised and then viewed him steadily with his one eye. He seemed to be weighing the urgency of the request and Pa's knowledge of his secret hives. Finally, he ushered Pa into his front room and asked him to wait. Pa described a room aromatic with clumps of dill, lemon balm, feverfew, alfalfa, and sage wrapped with cord and hung to dry from whitewashed beams. Bottles of shriveled leaves hand labeled "fever," "headache," "nausea," and other ailments crowded a small, rough plank table. The place was an upside-down meadow after a dry season. It soothed him.

Mr. Tatternook finally returned with a precious blue Mason jar full of honey wrapped in an old, checked cloth along with some leaves of feverfew he said would help with Ma's chronic headaches. He then bid Pa farewell. Puzzled, but with spirits lifted, Pa journeyed home.

When he handed his bundle to Ma, a wrinkled note fell out. Flattening it on the table, she read, "Dear Mrs. Smiley, cease worrying about your son. He'll return to you safely from prison. You may rest easy. Regards, R. F. Tatternook."

"Oh, what a demented old man!" Ma spat. "How did he ever know Tom is in Union prison? And he can't possibly guess Tom's fate." She dismissively tossed the note aside. I snatched it from the floor and read it. Mr. Tatternook is a soothsayer and a good man. Proof was his knowledge of Ma's recurring headaches. The note gave me hope.

Tish and I couldn't keep our thoughts from the jar of honey on the table. We yearned for just a fingertip's worth. Having been without for so long, we deserved just a moment of indulgence. But Ma was unrelenting. She guarded the jar with fierce protectiveness and secreted it in her room at all times. Daily she swathed the sticky sweet on the man's head as she swaddled it in torn sheets. She used every scrap of fabric in the house; bedcoverings, petticoats, nightgowns, and summer curtains were torn into bandaging. Sure that she would come after our last calico dresses, I hid away my favorite blue with the lacy collar—even though it is now threadbare around the cuffs and has patches on the skirt. Ma cut the boy's bloody clothes from his body, and Pa found some of Tom's pants and shirts to replace them. He was inches shorter than Tom, but with cuffs and sleeves rolled, the clothes were a fine fit. A homemade turban bandage crafted from brightly colored cloths transformed him into a Turkish sultan from my geography schoolbook.

After two weeks had passed, Ma burst into the kitchen, her cheeks ruddy with excitement. "Our patient is awake! He's finally awake!"

"Are you sure, Ma, or are you just wishing it's so?" I asked, as I set down my knife from chopping pine needles for tea.

"Oh, no. Come see! He opened his eyes and smiled at me. For just the briefest moment," she said as the three of us headed for the parlor. "What a beautiful smile it was!" But we found him unconscious again. In the days following, he was awake for longer and longer periods but couldn't speak coherently. Stuttering and gesturing, he finally made it known by signs that he'd like to write something. Tish ran to the library and grabbed an old textbook, from which she tore pages, and then found a pencil. He wrote in crooked letters that he was Lieutenant Franklin Spragins from Charlotte, North Carolina, and had been in the cavalry. When he was able to convey his father's name and home place, I wrote a letter that described his condition and location. Franklin languished in the parlor, unable to converse in more than a word or two. We hadn't counted on having an extra mouth to feed. Even with his diminished appetite, his presence meant we each had even less. Ma spooned corn grits into his mouth as there was always a little extra grain to be found in cracks and corners around the mill. And Tish surreptitiously saved bits of possum meat from her plate to share after a meal when Pa had been lucky with his traps. She and I took turns reading to Franklin, which seemed to soothe his agitation.

Tish had spelled Ma in the early days, and if you ask me, she liked to be in the parlor next to him far more than was necessary. She could talk of nothing else. What did we think his home was like? Did we think he had a wife or sweetheart back in North Carolina? And on and on. She burst into sobs when I teased her about him and was sullen with me for a full day after. Nevertheless, she shamelessly stared at his sleeping form whenever he was dozing.

She also gathered flowers from the garden every day for our patient. Pa nailed rough strips of pine where the windowpanes had been shot out, and the bedclothes and medical materials gave the parlor a disheveled look–but Tish's roses, daisies, field thistles, and blue cornflowers filled the room with a summer fragrance. I suppose she prayed fervently for a wartime romance to develop. Once Ma was able to wash the oily, blood-matted mess on his scalp, I could see why Tish might be sweet on him. He was a fine-looking man with the high cheekbones and fair complexion of folks from the lowlands of the Carolinas. Soft brown eyes shone out of a kind face, despite being so gaunt. We were all very excited when it became certain that he would live, but his sight was mighty poor and his ability to speak clearly did not improve. His left arm seemed useless as well. Perhaps with time he will heal better, but he'll be far away from Tish and our doorstep by then.

After the first Union skirmish, Pa hid the old moldy ham under a floorboard in the attic. Hoarding it in the smoke house no longer seemed wise. We wandered from room to room trying to imagine what would catch the eye of a thieving soldier, but there was simply too much to conceal. We were overwhelmed by the very notion and gave up. However, Tish and I did wrap the

silver forks and knives in a flour-sacking dishcloth and lugged them in a basket to the top of the hill. We had a tiff about where to put them. She favored
burial next to a fence post as a marker. I preferred a spot under the big oak
where chanterelle foraging is best. It's a site we know well. She finally agreed
that Yankees might carry off the fence post for burning but could never fully
remove the big oak. Chopped down, there would still be a stump to mark the
place. After digging a hole suitable for our bundle, we covered it with dirt and
a large rock, then tossed twigs and acorns around to make the ground appear
undisturbed. Prayer would have to provide security for the rest of our possessions. There was worry enough about the family's safety without overly much
thought for things that could be replaced.

Franklin Spragins's father came from North Carolina two months later,
in early August, to fetch his son home. By this time, Franklin had recovered
enough to sit upright for an hour or two a day but was still quite weak. Ma
had taught him to feed himself with his one good hand. He still only com-
municated clearly by scratching out barely legible letters, and that seemed to
tire him mightily. His father had navigated his finely built wagon around combat near Richmond and threaded through the mountains toward the Valley
where battles could spring up at any time. When he saw his son in our parlor,
both men burst into tears. Mr. Spragins clung to him until Franklin seemed
embarrassed by so much emotion and looked to Ma for help. She gently led the
man away to join us where Tish and I were discreetly waiting on the porch.
Mr. Spragins lingered for a week before chancing the hazardous trip home.

Ma, Pa, and he struck up quite a friendship during that time and talked
for hours in the library as Franklin rested in the parlor. One afternoon, I overheard them discuss how hopeless the Confederacy's prospects of winning this
war were. Mr. Spragins didn't believe the war was about ending slavery or even
honoring states' rights. He espoused the same nonsense as Ma, but just wasn't
crazed by it. "Mr. and Mrs. Smiley, do you think God damns the people of the
South for their sins?" Mr. Spragins asked. "This position is frequently taken by
our North Carolina churches, and I'm inclined to concur."

"I have no doubt," Ma clapped her hands, joyful to have found a kindred spirit.

Mr. Spragins said, "So many folks are concerned with the outcome of the November election—particularly those who pray Abe Lincoln's defeat will end the war—but they're looking for a solution in the wrong place. The war is God's doing, and until men of the South learn to be more devout, God will allow the war to persist."

Ma's repeated "Amens" could be heard beyond the parlor, and Pa's echoed hers. "But when will people of the Confederacy gain this wisdom?" my father wondered.

Mr. Spragins said, "I wish I knew. Obviously, our great losses haven't been enough to bring a necessary level of humility." But I wondered about the effectiveness of prayer, because months later Lincoln won the election.

I think Mr. Spragins was so overjoyed to see his son alive, he failed to notice how Franklin's chances for a normal life had been reduced. Mr. Spragins shares Tish's wishful view of his son's future. As he prepared to leave, he spoke with relief of Franklin's return home to help with the fieldwork now that all his slaves but one had been taken off by the Confederate army for labor. Pa helped him arrange a borrowed mattress in the back of the wagon for Franklin's comfort, and one morning, as we all stood on the porch and waved, Mr. Spragins and his son departed. Ma and Tish watched until the wagon was out of sight, and then they wiped at tears rolling down their cheeks, Tish for dashed romantic dreams and Ma who was suddenly more aware of Tom's absence.

Franklin's horse boarded with us until early September, as Mr. Spragins couldn't both drive the wagon and handle Franklin's steed. By the time his remaining slave Minis arrived to guide her home, the mare had added some bulk to her ribs. I had scoured the corners of the barn and the fields for bits of hay and found sufficient to bring her back to health. Fortunately, the mare was gone by some days when the burning came into the Valley.

Caring for Franklin Spragins had made Ma better. She was so busy being useful that she had no time to rant. Perhaps she thought her kind attention to another mother's son would earn her Tom's safety in the Lord's eyes. But then an awful thing occurred.

Not long after, the family headed off to church in the buggy for Sunday services. As the grounds came into view, we saw neighbors' wagons and carriages tethered to the fence at the side of the road as usual, but there was a crowd congregated underneath the ancient oak tree.

Pa was the first to notice and said, "What the dickens is going on here? The service should start any minute now. These people will be late to their pews."

"Over by the tree—that looks like Mr. Blue and Mr. Lucas, but what on earth are they doing?" Tish asked.

We craned beyond the buggy sides to see. Mr. Blue, who is a tall and hardy man for his age, stood at the base of the tree, and the shorter, slightly built Mr. Lucas teetered on his shoulders. He awkwardly tried to heave himself up onto the lowest sturdy limb, a knife clutched in his teeth.

"Look, there's something exceedingly strange hanging from that branch." I pointed toward the elongated object at the end of a rope. It softly twirled in the morning breeze. It looked like a long, lumpy sack of potatoes, but the men's horrified expressions and alarmed talk suggested that the object was something much more unpleasant. Buzzards crouched in the upper branches and hungrily eyed the scene. A cloud of them with outstretched wings swirled around the tree's crown, projecting their shadows on the tight knot of men below.

Ma spied them and began to scream, "Satan's fallen angels! They are descending upon us! Can't you see them? You girls take cover! They steal souls, and they're right here in our own church yard!" She tugged at her hair and cowered under her shawl.

Tish tried to calm her, "Hush, Ma. Those are just buzzards. Settle down. There's nothing to fear from these ordinary birds. You've seen them on the fields picking at deer carcasses more times than you can count." But no amount of reasoning would calm her. For a split second, her vision became mine—the wrinkled gray heads of the greasy creatures did look like those of small demons. Then I recalled that they are merely Nature's housekeepers who never kill anything for food. They only clear away natural deaths and the bad deeds of others.

Pa joined the crowd around the tree, and Ma, Tish, and I watched in horrible fascination as Mr. Lucas inched out over the broad limb and severed the rope. The sack fell with a dull thud and collapsed in an eerily still, shapeless pile. But you just knew that inside were arms, legs, and a lolling head. Everyone was struck dumb. They stared at the spot where the encased body lay, until several men roused themselves and half–carried, half–dragged the bundle to the edge of the cemetery for later interment.

Nervously twisting his hat in his hands, Pa returned to the buggy. He sighed and seemed to dread the effect of the explanation to come. He couldn't deny what we had seen, and we would demand to know more. Haltingly he began, as Ma whimpered inconsolably. "Now, Christiana, you and the girls needn't worry. It's all over. There's nothing here that can harm us." He stroked her hand. "Not anymore."

He then explained what the substitute minister, Reverend Brown, had just reported to the assembled men. Brown had been awakened at daybreak by a disturbance, and when he peered from behind a parsonage window curtain, he saw Yankee soldiers advancing up the road with a hostage. The man's wrists were bound by rope to the back of his captors' wagon. The poor soul stumbled and fell, his sobs for mercy audible from where the Reverend watched. The hostage was near naked, and his feet left bloody trails in the road's dust, the minister had said.

"He watched? Why didn't he do something to help the man?" I knew the answer the minute I said this, but I couldn't help myself.

"What could he do? He had no gun, and he was outnumbered," Pa said. Then he proceeded to tell how Brown heard the Yanks declare that the church was a perfect spot for a mock trial. They took places across the porch steps with an officer as judge and six others as jury to try the man for murder. He thought their captive must have killed a Yankee soldier to merit such cruel treatment. Well, the poor fellow was in no condition to offer any defense. Their pronouncement was: Guilty. Death by noose.

Reverend Brown told the group that the pitiful fellow didn't utter a word as they shrouded his entire form with a sack and encircled his neck with a rope. After they seated him sideways on a horse, they whacked the beast on the rump. He made a startled leap forward. Before you could blink, Reverend Brown said, the prisoner was yanked off and swung in the air, twitching and writhing until the job was done.

Pa lowered his head and told us, "God bless the poor man's soul. It seems that we must suffer the effects of their visit too. The scoundrels made off with the sterling silver communion cups as well as the Bible from the pulpit."

We later read details in *The Spectator*. The victim was Samuel Creigh from down around Lewiston, about seventy miles farther toward the western mountains. Some believed his wife had shot a raiding Yankee who had attacked him. Others thought Mr. Creigh killed the soldier in self-defense. This slaying had occurred six months earlier, but in recent days some enemy of Creigh's had reported him to the Yankees in the Lewiston area. The Yanks found the body stuffed in Creigh's empty well. He was then tied to the wagon as a lesson for all to witness. The image of the sack dangling below the buzzards still spawns nightmares, and Ma was worse again.

Tish and I had drifted along with the comfortable memory of the sensible mother who had guided our lives so admirably until recently. Now, after the lynching, she seemed to lose touch with our world again. We had to face the fact that her unpredictable, angry behavior was a persistent danger to her as well as to us.

Pa summoned Tish and me into the library not long after Ma went off again. He had seemed preoccupied for days. Now he cleared his throat and adjusted his glasses on his nose. "I've been thinking about Ma," he said at last.

"I'm worried we're running out of time. More than likely, the soldiers will come this way again. We can't let your mother face even one of them."

This was the topic I'd dreaded most, but Tish seemed to have thought about it. "What about the basement?" she asked. "We hid there last time. And the soldiers never even entered the house. Perhaps we'll have that good fortune again."

Pa frowned. "That was just a skirmish, and the Yanks were only passing through. We need to find a place where she won't be discovered, even if they storm the house."

Pa's voice dropped, and he couldn't meet our eyes. "She may heap invective on their heads, and if that's the case, who knows what may happen. Lucas told me of a man who was pistol-whipped when he called one of them a Yankee bastard. They then burned his house to the ground." Tish's face drained of color, and I'm sure I looked the same.

"Do you think we could persuade her to walk to the top of the hill to hide?" Tish stammered, remembering our hike with the table silver and the stout old oak's illusion of safety. She must have envisioned Ma warmly enfolded by the tree that had weathered so many storms.

"That won't do," I said. "She might refuse to go, Pa can't carry her that distance, and how would you keep her there? Bound to a tree?" Tears came to my eyes.

Tish snapped at me. "I'd stay with her." She paused. "But there would be no shelter. What if the weather is cold or rainy? We'd catch our death of pneumonia. I guess Mary's right. It won't work."

This conversation was sorely grievous to Pa. He insisted, "Her hiding place should be here. But I can't imagine where in the house we might conceal her." He sighed.

I thought of the small attic cubby over the back addition where I used to hide my broken china-head dolls. There wasn't much illumination in that area, as the gable windows are located at the other end. It also had the advantage of being far from the central downstairs rooms. Pa and Tish agreed this was a possibility, but it was no better for muffling her voice than the cellar. There was no barrier between the attic sections. It was simply a less likely place for a soldier to venture.

I steeled myself before I spoke, remembering that Ma's and our lives hung in the balance. "What if we tied a flannel around her mouth? The Yankees would be here for plunder, not lodging. There's no advantage to staying in tiny Bethel. They'd be gone mercifully quick. You know as well as I that we have few provisions for anyone's use."

Pa slowly shook his bowed head. "I think we first need to ask for the Lord's blessings and guidance. And pray that he keeps the enemy from our door so that we never have to consider these actions." He added, "God help your poor mother to come to her senses in the meantime." My heart broke to see him so sad. I reached for his hand and squeezed it. He said in a low tone, as if to himself, "I just can't reconcile her deep devotion and her purity of life with the angry, disturbed woman she's become."

We moved from the parlor, unwilling to meet each other's eyes, and found some solitary chores about the house or up in the barn to wipe away the bitter traces of our conversation. There was no solution that any of us could find conscionable, but at least we now had a plan.

In early September, when the enemy troops had moved from the Staunton area toward Lynchburg to rip up train lines, and the Confederates were able to restore telegraph wires from Charlottesville to Staunton, there was the possibility of news again. And what dreadful news it was!

Pa and Mr. Beard were curious to see if rumors of Staunton's ruin were accurate and to learn where our troops were fighting. They set out one morning for town in Mr. Beard's wagon drawn by his old mare. Hidden in a barn down on overgrown lane several miles off the Bethel road, both had been safe from army scavengers. Pa had brought several bushels of potatoes from this past summer's harvest, hoping to barter. But they had little hope of finding something of value. These days there is little to be purchased or traded in Staunton, thanks to the summer's occupation of fifteen thousand Union soldiers in this town of an already deprived four thousand. Pa returned empty-handed.

When he entered the back door, he found Tish and me trying to entertain an agitated Ma in the kitchen by singing old favorites like "Aura Lee." "What's going on here?" he asked.

"Ma's been so anxious, we've been trying to entertain her. She was convinced you'd be captured by the Yankees on the road," Tish said. I placed my hands on Ma's to calm their shaking. Even with Pa's return, she wasn't consoled.

He sank into a kitchen chair, and suddenly looked much older. Then he blurted out his news. "You remember Mr. Waddell, the newspaper editor in town? Well, we met him as he was running out of his office to alert folks on the street about what had just come over the wire from the Charlottesville paper." The creases in Pa's brow deepened as he recounted how someone in that town had got hold of an issue of the *New York Observer*. It had reported Grant's newest plan for bringing Virginia to its knees. Union troops had been ordered to eat out Virginia clean and clear so that a crow flying over the Valley should have to carry his own provender from end to end. "Those were Grant's exact words, Waddell said. And Grant has an even more diabolical plan in store for us."

"We are already eaten out clean and clear," I said. "There is barely anything left for humans or crows, as it is. What could be worse?"

"Oh, Mary. There is worse," he said. "Waddell told us that Grant has also commanded all Valley barns, mills, stored grain, hay for horses, and crop fields to be torched, and all animals to be either slaughtered or driven off. Yankee soldiers have already set out from Winchester to march south down the Valley to carry out his plan."

"God help us," Tish cried out. She grabbed the edge of the kitchen table to steady herself.

"How can we survive, and, worse, what will become of Ma if Yankees come this way again?" I said.

With Pa seated before her, Ma fell into one of her Last Days reveries, addressing someone none of us could see. "Glory, glory, you say. And what about God's blessed manna?" She cocked her head to listen. "Will there be an endless supply, that we may never suffer hunger? And will we enjoy eternal peace? Oh, precious angel, shine thy light upon my face as we sing God's praises in Heaven." She then recited a list of Heaven's glories for us all after Judgment Day. I hoped she envisioned an ample supply of sugar, bacon, honey, cakes, pies, real coffee, and cotton calico dresses. Nothing Pa had said registered with her, and I was having my own difficulties absorbing this bleak account. Tish's lips were quivering, and her face was ashen.

Two weeks later, a gentle, cool rain had been steadily falling in the late afternoon when Mr. Beard galloped into the yard. We had just finished supper when his footsteps pounded up the front steps. As Tish opened the door, he pushed his way past her and found Pa. "It's started. The burning has started! The enemy has torched all the barns in Waynesboro, and they're headed this way," he said. "I 'spect they won't get here until tomorrow morning but be prepared!" He barely spit the words out before he leaped on his steed and was down the road to tell the next neighbor.

My eyes nervously took in the room, imagining what a soldier might find desirable, but there was really nothing to be done outwardly to prepare. The shriveled smoked ham was hidden in the attic, the silver was buried, and all else of value to an army was already taken. What to do with Ma was the real problem. Solving it would take every bit of courage and determination we had.

We kept to ourselves, while Ma persisted with her constant litany of prayer and exhortation. Tish wept silently, but I was numb with apprehension. His face pinched with worry, Pa hugged each of us to him. "I'm going to shut myself in the parlor to ask the Lord's counsel. While I'm there, you girls might pray for guidance as well," he told us, as Tish whimpered.

"Now, Tish, we'll get through this. Just be calm and trust in your own strength and God's divine will." Pa strode into the parlor and closed the door behind him.

After persuading Ma to go to bed, we spent the long night tormented by our individual anxieties. I couldn't bear to discard my day dress, afraid I wouldn't be prepared if something happened before sunrise.

Near dawn, I heard Pa pacing in their room as I crept in my bare feet downstairs to sit on the porch. I hoped to be soothed by calls of owls perched in the cool, dark cedars and by the rippling sighs of the high creek. But one step outside brought a strong smell of bitter wood smoke. Off to the north, a faint orange glow capped the black hilltops with an eerie sunrise come too early in the day.

I stormed into the house, my cries of alarm drawing Tish and Pa into the upstairs hallway. Ma's enquiries of "What's going on? What are you all so upset about?" came from the bedroom.

"Don't you fret, Christiana. Everything's going to be all right," Pa called with a tremor that only we could hear. In a softer voice he said to us, "What in God's name will we do? The enemy will be here shortly if you can see fire in the distance."

Firmly I said, "Remember our plan, Pa. I'll take two chairs up to the attic, one for her and another for one of us."

"I'll stay with her," Tish said. "Just like last time. I've no desire to confront Yankee soldiers."

"But what if the Yankees set the house on fire?" I said. "Promise me you'll come downstairs with Ma at the first whiff of smoke, regardless of what you fear from the soldiers. Please promise." She glumly nodded assent.

Pa removed his glasses and rubbed his eyes. Putting them back on, he joined me as I stepped into the bedroom to reason with my mother. Taking a seat on the bed, Pa held her hand. He gently brushed a strand of gray hair from her forehead, saying, "Christiana, my love, Yankee soldiers approach on the road, and you will be safest waiting with Tish in the attic. Please come with us up the stairs and stay there until I give a sign." She glared at him, but he continued. "Tish is coming too. It will be exactly like the last time. It will be over quickly, and then all will be well. But you'll need to stay quiet while they're here."

Ma sat up straight and retorted, "William, if you think I'm afraid of the Devil's minions, you are sorely mistaken. If none of you have the backbone, I'll confront them myself and tell them of the power of the Lord." An expression of horror crossed my father's face. "They all suckle at the Whore of Babylon's bosom, every one of them. Let me greet them with word of the true Lord."

"No, no, Christiana, you'll bring harm to all of us!" he said.

"Nonsense. His mercy shields me. I'll be spared any harm." She threw back the bedcovers, placed her feet solidly on the floor, and fastened her long robe.

Pa gave me such an exasperated look. Ma was clearly not going to go peacefully to the attic. Stronger odors of burning wood and another power- ful and objectionable scent crept under the windows. Later we learned that the enemy had pitched living hogs on bonfires made of fence rails and posts at a neighboring farm. The sky had become murky with a low ceiling of gray. Where there should have been a glow of brightening dawn, there was none.

Tish peered out through the window. Suddenly she yelled, "Oh, my heav- ens, look at this! They must be at the Hogshead place now! Whatever will we do?" Orange fingers of flame clawed at the sky in front of us. It looked as though Hell had split open and was attempting to suck the town of Bethel in. Cries of desperate animals and gun blasts filled the air. There was no longer time to squander.

Before Ma could protest, Pa scooped her up into his arms. He cradled her for a moment against his chest as tears coursed down his cheeks. She hadn't realized that she wouldn't confront the soldiers at the door, and when the truth dawned, she twisted and writhed in his arms. "Now there, Christiana, be calm. This is for your own good, my Tina girl. Please be still. Please, please be still." He held her in a lover's embrace, trying to soothe her. Loosed from its daytime braid, her straight hair rippled in a gray stream down her back and framed her furious face, while her billowing, white cotton robe trailed down from his arms. "William, what are you doing? You're siding with Satan himself," she shrieked. I'd never seen her this bad off.

"You go downstairs, Tish, and watch for them. Call up and warn us when they're close," I said as I shoved my sister toward the door. I tore the bed sheets into thick strips. Now Ma sobbed, gasping for breath. Grabbing a handful of strips, I propped the attic door open as Pa wrestled her toward the stairs leading into the musty darkness above. He uttered tender, consoling words as she bellowed and frantically beat at his arms.

Ma's body was fixed in rage. We struggled to maneuver her across the attic floor toward the space over the back addition. Once there, she was so wearied by resistance that she crumpled into the high-backed armchair I had placed in the dimmest corner. Pa adjusted her in the seat. We were almost useless with weeping. I quickly grasped her wrists and bound them together as she pleaded, "No, no, Mary, how could you do this to your mother? Let me loose, let me loose. I pray you to free me."

"Ma, I beg your forgiveness." I paused to wipe my eyes. "Someday you'll understand that this was necessary to save all of us," I said as I quickly wound the sheeting around her waist and tied it to the chair. I secured her to its sturdy frame, but all the time worried that I might grievously squeeze her.

Tish's cry of alarm resounded in the front hall. "Pa, Mary—they're coming! I hear the horses!" Tish took the stairs two at a time and gasped in dismay when she saw our mother tied in the corner darkness. I dropped the extra strips of sheeting on the floor. Quivering from head to toe, I told her again, "If there's the first whiff of smoke in the house, grab Ma and run. Burning alive is more horrible than anything a Yankee might do." I then joined Pa at the front door.

Somewhere in the distance beyond the roiling smoke, a whistle pierced the air. Then, a company of about fifty indigo-clad cavalry soldiers charged into sight, with flaming torches of oil-soaked rags twisted on long stakes held high. They sang at the top of their lungs, "Mine eyes have seen the glory of the coming of the Lord, He is trampling out the vintage where the grapes of wrath are stored," as more lines of that dreadful song swelled closer. When they gained our lane, most cantered up the path to the barn. A man who appeared to be their leader and several others veered toward the house, dismounted, and secured their horses to the fence near the porch. Pa and I hastened into the yard, hoping to draw them away from the house. Flickering torches turned the Yankees nearing the big red bank barn into the stuff of nightmares. The farm animals were long ago claimed by the Confederate army, but Pa's farming implements—rakes, plows, and harrows—were stored inside, and he had bolted the large doors with a heavy iron padlock. Several soldiers strode toward the house.

"You there, old man," one spat at Pa. "Where are the keys to the barn padlock?"

Another demanded: "Give them to us or pay with your life!" He raised his rifle as if to take aim. Pa merely glowered at both of them.

Others were now on the porch, demanding whatever we had in the way of food. One had a patch that concealed his left eye, and they all looked ill fed and sickly. Their threadbare uniforms were stained with smoke, oil, blood and who knows what. Several of them were without footwear. Even if they were Yankees, I ached to think what it must have been like to charge in combat through fields of shattered corn stalks and knife-like branches, and then to hike on bloody feet for miles between battles.

"There is no key. It's lost," I shouted when I gathered my senses. Pa shot a fierce look to hush me up. The soldiers sped back to the barn door. One of them drew his pistol and blasted the lock apart. They then disappeared, shortly to re-emerge with the Pa's plow, harnesses, saddles, barrows, rakes, scythes, harrows, and wood troughs that they heaped on a bed of fence rails. Others collected dried cow patties and loose hay from the barnyard and added them as kindling, along with dry leaves and sticks. Torchbearers then spread out around the barn perimeter and, on signal, dipped their cracking torches into the pile.

Dampness from the previous night slowed the fire, but eventually small flames toasted the grasses and spread in a widening circle. More blazing torches were flung into the open barn doors, and soon an ungodly roar sucked at the air. The barn crackled like gunshot as flames devoured the dry floorboards and beams. Then, with a great thundering, the wings of the roof collapsed and left only a few skeletal outside beams standing. The sight rippled from earth to sky. Stunned, I idly wondered if sparks might leap to the house, and if we might lose it as well.

The officer and his men spun from the spectacle before them and rapidly approached the house, pounding up the porch steps. My heart lurched, and Pa and I followed quickly to keep up. They stomped into the library and pitched books from the shelves onto the floor, eyeing a copy now and then and thrusting an appealing one into a rucksack. The invaders cast cushions onto the floor, tore paintings from the walls, ripped curtains down, and upended chairs. Our refusals to meet demands for silver and valuables further aggravated them. The one with the eye patch ordered Pa and me to kneel on the floor in the library, while the others ransacked the downstairs. I could hear them travel from room to room, slamming drawers and cupboards. They exclaimed with pleasure when they found something to give a mother or sweetheart and swore when their search was in vain. One came back into the parlor chewing on the last candle that Ma put aside for an emergency.

"Missy, where are your potatoes and apples? I know you have something to eat in this house besides tallow wax. Something puts meat on those bones." He pinched my upper arm, and his rankness made me gag. Like some of the others, he had what appeared to be fresh blood on his shirt, and then I remembered the order to kill the animals. The Hogsheads managed to spare some of their hogs and sheep in the past by hiding them in a thicket of prickly bushes on a distant hill, but evidence that they'd been discovered discolored this man's clothes. Perhaps if I fessed up about the potatoes in the basement, they'd leave the upper floors unexplored. I held my breath, listening for oaths coming from the attic. Thank God, there were none.

All but the officer went below in the quest for fruit and vegetables put up in crocks and stored there for the winter. He headed toward the hall stairs. Footsteps soon passed from one room to another above our heads. His boots halted at the attic door, and the knob rasped. He ascended the last set of stairs and then rummaged about. My heart thudded so violently our captor would surely hear it. There was silence and then Tish's muffled voice, pleading most pitifully, although I could not make out distinct words. The man responded. There was still no utterance from Ma. Pa and I avoided looking at one another for fear of giving away our thoughts.

After what seemed an eternity, the officer clumped down from the attic and descended the main stairway. At the same time, men emerged from the cellar with knapsacks that bulged with all of this season's potatoes and the few apples that we had gathered. The officer grabbed the man by the collar. "Empty your sacks," the officer ordered, "and deposit everything that you've taken from this house here in the center of the hall. Leave it all behind now, or you'll pay later."

"What the hell?" one soldier demanded.

Another asked, "Have you lost your mind? We need this stuff."

"Do what I say. Now." the officer said and placed his hand on his revolver for emphasis.

There was much cursing as our provisions were spilled out on the floor. The officer wearily passed his hand over his eyes. "I don't know how much more of this I can stand," he said to no one in particular. If he wasn't a Yankee, I might have felt sorry for this man who had forgotten he was the enemy. He was attractive with his light brown, wavy hair and a tall, thin frame. But his weary, dispirited eyes revealed someone who had seen too much.

Pa and I hadn't recovered from our shock when the sharp sound of a whistle again split the air and the intruders departed. Hooves pounded the lane and then the road as they tore away in a mob, holding aloft torches newly ignited from our burning barn. We froze, straining to hear if the riders continued down the road past the mill, or if they would incinerate that too and destroy all hope. But the hoofbeats clattered into the far distance more and more faintly until they vanished altogether.

With an all's clear shout from Pa, Tish came down the stairs, guiding a mute and unbound Ma by the arm. She was subdued and seemed to understand the peril that had just passed. I asked Tish, "What in the world happened up there? That officer ordered his men to abandon everything they'd taken. It's a miracle."

Barely able to locate her voice, Tish softly said, "He was poking about the attic, I guess hoping to locate something under the floorboards or hidden in the eaves, when he spied Ma and me huddled back under the roof beams. When the Yankees raced up the lane, I was forced to gag her. There was just no other choice. I wound a piece of sheeting around her mouth. Oh, Mary, she didn't struggle. She just slumped against the bindings. It broke my heart." Tish paused to wipe away the tears, and I squeezed her hand in mine. She continued, "When the officer saw us crouched there in the half dark, he was speechless for a moment, staring. Imagine what a sight we must have seemed—a woman gagged and tightly bound in a chair with her daughter at her side! I was frightened witless, but I begged him to understand that Ma had gone mad with the war's hardships, and that her insanity might lead her to offend his men. I couldn't say anything but the truth. He told me not to be disquieted any longer. It was then that he descended and made his men return our goods." Tish plunked down onto the bottom step in relief and grief; her shoulders shook with raw sobs suppressed so long. Now I understood why the mill had been spared. The good officer knew we would starve without it and took pity on us again. Pa pulled Ma to him and held her tight, softly stroking her hair and begging her to forgive him.

Just then, the strong odor of wood smoke tugged me back to what was happening outside. Racing to the parlor window, I saw our Bethel neighbors charge up the farm lane, shovels and leather buckets swinging from their shoulders and hands. Mr. Beard and several men threw themselves into digging a ditch around the little flames lapping at the edge of the lawn. Heat from the barn was too intense for a person to stand in its proximity for very long. I tucked my skirts up and joined neighbors who relayed buckets of water from the stream and splashed it on the edges of the flames nearest the house. Men soaked neckerchiefs in the buckets before affixing them over their noses and mouths, and a torn strip of petticoat afforded me the same protection. We frantically worked, as we hacked and coughed to clear our chests. But before long, most of us were hampered by aching lungs and impaired vision. We were compelled to leave or go inside the house, where we clustered at the windows with dread. If rain had not fallen the previous night, we might have lost everything. As it was, the combination of the ditch and the dampness saved our home.

The barn ruins smoldered for days. Our hair and our skin stank of it. The acrid scent burrowed into the walls of the house and into the stuffed furniture and rugs. Charcoal-tinged drainage emitted from our lungs and nostrils for a week. Not one tool remained with which to turn the soil in the spring. Not even a rusty hoe to unearth a small kitchen plot.

Stories about the burning spread from neighbor to neighbor like the smoke. Local folks were abuzz about Old Tatternook and how, when the Yanks came by, he boldly pursued them through his barn doorway and put a curse on them.

Mr. Tatternook came to visit a few days later. "These are for your wife," he told Pa, as he extended a bundle of dried lemon balm and lavender bound by string. "Tell her to wear the leaves in a small, loosely woven sack around her neck. The aroma will calm her anxiety."

"You heard that she suffers from nerves? I'll make sure she makes use of these. Thank you. Come in, Mr. Tatternook, and tell us how you fared during the burning. We've heard stories," Pa said.

"I'll stay here by the door, thank you. You hold in your hand all that's left of my healing herbs. I saved a few dry bundles while the Yankees gathered tinder. I tried to warn them, but they wouldn't listen to a one-eyed old man. One even waved a revolver at me before incinerating my barn."

"Warned them of what?" Pa asked.

Tatternook said, "Their end was nigh. I told them to prepare themselves and their comrades to go in peace. The soldier spat and snarled, 'Get on your way, old bastard, or it's your own end that will be nigh.' At that point I gave up and left the barn and them to Fate."

He told Pa that he knew they'd be bushwhacked later that day between Bethel and Staunton, and not one life would be spared. Their shallow graves by the road would be disguised with leaves and brambles. Everyone in Bethel swears his story is true. But you never know. So much terrible has happened that truth and fiction no longer seem to have any particularities between them. I hope the kind officer was not among them.

28

IN THE SUMMER OF 1918, I FINALLY YIELDED TO TISH'S AND ELLEN'S entreaties to have a device called a telephone installed in the house. Ellen had witnessed the machine's remarkable benefits when she had stopped into the Bethel General Store to buy coffee beans. Mr. Jones, the proprietor, was speaking into his new telephone. People could now dial him up to inquire about produce in stock rather than arriving to find none. They'd even been placing orders for delivery. Ellen became convinced that such an invention was essential to our well-being as elderly people. If we had owned one when Mary was fading two years earlier, we could have summoned the doctor more quickly than my wild wagon journey through the night to fetch him and bring him back. Mary passed on from a tumor after declining for weeks while Ellen and Tish tenderly wiped her brow and read from the Bible. We muffled our voices and footsteps in the house so as not to disturb our patient, but the silence only made space for our grief to grow.

This bright summer afternoon, Tish and I gathered around to watch the telephone man in his gray striped uniform give the last turn of his screwdriver to the oak box on the kitchen wall. He inserted his finger in the hole of the black dial, spun it around once, and then held out the flower-shaped receiver with the wire dangling. "Put it to your ear and listen," he instructed me.

Amidst a snapping and crackling, I heard a faint voice. Someone was saying my name from a long distance away. "Hello, hello," I yelled into the receiver. More crackling, and then a faint but recognizable sound came through.

"Tom, is that you?" it said. For a minute, I heard Mary's voice.

"Mary? Mary, can that be you?" I cried incredulously, my heart racing.

Tish gently placed her hand on my arm. "It's the operator, Tom. I think it's Mabel Goodall from Bethel. I heard she's working for the telephone company."

Something similar happened when Phoebe returned to the house this past weekend. She has recently been reading books that Ma and Ellen would have burned with the fall leaves in the yard. They are old tooled-leather texts with titles like *Through the Darkness* and *Book of Spirit Communication*. A lopsided stack of them rests on the floor in the library, topped by a newer volume with a paper book jacket, *Intuitive Studies*. Phoebe lights a candle, reads pages from one book, then puts it aside on the sofa while she adjusts her posture to imitate Dr. Liebowitz's. Her feet are flat on the floor, her hands are on her knees, and her eyes are closed. Her breathing slows. An air of calm pervades the library. I've watched her do this numerous times for as long as an hour, not moving and totally silent. But today is different.

For the first time, I hear her voice without her lips moving. It sounds far away, like the first time I heard the operator's voice on the telephone. Her words come as though they travel across a long wire, and they speak directly to my heart. They are faint and reedy, and sometimes drift off and fade to nothing.

"Tom?" she repeats. "Tom, are you here?"

I reply, "Yes, yes! I'm here!" But she asks again. "I'm here!" I yell, and her startled expression tells me that she hears me. Can this really be happening? Phoebe looks as surprised as I feel. After so many years of trying to make myself heard, first to Ellen, then Cora, and finally to this couple, I can't believe it. But there she is. She has regained her composure and waits silently with her eyes closed, while the dog Emma has stealthily climbed upon the sofa, a spot normally forbidden to her. The dog cuts her eyes at me, sighs, and drops her head onto her paws. Soon she falls under the room's tranquil spell and is snoring.

Do I finally follow old Tatternook's advice to confess my secrets, or do I allow them to drag me closer to the inferno? Family and friends who might have judged me are long dead. And after reading Mary's journal, I've learned that my family had secrets of their own. We bound our shame tight to our chests and cloaked ourselves in lonely guilt for the rest of our lives. What if I tell this woman everything? I no longer have anything to lose. I've faded to something moldy and unrecognizable, and the tale spews upward, erupts like vomit, out of my control. Let it be.

After only two months in prison camp, bone-deep weariness and poor health marked us as old beyond our years—skin and clothing hanging from skeletal, filthy, vermin-infested bodies—many prisoners with angry red scars and disfigured bodies. Some rarely left their berths, preferring solitude to the company of men in the pen. When forced to go out, they sank motionless against the walls and stared off vacantly. Many hunched forward on the wooden bed ledges, heads cradled in their hands. They seemed to have lost all interest in living. John Bibb became one of these low souls. After a few weeks of good companionship, joining in our jests, he gradually withered into himself and never smiled.

His innocence had drawn me to him, but that's also what made him more vulnerable to the viciousness of our last battle and the harshness of our daily prison life. "You're like a hibernating bear. Come on out in the yard and aggravate the guards," I teased him one morning, giving his arm a playful tug. He muttered something unintelligible and looked at the stained floor.

"I mean it. You'd feel better if you'd get out in the sun and work your legs a bit," I said.

He finally looked at me. "What's the point of it? Just to have the strength to face another godforsaken, miserable day? Perhaps we'll be released soon, but I don't believe it. No one has any idea how long this hopeless war will go on. And then, what?"

"You'll go home, that's what. Isn't that what we all long for? Sooner or later, we'll all go home," I said.

"Sure, I'll go home. I'll return to Charlottesville to manage my father's general store. Every day, I'll look across the counter at men and women who have no idea of the hell we've seen. And I'll resent them for it. I'm not fit for any life."

"What about Margaret Ellen?"

"I'd have nothing to say to her. We'd live on different planets, and it would never work out." He turned his head away and made no movement to follow me into the yard.

There was nothing more I could say, and his lack of interest in living concerned me deeply. I reluctantly left him sitting on the sleeping shelf and stepped out into the bright heat of the pen.

I understood what worried Bibb. All of us boys secretly feared what our return might bring. As much as I longed for home, my protruding ribs, hollowed cheeks, and unsettled mind were so disturbing that I wasn't sure my family would accept what I'd become. Folks would want to hear stories of heroic deeds, not the turmoil going on inside my head. Even I tried to ignore it. On the other hand, Jim Blue declared that if exchanged, he would seek what was left of the 5th Virginia Infantry and fight Grant with all of his strength until he'd driven Yankees from the Confederacy forever or died, whichever came first. I'd have expected Zeke to join Blue in this sentiment, but Zeke rarely joined our regular conversation now. Instead, he slumped back on his bunk, his head against the wall. He and John Bibb frequently spoke quietly together.

John Bibb's days became exhausted escapes from nightmares. Almost every night, he snarled and screamed at invisible enemies, his arms thrashing violently. I'd reach across the aisle, shake his shoulder, and call his name until he woke up and gasped a response.

He wasn't alone in his terrors. The barrack nightly echoed the frightened shrieks of boys soaked with sweat. The pen also had its walkers—men so anxious that peace was possible only through constant movement. With heads lowered, they shuffled incessantly around and around the inside perimeter of the pen. That purposeless action was preferable to idleness that encouraged the shrieking voices in their heads.

One morning at breakfast, Bibb pushed his gristly chunk of beef across the boards toward me. "I'm done with eating this stuff. It makes me gag."

"No question it's awful, but you need to swallow it for strength," I said pushing it back toward him.

"I can't do it. What's the difference between this meat and dead soldiers' bodies on the Spotsylvania battlefield? None, as I see it. From the first time I saw horses and men with their innards spread out on the grass and the buzzards working away on it, all meat seemed the same."

We had all witnessed too many pounds of animal and human bodies sliced, split, and blasted into chunks of red muscle, creamy-yellow fat, shiny sinew, and marrow-spilling pearly bone—no longer with names or recognizable features—scattered randomly across hills and fields. I too was haunted by the dehumanizing effect of a field after combat. But I wasn't going to give up eating the measly bits of meat in the prison; I'd starve if I did.

"Don't dwell on it, John. It does you no good," I gently said. But he looked away and ignored my words. He continued to wonder aloud if we are no different from the animals we tear with our teeth. I wished he would stop.

Jim Blue tried to counter. "The Bible says man's meant to eat animals. Don't you remember all those fatted calves and sacrificed goats? Men have souls; animals don't."

Bibb glared at him. "So where is this purported human soul? I saw a lot of men utter their last breaths, but nary a one had anything like a soul fluttering from his breast." There was no point in arguing with him.

Meals were twice a day—breakfast and dinner—and sorry excuses for meals they were. When John Bibb stopped eating meat, he limited himself at breakfast to a one by three-inch piece of dry yellow cornbread, while the rest of us also ate the small chunk of greasy beef or bacon accompanying it. Dinner was not any better at sticking to the ribs—cornbread again, served with a meager chunk of rancid, flyspecked beef and a half a cup of "soup"—something so mean I could barely swallow it. The cooks claimed it was rice soup, but it was a thin, flavorless liquid containing hair, grit, a few rice hulls, an occasional piece of rice or corn, and dozens of half-inch rice worms. I could swear there were nail clippings in there too. Perhaps the worms were the source of John Bibb's protein.

Zeke cracked a joke about those worms. "Boys, don't worry about the squiggles swimming around in your gut," he said. A huge grin spread across his face. "They won't last for long."

"What the devil are you talking about, Zeke?" Beards asked.

"If there's too little liquid in your stomach to drown 'em, they'll still die."

Beards played along, "Why's that?"

"From starvation." We laughed doubly hard to hear Zeke quip again. It was so rare that his spirits were high.

More and more Bibb resembled the emaciated prisoners who had been confined to the island longest. I worried he might just fade away. But I also had noticed that some prisoners had more flesh than we did. Sergeant Sorrell and his mates were in this group. They would surround weakened fellows as they walked from the dining hall and threaten to beat them if they didn't hand over their rations. The guards looked the other way and then disciplined those who complained. Sorrell's fellows were the sort who plundered the bodies of their own fallen comrades for any coin or jewelry. But many of the healthier looking boys weren't of this immoral nature. So, how did they get by? If I found out, perhaps I might find something Bibb would eat. I asked Frank.

"It all depends on whether you're lucky enough to have a relative or friend in the North. If you do, mail is allowed from them, even mail with money. And money will get you bread, citrus, and even paper, pens, and pots and pans from the sutler's stall. That's why some boys are healthier than others," he said. "I wish I knew someone up North." He scuffed the dirt with his foot.

"Ah, that explains it. The guards took every single cent I had. This sutler business seems uncharacteristically generous of them."

"It's only because they take a cut of the sales," he said.

This suddenly gave me an idea. I remembered that in the summer of '61, Pa had expected a visit from his uncle Grier Ralston from Norristown, Pennsylvania. The uncle had planned to hunt for Indian artifacts, his hobby, but then the war intervened. I'd never met him, but there was nothing to be lost in letting him know where I was. I begged a scrap of paper from another boy, who had already found success with a Northern friend. If Grier Ralston responded, I'd then ask for money in the next letter. Every morning I waited fruitlessly at mail call. Finally, after two weeks, a letter from Norristown arrived. Hands trembling, I ripped open the envelope.

My great uncle addressed me as "Dear Enemy." He said he was disappointed that any of his kin had taken up arms against the government, and he assumed that my service in the Rebel army wasn't voluntary. But then he offered to help in any way the prison would allow. He said he prayed for the time when he could sign the letter "Your Friend." I could hardly believe my eyes. A rush of warmth toward this stranger filled my chest. This was far more than I had hoped for. Did the offer of help include sending a little money to buy food? He had not only answered my letter, but behind the talk of enemies, he acknowledged me as a family member by saying he trusted Ma and Pa were well. That afternoon I begged another scrap of paper, this time promising to pay the boy back, and wrote to ask if Uncle Grier would send coins to buy food.

He sent five dollars in gold pieces. Able to purchase a tin drinking cup, fresh bread, and lemons, I squeezed the fruit into a tart juice potion

I shared with John Bibb, along with slices of the bread. Perhaps I could keep scurvy away from both of us, and the sour taste was sharp enough to disguise the rankness of the water. With each sip and bite, I sent a silent thanks floating toward Grier Ralston in Norristown.

Another chance to avert starvation came unexpectedly from Beards, who hadn't lost his camp habit of roaming from group to group picking up news. "You boys better come see this. Come quick. You won't regret it." He ran ahead, as he guided Jim Blue and me toward a gathering of his new friends. They milled about a steaming kettle balanced on burning scraps of wood salvaged from a discarded packing box. A few others crowded over to the side above a hole in the ground, long scraps of wood readied in their hands. A scrawny fellow with a rag around his head said, "Alright, Amos, wait until I give the signal. Then dump your boiling water in this hole over here." Blue rolled his eyes at me. We had no idea what they were doing. The fellow said, "Not too fast, now. Don't get ahead of yourself. Wait for my go-ahead." He spoke urgently to a man with a metal bucket positioned a few yards away at a second hole. "Now get in position and be ready." He shifted the stick from his left to right hand. "Now go!" He raised the stick over his head and waited.

The fellow called Amos sloshed the container of scalding water into the farthest hole. Two sleek water rats exploded out of the one near us, and the club swept down for a kill. The rats were about the size of a grown rabbit. One of the fellows scrambled to grab up the furry bodies and passed them to a man with a penknife. Before you could blink, they were beheaded, skinned, and tossed into the kettle. Jim Blue and I were disgusted, but Amos smacked his lips and said, "You boys just wait until you taste these rascals. A little spice from the sutler's and a good boiling—they're as fine as any chicken or squirrel at home." He rubbed his hands together.

"I don't know about eating rat," Jim Blue said. "I haven't fallen to such a low place that you'd catch me eating one of those nasty critters."

But Amos chided him, "You eat plenty of hog at home, and a water rat sure's cleaner than a hog. Give it a try." It was white meat, and it didn't have an offensive gamey odor. I gave in and tasted the "fresh rat soup." He was right. It was fresher and tenderer meat than we were served in the dining hall, but I couldn't eat it unless we hadn't seen beef for a week, which happened more and more frequently as the fall turned to winter.

29

SHORTLY AFTER SUNRISE ONE MORNING, THERE WAS MORE THAN THE usual ruckus outside the barracks. When I groggily shoved my way to the window between other gawkers, I saw lines of prison guards with haversacks hoisted on their shoulders. On command, they noisily filed through the prison gates and boarded boats tied at the dock. Some boys had heard that our keepers were being sent back to combat. Zeke and Beards called after them, "Good riddance, you bastards." And "Get ready to meet your maker. You won't have a beggar's chance against our Rebs." The minute they were out of sight, a new crew of rowdy, blue-coated boys marched into our midst. We solemnly watched them cross the pen, puzzled that some spoke English mixed up with an unrecognizable language. They seemed awkward with their shining new weapons, and it made me nervous. Within a few minutes, Ahl marched the entire crew to Schoepf's chambers.

Curious about these strangers, Zeke and I loitered in the yard until they finally appeared above us on the pen. We leaned against the wall below, where we could eavesdrop. After detecting the words "*Ach, ein, das,* and *nicht*," Zeke decided they must be recent German immigrants. He'd encountered German Mennonites at the Waynesboro market at home and recognized the accent. By straining to decipher their conversation, we learned they were fresh recruits to the Ohio National Guard. They knew nothing about soldering except for Schoepf's explanation of Special Order Number 157. There hadn't been time to memorize the basic training manual on the train ride from Ohio to the Delaware.

The next day, I was hiding from the sun's rays in a wedge of shade by the barrack wall. Someone bellowed, "Hey, you lousy dummkopf, are you too good to stand out in the yard with the rest of the vermin?" I furtively looked around to spot the pathetic butt of this invective. Turns out it was me. A new recruit stood above on the wall with his rifle pointed at my chest. Ahl stood next to him, sporting a malevolent sneer. Muttering "son of a bitch" at him below my breath, I lost no time moving into the pen's scalding heat.

Late one night toward the end of August, I woke up to gunshots and a wild commotion in the captive officers' pen next door. You could hear the ruckus over the violent evening storm that ripped at the corners of the fort and drove the rain horizontally. Waves threatened to breach the levees, and claps of thunder echoed across the empty yard. I gave up on trying to make out words and eventually went back to sleep. In the morning, the sutler, who had access to both officers' and enlisted men's pens, told us what he'd learned.

Just over the pen wall, E. Pope Jones, a wounded officer with a virulent foot, had headed for the sinks on his crutches. He met a friend who steadied him with a hand to his back as they made their way on the long, wooden walkway in the storm. At that moment, Ahl, who was patrolling the top of the pens, saw them. He then asked one of the new guards, a young private named Wilheim Douglass, if he knew he was under orders to shoot any prisoner who doesn't respond to a command to move double quick along the sink plankway.

"Ja, your orders are perfectly clear. No cause to worry here, sir."

Satisfied with the pimple-faced novice's earnest response, Ahl, strolled away toward the next new guard.

Shortly after, prisoners on both sides of the pen wall heard Douglass yelling like a madman from the top. Most of his words were muffled by the storm, but some witnesses heard him scream, "Move along, you—double quick! Double quick I say! Now trot, you dummkopf!" His flailing arms made it clear he'd worked himself into a blind fury. "*Gott verdammt*, I'm going to shoot one of these Rebels before midnight!" he yelled.

About that time, Colonel Jones finished his business. Leaving the privy, he met some fellows on the path who started a conversation, huddled together with their heads down and backs to the rain. Private Douglass began to rant, "Break it up, move on, double quick! Move on!"

Jones lagged behind, struggling to stay upright on his crutches on the slippery boards. Douglass adjusted the large lantern that illuminated the sinks at night, and there the crippled man was, caught like a moth in a circle of lamplight. Douglass took aim and bellowed at the top of his lungs, "Double quick, double quick! Damn you, run! Run!"

Some said Jones was partially deaf from the roar of cannons and didn't hear the order. Others said he called back, "Sentry, have some mercy. I'm lame. I'm going as fast as I can." Whichever is true, Douglass fired his rifle, and the force of the bullet blasted through Jones's chest, lifting him from the bridge. He splashed into the black water and his crutches bobbed on the waves in the darkness. Several men leaped from the privy platform and dragged him from the river. He died the next day in the hospital.

Private Douglass got a promotion and a glossy blue and gold chevron stitched onto the serge of his uniform sleeve for faithfully following Ahl's instructions. Now a clear message had been sent to the new guards that the quickest way to advance was to shoot one of us.

The day after the shooting, gut problems got me down too. I stayed away from the dining hall, certain that rotten grub was the cause. But Jim Blue returned from breakfast sputtering. "Have you seen the new order nailed to the cookhouse wall?"

I groaned from my place on the shelf. "Tell me quick, and then leave me be." I rolled over with my back to the others.

"It says that any order from a guard must be obeyed, never mind how unimportant. You have to obey. Otherwise, there will be unfortunate consequences," he reported. "That means they can shoot us for no cause at all, just like they did to Jones. No cause at all, goddamn it."

Beards shook his head. "The odds are stacked against us, no matter what. Half the time, I can't even understand these new guards with their thick accents. We'll be shot because we don't know what the hell they're saying."

This new order was the last straw. Some prayed for an end to the conflict. But I came up with a plan while lying there on the shelf with cramps in my belly. With the remaining few chits from my uncle's gift clutched in my fist, I hobbled the distance from the barrack to the sutler's stand. I bought one page of paper and an envelope. Once back to the relative comfort of the shelf, I wrote an anonymous account of the abuses at the prison and directed it to the Union commander of prisons in Washington, DC. Surely this official wouldn't approve of Schoepf's new rules. Prohibiting pissing next to the barracks was one thing, but I was convinced that killing a man for doing it or for ignoring a simple command was more than even Union officers could stomach. This cruelty had to stop. I addressed the envelope to Uncle Grier in Philadelphia and inserted a scrap asking him to forward my note to the authorities. Grasping my sides, I made the painful trip to the postal box in the wall. If there was a chance my relative would take pity on us and grant my request, it seemed worth the risk.

Ahl singled me out at the next roll call. He eyes traveled ominously up and down my body before announcing, "Well, boys, turns out we have a sniveling tattler in our midst." My breath caught in my throat.

"And who can it be?" He paused and a sinister smirk twitched at his lips. I watched in horror as he raised his arm and jabbed his hairy finger in my direction. Sarcasm oozed from his words. "It's none other than this goddam fool Smiley standing before me. A sissy pants who runs to his uncle with false stories of abuse. Poor boy."

He abruptly motioned for one of the guards to seize me. The bottom dropped out of my stomach and my bladder let loose. A burly guard seized my left arm and wrenched it behind my back. His body odor was over-powering as he shoved me toward the ladder. I hoped he couldn't smell my stink. With his arm across my chest, he dragged me rung by rung to the top of the pen. Pain rippled from my twisted wrist to my shoulder. Once he had me on top of the wall, Ahl struck me hard on the shoulder with the stout club he wore in his belt. "Well, Smiley, you thought you could get your little note by the censors, didn't you? No such luck, my boy." He struck me again, this time harder. I would have crumpled to my knees if the guard hadn't squeezed me tightly. "You'll enjoy the next four days in solitary with water as your only fare. See if you try the same trick again. Next time, you'll join Lieutenant Jones." He glowed with satisfaction as iron shackles clanged shut around my ankles. "You'll be across the river eaten by lime in a mass grave. No one gets anything by me. And none of you better try," he said to the group of prisoners standing below him.

Two soldiers grabbed me under the armpits and hoisted me down the ladder, my head and heels thwacking against the wooden crossbars. They dragged me across the yard to a small plank shed, my body carving a wob-bly track in the dust. When the guards slid back the massive iron bar and thrust the door open, a urine and defecation fog ballooned into the open air. There was not an inch on the floor without filth, and a reeking pot overflowed in the center. Vomit surged in my throat.

As I squatted in a narrow spot against the windowless wall, scenes of revenge played out in my head until they finally wore me out. Loathing for Ahl and his new guards had consumed me for hours and then turned to humiliation for not suspecting I'd be caught. After all, Frank had warned me about Ahl's censors. When the sun went down, a guard shoved a cup of murky water through the slot window for my "supper." In the dark-ness, I recalled the bodies I'd seen dragged out of this shed. Ahl probably expected I wouldn't survive this extra assault on my body, just as so many other weakened boys hadn't. But I wouldn't give him that satisfaction. I'd get home to Virginia alive, by damn. For four days, I clung to an image of the farm's emerald hills and fields in early spring, reaching deep for it whenever the picture slipped. The pungent walls of the plank shed evaporated, and the calls of tree frogs and the yellow flicker filled the void. I strolled through the oak and cedar trees, reliving each footfall, hearing the leaves rustle and the twigs snap on the ground as my boots kicked through them high on the hilltop above the farmhouse. Over and over, I retraced those steps, imagining the dome of blue sky over it all and the occasional glide of a red-tailed hawk.

At last, when the door creaked open to let in blinding light and sweet air, one guard stood at the entrance. "On your feet, Smiley. Your time in here is up." As much as I wanted to stride out in defiance, I failed miserably. My knees wouldn't work when I tried to stand. They'd been bent for too long. As the guard roughly jerked me to my feet, through bleary eyes I saw Bibb and Beards peering in at the doorway. "If you ain't coming out, I'm not staying in here with you," the guard said and shoved them aside as he tore past.

Bibb's eyes widened as they adjusted to the dark. "My God, Tom! This reeks! How did you stand it for four days?" He cupped his hand over his nose and looked down at the slime on the floor.

"Cut the comments and let's get him out of here. He can't do it on his own," Beards said as he raised my left arm over his shoulder and began to lift me. "Get on the other side." Bibb dropped his hand and quickly came to my aid. My two friends supported my weight all the way as I lurched to the barrack on board-stiff, throbbing legs.

30

INMATES HAD DROPPED ALL HABITS OF SOLDIERING WITH THE EXCEPTION of marching around the pen during the guard-ordered drills. Half-baked imitations of leisure activities at home brought more comfort. Frank Armstrong and a number of fellows from his company organized relay races against men in our division, or at least those with two fit legs. After morning drill on cooler mornings, the boys formed one long line parallel to a line of fellows from the other division and passed off a button, competing to see which division had the swiftest runners. Even a week after my time in isolation, my gait wasn't back to normal. I could only watch, but at my best, I had never been as fast as a Fishersville man in our division who regularly won.

In August, my great uncle in Philadelphia had mailed a copy of Milton's *Paradise Lost,* which passed muster with the prison censors, along with another precious five-dollar gold coin and his usual brief note regretting my choices. I bought more lemons and bread to share with John Bibb but had no use for the book. From the little I knew, it seemed a wildly embroidered version of the Old Testament's account of man's fall from grace. In my home, there was already too much discussion and reading of the Old Testament. The book made a loud thud as I pitched it to the rear of our sleeping shelf and gave it no more thought. I spent most of the scorching days leaning against the pen wall next to Bibb, limp from the heat but comforted by his presence.

In early September, Schoepf decided that allowing men access to the sutler's goods made him appear too soft. Once again, this was Ahl's doing, I was certain. He had found another way to torture us by playing on

Schoepf's insecurities. The sutler was banned and didn't return for three months—not until too many men died from scurvy and starvation.

When the prison's meat supply spoiled, we were forced to eat John Bibb's diet, for which he teased and fretted us. Breakfast was nothing but crumbling cornbread, and at supper there was more cornbread and a cup of paltry soup. When we grumbled, Zeke reminded us, "What are you whining about? The meat for the past two weeks was crawling with worms, and you had to hold your nose to eat it!" Zeke, with his usual irony, also described our drinking water as "a turgid, salty, jellied mass of waggle tails. It's got dead fish, leaves, worms, and other putrescence that show up in my cup and then get cast out by my gut."

One day in late September when the days had cooled slightly, Frank Armstrong joined me at the wall's edge where I watched boys play catch with a bound rag. He whistled for a few minutes, glancing warily around with his hands crammed in his pockets. When it seemed safe, he leaned toward my ear and said in a low voice, "Zeke and I are scheming to get out of here. We've got some other boys you know on board too. Why don't you join us?"

I kept my gaze forward, but my jaw dropped. "Have you lost your minds? You'll never get past these idiots with rifles."

"Come on now. It isn't such a bad idea. Last year, two hundred escaped by slipping into the river one night. We're talking about only a handful this time."

Zeke leaned on the wall in the shade several feet away and overheard a few words of our conversation. He moved closer. "Come on, Tom. This is a solid chance. Frankly, I'll go mad if I'm here for another month. I'd risk everything to get out, and this plan is as good as any. "

"And what is this plan?" I asked.

Zeke ignored my skeptical tone. "The guards go on leave just before next week's waning moon and will be back when visibility is poorest, loaded down with bottles of fresh liquor. We're waiting until then. Frank has already loosened a board on the division's back wall, just where the canal emerges from the barracks. We'll use the building as cover to gain the river gates."

"Even with no moonlight, the guards will notice," I said.

"Not a chance. You saw how much liquor they hauled back from their last leave ashore. Once they start sousing it up at night, they're oblivious." Frank explained how the conspirators were trading pans, penknives, and other sutler goods for federally issued canteens. They would become floatation devices, attached by ropes around their waists. Quite a few boys had agreed to sacrifice theirs to help their bolder friends. But the owners were hanging on to them until the chosen night so suspicions wouldn't be aroused by any one man having too many.

"I could get you some, easy," Zeke said.

Because I only knew the shallow creek below the house, I was ignorant about swimming. "No thanks, Zeke. I'll take my chances here. But I wish you fellows the best of luck." Zeke and Frank exchanged disappointed glances and then strolled away.

Our bunk gang impatiently watched for the waning harvest moon. When the guards returned from furlough with bottles clinking in their haversacks, the group gathered that night in our barrack. We wordlessly watched Zeke while he tied his canteens around his torso. He was lucky to have found some unclaimed rope in the pen and had hidden a coil under a floorboard. Usually hoarded to prevent pants from drifting below shrunken waistlines, it was now cut with the whittling knife and divided among the twelve "swimmers."

"We'll send you poor wretches leftovers of the delicious vittles we'll be eating every day. What shall it be? Cake? Roast pork? Apple pie?" Zeke joked. Frank added, "Or maybe we'll write you a line or two saying how many times we've been kissed by our sweethearts—if we have energy left over for the task." There was much guffawing and pounding fellows roughly on the shoulder.

I threw my arm around Zeke, feeling his shoulders' broad sharpness and the rough texture of his worn shirt. I wondered if I might ever see him again. During the past three years, his wry humor and quirky perspective on the world had meant a lot. He always made me see the hidden side of things that were, in fact, the most important. I'd miss him mightily. But I wouldn't begrudge anyone a chance to get out of that place. John Bibb couldn't conceal his sorrow. He'd known Zeke for only a brief time, but Zeke had understood him when he was most downhearted. "I'll be thinking about you, hoping you are living on the high side," Bibb told him. "Maybe someday, when this madness is over, we'll meet again." Zeke looked away without speaking.

Frank and his fellow escapees slipped through the loose board and eased into the canal. The night swallowed them, and we returned to our sleeping boards, each of us vaguely regretting our decision to stay. Blue and Beards were alert on their backs as rigidly as I was, dreading any sound of trouble. After about ten minutes, a cry erupted from the river, followed by a guard's shouts of, "Escape! Prisoners are escaping!" I held my breath as boots thudded in the direction of the water, and rifle blasts sliced the air. One guard screamed, "They got no weapons—shoot to kill!" After a few minutes, all fell quiet.

"Holy Lord God," Beards said. We strained to hear what might come next. But there was nothing.

"Maybe they got away. Maybe that's what the silence means," I said, rising up on my elbows.

But then footsteps sounded near the barrack, and a guard gloated, "By hounds' teeth, I finally got to shoot at the dummkopfs! I hope I sank at least one." My blood boiled. I fervently prayed that liquor had destroyed his aim.

I heard Bibb whisper after a while. "Do you think they made it? I can't sleep for worrying about Zeke."

"Sure they did. That Zeke is strong as a horse," I assured him. "He can handle anything." Then I lay awake, counting the hours to dawn.

Racing to the sinks at sunrise, I spied a body face down in the murky shallows of the beach. Its arms and legs loosely bobbed to their own secret tune in the tide's flow. Three guards had also spotted the floater, and they waded into the foaming brown water. They grasped the corpse by the collar and seat of its pants and tugged it, face down and dripping, to shore. When they pitched the body up on the mud, I could hardly breathe, fearing the worst. They flipped over the limp form, now gray-faced and bloated but still identifiable. It was Zeke. I gasped, and my legs gave out from under me. Then, through my own darkness I watched the wheelbarrow man collect Zeke's body. I couldn't imagine how I'd break the news to Bibb and the others.

Days later the rumor spread that someone at the sinks had heard a man cry out in the water. The waves surged over Zeke's head before the guards' bullets could find their mark. He must have gotten a crippling cramp.

The weather was chilly by early October and provided a foretaste of winter in our drafty, oversized shack. Many of us were captured in the late spring and early summer after the last prison distribution of socks and underwear had been made. Most had no coats, other cold-weather clothes, or boots. We had only what we wore when we were taken, and was so threadbare now that it offered only modest cover in warmer months.

By November, we shivered all day in bed, shrouded in thin prison blankets. Or we hovered near the wood stove in the center of the division aisle. Boys formed double and triple lines to take their turn standing near the heat for a few minutes, then would move so that another could take his place. The rotation would go on until we wearied of standing and crawled back to our shelves to cocoon under thin, scratchy cover. When the barracks emptied for trips to the dining hall, we were an exodus of army-issue bats, blankets pulled around our heads and flapping at our sides as we trudged across the yard to the dining barrack.

One chilly morning, an idea about how to help John Bibb surfaced in my head. He now was thin as a reed. When there was meat in the dining hall or good rat hunting, I gave him my morning and evening cornbread, but it wasn't enough to put flesh on his bones. His spirit was diminishing as quickly as his body. Intent on keeping my mind active and thinking it might distract him from morbid musings, I suggested that we memorize *Paradise Lost*. The book was still where I'd thrown it at the back of my bunk. If the poem was merely a form of mental exercise, I might overcome my disdain for it. I didn't anticipate how seductive the tales would become.

Every day after drill and breakfast, when light was brightest in the barrack, John and I took turns reading aloud a verse, and then we'd see how many words we could remember, reciting lines until they were firmly fixed in mind. Gradually, the others, wound in their blankets, huddled around on the tiers to listen. Jim Blue, Beards, and the boys in nearby bunks became regular spectators, memorized the lines too, and then called out the correct phrase when John Bibb or I faltered. The exercise became a competition. Boys took sides, betting shirt buttons on which of the two of us could recite the most lines without a slip. Cheering erupted whenever one of us was able to recount first a line and then an entire verse flawlessly. There was plenty of material to keep us occupied—the longest was Book IV with 1,189 lines! These were first-rate stories. When John and I recited Book I, which describes Satan's legions of fallen angel warriors and the horrors of the Hell world where God banished them, listeners were spellbound. The two of us spent a week repeating the monstrous descriptions all day and chiseled the words in our brains until we could declaim them without consulting the text.

The first section told of a monumental three-day war between good and evil. All had been perfect between God and His favorite archangel, with whom He shared the benefits of His power. But then He created a Son. Jealous, the archangel vowed to overthrow the kingdom and duped a multitude of angels into waging a violent rebellion. Some fellows joked that it reminded them of the battle at Spotsylvania Courthouse. In the story, both sides abandoned weapons and wrenched vast mountaintops out of the ground and hurled entire forests—as well as streams and giant boulders—at the enemy, flattening them beneath otherworldly weight.

Witnessing Heaven perilously close to annihilation, God charged His Son with dominion over the realm. The Son righted the mountains and steered His chariot over the enemy, crushing their skulls beneath. He then pitched their shattered bodies through Heaven's crystal gates into the eternal void of Hell.

At this point, Bibb addressed the group. "Don't you fellows see how the men who got us into this are like Milton's Satan? And aren't we like his deceived angels? How could secession be worth the cost? We've thumbed our noses at the federal government, a force mighty as God."

"Oh, for Chrissake, John, spare us the sermon," one fellow said.

"But can't you see? Union troops have stolen, burned, chopped, and trampled their way across our homeland. Worse than anything in this tale. And the Confederacy hasn't a chance in hell of stopping this business we began."

"Come on, Bibb. It isn't as bad as you make it to be. Let's get on with the game," another said.

"You'll see," Bibb said. "We Southerners will pay the whole price. After this conflict is settled, we'll be the ones with broken lives and ruined landscapes. Not the Yankees. And for what gain to us?" He looked at me for a response and then glanced around the room, but no one wanted to answer him. In my heart, I heard the whisper of a more important question, "And at what cost to our souls?" I couldn't give voice to the dark thought that constantly tormented me: Why so much death and destruction to preserve an evil? Was there any good reason? I hadn't found one.

Each day, the listeners multiplied, crowded into the bunk shelves and squatted on the floor until no one could budge. When Satan's serpent lured Eve into feasting from the Tree of Knowledge, the crowd loudly hissed and booed. Milton had painted her as an adoring and compliant companion to Adam, sensual and loving in every way. Eve was such a glorious creature that Adam couldn't tear his eyes away. The poem's Eve set many to recalling and longing for a soft female hand on the arm, a head gently leaned into a shoulder or chest. We too would have been lured to take a bite of the apple and wouldn't have given a second thought to breaking God's rule. We understood why Adam couldn't deny the stirring in his loins.

Memorization of *Paradise Lost* was finished in early December. I had etched every word in my mind, without a single lapse of recall. As the story wound down, more than the everlasting fate of a flawed mankind saddened the barrack. What would we do now that the weather was too frigid to stir beyond our bunks? There was still singing at night, but less of it now. Sometimes a lone voice would croon "Aura Lee" into the dark, and then one man after another would take up the lyrics, as we bunched together for warmth. But many fellows by this time were too down at heart to pay any mind. Singing sparked feelings of longing for home that ambushed me with their intensity, so I refrained from joining in.

31

IT WAS IN LATE NOVEMBER WHEN TEMPERATURES PLUMMETED BELOW freezing and held there for weeks. The Delaware River crackled with ice, and brittle wind blasted across the frozen surface every day. Frozen waste at the sinks and in the canals mounded in piles with no movement of water to dislodge it.

Schoepf requisitioned more guards. When we had arrived, the prison held four times the number of men it had been constructed to house. Thousands continued to pour in. The inexperienced Germans from Ohio finally had been joined by veterans from a Massachusetts company. In this group was a Union guard named Israel Adams. After his brutal cudgel beatings of several prisoners for reasons that no one could fathom, Ahl found merit in the man. He became convinced that Adams, with his hair-trigger temper and profound disdain for his charges, would instill discipline in the younger, softer-hearted guards. He might even serve as a role model. In a matter of days, this stocky, puffy-faced man was promoted to sergeant of the guards. His florid complexion betrayed his fondness for alcohol, even in the daytime, and slurred speech and unsteadiness on his feet warned us to stay out of his way. It didn't take him long to figure out how to curry favor with Schoepf. He made a show of keeping the barracks sanitary—whitewashing and scrubbing obsessively. Snarling, he would cry, "Hike out, hike out, you damned Rebel sons a' bitches!" He quickly earned the name Old Hike.

Shortly after breakfast on the seventeenth of December, with the divisions assembled below, Old Hike stood atop the pen wall next to Ahl, arms folded across his blue-clad chest. "The United States Army has taken pity on you sons a' bitches, and they've provided overcoats and woolen clothing. Strip down to your shirts and hand off your old pants and other clothes to the guards passing among you. Do it on the double quick." He turned toward Ahl and grinned. Ahl offered a mock salute with his cane.

When all prisoners were half naked before him, he bellowed, "Right face, face forward, double quick hike!" Beards, Jim Blue, John Bibb, and I looked at one another in astonishment, then total dismay, as we were marched back through the freezing, slushy mud into the barracks. It was a bitter day, and we had no warm clothing to begin with, much less any extras. By this time, we prisoners were so demoralized that no one challenged Old Hike's order. Tears trickled down the cheeks of some. Our dejected mass gripped blankets and huddled, naked body to naked body, with no hope we'd survive the Delaware winter.

The following morning, the same cry issued from the wall top. Old Hike lorded above us amidst piles of our old filthy rags, which he and the other guards then kicked with their muddy boots down into the pen. A wild melee of tossed garments ensued. I was forced to settle for someone else's stained canvas pants slit from knee to ankle, worse than the ones I lost. Fistfights erupted when boys were caught improving their lot with someone else's better cover.

"Form lines, face forward, stand at attention!" Old Hike commanded when most of the men were clothed again. "The barracks will be scrubbed and searched while prisoners wait in the yard. Any more than one blanket per man, and it'll be confiscated."

The sound of the guards stomping through the barracks caused my spirits to fall even lower. They'd claim whatever we'd purchased from the sutler with those precious bits of money from Northerners. Some men had begged enough to purchase an extra blanket. Beards had gotten a second one from a crate sent by a Quaker group. He, Jim Blue, and I had been spreading it over our three bodies, lying motionless and grasping the corners to keep it in place. We flipped a button at lights out for the spot in the middle, but even so, our teeth chattered through the night.

For two hours, we were forced to stand in formation in the icy yard while the guards scrubbed and performed their mischief. My fingers turned blue, and it was only by rubbing them together constantly or tucking my hands in my armpits that I kept them from freezing. The barrack reverberated that night with the sound of hacking coughs, sniffling, and feverish moans.

During the early morning hours of December nineteenth, the first snow fell ankle-deep and a blast of wind careened across the solid river. No one had warm footwear, and we stayed in our blankets, dreading the need to go outside to wait at the sinks. Guards delivered coal to the barracks daily, but it was only a half-day's supply for the small cast-iron stove. Even the guards clutched at their thick overcoats, shoulders hunched inward as they paced on the walkways.

The Ohio fellows were particularly surly. Their "one-hundred-day tour" was to have ended in early December, in time to be home for the holidays, but Ahl announced several weeks earlier that they'd be staying on that godforsaken island through January. Whiskey around the clock would console them until their tour was up.

Later that morning, but before breakfast, Old Hike howled his devilish command under a steely sky. "Hike out, hike out, you lazy bastards!"

Many men were too ill to stir, including John Bibb. Phlegm rattled in his chest. His ragged hacking during the night was another reason for my sleeplessness. He pleaded, "Could you answer for me if there's a roll call? Standing out in the snow will be the end of me."

"Of course, I'll speak for you. Just try to be well enough to be out there yourself tomorrow." Grabbing my blanket, I headed for the barrack door.

On the pen wall, Old Hike was joined by Ahl, whose face was barely visible within the shroud of a woolen scarf. His flinty eyes gleamed between a cap pulled low and the cloth over his nose and mouth. Old Hike clutched the roll list in his gloved hands as puffs of steam floated from his mouth. He bellowed out each name as usual, and a man's voice responded every time, hanging in the frigid air. At the end of roll call, Ahl scanned the group. "We have here an epidemic of escapees or an epidemic of cowards. Which is it? Where is everyone?" He tugged his scarf higher around his neck.

Old Hike growled, "I know how to rout the lily-livered rats. Leave it to me." He shuffled down the stairs on the other side of the pen. A heavy wooden truncheon dangled by a strap from his ham of a hand. Soon the sounds of Old Hike's cursing, wood impacting flesh and bone, and cries of anguish rang from the barracks across the frozen yard. Ahl rocked back and forth on his heels as he listened with his gloved hands clasped behind his back. When Old Hike entered our division, my heart sank. I knew there would be no mercy for any of the ailing fellows, including Bibb. After a time, boys with bloodied noses and heads staggered out, and a few clutched an arm dangling by their sides.

Bibb's face was ashen and drawn in the morning light. He stumbled at the doorway, but I gained his side before he tumbled onto the ice. They had broken his arm. Jim Blue and I held him upright until Ahl finished calling roll again.

"Now, that's more like it. All the rats have been routed from their cozy nests. Be sure you are all—every last one of you—out in the yard tomorrow," Ahl said. He turned toward Old Hike. "You may give the order to disperse."

With an arm around Bibb's waist and his good arm draped over my shoulder, I supported him back to his tier. His weakness was now so great that he seemed insensitive to pain. Blue and I helped him to lie down on his tier and tucked his blanket around him. I then went out into the cold pen and returned after an hour with tears blinding my eyes and a nose like a frozen radish. But I had found a discarded strip of packing crate.

"What do you plan to do with that?" Beards asked.

"Make a splint," I responded. "But first I need a scrap of cloth to bind it to Bibb's arm." I held out the edge of my ragged shirt to show that it had too many tears to be useful. Blue yanked his shirt over his head and tore at a small rip with his teeth until a strip of fabric was free. After shivering back into his shirt, he held the stick while I wrapped the fabric around and around to keep the bone in place. Bibb cried out only once. Another fellow volunteered a strip of shirttail to then bind the arm to Bibb's chest. When I was done, he gave me a faint smile of gratitude, squeezed my arm with his good hand, and drifted off to sleep. I sat by his bunk, hoping that my presence might give him some comfort if he awoke.

In my heart, I was roiling with a dark rage. Bibb deserved this punishment the least of any of us. If Ahl and Old Hike despised us for being Rebels, they should have picked on a seasoned soldier like Beards, Blue, or me. Why pick on the least experienced and weakest?

I spent the afternoon of the nineteenth seething. There was nothing I could do to avenge Bibb or, as their former sergeant, to protect any of these men. I was obsessed with how the guards had humiliated and bullied us too many times. But I knew it was at Ahl's direction. Three frigid months now stood between us and the advent of spring. I couldn't see how we'd survive until then.

More than that, I knew that my family was suffering from hunger and the cold. I was helpless to do anything about that, too. Ever since captives from the battle at Cedar Creek had been admitted in late October, I'd been distraught with worry. As usual, a horde of us had gathered at the gate to learn news of the outside. "Sons a' bitches burnt the whole Valley," one had said. "Grant targeted it all the way from Winchester to New Market, and they went at it from June until now."

Another had said, "We're finished. Our army is washed up, thanks to this last battle. The Yanks have the run of the whole Valley." He told us he'd heard that the burning continued south of the targeted area all the way to Lexington, with small bands of a thousand or so spreading the flames. I had gasped. This meant the troops had marched past the farm. "They set fire to anything that could supply the Rebel Army, whether barns, mills, blacksmith shops, or animals. And even the occasional home, just for good measure." I had groaned and covered my eyes with my hand.

He went on to say that citizens now halted soldiers on the road to beg for just a crust of bread and a few sticks of firewood. "Imagine that. They're turning to us for help, after we've depended on them for food. It breaks a man's heart." There was no stomping and cheering. This time an eerie silence had fallen across the prison yard.

Now it was only a few days until a Christmas that would be nothing like earlier ones. On the way back from the dining hall as the sky turned from gray to black, Beards reminded me. "I never thought times would be so bad that I'd fondly recall Yule celebrations in camp. Remember the smoked hams your father sent, and the rum-soaked fruitcakes from my mother? And how Zeke got so soused on contraband liquor that Blue had gotten from someplace at the end of '62?"

"How could I forget? Particularly the two of you fancy stepping around the campfire to strains of Blue's mouth harp. I think you were a little soused yourself." Beards took a swipe at me and laughed. Then we both fell silent. The image of a dancing Zeke was too painful.

"Looks like snow again. I can smell it," Beards commented just as we entered the barrack.

He was right. When I awakened, I could see through the cracks that the putrid pen had been transformed to a softly sparkling landscape, this time by knee-deep snow. Small drifts had blown through and blossomed on our sleeping shelf in front of each opening.

It was a holiday blessing, however, because the powdery ice was now deep enough to be a source of clean water. There were no wiggle waggles or green slime. The snow had drifted pure from God's Heaven and lay white across the ground under the open sky. Now that the river had become a slab of ice, the barges couldn't reach the island and water was scarce. No one wasted it on bathing. There was barely enough to drink. That morning, Jim Blue organized a group of men who'd purchased pans from the sutler; they darted into the snow and forced as much into a pan as possible and packed it hard. The containers filled the space around the coal stove in the center of our barrack and quickly yielded warm water.

The men called a division meeting by midday. All voted that the pan contents would be used for washing. Fellows who wanted something to drink could scoop snow in their tin mugs. We took turns sponging off, the water floating gray scum with use. Even Bibb, with help from Beards, joined us. My body hadn't enjoyed warm water since the two summer baths in the first months after capture.

Although a day had passed since Bibb's injury, I couldn't calm my fury. At home I'd have smashed a fallen limb against a tree until the anger was spent. And cursing the guards might get me killed. I had to find an outlet, or I would explode with helplessness and outrage. My eyes fell upon the pans of water surrounding the stove. An idea was born.

"I'm goddamned sick of these tyrants playing with our lives. They make up nonsense rules and then murder us when we don't obey," I sputtered to Beards, who crouched next to me on our shelf.

"There's nothing we can do about it. Calm down. No point in getting yourself so riled up," he said, his chin in his hands.

"No, listen to me. There is something we can do. What if, when the federal inspectors are here, we expose Ahl and Hike's barbarity? Maybe even implicate Schoepf?" I asked Beards. "Maybe they'd be replaced by someone a little less crazy."

He jerked his head in my direction. "What in God's name are you thinking? We're totally vulnerable down here in the pen. You know we're forbidden to speak to guards, much less the Feds. Didn't you learn anything from your time in solitary?" He pulled his blanket up around his ears and looked away.

I shifted my seat so he couldn't ignore me. "Sure, it's risky, but listen. Tomorrow the federal inspectors will be on the wall with Ahl and Old Hike at 7:00 a.m. for their monthly tour. What if we get some fellows together, and when the guards are changing shifts, we pitch pans of dirty water out of the windows?"

"What the hell will that accomplish? And have you forgotten? Special Order Number 157 states that men aren't to throw filth into the yard."

"This won't be filth—it'll be wash water. The guards will fire warning shots, but we'll quit before the third one. The Feds are bound to ask what the disturbance is about. Then Ahl and Hike will have to tell them about Special Order Number 157, and more than that, the guards will look like maniacs for shooting at men who are just pitching out water."

Beards shook his head. "I'm not so sure about that, Tom." He said he thought I was delusional, that I should know that nothing made sense in how the prison camp worked. He was silent for a minute, considering. "You're counting on the guard not aiming to kill the first or second time, and on the Yankee inspectors paying attention. The payoff is way too small for the risk. Give it up."

I don't know why I couldn't hear him. How could I have been so stupid as to expect logical rules in a prison camp when there'd been none in war? Instead, I rattled on. "Doing nothing is just as dangerous. You know that living in daily fear does real harm to boys with wounded minds. We've both seen it. There's Bibb, for instance." I paused. "And there's a chance the guards are softening a little. Don't you remember when the fellow from Division Eight pissed outside the barrack door. When he didn't stop, the guards aimed above his head twice and then didn't shoot him. They just gave him a scare."

I believed the guards wouldn't dare shoot five or six boys at one time. Not in front of big men from Washington. "I swear I'd be willing to risk my life if I thought it would destroy Ahl and Old Hike."

"For Chrissakes, Tom." Beards was silent for several long minutes. "Well, I'll tell you what," he finally said. "I'm not fully convinced, but if you can talk the rest of the fellows into it, I'll join in." He grabbed the corners of his blanket tighter around him and walked to the far end of the barrack. I'm sure he thought I'd never convince the others, and he'd be off the hook.

It was tough work, but I persuaded Blue and two others. Beards lived up to his promise, making five of us. "But I'm not joining in until you promise that after the second warning, you'll stop. And I mean it. Stop dead in your tracks." Beards glared at me.

"I solemnly swear I'll stop," I said. "I'll shake on it. You have my word." I extended my hand, and he shook it. I only wanted a chance. If my trick succeeded, Ahl and Hike would be gone, and all of our lives would be less miserable.

The sun rose shortly before guard changeover. Sleep had eluded me the entire night—what with jangling anxiety and then despair at John Bibb's discomfort.

It seemed a shame to waste the warm water without first using it, so several of us sponged off one last time. Jim Blue kept a look out through the window for Ahl and the inspectors to appear on the wall. Finally, he signaled with a raised hand, and I slipped into the shadows behind him. Right on schedule at 7:00 a.m., Ahl swaggered across the top of the pen, boasting loudly to two portly, imposing looking fellows, stiff overcoat collars cupping their ears against the river wind. One inspector stroked his dark beard, absentmindedly nodding as Ahl extolled the sanitary conditions and fair treatment of prisoners. The other was grinding away with a fingernail in his ear while he surveyed the horizon. Neither was listening to what Ahl said. Old Hike scurried behind, trying to insert himself into the discussion.

Jim Blue's hand went up again; the trio was close by and the moment for action had come. We hoisted buckets to the windows and, at my word, heaved their contents forward. Steam hissed as warm liquid splashed the snow. A startled yell burst from the guard on the wall far across the pen. Ahl was pointing and then waving his arms angrily. The inspectors peered curiously in our direction as Old Hike barked oaths. The wind was fierce, and the guard's thready voice drifted off across the pen. A satisfied smile spread across my face as the little Yankee flailed his arms and his pudgy face darkened with rage. Beards and the others speedily recoiled from the window and crouched behind the barrack wall. Reserve buckets were ready at our feet, and Jim Blue and I each emptied out another. This time, the guard raised his rifle and yelled more heatedly. Ahl seemed to be encouraging him. When Blue saw the gun barrel pointed his way, he shrank back. But I was like someone intoxicated. Danger didn't cross my mind.

"Come on, Tom, quit now while no harm's done! We've made our point." Beards' voice was sharp with urgency. "You promised. Now keep your promise!" I could hear the other fellows' entreaties as if from a distant shore.

Then John Bibb struggled upright from his sleeping tier and stretched his hand toward my shoulder to pull me behind the window frame. "Tom, I beg you. Stop. This is pure folly!"

A surge of the old fighting spirit coursed through my veins. I brushed Bibb's hand aside. "Look at that little fool bestir himself!" I leaned out the window to pitch the last bucket of water. "Take that, you Yankee bastards!"

A second later, a bullet whizzed past my ear. "It's Bibb! The sons a' bitches have shot Bibb!" voices behind me cried. He'd made no sound but for a thud when his body collapsed back on the shelf.

My breath stopped. Perhaps he had only received a nick in the ear that stunned him, or a wound to the arm. I dropped to my knees and gently shook him, oblivious to the scarlet fountain that spurted from his chest and stained those of us close by. "Answer me, please answer me, John," I begged. His bad arm dangled from the tier as his body sprawled in a widening puddle. Faintly I could hear someone saying, "I knew it. I knew this crazy scheme would get someone killed." My whole body seemed to dissolve in that moment.

Another voice cried, "He'd still be alive if it weren't for you!"

Even Beards, standing next to me with his hand on my back, softly said, "You gave your word. You promised."

Every instant of my life was reduced to this wretched place and time, crouching at Bibb's side with the realization that he was gone. Nothing else mattered. I dropped my forehead to his chest, oblivious to the warm, sticky liquid dampening my hair and beard. In death, his face had a purity that belied his eighteen years. After a time, someone's hands pulled me away and guided me toward the shelf across the aisle. I turned toward the wall to hide the unstoppable tears.

When the wheelbarrow man arrived to cart away Bibb's body, I stood apart from the others. Jim Blue solemnly tucked Bibb's blanket over his head and torso so that his blank, staring eyes and gaping mouth would no longer be directed at the wintery sky. But the others persuaded Blue that John's blanket would be of no use to him and might save one of us. He reluctantly removed it. Someone hid John's knapsack with Margaret Ellen's image to safeguard it from the guards. Lanky legs and arms flapping over the wheelbarrow's sides, John Bibb was hauled away. The rumble of the iron wheels across the rough barrack boards and over the doorstep haunts me still.

Schoepf convened a court of inquiry within his quarters that drab afternoon to investigate the fatal shooting. The federal inspectors were long gone.

Earlier in the afternoon, a guard had arrived at our division and led away Private Leonidas Tripplett, the man bunked on the boards next to John Bibb. Tripplett's blanket, soaked by John's drying blood, was his only barrier against the cold. The guard also summoned Privates William Kelsoe and R. M. Retherford, the only prisoners in the

snow-covered yard at that hour of the morning. We watched them trudge
away to Schoepf's rooms in the fort.

After Tripplett's return several hours later, Beards asked the question
for the rest of us. "Are those bastards Ahl and Hike and the guard going
to suffer for this crime?"

Tripplett surveyed our downcast faces, wiped his palm across his forehead, and began in a despondent voice. "It was nothing but a charade.
They simply wanted to judge Bibb guilty and to prove his execution was
deserved, in case there were queries from Washington." His mouth was a
grim slit in his bleak face. "It was just a whitewashing. That's all."

"Goddamn it!" Beards exclaimed, as a chorus of expletives followed
from the others.

Triplett had told the jury how, as he was going out to breakfast, he'd
seen us bathing by the coal stove. A man then pitched out dirty wash
water—not urine—against which there are no prohibitions. Besides, Bibb's
injured arm rendered him incapable of dumping out a heavy bucket. It
was a task that required two hands. At this point we all cheered a strong
round of "Huzzah! Huzzah! Good man, Triplett." He nodded and kept his
eyes to the floor.

Kelso and Retherford had said the guard Deakyne was too far away
to have any idea what was being pitched out of the window. But the tribu-
nal only wanted to know if the two witnesses were familiar with Special
Order Number 157. They didn't want to hear anything that might imply
the guard's guilt.

"Last came the lying guard Deakyne. First, he had no doubt it was
urine; he was only twenty feet away," Tripplett said. "And that he'd shouted
a warning four or five times. The sorry louse said he was only fulfilling his
duty," Tripplett concluded. A furor broke out at those words.

When the boys quieted, Blue asked, "And did the officers want to
know who was actually throwing the water? Did they ask you anything
about that?" Everyone looked toward me.

"No, not a word on that matter or the others, either. Or they would have had to ask incriminating questions about the Fort's policies and Deakyne shooting to kill without just cause," Tripplett said. "The only thing they cared about was Bibb's innocence." He paused and finally met our eyes. "I'm sorry, fellows. He was a mighty good man who didn't deserve this ending." He sank down on his bunk.

The guard Deakyne was absolved of any wrongdoing. I too had gotten away scot-free. Bibb was the only one who paid.

32

OBLIVIOUS TO THE FREEZING TEMPERATURES AS NIGHT FELL, I STUM-
bled across the snow-covered ground to the farthest edge of the
pen, while blood roared in my ears. I was no longer worthy as a leader
of others. Maybe I'd never been. Fragments of conversations with Bibb
haunted me. Now he would never see his home and family again. He'd
never experience the adventure of California, or the satisfactions of holding Margaret Ellen in their marriage bed. My thoughtless actions had
destroyed all those possibilities.

That lead bullet had been meant for me. Meant to burrow into my
chest. I wished it had. I'd withstood sickness and battles when so many
others hadn't—to do what? To be responsible for the death of a shattered
man who was straining to save my life for the second time. In combat, I'd
dispatched strangers, but Bibb was my friend and a member of my circle to
protect. The killing field was behind us. How could I have been so stupid?
I had loved this boy as I had loved the memory of my younger self, before I
had been undone by so much carnage.

I couldn't conceive how I'd face the boys in the bunks again. I knew
the consequences of violating Special Order Number 157 as well as anyone; yet only I taunted the guard past the edge of danger. I was convinced that, somehow, I could change the prison circumstances. That I
alone could make a difference, when no one else had. What vanity, what
false pride!

I had lost not only John Bibb that day, but these other comrades as
well. As their sergeant, I had held their trust and confidence. Now I'd
violated that trust and led those closest to me into this dangerous stunt.

That afternoon the fellows ignored me, their eyes purposely fixed on the opposite wall or engaged with one of the others. I couldn't go back into the division, even if the last vestige of light had faded and my teeth were clacking. I'd stay in the frigid yard until I found my own place of final darkness.

Just as I was overcome by convulsive shivering, Sam Lucas appeared across the yard. I squinted my eyes to sharpen my focus, not believing what I saw. It was Sam! He'd stepped out of the shadows of what appeared to me to be a darkened rail station. My heart split asunder, and I sobbed as I hadn't since William Valentine's death at Manassas. Next to Sam strode Tayloe, Zeke Skinner, and all the Augusta boys who had perished. William Valentine was there too, with his hand resting on Old Suzie's velvet head. Behind them marched a crowd of soldiers, Blues and Grays, Blacks and whites, some without an arm or a leg, some without heads, hands, noses or ears, some barely there at all. And then swaying toward me were mourning women, thickly veiled in black crepe, their ebony skirts rustling around them. Mothers, sisters, sweethearts of both races. A horde of Blacks in chains—men, women, and children—stepped quietly behind, followed by the entire New Jerusalem Church choir, swathed in yellow robes, voices soaring in a requiem. At the rear, there was Tatternook in his white shirt and black suit. I saw myself as a young boy, then as a tall, melancholy old man. My fingers and toes were in agony, but I hardly noticed as the advancing figures drew me to them.

Piercing the fog that shrouded my senses, a familiar voice called to me from the barrack door. I couldn't respond and wouldn't have, if capable. Beards's strong hand was suddenly on my shoulder, and I was being shaken, then supported between two men who directed my frozen feet toward the brightness of the barrack door. They propped me near the stove, my head fallen against the bunk, and swaddled me in their blankets. Finally, they rubbed my arms and legs until warmth began to circulate, and full alertness returned.

"Man, have you gone mad? John wouldn't have wanted you to pay for his death with yours. That cur of a guard killed John, not you. It was just damned bad luck." In spite of what Beards said, I knew that if I'd quit my taunt when the guard barked the second warning, John Bibb would have been traveling home when the war ended. I would have found ways to keep him alive until then.

As January plodded along, I craved punishment for John's death. Repeatedly, I asked myself why the official review had ignored the identity of the "nuisance" instigator. Eventually, I concluded that we were punished if we tried to break rules, but not after the rules were broken. And after the war, I learned that the federal authorities couldn't have cared less about the welfare of their prisoners. Nothing was enough to make up for what their boys had endured in the Confederate prison at Andersonville, Georgia. The more we suffered, the better. The inspectors probably knew about Special Order Number 157 before they visited Fort Delaware. I was a moron to think my trifling plot would dislodge Ahl and Hike or affect Schoef's hold on the place.

Every day, my ears echoed my father's voice when I'd committed some stupidity at home. I remembered Pa's anger when I'd risked his horse by riding her to Sam's house without allowing her to cool down after his ride to Staunton. And his harsh words when I'd once forgotten to lock the hen house. A nighttime marauder had eaten them all. The list went on and on, a running narration of worthlessness. Bibb's death taught me as nothing else had why anger shouldn't be allowed to swallow reason. Now it was too late.

Nights were worse than days. Images of Milton's Hell crowded my dreams, and demons lurked at the edges of my bunk to pluck me into their world. I stayed to myself and didn't enter into pen games and harmonizing. Failed attempts to draw me into play or our old memorization contests convinced the others to leave me alone.

In my self-imposed silence, I relived John's and my times together. I missed the sound of his deep voice, his thoughtful conversation, and his kind nature. Sometimes I caught a flash of his crooked grin and crinkled blue eyes on the edge of my vision, but when I looked in that direction, there was nothing.

Finally, in late January, I decided to write a letter to John's family in Charlottesville. He'd want their minds to be eased with details of his last days. I was obsessed with composing just the right words in my head, trying out one version and then another. Finally, I used my last sheet of paper, hidden until now under the shelf. I wrote only that John had been fatally wounded by a prison guard and assured his family that he was a brave man of faith and goodness well prepared to meet his Maker. I reported where his body was buried on the river's New Jersey shore. The mass grave was hundreds of miles and many days from Charlottesville, but maybe his father could manage a trip after the war ended. I concealed the details of the shooting. The family would find no solace in discovering their loss was an accident caused by someone's idiocy. When the letter was finished, I tucked it deep in my haversack until prisoner letters to the South might be allowed. I'd hoped that putting those words on paper would give me some relief, but it didn't.

On February 8, just when my spirits could go no lower, Beards burst into the barrack so excited he could hardly spit out the news. "Prisoner exchanges are going to start up again! By the end of the month or by early March!" The Confederacy was so desperate for soldiers that it was granting freedom to any male slave willing to serve in the Confederate army and had vowed to trade a Black Union soldier for a white Confederate one, man for man. Lincoln then had agreed to prisoner trades.

"How can you be sure?" I asked, knowing the commander forbade any communicating with guards. Only they would be privy to this sort of information.

He grinned, "Let's just say that somewhere along the line, a guard leaked the news."

"Probably a fellow from the Maryland unit. Some of them take a little more pity on us Southerners," Jim Blue said.

"I'm not saying, but one thing I'll tell you—no one's going anywhere unless they swear to the United States Oath of Allegiance and pledge to quit the rebellion," Beards said.

"You won't catch me swearing allegiance to these sons of bitches," Blue blurted.

"Not even if it's a chance to be free?" I asked.

"Free? Where? You won't be going home," Beards said. "The Yankee boats are standing ready to take us north, not south. We're still at war, remember."

"Do you think your Pennsylvania uncle would be willing to take in three former enemies?" Blue asked me. "Otherwise, we'd be without shelter and food."

"No, I don't expect so. He doesn't even know me." I thought for a moment. "If we sign that oath now, we'd be considered traitors at home. Probably for the rest of our lives. Our families and neighbors are still suffering, and we'd have taken the easy way out."

The other two nodded their heads and then fell into silence. I finally spoke. "I recommend we stay. This hell can't go on much longer. Lee's going to have to surrender soon. The last group of captives made that clear. We've lost every battle for months."

"You're right. Even if there was some way to get south, we'd be forced back into combat, and I'm not about to risk my life again for a losing cause. This place is dangerous enough," Blue said.

We made a decision. Not one of us would abandon the other two. We'd wait until Lee surrendered.

On February 27, over one thousand men pledged loyalty to the Union and left Fort Delaware on the steamboat Cassandra headed north. The boat left only twenty-four hours after Ahl made the announcement from the pen wall. Beards and Jim Blue were as downcast as I'd been for the preceding two months as they watched the chaotic leave-taking. Even though their reason told them staying was the right thing to do.

I still was in the grip of such profound heartsickness that I gave it little notice. There was strange comfort in being in the sole company of fellows who knew the worst about me; I could wallow in self-contempt without having to explain myself. Once home with its demands, and removed from the inactivity of prison life, how would I satisfy the curiosity of keen observers like Mary, Ma, and Tish? They'd notice immediately that something wasn't right with me.

33

NARY A JUNE COMES AROUND THAT I DON'T RECALL THE FIRST
minutes of freedom from the Fort. This morning's sun-laden, leafy
fragrances put me in mind of that bright June day. Lee had surrendered in
April, two months earlier, and the war was finally declared over in May,
yet it was still several weeks until our release.

Schoepf and Ahl presided over a table laden with stacks of official documents while a double line of prisoners snaked across the pen. The men
shifted from foot to foot as the officers slowly filled out forms for each
and rubber stamped them. When my turn came, Ahl's eyes hardened. I
wondered if he still had power to harm me. While Ahl glared, Schoepf
looked me over. He then wrote out a line describing my hair and eye colors
and approximate height. Nothing had changed there, although so much
else had. At long last, he signed my release slip and passed it to Ahl. For
what seemed an eternity, Ahl did nothing but watch me squirm. Finally, he
signed the form and thunked down the US government stamp. I breathed
a great sigh. The last step was to raise my right hand and swear allegiance
to the United States.

At long last, the gates were thrown open. Waves of happiness rose in
my chest for the first time in too long to remember. Those with the energy
cavorted and frolicked on the grass beyond, oblivious to the streaks of
green stain on newly issued pants. I solemnly regarded the outside of the
pen wall, a sight I had doubted I would live to see again, and remembered
a year earlier when I viewed it for the first time with Zeke, Tayloe, and the
other boys. With a strange mix of sadness and relief, I threw my haversack

over my shoulder and tramped up the loading plank of a packet boat headed for Baltimore and finally a journey south.

The port of Richmond was our destination after boarding a second packet boat in Baltimore. It was a malodorous two-day journey, spent leaning against the next man for support. Pull one out, and the whole stinking bunch might fall. An hour or two out in the Bay, gray clouds mounded to the west of the horizon, and soon a strong wind churned the water into agitated waves. We pitched against one another, grabbing for a shoulder or arm for support. My stomach lurched, and I clasped one hand over my mouth to unsuccessfully stem the rising stream. Beards and Blue were spewing the contents of their guts too. Once the wind died down and the sea smoothed out, the boat's interior was filled with an eerie silence and an even fouler stench. There was only the sound of the paddle wheels slicing through water, accompanied by frequent sighs or nervous coughs.

Apprehension had taken root in men's minds. What might their wives or family think when they first spied a crutch standing in for a leg, or a sleeve pinned back on a one-armed jacket? Would there be revulsion? Or pity? I studied Beards and the others, imagining their folks seeing them for the first time. I was used to the shadows of Beards's hollowed-out cheekbones and purple-haloed eyes. The others were just as ghoulish. I was no better, but I was also weighed down by a spectral John Bibb. His body might have been rotting in a ditch by the Delaware River, but his presence was palpable the minute I left the fort, when I first savored the exhilarating, chest-expanding sense of freedom, something he would never know.

A collective gasp arose as the splintered landscape of Richmond came into view along the James River. We pressed against the railing. I had never visited the city, but Jim Blue had accompanied his father by train a few years before the war. "I'll be damned," he said. "This isn't Richmond. This is a nightmare." He was right. Brittle, empty facades stretched as far as we could see. Some tobacco warehouses were as much as four stories tall with windows nothing but open frames for the sky—the interiors and roofs gone to ashes.

Shoving forward, we filed onto the wooden gangway and spilled out onto a loading dock jammed with hundreds of jostling freed prisoners and those who'd come to meet them. Beards, Blue, and I staked a position in the center of the cobblestone street, as sweethearts, mothers, fathers, and siblings cried out and hugged their boys to them. But for us there was no familiar voice from behind or a tap on the shoulder. No one was there to greet us.

Did this mean that Pa was injured or ill, unable to make the trip? Or worse, could he have died while I'd been in prison? After all, he wasn't a young man, and there had been no word from home for more than a year. I was beside myself with worry.

After an hour, when the crowd had wandered off and only massive tobacco barrels stood like sentinels on the dock, Beards said, "We might as well find a way home on our own." He saw my anxious expression and added, "I suspect our folks had no way of knowing that we were coming today."

"I'm not sure I have it in me to walk that far," Jim Blue said. He sank down on a stone curb. I agreed. We would have to cover a hundred and twenty miles, a ten-day walk if the train wasn't running, with no money, no food, and no transportation but our legs. "We have no choice," Beards said. "Grab your packs, and let's get moving." He briskly stood up and strode off.

I reluctantly hoisted my haversack to my shoulder and followed Beards through the streets. Jim Blue lagged behind. The place was overrun with Union soldiers, rifles on their backs and strolling the rubble-littered sidewalks as if they owned the city. I flinched every time I saw one, and we crossed to the other side of the street whenever they approached. I itched to get out of that place.

In front of warehouse ruins at the end of the street, a tall Black man struggled with a wood barrow full of bricks. He lowered the handles and passed a rag over his brow and face. His faded homespun shirt swung loose from his bony shoulders and thin arms protruded from its sleeves. As we approached, he ignored us, instead concentrating on his barrow's passage through the debris and across the rough cobblestones.

"Hey, can you please help us?" I called.

He paused and looked over his shoulder, his eyes crackling with wariness. He then dropped the barrow's handles and turned.

I gave our names, and then said, "We want nothing more than to get home to Augusta County. We've fresh out of a Union prison." The words caught in my throat. I held my breath. Why would this man assist former Confederates? But then, he must have taken account of our hollowed cheeks, sunken eyes, and frail limbs and decided we posed no harm. He nodded and told us, with a faint tremor to his words, that he was Bill Stewart.

Beards asked, "Are you from around here?"

"Nope, not from Richmond. I'm from down around Hampton— raised up on the Stewart plantation."

"How'd you come to be here?" I asked.

"I spent the last year of the war as a refugee at Fort Monroe after the Yankees took it. Then came up here two months ago to get paid work with the federals cleaning up the city. I know the area right well now."

"Can you help us find our way?" Blue asked.

"We're looking for a train. We need to find one running toward Charlottesville or Staunton," I added.

He grudgingly offered to guide us to the terminus of the line going west, although he'd be losing time from his work. "I heard that the rails from Richmond to Charlottesville are repaired now. Have been for about a week," he said. "Don't know about going any farther west or north than that."

"We'd be mighty grateful if you'd point us in the direction of where the freight trains run. We hope to jump one to get home," Beards said. He looked around at the wreckage towering over us. "What happened here? We heard the Confederates torched the city in April to keep the Union troops from getting supplies from the warehouses, but this is unbelievable destruction."

Bill said the buildings were still smoldering when he arrived, two weeks after they were torched. A mob lost control when they saw wheat, oats, and rye spilling from crumbling warehouses. The city had starved while speculators secretly hoarded grain and drove the prices so high no one could afford them. In their fury, the mob set fires far beyond the area designated by the Confederate army.

"I heard that Mr. Pollard, the owner of this big one behind us, suspected maybe ten or twelve paupers camping inside was burnt up too," he said. He told us that shells exploded all day after flames reached the nearby armory. "Now I'm pulling a good wage cleaning up, so I don't mind the mess. But I sure hope I don't find any of those paupers," he said. He parked his barrow against a ragged wall. "You boys can follow me."

Apologetically, I put my hands in my pants pockets and yanked them inside out. "But we have nothing to give you."

"Never mind."

We trailed behind as he marched confidently through the few streets cleared of charred timbers and mountains of bricks. He also knew the street corners where the federal army was dispensing rations for those who'd signed the United States loyalty pledge. I fumbled in my new shirt pocket for the allegiance document and unfolded it.

A gray-haired white woman with rounded cheeks and a sweet expression dipped water from a crock into a canteen and tied up some cornbread in a red cotton kerchief. "Here, son, you'll be needing these on your travels," she said. I murmured my thanks and put them in my bag, stepping back to make room for the other boys. She reminded me of women from Bethel, with her mild manner and soft face, and home seemed a little nearer.

Bill led us to the rail tracks at the western side of the city. "I hear the whistle blow morning and evening, and I haven't heard the evening one yet, so a freight is bound to come by sooner or later," he said. We pumped his hand, thanking him profusely. He turned without glancing back as he set out for the trek back to his wooden barrow. Then we waited. As a freight train finally chugged toward us, Beards yelled and I frantically waved my shirt in the middle of the track to force the engine to halt. The train slowed, and the engineer leaned from the cab window. His voice was drowned out by the engine's blasts of steam, but he beckoned us to get aboard. I jumped through the wide doors of an empty freight car and grabbed Beards' and then Blue's outstretched hands to pull them aboard. Now we were off toward those fair mountains seen in the past months only in dreams.

Bibb's presence intensified as we disembarked in Charlottesville, the last stop where the rail line was in good repair. But for me, he would have been greeting his mother, father, sisters, and perhaps sweet Margaret Ellen right there at that track, laughing as they embraced him and drew him into their healing warmth.

For a few seconds, I considered delaying our return to Augusta, if only a day, to call on the Bibb family. I could give them news of John's last moments, his time at the Fort, and could perhaps pass on that letter I'd written months ago. But a voice in my head whispered that they would want to talk about their son and would expect some answers about his death. I couldn't possibly tell them the details. Not for the life of me. Cowardice won out, even if I was denying Beards and Blue a night's rest in a real bed and an opportunity to wash off the journey's accumulated filth. I tore the letter into pieces when the boys weren't looking and dropped them into a laurel bush. When Beards suggested a side trip into town to see if more rations were available, I snarled at him so fiercely that no one dared venture in that direction. Bibb in tow, I stumbled forward with the others on the path home.

34

B Y WALKING BESIDE THE SCORCHED WOOD TIES AND TWISTED IRON rails west from the city limits, we found Rockfish Gap Turnpike, the route we sought over Afton Mountain. Having gobbled the federal hand-outs of cornbread and swallowed all the water in our federal-issue canteens on the overnight trip from Richmond, we now had nothing to eat or drink. The June sun was merciless, and we wouldn't feel relief until early evening when we reached the mountain's higher altitude. After several hours of tripping over ruts and ignoring complaining stomachs and parched throats, Blue, who was yards ahead of Beards and me, spotted a tree with a small strip of wood nailed to it. He brushed away a crust of dirt and peered at the faint letters scrawled across it.

"There's water through these woods off to the right," he called. "I can hear it. It must be Lickinghole Creek, like the sign says." He disappeared down a slope through the pines and wild wineberry bushes. Rippling over rocks, the stream had plenty of icy water for rolling up our pants legs and wading, filling our canteens, and splashing our reeking clothes and sweating foreheads. Beards sank down in a rock depression and let the creek cascade over his body up to his neck. Blue and I found our own rock hollows and joined him. Then I lay back in sopping clothes on the cool ferns and poured water into my mouth until I thought it might seep from my ears. Now, if we just had something to eat. My eyes drifted to the cloudless sky above our heads. Beyond the treetops, smoke threaded faintly off to the west.

"Do you see what I see?" I leaped up in my excitement. "Maybe that's a hunter with deer or bear meat to share."

"Forget it. I want to get home. As long as there's water, I can go without food for a day or so," Beards said.

"Well, I can't," Blue responded. "I need something to eat, or I won't make it much farther."

"I'm with Blue," I said. "This may be our last chance for a while. That smoke isn't far away, and if there's someone else on this mountain, they're bound to have more to eat than we do."

"I guess I wouldn't mind some food," Beards said. He stood up and brushed twigs and fern fronds from his wet pants.

We followed along the bank of the stream until a footpath meandered upward through tall oaks and maples. The smoke came from that direction. After a hike of about a mile, a sunny clearing opened before us. A one-room wooden house stood in the center and its stone chimney spouted smoke. "Wait here," Blue said as we stopped at the forest edge. "Is anyone home?" he called out, but there was no answer. "Maybe they just stepped out."

"I don't know. It seems strange someone would go out and leave the door wide open like that. Who knows what critters might take advantage? Seems fishy to me," I said.

Beards tilted his head back and sniffed. "I smell something cooking, so I say we should go in."

Slowly I crossed the clearing, still convinced this was unwise. The smell of food grew stronger. "Who in their right mind would go off and leave vittles cooking?" I said. We crossed the board porch and peered into the shaded interior.

"Look at that," Beards said. Strips of meat still smoked over coals in the large stone fireplace. Potatoes boiled in a pot of water suspended by an iron rod over the heat. My warning had no effect on Blue and Beards, who stepped through the door and approached the fire. The hairs on the back of my neck prickled, but I followed.

The house was tidy but sparsely furnished. A table and two chairs were pushed against one wall, and there was a bed with missing legs against the other. Within the frame lay a bear hide with green pine boughs poking out from beneath. A brightly colored quilt was folded neatly at the end. Through a small window, I saw two graves. One was freshly dug, and both were marked with crosses of vine-bound branches. That's when I detected a flash of movement headed in our direction across the yard.

"Watch out!" I yelled as a Black boy burst in the door like lightening and threw himself upon Beards. They tumbled to the floor, and in the tussle, I saw that Beards's attacker clasped a large hunting knife. "Help me grab him!" I yelled at Blue. When the boy managed to roll on top of Beards, Jim Blue and I seized him by the upper arms and peeled him off. We set him down in one of the two chairs and stood over him. But not before I firmly held his wrist and opened fingers clutching the knife. The antler-handled weapon clattered to the floor.

"Goddam it. Get your hands off me!" the boy hollered. "I'm not going. No matter what you say or do! I'll kill all three of you before you can take me away!" He spat in our direction. His arms trembled, and he looked to be about twelve years old. Beards had gotten to his feet and stepped forward with his palms raised.

"We mean no harm," he said. "We're only trying to get home across the mountain. We saw your smoke and hoped you might have some vittles to share. We've had nothing but cornbread in the past several days, and prison rations before that."

"You ain't going to take me away like you took my cousin Ellis. I'm not fighting for anyone, especially not you people," the boy said.

Beards was silent, trying to understand the meaning of the boy's words. Then he said, "The war's over. You're free. And anyway, we aren't here for that reason."

"I've always been free, Mister," he spat out. "My Granny, and the rest of my family too. But white soldiers like you found their way up here this past spring and took my cousin Ellis off at gunpoint to fight in the war. It didn't matter a whit that he was a free man." He glared at us again. "You better not be trickin' me, or you'll regret it."

The memory of what I'd seen at Gettysburg came roaring back. "I've known too much of that kind of thing," I said. "It's despicable. We'd never do that to you, or anyone else, for that matter." The tension left his thin shoulders and his hostile expression partially melted. I said, "Tell us more about what happened to your cousin."

He haltingly explained that Ellis had been into town one day in late winter for supplies and had seen hundreds of slaves lined up on the court-house steps. Confederate soldiers held them there, threatening them with weapons. He said his cousin then noticed a flyer posted on a tree that ordered all slaves to gather that day at the Albemarle Courthouse before 10:00 a.m. Owners not willing to give up their male slaves would have them seized by the Army at gunpoint. Instantly, Ellis forgot his errand and slipped back up the mountain. "But they found him anyway," the boy told us. "People in town knew that freed people live up here. When I heard someone thrashing up the hill, I hid in the hollow of a big log, just like today. Didn't come out until the soldiers were gone." He said Ellis's wife and baby took off the next day for her family who live near Waynesboro. She had tried to talk him into going, but he wouldn't. "Who'd be here when Ellis comes back? I wish I could have saved him from goin' off, but there were too many of you people," he said. "At least I can wait for him. He taught himself to scribe, but I've heard nary a word."

"Where is your Granny? Are you alone now?" I asked.

"Granny passed on in February from consumption. She raised me after Momma died birthing me. Ellis and I dug Granny's grave right next to Momma's over by the woods. But from the time I was little, Granny taught me how to trap critters and grow plants. We had some laying hens, but the soldiers took them too."

Beards looked thoughtful. Then he said, "You haven't told us your name."

"Lewis. Lewis Hornsby."

"Don't you get lonely up here in this cabin by yourself?"

Lewis glowered at him. "I can take care of myself. Anyway, Granny's watchin' over me. And I couldn't leave her alone on the mountain either."

We were silent for a moment. Then the smell of the food and the cramps in my stomach reminded me why we were there. "We don't have anything to offer you, Lewis. Not one thing except conversation, and you may not have a need for such. But is there any way you could see fit to share some of these vittles with us?"

Lewis looked us up and down one more time. There was still a flicker of fear in his eyes, and it was clear he suspected we'd simply seize his food if he didn't agree. Or worse, might kill him for it. Finally, he turned toward the fireplace and said over his shoulder, "I expect I have enough smoked rabbit here to share, and I could split the potatoes four ways, if you care for some."

It was late afternoon by the time we finished eating and telling him what little we had learned about the end of the war. Lewis had boiled two more potatoes. He knocked dirt from carrots pulled from his garden and offered them to us. Those, with the potatoes, would last until we reached home.

"You were mighty generous to share your vittles with us. Thank you. Now we can make it home."

Lewis wouldn't meet my eyes but waved his hand in dismissal. We bade him farewell and returned to the mountain road the way we'd come.

Jim Blue suggested we walk as far as we could that night. We all wanted to make up the time lost on the side trip to Lewis's cabin. The moon was full behind us, making the trek easier, and long moon shadows fell in front of our feet as the road ascended. Silently, we climbed, but my mind was anything but quiet. As the hours had lengthened, I couldn't shed the image of Lewis with his defiant loneliness. I moved from concern about him to wondering if I, too, might find myself alone, uncertain where my family was. I puzzled again over why no one was at the Richmond dock to meet us. Had my family fled Augusta to avoid harm from Yankee troops, and was now too far away? Had the house been burned? Anything could have happened. In this disturbed state of mind, I flinched with every screech owl and wild animal cry. Each twig crackle made me jump.

We plodded on in glum silence, ascending more slowly toward the top of Afton Mountain until exhaustion forced us to lay our haversacks down out of sight of the road and rest our heads upon them.

35

WHEN WE REACHED AFTON'S CREST IN MID-MORNING, A WESTERLY wind stirred gray clouds of insects above our heads. Where oak trees and cedars parted to give an open view of the valley, farm after farm was circled by charred land, scorched barns, and shattered fences. Collectively, we gasped. Is this how we'd find our homes? The sounds of distant cattle lowing might once have ridden on mountain updrafts but now were gone. Hawks soaring above the mountain crest made the only creature noises.

At one point on our descent, we heard horses' hooves clopping on the road beyond the mountain's curve. We slipped into the shadows of some oaks until we could see who approached. A band of blue-coated men, federal militia with rifles across their saddles, meandered into sight. We thought we were well concealed, but the leader spotted us and called out. "Step into the center of the road where we can see you." There were ten of them, and they halted their horses in a double line across the road. Beards had startled when the officer called out, and his face was ashen. I noticed that his fists were clenched.

I told him, "It's okay. No need to worry." He looked at me sideways and said nothing.

"Show your papers before you pass on," the fellow in charge demanded. I fumbled in my pocket, rattled by the command. The officer snatched for the folded scrap and glanced at Schoepf and Ahl's signatures. He looked me over. "A prisoner, eh?"

"We're headed home."

"Well, keep moving," he said and geed his horse forward. He threw the papers in the dust behind him. Beards scurried to gather the documents, and then we watched the soldiers ride out of sight.

"Sons a' bitches," Jim Blue said. He spat in the dust after them.

The ground flattened when we reached South Fork, a river too swift and deep to ford on foot. The three of us had been resting for an hour by reeds at the water's edge, when Blue set up a whooping and hollering. Through the oaks, the prow of a rowboat floated into view, followed by the sight of an old man plying the oars.

"Hey there, can you help some Johnnie Rebs get home? We need a way across the river," Blue yelled. The boat drifted slowly into the cattails on the river's edge and lodged in the mud. Its occupant, gray hair drooping in sparse clumps around his wizened face and a homespun shirt flapping on his stooped frame, examined us warily. Jim Blue explained that we'd been prisoners at Fort Delaware. The expression on the man's face changed to sympathy.

"Where's home for you boys? You headed to Staunton or parts south? Because if you're headed to Staunton, you'll find more federal troops than you ever witnessed in prison."

My heart sank. There'd been Yanks on horseback on the road from Charlottesville, and Richmond was full of them, but I hadn't expected them to be so plentiful near home. "What do you mean?"

"There are two Yanks for every man, woman, and child, some say. Soldiers toting guns patrol the streets every night. There's a ten o'clock curfew."

Beards gave me a sharp look, impatient to move along. "We're headed out the Bethel road," he said brusquely.

"Alright, fellows, I can see you're in a hurry." The old man stiffly settled down at the rusty oarlocks.

We floated quietly for few minutes, but then I couldn't help myself. "Do you know anything about folks living along the Bethel road? Whether there was much burning there?" I asked.

"I heared there was some, but I don't know much about it," he said.

"Do you know anyone living in Bethel?"

"Can't say that I do," he said.

The boat ground into the mud on the other bank. We jumped over the side of the boat and waded to shore. He muttered to himself as his oars splashed away from us in the river.

It was time to part from Blue. Beards and I were headed south, while Blue was headed north to the Staunton outskirts. Blue and Beards hugged in a rough embrace. "We'll see each other soon, right?" Blue said as he slapped me on the shoulder. I didn't have it in me to answer. I'd been with Blue for four years, side-by-side, suffering together and making sure the other one made it to this moment. Until he passed out of sight around the curving road, my eyes lingered on his departing back.

"Well, that's it," Beards said, and we trudged off through wild blackberry brambles toward Bethel, silent for fear of letting our feelings show.

36

I HEARD MA'S VOICE CALLING TO MARY AS I MOUNTED THE PORCH STEPS. They were in the upstairs back of the house, and Ma was asking for help in finding something. For a moment I remained there quietly, soaking in the hot smell of oak and cedar trees across from the house, the indigo hills behind the fields, and the longed-for familiarity of the voices within. I also needed a moment to rein in my feelings before I was swept away by those of my family. Finally, I opened the door and called out. "Ma? Pa? I'm home!"

Tish was the first to reach the door. She looked as if she had seen a ghost. She called over her shoulder, "Ma, come quick! It's Tom!"

Tish threw her arms around my neck, and over her head I could see the others running toward us. The women smothered me in hugs, as Pa beamed, waiting for them to finish so that he could greet me. He sheepishly wiped at the tears rolling down his cheeks. Ma clung to my arm as if I might run off at any second.

Eventually, Mary said, "We should leave you be for a while. You might like to wash some of that travel grime away." Tears filmed her eyes as she smiled at me.

Ma reminded me that my shirts and pants were hanging in the cupboard where I'd left them, and Pa had an extra pair of boots for my use. They were worn but at least had intact soles. I went to my room, closed the door, and collapsed on the bed, where I wept into my pillow like an infant. During the past year, I'd never thought I would see home again.

While they waited for my return downstairs, Tish and Mary planned a celebration dinner. Four months after the war's end, the shelves of

Staunton stores were still bare. So my sisters had set off through the woods with their foraging basket and returned with their finds. The three women sauteed mushrooms, boiled dandelion greens seasoned with apple vinegar, and used the last of Pa's secret garden potatoes. For dessert, there were wild grapes and mint drizzled with a spoonful of Tatternook's honey. Mary was bursting with questions, but thankfully had gained new patience in the time I'd been gone. Distressed by the looks of me, I believe Ma, Mary, and Tish took a vow not to press me about what I'd seen and done. Lord, all you had to do was glance into my eyes to recognize there was a chasm that was too dark to explore.

Mary didn't ask about Beards, why he'd stopped writing, and if he might still care for her. When Pa asked me about his well-being, her flushed face and downcast eyes were the only signs that she still had feelings for him. I couldn't have answered her questions, but I knew the past four years had changed him too.

When we were all exhausted from so much feeling and talk, I bade them good night and returned to my room. I lingered by the bed, wanting to savor every minute of turning back the smooth sheets and sinking into the down-stuffed mattress. With the covers folded back, I slipped between the cool linens, my head swallowed up to the ears by the pillow. I thought I'd departed this earth and gone to Heaven, with a belly full of food and shrouded in a silken cocoon.

But the happiness of those first days wore off, and my melancholia crept back. I was damaged, and so were all the folks around here. No one wanted to discuss the bad times, and they were timid about prying into mine. But the war's toll was visible in my parents' stooped shoulders, lined faces, and the girls' silences. At first, after the joy of my return, my mother's transformation was less apparent. But within several days, it was evident that she had changed the most. She'd become more subdued and tentative. The resolute, self-assured mother I remembered seemed defeated. She deferred to the other three most of the time, speaking infrequently and then in a quiet tone. Always tidy in her appearance, she was less so now, with hairpins often dangling from her loosely coiled braids and her collar askew. When I asked Mary about it, she shook her head sadly. "The war was especially hard on her." That was all she'd say. It made me grieve to see my mother like this, but nothing was the same anymore.

37

EARLY ON, I DEVELOPED THE HABIT OF CONVERSING WITH JOHN BIBB. He dwelled there with me in Augusta. I saw him every day. The mornings were the worst, when cobwebs of sleep still clung to my wits. He was present when I dashed icy water on my face from the basin and peered into the wavy glass framed on the wall above. His flat, dead eyes stared back, sweeping me with blame. To shorten the time I spent before the damned mirror, I grew a beard.

One day, after I'd been particularly surly to Pa at breakfast, Mary materialized before me on the porch, anger alight in her blue eyes. "What got into you this morning?"

"Nothing. I'm just fine."

"You're not fine. Every day you sit in that rocking chair where you mutter to yourself—huddled in a blanket as though it was winter. Have you given any thought to helping Pa at the mill?" She paused. "Maybe if you busied your hands, your bleak mood might lift. Law, that snapping at Ma and Pa needs to stop."

I thought how simple it was for her to be critical. Hands chalky with flour, she brushed wisps of auburn hair from her eyes with the back of her wrists as she waited for some response. She and Tish were baking bread that morning. What could she possibly know about the hell I'd been through? Folks complain that old scars often act up when it rains, but these invisible ones act up regardless of weather.

"Why don't you just go back in the house and mind your own business?" I said.

She stomped from the porch, slamming the door, and rejoined Tish in the kitchen. Her indignant voice floated toward me as I continued rocking. Reluctantly, I conceded that maybe she was right. Pa could use help, and I certainly couldn't be any more miserable at the mill than squandering my days on the porch. Besides, guilt for my sharpness toward my well-intentioned family was eating at me. I wasn't ready to apologize to Mary, but I slinked off the porch and rounded the side of the house away from the kitchen windows, cutting through the field down to the mill.

I took to working steadily with Pa. The regular rhythm of creek water against the massive millwheel's paddles, the grinding of the coarse stones against the corn, and the conversation of farmers hauling in their sacks kept my mind from festering old wounds.

But I missed all my old fighting comrades. In my heart-sore state, I idly considered visiting Beards, just to hear what news he'd scoured out of the neighborhood—up to his old habits again. Now and then, I puzzled over his absence at our place. Then one day, Mr. Beard, one of the earliest to bring his harvest in, arrived at our mill with a cow lagging behind on a rope lead. He was followed by Beards and his brother Jackie driving a wagon creaking under a load of bagged rye. Thanks to their remote location behind the hills, the family had managed to keep this beast, all skin and bones, throughout the war.

One more curious thing about those times was what passed for money now that no one had any. "Smiley, would you consider taking this cow in exchange for services? She's not much to look at now, but with time and care, she'll be a fine milk producer." Mr. Beard puffed his chest and pulled at his suspenders with his thumbs. "She has more than a few years left on her, and if you can find a bull hereabouts, you might even get a calf or two outen' the trade." Pa pretended to consider the offer and then eagerly accepted, anticipating a later barter of milk and butter. Miss Baldwin was now taking such exchanges for tuition at her finishing academy in Staunton, where my sisters would return to their studies of history, literature, mathematics, and philosophy.

As the two younger fellows positioned sacks against the wall, I emerged from the mill and embraced them warmly. It was so good to lay eyes on my old friend. "Beards, where've you been keeping yourself? You know Mary and Tish would be mighty pleased to see you at the house." I gave him a pointed look. "Especially Mary." I didn't tell him that Mary was deeply hurt that he'd made no attempt to contact her. She was now after me constantly, speculating about reasons for his absence from our lives. "They ask after you frequently, and I wouldn't mind catching sight of your old mug from time to time." He looked through me, as if I hadn't spoken.

Beards had always been fastidious about hygiene, but his brown hair was now matted in a greasy skullcap. I swear the stain-mottled wool pants and soiled muslin shirt hadn't been washed since we were set free. He lowered his gaze, "Well, you know how it is; there's so much necessary work on the farm. But maybe I'll come by someday soon." He turned back to unloading the wagon as if I were a mere acquaintance. His rebuff was nothing like my old friend. Jackie threw an apologetic look at me over a bag of rye and shook his head. But I already suspected Beards wouldn't be coming around, and I knew it had nothing to do with farm work. I let him be and busied myself moving sacks—brought low by yet another loss.

One afternoon not long after Beards' mill visit, I found Mary huddled on the parlor loveseat. She gazed absently at a point beyond the window. "You seem miles away; why such a long face?" I said.

"Shh—I'll tell you when Ma and Pa are out of earshot," she whispered. Waiting until their conversation was no longer audible as they strolled toward the garden with basket and hoe, she began: "I'm just back from calling on Sarah Beard. I couldn't stand Beards' absence another minute and thought I'd ask his sister why he's stayed away. But instead,

I saw the most distressing thing." Her voice shook. "It's in the corner of the Beard's yard. A cemetery of small graves has sprung up by the old picket fence. Field flowers poke out of apothecary bottles dug into the earth everywhere. Sarah says it's Beards' doing. He wasn't there but was off spending the day in ways he's taken up since the war. She says he drags home decaying deer carcasses from the woods, takes brood hens fallen over from old age, broken mice from his mother's traps, and gnawed birds that the tabby brings in, and buries them all in the yard. He sets out every morning with a burlap sack over his shoulder and returns with dead creatures. His ma and pa haven't been able to persuade him in all this time to provide much of a helping hand around the place." Beards' sister then told Mary that he had no interest in anything else, and that this is his sole industry. "His family doesn't know when this madness will end," she said, wiping at her eyes. "It's hopeless. I wish I'd never gone."

I didn't tell her what I knew. We'd done too much burying, and Beards hadn't yet let loose of it.

As days grew shorter and wheat was long ago cut and shocked in the fields, afternoons at the mill stretched out in solitary boredom. Farmers were now infrequent visitors, and there was little grain to grind. Idle time wasn't my friend. Bibb's grip tightened when there was nothing to occupy my thoughts. Remembering how I'd seen boys in prison whittling wood scraps to pass time, I took to wandering up into the grove at the top of the hill, looking for just the right fallen limb.

One late November afternoon, lifting my eyes from the forest floor where I'd been surveying broken maple branches, I was startled to see old Tatternook ambling quietly along our fence line. Clad in his usual black suit and hat with a patch over his eye, he sensed my stare and turned. He tipped his hat. I shifted my gaze and moved rapidly through the shorn pasture toward home. But I couldn't shake the sensation of being followed. When I glanced back over my shoulder, there he was, striding in my direction and peering intently at me with his lone eye. He seemed bursting with something to say and was trying to match my pace. I picked up speed and arrived at the house out of breath, firmly closing the back door before he entered the gate.

That unwelcoming gesture didn't deter him. He forced his way into my dreams and wandering thoughts. However, his indistinct words never quite jelled there, although I was certain that he perceived Bibb astride my back that afternoon in the field.

"Pa, what can you tell me about old Tatternook?" I asked one day at the mill. My father was taking advantage of the seasonal lull to tidy up and to sweep cornmeal from the corners.

He leaned on his broom and considered before answering. "Well, son, your mother and I always shunned him as a strange bird. You know, he has no use for churchgoing, and one always wonders if there are gaps where the Devil intrudes for heathens like him. But everything changed during the war, including our opinion of Tatternook."

"How so?"

"Well, he proved himself to a be an honorable man, if not any less eccentric. If I didn't fear being judged for blasphemy, I'd say he performed miracles around here. His hives have provided the sweet in our food and helped heal that wounded boy Franklin Spragins that we told you about. And he's to be thanked these days for trading his precious honey in exchange for grinding a few bags of corn. So, if you see him about, doff your hat and speak politely."

And lo and behold, there he was in the mill entry, a black outline against the white winter sun. "William, may I impose on your boy here to help me unload the last of my burlap sacks?" he requested while staring almost through me. A shudder coursed down my spine, and I tripped over my own feet, as we approached his rundown wooden wagon. I hefted one of the cumbersome bags to my shoulder, as he turned and spoke: "Clemency, Tom, clemency and compassion are what you need.

Forgive yourself, boy. Don't wait for the Almighty God to do it. It's up to you."

"What did you say?" I asked from behind a sack.

"You are like a wolf cub with its paw caught in a sharp-toothed trap, desperately gnawing its limb to flee. But the more you gnaw at yourself about that young fellow in prison, the tighter will grow his grip around your shoulders until the life will bleed right out of you." I was speechless. I could only stare at the ground littered with grain. "It was an accident," he continued. "Confess to your pa. He's a generous soul, and the telling of it will lighten your burden. Tell as many good folks as you can. None will be as hard on you as you are on yourself. With time, the guilt will ease."

But I was red-hot with shame and abruptly turned my back on the man. I had little faith that he was correct about the leniency of folks' judgment, especially Pa's. If I told my family, they'd know a man had died because of my recklessness. No matter how much time passed, I would feel blame, believing that behind their eyes lurked young Tom and his deadly mistakes.

Tatternook touched my arm sympathetically, and his piercing eye locked mine. I shook off his hand and grimaced.

38

AFTER MY PRISON RELEASE, I HAD BEEN STONE-DEAF TO MY MOTHER'S constant pleas to join the church. But then she proposed something that changed my mind.

The mill was closed for the winter season, and farm work was reduced to scattering hay twice a day for Mr. Beard's cow. Sunny days were in short supply, and I fell into a deepening gloom. Long, constitutional hikes were my way to escape the women's hovering concern. I stalked the upper fields, counting footsteps on the butter-tinted hills and pacing off the bristling tree line. But as days shortened and the anniversary of Bibb's killing approached, even that practice wasn't enough.

Dressed warmly for the weather in shawls knotted tightly around her woolen cape, Ma found me one afternoon again in a blanket on the porch. Full of righteous purpose, she pulled up a chair next to me. There was a hint of her old self in her assertive tone. "Son, I worry day and night about what ails you. I lose sleep over it."

Refusing to meet her probing eyes, I looked across the porch railing as if there was something of extreme interest tacked to the tree by the road. "Ah, Ma, I just wish you and the girls would leave me be. Can't a man even find peace in his own home? Sometimes I long for the war again—to get away from all this prying and picking." As soon as I saw her wounded expression, I regretted those spiteful words. She was so fragile these days.

Unexpectedly, she persevered. "You may be as rude as you like, but I'm going to get to the bottom of this moping about." She then went on to address her theory for my melancholy. A lack of devotion caused my low spirits, and the only solution was to get myself to New Jerusalem Church to pray for forgiveness. She told me how she was distraught when I was in prison. "But I turned to the Lord for salvation, and we were blessed with your homecoming. You should praise your Maker for bringing you safely back to us." She continued on in this vein, and eventually veered into some nonsense about a coming apocalypse. I ceased to pay attention and fell back into my own musings, her irrational conversation deepening my solitary misery.

But then Ma said something that sparked my interest. "There are so few who are able-bodied in the neighborhood these days. Reverend Brown says he'd welcome your assistance keeping the church account books when you aren't busy at the mill. You are a good man, but you need to get busy before the Devil discovers you."

Something shifted in me that day. An idea began to grow. My greatest dread was to be found out by my family; I needed to do something to redeem myself, something that might tip the scales more in my favor than against. An adult life of charity and church involvement might do it. People would say, "Yes, as a young man he behaved recklessly, but what an upright person he's become—always constant in his faith and helping others." Obituaries in *The Spectator* consistently cite regular church membership as proof of a life well lived.

But pride kept me from relenting in that moment. Believing her argument had been in vain, Ma arose with a heavy sigh and went back inside, leaving me to my doldrums. And yet, to her immense surprise, on Sunday I awakened with the rest of the family, donned a pair of brown canvas pants and a homespun linen shirt from before the war, and joined them in a pew at New Jerusalem, toting Bibb along with me. If Ma wanted to believe that by some miracle I'd been called, I wouldn't dissuade her. I belted out the words of hymns as though I meant them, and I even allowed myself to become her attentive student, studying the Bible chapter and verse every afternoon in this very library. Gradually, my show of interest seemed to bring her out of the shadows, and, I hoped, made up for my surliness.

My habits changed, but not my lack of faith in a benevolent God. Every Sunday I endured sermons that warned of wrathful Old Testament fire and brimstone. Preachers invoked a harsh paternal God, and I rejected Him before He could reject me. But there were other consolations.

The greatest was meeting my dear Ellen that long-ago day in church. The second was that the Presbyterian Church required its members to live by the Ten Commandments' rules and then those made by the Presbytery, the Church's governing body. If you were guilty of murder, fornication, failure to tithe, adultery, drinking alcohol, and fighting, you were banned from the church. I felt I needed rules. For four years, I'd lived by the only rule that mattered: kill or be killed. During that time, my own choices were often flawed. I no longer trusted my judgment. In the church, rules were crystal clear. Boundaries were unconditionally drawn in black and white.

I wholeheartedly embraced that system and worked my way through it. The first step was to become a Sunday School teacher; then I was promoted to Superintendent, overseeing four hundred students and their teachers. By the time my moustache was white, I was elected an Elder sitting judgment on others. My veneer of goodness was irrefutable, bolstered by my fellow congregants who voted me into office year after year. The die was cast, and the obituary's favorable text assured. I would be lauded as an admirable man in everyone's opinion but my own.

39

PHOEBE AGAIN CALLS TO ME WITHOUT MOVING HER LIPS. HER VOICE IS still faint, far off, but I make out her question. "Why do you torment yourself so for Bibb's death? He was just one man during four long years of combat, and you've told me about Sam, Zeke, and the others," she said. "You lost them too. And you must have killed lots of Union soldiers. Why is Bibb different?"

The sun has gone down without my notice or Phoebe's, and objects in the room are now only blue outlines made by the full moon beyond the windows. I sense another person in the room before I see him. His shirt sparkles turquoise in the moonlight. It's Tatternook, his black suit and hat merging with the dark. He nods in recognition. A gasp escapes me, but then there's a second visitor. John Bibb stands beside him. With a slight movement of his hand, he greets me. How long have they been there? I was too wrapped up in the worst of my past to note their arrival. Now all three await my response to Phoebe's question.

The images still vibrate in the room: Ahl and Old Hike in the pen, Beards' reaction to my desperate plan, Bibb's motionless body as I crouch over it, Lewis and his lonely cabin. These memories have been buried for so long, hidden below recollections of my family life in Augusta. They have the shock of a fresh wound. But curiously, the pain is less than I feared. There my secret is, out in the open for the first time. What if I'd heard myself say these things to Mary or Ellen long ago? Might my family have been as understanding? Spoken aloud over time, would my guilt have lost its power? The words no longer weigh so heavily that I think they'll crush me. I see no blame or disgust on the faces of my present audience. They don't condemn, but instead seem curious and accepting. Warmth floods my heart as I watch Phoebe sitting so attentively, so receptive to my confession. I feel a bond with her I haven't felt with anyone since my death. But I can't help thinking: if only my wife or sister were sitting there instead.

At first, the answers to Phoebe's question are formless bits careening in my mind, trying to coalesce but unable to find the proper joining. As I wait for a response to surface, Bibb has seated himself in the parlor's ladder-back chair. He observes me carefully. The silence deepens. Haltingly, I begin. "I understand why you'd ask that question. Why my heart ached so because of one man's killing when I experienced so much slaughter," I say. "But the war's slaughter wasn't of my doing. I had no control over the war, but I did have some control over the welfare of my unit. Once Bibb joined us at Spotsylvania for the journey to Fort Delaware, he was one of my men."

I pause for a minute, guilt tightening my chest. "Remember, Bibb risked his life to save me at Spotsylvania Courthouse and then died trying to save me from myself at Fort Delaware. I owed no one else such a debt. If he hadn't been so young and innocent, hadn't depended upon me . . ." I drop my head in my hands. "He could have lived a long life. The fighting was over, for Chrissake." I look across at Bibb. "You hadn't been through the horrors we had; you might have healed when you returned home."

"Perhaps. But we'll never know." He regards me sadly. "Don't you think there is more to your melancholy than that, Tom?"

"What do you mean?" I can't believe my ears. "How could there be more?"

"Look deeper. There's more," he says gently.

I'm confused by his words. "There's nothing more. Your death and your family's loss have filled every corner of my heart."

"Why is that?" he asks.

I'm irritated by his questions, until the truth breaks free. "So there would be no space to consider the rest. All those young men, especially the ones I loved best, who lost their lives." I'm stunned by this admission. "And for something so foul."

Even as I speak, a frozen stream is melting within. I feel Bibb's mind lock onto mine. Tayloe's gaunt face, Sam with his bloody teeth, and Zeke's blank, drowned eyes—all appear before me. And more. There's McCorkle, who fought on after Spotsylvania but never made it home to his wife and babe after Appomattox. There are the nine boys, almost a third of us remaining in Company D as prisoners, who died under my helpless watch as sergeant in Fort Delaware. I could do nothing to stop disease and starvation.

And there are all the men who didn't die, whom I saw every day in Augusta County, but whose war damage was visible to all lookers. There was Mrs. Calliston's son Ralph who shelved goods in the General Store with his one arm, the other a stump disguised by a pinned-up shirt sleeve. There was the owner of Staunton's American Hotel whose guests averted their eyes to avoid the disfiguring burn scars across his left brow, eye socket, and cheek. There were the numerous one-legged men every Sunday at New Jerusalem, a thicket of crutches sprouting from the pews.

Blue and many others simply passed away before their time. Four years without adequate food and the effects of war-contracted diseases took their toll. Poor, disheveled Beards buried carrion until the end of his shortened days. He, like so many others, was crushed in spirit and remained a ward of his family, incapable of a normal life. Although Mary would have cared lovingly for him, he had traveled beyond anyone's reach. For the rest of my life, I couldn't escape all those in town or on the county roads who'd lost a limb or their good sense to that conflict. They were everywhere one turned.

"There's more, Tom," Bibb says. His eyes soften with kindness.

"I could never live up to the blessings of my life in the midst of those poor souls." I continue. "Who was I to deserve such good fortune?" The words pour out of me. "My wedding night, the birth of our first son, the awakening of spring in the mountains, the presentation of my daughter Cara in marriage to a neighbor's boy—all these joyful times were marred by the shadow of what you and all the others were missing."

I can't stem the flood. "Twenty-six major battles. That's how many I survived. And I escaped smallpox, cholera, and diphtheria that killed as many as the bullets and the cannon balls. Every day I'm tormented by the question of why me and not the others." Tears flood my eyes until the room wavers.

Disappointment clouds Bibb's face. What more could he want to hear that I haven't said? I sit in quiet bewilderment. The answer should come easily to me; after all, I've always thought of him as my younger, more innocent self, the part that died during the war. I know him so well. In some timeless place, our bond seems to have grown lighter and sweeter, beyond my guilty obsession. And then a bitterness arises from my stomach, pushes against my ribs, and explodes from my lips like bile after a bout of purging. A blindfold has been lifted from my eyes, and I understand what Bibb has been waiting to hear.

"Oh my lord, all this grief, pain, and death . . . yours as well, would never have happened but for one thing. And that was the greed that kept slavery alive. The deep truth, the hard truth, is that I murdered men so that white people could continue to torture other human beings, could use them however they wanted, and could deny they were human like themselves. I've been terrified of the painful clarity that ripped through my heart and soul during the war. I didn't have it in me afterward to live day to day viewing humankind in that strong light. Instead, I've traveled in a fog, unable to navigate its sharp edge of truth." I hold my hands before me as if I can see blood on them. "I'm ashamed, so ashamed." The room falls still, even the creek's whispering and the calls of night birds are muffled. It occurs to me—is my repentance Bibb's also? He wasn't on the killing fields for very long, but he desperately wanted to be there, just as I did, while fooling himself about the cause he was joining.

He steps toward me. He speaks slowly and with gravity. "Tom, you are forgiven for my death. You always were. Let go of that guilt. But all of us bear the larger guilt."

Tatternook holds out his hand. A ray of light flashes like a shooting star and enters my heart. The tears that have been falling there for so many years dry up. The ray goes deeper and deeper, a pebble sinking into an ocean. I find myself in the station I glimpsed long ago in that icy prison yard the night Bibb was shot. There is the sound of an unearthly harmony, rising and falling in a multitude of divine voices. A golden train arrives, not on wheels, but borne on the backs of winged creatures from whom the singing comes. The brilliant glare of the rail cars almost stuns me, and I feel a great urgency. I must get on board.

But I owe Phoebe a debt of gratitude—one as deep as I owed Bibb for saving me at Spotsylvania Courthouse. She took pity on me and led me to this point of release. Ignoring her fear, she found an unexpected well of courage. She was as valiant as any soldier. One who should never again feel shame. I lay my hand on her shoulder as a father might his daughter and think how fond I've become of her. Despite my resentment of Phoebe and Harry's changes to my house, I recognize that they've made it a place that will now last for generations to come. It will stand firm and strong for others to enjoy as I did. Maybe they'll be my descendants, and my story won't be forgotten. I give her shoulder a squeeze of farewell. Phoebe shivers, her eyes brim with tears, and her face glows. She knows.

The station door has sailed open, and I must hurry. I take one departing look at my home and Phoebe in the library and then rush through. But just as my foot touches the embossed metal step and I grab the shiny hand rail, everything disappears in a burst of light. There is the ear-splitting sound of something crashing down, falling apart, shattering into jagged pieces. At my feet lies the shriveled, lifeless body of Moloch, Milton's dark god of guilt from *Paradise Lost*. The station and the train no longer exist. My house, the farm, Phoebe, Tatternook, and John Bibb are gone. Tom Smiley is disappearing too. Everything I treasured about myself has almost evaporated. But I have no fear or sense of loss as before. There is nothing to lose. I have no gender, no name, no position in society, or any possessions. But I am awash in peace and contentment, pulsing with the expanding and contracting vibrations of the universe. Bibb, Tatternook, Phoebe, and I are all particles of a grand, luminous wave of life. I am pure awareness, nothing more and nothing less. This is the first and last of what I am.

Afterword

This book is about the gritty, devastating effects of war—in this case, the often-dissected American Civil War—but isn't about officers, battle statistics, or strategies. It's about young Confederate soldiers without rank, infantrymen on foot for as many as a thousand miles a year carrying out war's grimmest chores, sometimes for a cause they didn't support. The story places its protagonist, Tom Smiley, on the Southern side because that's where conditions were harshest, the cause hardest to justify, and the site where most of the killing happened.

I was barely an adult during the Vietnam War, when many American soldiers were injured and killed for a cause with little connection to their lives. I wondered if the same was true for Confederate soldiers during the Civil War. I suspect most of the Southern combatants were racists, but only one in four families in the South owned enslaved people and had anything to lose if the institution was abolished.

Wars are often instigated by a proportionately small number of people whose wealth makes them politically and socially powerful, some of whom become military officers. Most white Southern wealth at that time was related either directly or indirectly to owning and selling Black humans. This white group was hell-bent on retaining a barbaric institution to enrich themselves and avoid daily labor. And ordinary citizens were the majority of those who paid the terrible price of death, injury, PTSD, and destruction of property. Men like Tom quickly became cogs in a vast military machine. The Confederacy established a draft in April 1862, ten months after the first battle, and consequences of avoiding enlistment or deserting were beatings, imprisonment, or death. Just as in the South, many folks in the North didn't believe in equality, but their Black and white leaders correctly convinced them slavery must be abolished.

Slavery began in the colony of Virginia, and by the time of the Civil War, the state rivaled South Carolina and Louisiana for sales of enslaved people. Auctions were held in Richmond and in smaller towns along primary transportation routes leading into the deep South where larger, even more brutal cotton and sugar plantations existed. By the time of the war, selling humans south into killing labor was more lucrative than any crop a Virginia landowner could raise. There was a steady current of enslaved people through Virginia to plantations in Louisiana and Mississippi.

In Augusta County in southwestern Virginia, the setting of this book, farmers weren't necessarily more humane than those in the rest of the state, but their crops of wheat and rye required much less field work. Farms were smaller than those growing tobacco and cotton, and they most often required only family members and hired hands as laborers. One in five Augusta families owned other people, but a third of those owned no more than one person. Often, enslaved people were rented out to wait on hotel and tavern tables, tend stables and animals, erect telegraph poles, work in breweries, lay rail lines, and provide domestic labor. Across the South on the eve of the Civil War, when an annual salary for an upper middle-class white man might be $500, a healthy, young, enslaved Black man sold for as much as $1,500. Today, that individual person's purchase price would be approximately $100,000 or more. By the time of Emancipation in 1863, the combined value of all the South's slaves, adjusted to today's prices using the relative share of GDP, was close to thirteen trillion dollars and, even as early as 1805, never fell below six trillion dollars. This is what Confederate leaders knew, and why they wanted to secede. They wanted to protect their wealth, built on the backs of enslaved people, even if it meant bloodshed.

Virginia was a border state during the war, and the southwestern region was strongly populated by Scotch-Irish people who had migrated from Pennsylvania. Many of them had strong connections with family members and friends in the North and shared anti-slavery views. Again, this isn't to say they weren't racist. The reasons men from this region volunteered and then stayed as enlistees in the early part of the Civil War differed across social classes. After the draft was created, wealthy young men hired substitutes. Upper-class white people told themselves and others that the reason for fighting was to preserve states' rights, disguising the fact that less fortunate people were dying to defend a privileged way of life made possible by enslaving Blacks. As Northern troops marched into the South, purpose for the ordinary, powerless Confederate soldier had to become survival and defense of a homeland. I asked myself while researching material for this book why those opposing slavery didn't leave the South as war was brewing. An admirable few had that courage, including Presbyterian minister Dr. George Junkin, the real person Reverend McIntyre is based on, but most couldn't give up the security of family, friends, and land from which they earned a living. And some even believed that enslaving Black people was encouraged by the Bible.

Tom Smiley, Civil War veteran and ghost narrator of *The Last of What I Am*, is tormented by war memories and is trapped by them in an increasingly personal hell. But he's also a stand-in for this nation, one unsettled by a history rife with injustices and motives many of us still can't face, not even generations later. Until we embrace that history and its long shadows, the nation won't be able to fully rectify those injustices and heal. This novel is a cautionary tale about what happens when a country is divided against itself.

Acknowledgments

I learned about writing from editors Jane Rosenbloom, Judy Sternlight, Stefan Merrill Block, and Phil Ehrenkranz. And had the confidence to persist thanks to encouragement from many friends and readers but especially Geraldine Brooks, Susanne Page, Nancy Worssam, Kay Rodriguez, Sheela Lampieti, Barbara Lucas, Tony Horwitz, and my family, David Tiller and Ana Patel, who gave thoughtful critiques. I'm especially grateful to Bowman Cutter, who read the manuscript nine times and was my patient sounding board and supporter through an eight-year process. I'm also grateful to book agent Jacques de Spoelberch for his faith in my writing, and to She Writes Press for publishing in July 2022 the first iteration of this novel, *Long Shadows*. My daughter, Anne Tiller, designed the award-winning cover which captured its mood so well. Thanks also go to Union Square & Co., for publishing this revised edition. Thank you to my Union Square & Co. editor Barbara Berger, and especially publisher Emily Meehan and Barnes & Noble CEO James Daunt, who believed the novel deserves a larger audience. They have reissued the book as *The Last of What I Am*, with a cover designed by talented cover creative director Jo Obarowski.

Without the extraordinary database and website "The Valley of the Shadow" created by eminent American historian Dr. Edward Ayers and his award-winning books *In the Presence of Mine Enemies: The Civil War in the Heart of America 1859–1864* and *The Thin Light of Freedom: Emancipation in the Heart of America*, I could never have found such detailed material about the Civil War in Virginia. Those sources, and Drew Gilpin Faust's book *This Republic of Suffering: Death and the American Civil War,* were the foundation for two years of research. My novel is as historically accurate as I knew to make it, with one exception. The Gatling gun, the first American rapid firing weapon, was first used in 1864 during the Siege of Petersburg, not a year earlier as my story states.